CAPITANA

CAPITANA

CASSANDRA JAMES

Quill Tree Books
An Imprint of HarperCollinsPublishers

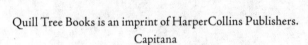

Quill Tree Books is an imprint of HarperCollins Publishers.
Capitana
Copyright © 2025 by Authorznote, LLC
Map illustration by Leo Hartas
Interior art © 2025 by Micaela Alcaino

www.epicreads.com
ISBN 978-0-06-334561-4
Typography by Laura Mock
24 25 26 27 28 LBC 5 4 3 2 1
First Edition

For Daddy.
You held the ladder.

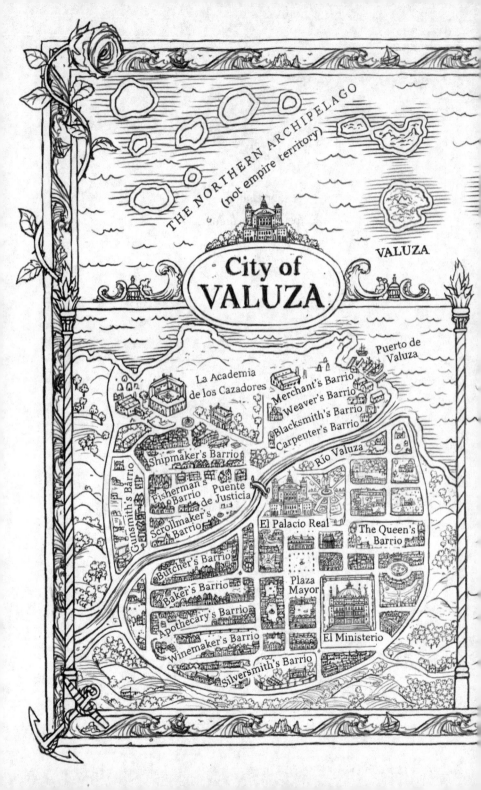

Capítulo Uno

It was a fine day for an execution.

The sun had just hit high noon, the sky was cloudless, and the candidates of la Academia de los Cazadores stood in long, crisp rows, looking appropriately grim in their black uniforms. Not a sound broke the silence; the air smelled of freshly cut grass. In the exact center of the hexagonal courtyard, a large wooden gallows awaited its victim, and the colors of the Luzan Empire—black, white, and gold—stirred in a mild sea breeze. So it was a fine day to die, and everything was just as it should be.

Ximena Reale had arrived an hour early to ensure she would be standing in the front row. Her uniform was pressed to perfection, her spine was as rigid as a ship's mast, and the three gold badges on her chest gleamed from a recent polishing. She had even taken the time to shine the patch that covered her missing left eye. After all, she was the reason that a man's life would end that afternoon. She couldn't look anything less than her best.

"De la preparación surge la perfección."

From preparation comes perfection.

It was the compass that guided her life.

She muttered the words under her breath, drumming her gloved fingers against her thigh as she and the other cazador candidates watched la academia's clock tower, waiting for the bell to toll. The seconds crawled by like centuries.

At last, the noon bell rang. Admiral Gabriel Pérez stepped onto the gallows platform, looking every bit like the hero he was: broad-shouldered, black-browed, with the bronzed and weathered skin of a man who had traveled to the furthest reaches of the Luzan Archipelago and back. No one could deny that he was the greatest cazador alive, with more pirate captures to his name than any other hunter currently serving the empire, and the youngest admiral to ever lead the armada, the fleet of cazadores. In other words, he was everything Ximena aspired to be.

So when his eyes found hers in the crowd, her heart tripped over itself in her chest.

"Treveda Ximena Reale."

She waited a moment as her name and rank echoed over the courtyard, savoring the sound of it. Then she stepped forward.

"I am yours to command, sir."

"Approach."

Obedience came naturally to Ximena. She strode up the platform steps and came to a stop in front of the admiral, placing two fingers to her lips in a salute. He acknowledged her with a nod. His shark-eyed stare cut through her like a rapier blade.

"Treveda Reale, do you confirm that you are responsible for the capture of the accused?"

"Sí, señor."

"And will you carry out the sentence as it is declared, in the name of your law, your queen, and your empire?"

"Sí, señor."

"Very well then," said the admiral. "Bring forth the prisoner."

At the foot of the gallows, a pair of drummers struck up a solemn beat. The iron doors of la academia's west wing swung wide open—four grim-faced cazador candidates stepped into the afternoon sun, flanking the prisoner. To Ximena, there was no sound in the world quite as satisfying as the metallic clank of a pirate in chains. She pulsed her restless fingers against her thigh while the candidates positioned the prisoner beneath the noose, saluted the admiral, and retreated back to the courtyard. She was so close now. Victory dangled in front of her like a fisherman's hook.

The admiral lifted a fist. The drums stopped; silence fell. All eyes landed on the man in chains who waited with his head bowed. In the colorless courtyard, he was a parrot among ravens: his loose-fitting clothes were an obnoxious tangerine color, and every one of his fingers and toes (the man was noticeably barefoot) sported three silver rings. The candidates of la academia knew his crime before it was even announced. Only one kind of person would dress with such a garish disdain for propriety.

A pirate.

"Captain Salvador Domínguez," the admiral boomed. "You have been found guilty of piracy, murder, and treason against the Empire of Luza. Therefore, you have been sentenced by the high court of el Ministerio de Justicia to hang by the neck until dead. Do you wish to repent for your crimes before your sentence is carried out?

For the first time, Captain Salvador Domínguez looked up. He was not a young man, falling somewhere between forty and fifty, with eyes like black mollusks and an overgrown nose. Most pirates were caught and killed long before they reached his age. His survival up until this point was indicative of his skill.

Just as his death would be indicative of Ximena's.

"Repent?" The pirate laughed. "What do I have to repent for, admiral? I gave my life to the only cause worth dying for." He smiled at the admiral with blackened teeth. "Freedom. So no, I won't repent. ¡Viva Gasparilla! ¡Viva la libertad!"

Gasparilla. The word struck the courtyard like a lightning bolt. An uncomfortable rustling moved through the assembled candidates—declaring that name aloud, as everyone knew, was an act of treason. After all, it belonged to the most notorious pirate captain in the Luzan Empire's history, the man who had led the bloody Scarlet Siege against the capital island of Valuza and ransacked its silver vaults.

Captain Domínguez sensed their fear; his black-toothed smile grew wider. "¡Viva Gasparilla!" he shouted again. "¡Viva la libertad!"

Ximena frowned. A few years ago, the candidates of la academia would have laughed at such a threat, and they would have been right to do so. Gasparilla was two hundred years dead, caught and killed by the armada of cazadores at the end of the Scarlet Siege. But whispers had traveled to Valuza from the furthest reaches of the archipelago, carried by merchants and fishermen and pirates alike, whispers that infected the islands like plague. They said Gasparilla had returned. They said he'd been resurrected from the dead using el idioma prohibido, the forbidden language of magic.

They said the legendary pirate was preparing to strike again.

Even worse, pirates captured by the cazadores had begun invoking Gasparilla's name just before their executions in direct defiance of the Luzan Empire. They declared it boldly, proudly, in the same breath as *liberty*, as if the sound of it were a threat or a prophesy or a battle cry. As if they knew something the cazadores did not.

But the time for guessing games and superstition had long since passed. El ministerio had delivered its verdict, and Domínguez was doomed to die. So the admiral raised his fist again, restoring order with a single glare.

"Enough," he said. "The accused has elected not to repent for his crimes. Therefore, his execution will be carried out forthwith."

Domínguez laughed again. "I hoped you would say that."

He slipped his head through the noose. The candidates let out a collective gasp. No pirate had ever noosed himself before.

"Well?" said Domínguez, raising his eyebrows. "Dispatch me to a better world, admiral. Then we will have both done one another a great service."

The admiral ignored him; he was far too noble to engage with a pirate's antics.

"Treveda Reale," he said. "Carry out your orders."

It was time, then. Ximena moved to the wooden lever on the other side of the platform. With careful precision, she curled both gloved hands around it just as she had watched older candidates do so many times before. The drummers struck up their beat again. Her heart pounded along with the rhythm. *Boom ba-boom. Boom ba-boom.* She took a long, slow breath.

"De la preparación surge la perfección," she repeated in a whisper.

Ximena had spent the last four years training for this moment. Four years of brutal courses and examinations in maritime history, combat, seamanship, espionage, and battle strategy. Four years of sleepless nights and sore muscles and endless study sessions, moving from the lowest rank of uveda to dotreda and then to treveda, the stage of training when candidates were finally deployed on their first pirate hunting expedition with the cazadores. Four years of preparing to stand on this platform next to a pirate whom she had brought to justice.

Now the moment had come. She was staring into the eyes of Captain Salvador Domínguez, and she held his life in her hands. But the pirate didn't look the slightest bit concerned. In fact, he was smiling still, his eyes as bright as stolen silver coins.

"Do it, little cazadora," he said. "Orders are orders, no?"

His arrogance made up her mind for her. Ximena breathed out. She pulled the lever. There was a creak, a pop, and a snap like the crackle of fish bones—then it was over. The great Captain Salvador Domínguez was dead.

As his corpse swayed in the wind, quiet descended once more over the courtyard. Ximena stepped back from the lever and reminded herself to keep breathing. Some candidates swooned or vomited the first time they executed a pirate, but she would be hanged herself before she revealed that kind of weakness in front of anyone at la academia. Thankfully, the admiral's booming voice was enough to distract her.

"May this violence not be in vain," he declared. "Rather, may it remind us of our duty to the law, to the queen, and to the empire."

"To law, queen, and empire!" the candidates chanted in response.

Two candidates hurried to remove the pirate's body from the noose and carry it off the platform toward the north gate. From there, Ximena knew it would be paraded through the city by cart to el Cementerio de los Traidores, the Traitors' Cemetery, where all the empire's pirates were buried. The captain whose name had once echoed throughout the empire and its archipelago would rest in an unmarked grave, condemned and forgotten. *As it should be*, thought Ximena. That was the price one paid for defying the law.

But the ceremony was not finished yet. The admiral beckoned her forward. She stood at attention and performed a second salute. In response, he unsheathed the rapier that hung at his hip and addressed the assembly.

"As you are all aware, there are two channels by which a candidate of la academia may be promoted to a higher rank. The first is by being selected to take the Royal Examination, offered every two years. The second is by demonstrating undeniable and extraordinary merit. Treveda Reale . . ." She liked to imagine that there was an edge of pride in his voice. ". . . you have proven your commitment to the law and to your queen by capturing the notorious pirate Salvador Domínguez during your deployment. You have demonstrated the highest standards of honor, valor, and love of justice that la academia strives to reflect. For these reasons, I hereby promote you for exceptional merit to the rank of cuatreda."

Ximena dropped to one knee. The admiral touched his rapier to her head.

"With this rank, you have reached the final and most rigorous level of training at la academia. Should you prove yourself worthy, you will be chosen for the Royal Examination and have your chance to earn the title of cazadora." The admiral offered one of his rare half-smiles. "May the seas be with you, Ximena."

"And with you, admiral," she replied.

She stared straight ahead as the admiral took a gold rectangular badge from his pocket and pinned it beside the others on her chest. Though her expression remained blank and her posture impossibly stiff, the flush on her cheeks betrayed her excitement. She was one step away from becoming Cazadora Ximena Reale, weapon of the empire, bane of the lawless.

A pirate hunter.

"You've set an academia record," said the admiral as he fastened her badge. "No one has ever reached the rank of cuatreda so quickly."

Pride burned in Ximena's chest. It took most candidates eight years to earn their cuatreda badge. They were recruited at thirteen years old and spent two years in each rank, moving steadily upward through their training and examinations until they graduated at twenty-one with their Cazador Cloak. That is, if they even made it that far—it was a well-known fact that only one out of every ten candidates recruited to la academia would become cazadores themselves. Half were cut in their first year; the rest would be slowly eliminated by examination until none but the best of the best remained.

So it took most candidates eight years to earn their cuatreda badge.

Ximena had done it in four.

"I serve under an excellent commanding officer, sir," answered Ximena.

The admiral's half-smile returned. He was her commanding officer, after all. She had been assigned to him when she was promoted to treveda and had served her deployment under his command. She wouldn't be where she was without him.

"I am proud to have you in my service, Cuatreda Reale," the admiral said. "But it's a pity your sister wasn't here for the ceremony. It might have served to motivate her."

Scanning the section of the crowd reserved for archivists, Ximena searched for a pair of familiar hazel eyes. But in the place where her sister should have been, there was a sneezing archivist who was missing a glove. Her stomach sank. Marquesa was gone. Again.

"My sincerest apologies, admiral," Ximena said. "I'll correct my sister's behavior personally."

"See that you do."

She saluted and retreated from the platform. No sooner had she taken her place in the front row than the whispers began to fly.

"Pirate spawn."

"She only gets promoted because she's the admiral's little pet."

"We'll see how well she does on the Royal Examination."

But Ximena was hardly listening. Her golden badge gleamed on her chest. She was finally a cuatreda. Her Cazador Cloak was within reach. If she had been capable of smiling, she would have grinned. She had never come so close to true happiness in all her life.

So naturally, Dante de León had to spoil it.

"Bien hecho, Cuatreda Reale. The highest standards of honor, valor, and love of justice. High praise indeed."

Her shoulders stiffened. She would have recognized his voice anywhere in the archipelago; though he spoke in a whisper, it grated on her nerves like a gull's screech. She didn't know how or when he had come to be standing behind her. But as far as she was concerned, he didn't exist if she didn't acknowledge him. So she kept her gaze fixed on the admiral as Dante de León drawled on in her ear.

"Truly, I have nothing but the utmost respect for you. It must have been incredibly difficult to end poor Domínguez's life yourself, given your background."

Background. The word was a knife pressed between her shoulder blades. But after four long years, she was used to Dante's jabs. So she answered calmly, "No more difficult than it would be for any other candidate."

"¿De verdad? I'm glad to hear it. We were all concerned on your behalf, you know. The sound of the lever, the snap." She heard him click his tongue against his teeth for effect. "You never know what memories that might bring to the surface."

"Your concern is appreciated, but ultimately unnecessary," Ximena replied, though she would have preferred to toss his concern into the sea.

But Dante wasn't finished. He leaned closer—she could smell the expensive perfume on his skin—and she just barely resisted the urge to unsheathe her rapier.

"Remind me again," he said. "How many years ago was your parents' execution? Six? Seven?"

"Five."

"Ah, claro que sí, of course."

He spoke as if he had forgotten, though of course he hadn't. Not a single person at la academia had forgotten that Ximena's parents were fallen cazadores, hunters who had betrayed the empire by resorting to piracy for their own personal gain. She was reminded of it every waking moment.

"Well," Dante continued, "if you need someone to process your feelings with, you know that I'm always happy to assist a fellow candidate—"

"As I said, that won't be necessary. I have no sympathy for Captain Domínguez, just as I had no sympathy for my parents. I would expect the same punishment to be dealt to me if I committed their crimes. It is the law."

Dante sniffed, drawing back. "The perfect little capitana, siempre."

"Not everyone has the privilege of surviving on their family name alone, Treveda de León."

"True enough," he acknowledged. "But isn't it fantastic when you do?"

As if to prove his point, the admiral's booming voice interrupted them: "Dante de León!"

"Duty calls."

Dante winked at her over his shoulder and swaggered up to receive his promotion to cuatreda. Ximena grimaced, her mood soured. If Dante de León had been anyone else, she believed he would have been cut from la academia years ago. His grades were abysmal, his combat skills a disgrace, and in Ximena's estimation, he possessed the cumulative intelligence of a small, dull rock. But he was a de León. His mother was high minister of Luza, head of el ministerio, second only to the queen. His older brother, Mateo, was one of the most promising young cazadores currently sailing for the armada. In other words, Dante de León was as untouchable as the sun over the sea.

Of course, that didn't stop Ximena from hoping that, one day, he would make a mistake so terrible that the admiral would terminate his candidacy without hesitation. But the boy had an incredible talent for disappointing those hopes. Every two years, he managed to accomplish a feat so extraordinary that the admiral had no choice but to promote him. In their uveda years, he had saved another candidate from drowning (though Ximena was convinced the drowning had been staged); in their dotreda years, he had successfully commandeered a rival ship during a training exercise (though Ximena was certain he had bribed the candidates crewing the other ship).

Then, on this latest deployment, he had assisted her in the capture of Salvador Domínguez, which really meant that *she* had captured the pirate and he had unsheathed his rapier just in time for the admiral to see him standing there, triumphant. So while Ximena fought every waking hour for her perfect grades, top examination scores, and flawless displays of extraordinary merit, Dante de León coasted by with nothing but a flash of his perfect smile.

Perhaps she should have told the admiral that the boy had spent half the voyage drunk out of his mind. Maybe then he wouldn't have been so quick to hand Dante a promotion to cuatreda. But Ximena Reale was nothing if not honorable. She wouldn't be accused of betraying her crewmates. Ever.

After the admiral had pinned the cuatreda badge to Dante's chest, he half-skipped down from the stage and returned to Ximena's side.

"Felicidades," she said through gritted teeth.

"Couldn't have done it without you, capitana," he replied.

No, she thought. *You couldn't have.*

"Shall I write a poem of gratitude in your honor? Songs praising your courage and beauty? I've been told I'm a great singer, and an even better liar."

Ximena remained silent; Dante grinned, victorious. This was the game they had played for years. He would bait her, and she would say nothing because he could afford to say whatever he wanted, and she couldn't afford to say anything at all.

So Ximena Reale hated piracy.

But she *detested* Dante de León.

After giving out two more promotions, the admiral finally dismissed the candidates from the courtyard. They filed back to their respective wings in la academia: Uvedas to the northwest wing, dotredas to the northeast, trevedas to the east wing, and cuatredas to the southeast. Only the cazadores were allowed into the southwest wing, and the west wing, of course, was reserved for prisoners and the Maritime Archives. This would be the last time Ximena would leave the courtyard with the trevedas. Tomorrow, she would pack her things and move to the cuatreda dormitories, where she would begin the most difficult stage of training at la academia. The thought made her heart drum against her ribs.

When they entered the familiar halls of the east wing and the iron doors were shut behind them, the candidates relaxed. They stripped off their gloves, loosened their collars, and wiped the midday sweat from their foreheads, congratulating the two other trevedas who had been promoted. No one congratulated Ximena, of course. She lurked in the corner as she always did, tall, severe, and alone. If a candidate accidentally made eye contact with her, they were quick to look away, and when one stepped too far backward and stumbled into her, he recoiled as if he'd seen a ghost, muttering, "Lo—lo—lo siento, Cuatreda Reale."

None of this surprised her. After all, Ximena did not believe in friends. She considered them to be the second most dangerous distraction to her training (the first being romance of any kind), and therefore endeavored to dwell on the outskirts of all social circles. Over the course of her career at la academia, she had been mostly successful. Her peers considered her to be cruel, taciturn, and more arrogant than the daughter of infamous pirates had any right to be. So they left her alone, whispering about her from a distance, and that suited Ximena well enough. The only person she could bear to talk with was Marquesa—and Marquesa was usually missing.

Idiota, thought Ximena. Her sister would get an earful before the day was through.

So while the other trevedas laughed and chattered among themselves, Ximena slipped around the crowd toward the stairs. She still had a few hours before dinner. If she hurried, she could make it to the archives to see her sister and still have time to spare. She didn't have the luxury of celebrating her promotion any longer than was strictly necessary. She had to get back to training, for both her and her sister's sake.

But just as Ximena's boot hit the first limestone tread, she felt a hand catch her sleeve.

"Where are you running off to, Cuatreda Reale?"

She turned. "To the archives to register Domínguez's execution. But fortunately for both of us, you are not my commanding officer, Cuatreda de León. So I have no reason to inform you of my plans."

Ximena may have only had one good eye, but she was fully aware that Dante possessed the same beauty all the de Leóns shared. His square jaw and broad shoulders were offset by his full lips and delicate nose; his eyes, always laughing, were wine-dark and framed by lashes any girl would envy. If only Dante himself weren't also aware of it. But he knew the effect he had on the people around him all too well. Worse, he reveled in it, winking and swaggering his way through life without shame.

Even his hair—curls so blond they were almost silver—was a reminder of his superiority over her. La academia's rules forbid candidates from altering their appearance in any way. But Dante knew none of his fellow candidates were brave enough to report his indiscretions, so he dyed his hair with abandon, just as he kissed girls he wasn't supposed to kiss and drank liquor he wasn't supposed to drink. Ximena had tried to report him for it once, years ago, when she was thirteen and naive, brand new to la academia. But Dante had slipped his dye canister into her dormitory and blamed the whole incident on her, resulting in her getting disciplined and him receiving praise. She had learned her lesson quickly then: She was a Reale. The daughter of pirates executed for their crimes against the empire.

She would never best Dante de León, no matter how hard she tried.

"According to Section 857 of the Cazador Code of Conduct," he said, furrowing his brow in a mockery of thought, "candidates are forbidden from leaving their fellow peers behind in the line of duty."

"Section 857 of the code is only applicable at sea, pursuant to Addendum 4."

"'Only when one is certain of the law may one begin to break it,'" Dante quoted. "Alessandra, esteemed founder of the Luzan Empire."

"'If one argues with a fool, one is certain to become one,'" replied Ximena. "Also Alessandra."

"Well," he said, "then I must never argue with you again, capitana."

Laughter ricocheted off the polished limestone walls. Predictably, a crowd had gathered around Dante de León, girls and boys alike ready to shower him with compliments at a moment's notice. They were mostly other patrimonios, the children of ministers, merchants, or royal family members, admitted to la academia because of their last names rather than their abilities. Perhaps they thought that if they could please the high minister's handsome second son, he would snap his fingers and have his mother crown them with the title of cazador. But Ximena knew better. The minister's son had never cared about the cazadores, and he never would. He only attended la academia because if he didn't, his mother would disown him.

"We're going into the city to celebrate my—*our*—promotion," Dante said. "You could come with us, capitana. Get your head out of those books for a while."

"Leaving academia premises without permission is a violation of the code, according to Section 368—"

"Hang the code."

"I must make our report—"

"Hang the report." Dante waved a hand dismissively. "You don't become a cuatreda every day. Besides, my mother isn't high minister for nothing. We won't get anything more than a slap on the wrist."

Ximena's good eye narrowed. "'One doesn't follow the law for fear of punishment. One follows the law because they love it as they love themselves,'" she quoted.

"And who said that?" asked Dante.

"Your mother."

As Dante's grin faded, she twisted her wrist from his hand and marched up the stairs.

"Suit yourself, capitana," Dante called after her. "I've already asked Marquesa to join us. I'd be happy to buy her a drink in your place."

Ximena didn't look back. She even pretended not to hear when he turned to one of the many girls at his side and said, "It's not like either of them will be any competition. My mother will see to that."

He was baiting her again, she knew. Perhaps he hoped that one day she would snap and spear him through with a rapier. He didn't share her scruples about betraying fellow crewmates. He would report her to Admiral Pérez for untoward conduct without a second thought, and just like that, their four-year battle would be over. No doubt that was why he had asked her to join him in the city—he would have reported her, had her disciplined, or even expelled, and exonerated himself with a well-placed mention of his mother's name. And since he had failed to entice Ximena, she knew he would hunt for easier prey: Marquesa.

Which meant that Ximena had to get to her first.

She made her way down the long hallway that led to the west wing. As she walked by, wide-eyed archivists in training leapt from her path, straightening their rumpled uniforms.

"That's her," one whispered. "The one who caught Domínguez."

"Heard she lost her eye to a pirate," said another.

"What's she doing here?"

"Hopefully nothing to do with me."

Ximena paid them no heed. With her chin up and eye fixed ahead, she made her way to the archivist dormitories, stopping at the door labeled 142—Marquesa's room.

"Open the door, Marquesa," she said.

No answer.

"Open the door, ahora mismo."

Still no answer.

"Fine," said Ximena. "Then I'll tell Dante de León you're too sick to join him in the city tonight."

Silence. Then the turn of a lock, and two hazel eyes peeking through the crack in the door. That was all Ximena needed. She burst into the room, ignoring Marquesa's squeak of protest, and spun on her sister with her good eye blazing.

"How dare you dishonor us this way," she said.

"Lo siento." Marquesa's voice was like seafoam melting away. "I couldn't . . . I didn't . . ."

"By the law, finish your sentences, Marquesa," Ximena said. She'd been trying to correct her older sister's habit of letting her words dissolve for years to no avail. "You skip class, barely pass your examinations, and miss the most important execution of the year as if it were a birthday party."

Marquesa shivered, folding her skinny arms around her ribs. "You know I hate executions, Ximena."

"Did you stop to think about how that would look? What people would think?"

"I'm sure they don't think . . ." Marquesa began.

Ximena shut the door, ensuring no one would overhear them. Then she swiveled back to her sister and pulled herself to her full height. Though she rarely lost her temper, Marquesa's weakness never failed to provoke her.

"They think we are the unholy spawn of two convicted traitors. They think we are a disgrace to the law and the empire. They think we don't deserve our place in la academia. And you are doing everything in your power to prove them right."

Marquesa sat down on the bed, hands trembling in her lap. In times like these it was easy to forget that she was nineteen, two years older than Ximena: Her eyes were large and glassy like a doll's, and her uniform sagged like melting wax. Her legs were bowed, and her chest caved, likely from the asthma that prevented her from participating in la academia's exercises. When she was nervous, she bit her nails with her small, sharp teeth—and Marquesa was always nervous. So her fingers were red and sometimes blood-crusted. Ximena made her hide them beneath thick, black gloves, but she always forgot to wear them. Watching her quiver, Ximena's lip curled in disgust.

"Get up," she said.

Marquesa obeyed without complaint, gnawing at her thumbnail.

"Basta," Ximena said, swatting the hand from her sister's mouth.

"Lo siento."

Ximena walked across the cramped, sparsely furnished room: the dormitories in la academia were equipped with nothing but a bed, dresser, and chair. Upon reaching the dresser, she sifted through the bottles of half-finished rouge that were strewn over the top.

"Where did you get this?" she said.

Marquesa bit her lip. "One of Dante's friends. She said it would look nice, so I . . ."

"Makeup is against the code," Ximena said.

"Lo siento," said Marquesa for the third time that day.

"Turn."

Marquesa shifted on the bed until her back faced her sister. Then Ximena pulled her own gloves off, tucked them into her trouser pocket, and dipped one hand into a clay pot of whale oil. She raked it through her sister's unruly curls without a hint of gentleness. Marquesa flinched.

"I wish you didn't have to . . ."

"Cazadores don't wish," said Ximena, and that was that.

When Marquesa's hair was dark and slick with oil, Ximena reached for a ribbon, tying it off into a neat ponytail. It was as if they were children again—Marquesa fourteen and Ximena twelve, gangly girls preparing to attend their parents' trial. The Reales' execution had reduced Marquesa to a ghost, neither living nor dead. She had lost all her zeal for the law and her purpose along with it. So the task had fallen to Ximena to ensure they wouldn't end up on the streets, which began with concealing their signature Reale curls.

She refused to give people one more reason to believe they were the rebellious, unruly daughters of rebellious, unruly pirates.

This, in the end, was Ximena's one weakness. She loved her sister. She loved her so fiercely that she hated her—for giving up, for becoming this shell of herself, for being so easily shattered on the rocks of life by every passing storm. But Ximena had sworn the day their parents died that she would do everything in her power to keep Marquesa safe under the law, and that was not the kind of oath one broke.

If only Marquesa didn't make it so difficult to keep.

"You're not leaving me many options, hermana," Ximena said. "Do you even know how hard I had to beg the admiral to move you to archivist training when you failed the cazador track two years ago? He's already made an exception once. He won't do it again."

"Tal vez eso sería mejor," Marquesa whispered.

"Louder."

"Maybe that would be better," she repeated. "We both know I'm not going to pass the Royal Examination."

"You will if you listen to me and study, for once."

"But I *have* studied. I just don't . . . I don't have the talent for it that you do."

"That's not true."

"But it is true. Maybe if I left la academia, things would be . . . easier."

"Absolutely not."

"For both of us," Marquesa insisted. "You could come with me, you know."

Ximena sniffed. As if she would ever leave la academia. This place was her lifeblood, her reason for being. She couldn't leave it any more than she could become someone else.

"I know you don't want to hear this . . . which is why I don't ever . . ." said her sister.

"Speak up, hermana."

Marquesa lowered her eyes. "I know my odds of passing the Royal Examination. Do you . . . know yours?"

"What is that supposed to mean?"

"I only meant . . . it's just . . ."

"Por favor, Marquesa, finish your sentences."

"They aren't going to let you win. They aren't going to let you become a cazadora."

The words, spoken so softly, may as well have been a cannon blast. Ximena's good eye narrowed to a slit. It was one thing to hear it from Dante de León. It was quite another to hear such thoughts from her sister.

"This conversation is over," she said. "Cazadores who doubt are cazadores who lose. We have our heading, Marquesa, and it is the same as it has always been. You'll become an archivist, and I will become a cazadora, and we will work together for the law just as we always planned. The second I leave this room," she added, toweling off her hands, "you're going to see the admiral in his office."

"Ximena . . ."

"You're going to apologize for your absence at the execution this afternoon, tell him that you were feeling ill, and that you will serve double the usual number of shifts in the archives."

"No," her sister whispered. "No, I couldn't possibly . . ."

"You can, and you will. Now stand up so I can fix your uniform."

It was at that moment that Marquesa's frigate bird flew in through the open window and landed on the bedpost. Watching the girls with eyes that knew too much, it tipped its beak, puffed out the rubbery red pouch that dangled from its throat, and flapped its black wings, which were sharp and curved like knife blades. Marquesa had rescued it from drowning and decided to keep it as a pet a few years ago. She greeted it now with a smile and offered it a salted fish from a jar under her bed, cooing to it in a soothing whisper.

Ximena, who was afraid of birds but would never admit it, only glowered.

"I thought I told you to get rid of that creature. If anyone else finds it in here, they'll have enough reason to expel you."

"*That creature* has a name, you know," said Marquesa.

"And what is it, pray tell?"

Marquesa's smile was a shadow of things long gone.

"I call it Ximena," she answered.

A stray wind blew the window shut. The heat was stifling.

"Go and see the admiral," Ximena said, turning to leave. "Tonight. This might be your last chance, hermana. ¿Entiendes? Your very last chance. If you obey the law—"

"The law will protect you." Marquesa's voice was hollow. "How could I forget."

The frigate bird squawked. Cringing, Ximena opened the door and stepped into the hallway. But her boot paused over the doorframe, and she said over her shoulder:

"I was promoted to cuatreda today."

"Felicidades," replied Marquesa, though there was no joy in it.

Ximena sighed. "Don't go with Dante de León tonight. He only invited you to get under my skin."

But Marquesa wasn't listening anymore. She was sitting on her bed and petting her frigate bird—she had shaken her hair out, resurrecting her mane of black curls.

How long would it take? Ximena wondered. How long would it take before the admiral lost patience and expelled Marquesa from la academia for good? Ximena knew exactly what would happen to a girl without fortune or family to protect her: She would end up on the street, begging for scraps, sleeping in the gutter, or worse. The law could not protect those who did not follow it.

"Did you hear what I said?"

"Yes," said Marquesa. "I heard you."

"And you're not eating enough. You've lost weight."

Long afterward, when she took time to consider what had gone so terribly wrong, Ximena would remember that curl of Marquesa's lip.

"Gracias, hermana," her sister said. "For everything."

Ximena wanted to warn her one last time about the dangers of going anywhere with Dante de León. But it was almost dinner-time, and she hadn't been to the archives yet. So she straightened her spine, pulled her gloves back on, and strode out into the hallway without another word.

If the guard in the hallway saw her remove her eye patch and swipe at the scarred skin beneath it, he didn't say anything. No one in their right mind would dare assume that Ximena Reale had the capacity for tears.

Capítulo Dos

Ximena knew as well as anyone that she was not going to become a cazadora. Her efforts and the admiral's favor had gotten her this far, to be sure. But she was a cuatreda now. The only step that remained was the Royal Examination, and that was not judged by the admiral as her previous examinations had been. It was judged by el ministerio.

In other words, by High Minister Elena de León.

Dante's mother.

The woman who had overseen her parents' execution.

So Ximena Reale would never become a cazadora. She would never achieve her dream, and she would never be able to protect her sister from the people who wished to destroy them both. Unless, of course, she accomplished something so extraordinary that to deny her a Cazador Cloak would be an embarrassment to the empire itself.

"De la preparación surge la perfección," she repeated to herself as she walked.

Ximena Reale was many things, but she was no fool. She'd understood the odds were stacked against her since she'd begun her training as an uveda. So, she'd spent the last four years devising a plan—a secret plan—that would be her best and only chance of earning her cloak.

That plan began in the Maritime Archives.

As she walked, her boots clicking against the stone in a steady, measured beat, her frantic heart began to slow for the first time that day. La academia always had this kind of effect on her. After all, this school was the embodiment of everything Ximena loved about the empire: its limestone walls were both elegant and impenetrable, its corridors and stairways organized, efficient, pristine. Every moment of every day was timed to the toll of the clock tower bell, so that the rhythm of life was as predictable as the tides, leaving nothing to guesswork.

In fact, over the course of the empire's two-hundred-year history, la academia had hardly changed at all. Hundreds of cazadores had walked these halls before her, and hundreds would follow after, all fighting to protect the empire and the principles it stood for. She felt that history in every step she took; it filled her with unswayable purpose. Ximena had always been certain of her role in life—she would be a cazadora, and she would defend the law with her very last breath. Nothing and no one would take that destiny away from her. Not while she could help it.

This conviction settled on her shoulders like a Cazador Cloak as she came to a stop before a pair of impossibly tall iron doors engraved with the Luzan Empire's motto: *Of the law, by the law, for the law*. She had arrived at the Maritime Archives, the beating heart of la academia. Now it was time to work. She reached for the door handles and pulled, stepping into the comforting smells of leather, ink, and dust.

The archives were the only part of la academia that were not made entirely of limestone. Thousands of mahogany bookshelves, organized into rows and categorized by subject, stretched into the distance, towering so high overhead that a system of wheeled ladders had been invented to give people access to certain records. The archivists rode these ladders at blinding speeds, their arms full of scrolls, muttering to themselves as they filed and rearranged records that had been checked out. Every notable moment in the empire's history was immortalized in those record scrolls, from the archipelago's war-torn origins to its unification under Alessandra to the present day. For that reason, it was the most important room in la academia, on the island capital of Valuza, and perhaps even in the entire Luzan Empire.

Though she had chosen the cazador training track, Ximena had a profound respect for the archivists of la academia. The cazadores were responsible for hunting down and capturing threats to the empire, of course. But the archivists were responsible for providing all the necessary information for those missions, and when a pirate was successfully captured, they served as attorneys before el ministerio, providing the legal case that would condemn the traitor according to the law and its tenets. Cazadores and archivists—one could not exist without the other.

It was the future she imagined for herself and Marquesa. The Reale sisters would be the greatest team la academia had ever seen, cazadora and archivist, working together in the name of the law. Except that Marquesa would rather be drinking with Dante de

León than studying for her exams . . .

But Ximena couldn't think of that now. There was work to be done, and she was already running out of time before the dinner bell rang.

She strode through the whirring ladders to the center of the archives, where the head archivist worked at his mahogany desk. She rang the small gold bell and waited.

After several moments, the head archivist raised his head. He was a little man with an absurdly large gray mustache and a pair of leather-rimmed goggles, which made his eyes look several times wider than they actually were. It was impossible to tell how old he was, though it was generally known that he had been serving in the archives since the reign of Queen Catarina, great-grandmother to the current Queen Dulcinea, and that he believed nothing good had happened in the empire since Queen Catarina's death. He spent most of his time muttering, pursing his lips at the other archivists, and putting up with Ximena.

"You're back," he said.

Ximena nodded.

"I heard you were promoted."

"Yes, sir."

He didn't offer congratulations. "Have you come to make your report?"

"Yes, sir."

He sniffed, then leaned down to pull a fresh record scroll from his desk. He grabbed a quill, dipped it in black ink, and looked up at her with an irritated purse of his lips.

"Name?" he said, though he already knew it.

"Ximena Alessandra Montoya Reale," she answered.

"Rank?"

"Cuatreda."

"Ship?"

"The *Pérez*."

"Notable crewmates?"

She grimaced. "Dante José Alejandro de León."

"Date of voyage?"

She answered him. The head archivist scribbled in the scroll, filling out the chart that would memorialize Ximena's exploits for all time. Every journey had to be recorded, even those that failed. This served several purposes. For one, future candidates could access the records and study them, learning from both the successes and mistakes of those who'd come before them. Additionally, if a candidate's expedition went horribly wrong, the records could be used as evidence before el ministerio. Ximena had heard of a cuatreda who had been tried and expelled from la academia after a discrepancy in the record was found. Thankfully, she had never had to experience such an evaluation herself.

The head archivist sniffed. "And which unfortunate lawbreaker did you capture?"

"Captain Salvador Domínguez. Known aliases include 'El Delfín' and 'El Sabueso.'"

"Method of capture?"

"We flew a merchant's flag, so he attacked us of his own free will, thinking we were carrying silver onboard. We had him outnumbered and outgunned." Ximena lifted her chin with the slightest edge of pride. "It was a short fight."

"How clever of you," said the head archivist, though he didn't sound impressed. "Any deaths?"

"None."

"Injuries?"

Ximena considered telling him about the blow she'd given Dante when she'd found him drunk in his cabin after celebrating Domínguez's capture but decided against it.

"None."

"Charges against the accused?"

Ximena listed them.

"Date of execution?"

"This morning, ten past noon."

"Method of execution?"

"Hanging."

"A classic. Standardized, you know, by Queen Catarina herself."

"Yes, sir."

He sniffed again. No one appreciated the brilliance of Queen Catarina the same way he did.

"That completes the record. Sign here."

She swept a perfectly symmetrical XR across the bottom line of the chart.

"You may be on your way," said the head archivist.

But Ximena didn't move. He sighed, adjusting his goggles.

"I assume you wish to speak to Archivist Sánchez again."

"If you would be so kind as to summon her."

"Kind," scoffed the head archivist. "When Queen Catarina was alive—may she rest in peace—no one would have dared to use such a word. Kind." He sniffed again. "I fought its addition to the general dictionary, you know. But they added it anyway. Gave some excuse about the volume and regularity of usage, etcetera. Utterly ridiculous. At least they haven't added 'compassionate' yet. With any luck, I'll be dead before they do.'"

Despite his grumbling, the old man reached up to the board behind his desk, which was decorated with several hundred silver bells, and pulled a string for the bell at the top left corner. Each one had a particular chime that would summon the archivist it was designed for. Archivist Sánchez's was a chipper ping—it sang out through the shelves like a bird's call.

While they waited, the head archivist peered at Ximena through his goggles and twisted the end of his mustache.

"If you weren't the finest candidate in la academia, I'd ask you to be an archivist, Cuatreda Reale."

Ximena stiffened at the rare compliment. "Thank you, head archivist."

"After all, you spend far more time here than your sister does. And quite a bit of it with Archivist Sánchez, though I'm sure I will never understand why. What is it, exactly, that you're looking for?"

She kept her response carefully neutral. "I will let you know when I find it, head archivist."

His enormous eyes narrowed with suspicion. But before he could ask her anything further, a small, high-pitched voice rang out.

"Cuatreda Reale! A most sincere congratulations on your promotion. All of us here at the archives are so very proud of you. Of course, it's only natural that you should be promoted, considering you're the greatest candidate in la academia's history. Well, besides the admiral of course. But who knows, maybe one day you'll surpass even him!"

"Archivist Sánchez," snapped the head archivist. "That will be quite enough. Such enthusiasm is entirely unbecoming for a candidate of la academia. Please escort Cuatreda Reale to the records of her choosing. *In silence.*"

Under his scrutiny, the archivist wilted, her smile wavering. Pía Sánchez always vaguely reminded Ximena of a goldfish. She was squat and round-cheeked, no older than sixteen, her blue eyes wide and roving as if the entire world surprised her. When she talked, she tugged anxiously at the tendrils of red hair that sprouted from her head like fire corals; someone should have introduced the girl to whale oil long ago. But odd as she was, Pía Sánchez also happened to be one of the most brilliant archivists currently in training, which meant, unfortunately, that she was useful. And Ximena had learned long ago not to dismiss anyone who was useful.

Pía recovered from her embarrassment with remarkable speed, offering them both another gap-toothed smile.

"Absolutely, sir. I will endeavor to be the epitome of silence and discretion. Right this way, Cuatreda Reale."

Pía did not endeavor to be the epitome of silence and discretion. As they walked, she peppered Ximena with questions about Captain Domínguez, his capture, and his execution, and her promotion, chattering on as if she hadn't spoken to another human in days. In truth, she probably hadn't. Ximena knew that Pía, in all her strangeness, was just as much of an outsider as she was—it was part of the reason she had chosen the girl as her research partner in the first place.

"And after all that, you come to the archives to continue working," Pía was saying. "A great candidate never rests, and you, Cuatreda Reale, are most certainly a great candidate—"

"Pía," Ximena interrupted her. If she let the girl prattle on any longer, she wouldn't leave the archives until midnight. Thankfully, the archivist fell abruptly silent at the sound of her own name, looking up at Ximena with an expectant smile.

Ximena continued. "Domínguez mentioned *him* at the execution today."

If it was possible, Pía's eyes grew even wider than usual. "*Him?*" she echoed.

"Exactamente. So we need to find every record we have on Captain Salvador Domínguez."

"Yes, yes, of course. That will be between the Year 205 and the Year 247, categorized under the letter D, about seventy-six shelves from here." No one knew the shelves of the archives quite as well as Pía, except for the head archivist himself. Her memory for numbers was so perfect that it was almost frightening. "This way."

Ximena followed her guide through the maze of shelves until they stopped in front of a sign that read *Año 205*. She watched Pía clamber up onto the closest ladder and begin pulling scrolls off the shelves, humming the Luzan anthem to herself as she did so. It took every ounce of self-restraint in Ximena's body to not inform her that she was completely off-pitch.

"There we are," Pía announced after several minutes. Her stack of scrolls was so tall that Ximena couldn't see her face. "Every record on Salvador Domínguez. He really was a very prolific captain. Until he came up against you, Cuatreda Reale."

She swayed down the ladder and heaved the scrolls onto one of the many mahogany desks that were positioned throughout the archives.

"Did you bring our scroll?" Ximena asked.

Pía bobbed her head, reached into the fold of her long black archivist's robe, and pulled out a scroll covered in ink.

"I carry it with me always."

She unrolled it onto the desk—a carefully drawn map of the archipelago covered in small, inked points. Each dot stood for a pirate attack that had occurred in the last four years. They'd spent every hour they had outside of training making it together.

Ximena took a seat. "Then we start at the beginning."

Pía sat beside her, and together they began reading through each and every scroll on Salvador Domínguez until the candle on the desk had burned halfway down and the sunlight from the archive windows grew dim. As they went, they added several more dots to the map, marking each place Domínguez had struck before his death. Pía was right; he had been a successful pirate in his time. He'd likely cost the empire several thousand pounds of silver before Ximena captured him.

"Look at this, Cuatreda Reale," Pía said, pointing to the map. "This corroborates the other data we've collected. The majority of Domínguez's attacks occurred in the southern islands. But over the last year . . ."

"The attacks moved northward," Ximena said, half to herself. "Toward Valuza."

The capital of the empire. The central island of the archipelago. The seat of el ministerio, the queen, and la academia.

Their home.

"It's the same pattern, Cuatreda Reale." Pía only grew more excited as she continued. She dragged her finger across the map, tracing the dark clouds of dots that increased in size as she drew closer to Valuza. "Attacks moving steadily northward toward the capital. Just as the archivists logged centuries ago, right before Gasparilla's Scarlet Siege."

Ximena looked over their map. Her heart pounded at breakneck speed; the blood rushed in her ears like an ocean current.

"By the law," she whispered. "My parents were right."

Pía's eyes went suddenly soft. "Your parents? Is that what made you come up with this plan in the first place?"

Unable to speak, Ximena nodded. She'd never told Pía the real motivation behind this mission of theirs. It hadn't been necessary. So she'd never explained that five years ago, when her parents had stood on la academia's gallows to be hanged for piracy, High Minister Elena de León had asked them for their last words, and Alejandra Reale had responded with two sentences that were burned into Ximena's mind forever.

¡Viva Gasparilla! ¡Viva la libertad!

At first, Ximena had taken those words for what they were: the traitorous ravings of a convicted pirate, chosen to remind the empire of its greatest shame. But then the whispers began arriving on Valuza's shores, warning that Gasparilla had come back from the dead. Other pirates gradually took up Alejandra's battle cry, swearing loyalty to Gasparilla before facing the hangman's noose, and Ximena started to wonder. Magic, of course, was forbidden in the Empire of Luza. But what if someone had broken the law? What if they had used el idioma prohibido to resurrect the one man who had succeeded in sacking the capital?

What if Gasparilla really had returned?

Then the person who caught him would be the greatest pirate hunter in history. And if Ximena Reale was going to earn her Cazador Cloak in spite of el ministerio, that was exactly who she needed to become.

The candidate who caught the most notorious pirate the empire had ever known.

Or at least the candidate who was desperate enough to try.

So in her second year at la academia, Ximena's instincts had brought her to the Maritime Archives, and to the only archivist who was strange enough to pursue such a ridiculous line of questioning. Together, she and Pía Sánchez had relentlessly researched the original Scarlet Siege. Together, they had discovered a pattern: In the years before Gasparilla's infamous attack, every notable pirate in the archipelago had turned their attention from the weaker southern islands to the seas surrounding Valuza. Pirates, after all, were no different from any other sea scavengers. They only attacked when they thought the reward outweighed the risk, and they were emboldened by one another's successes. As Gasparilla gained power, they grew more daring, hunting prizes closer and closer to Valuza.

It was the exact same pattern that she and Pía were now tracing among the current pirates in the archipelago. Multiple vicious attacks on empire ships and pueblos, too close to the capital. History, it seemed, was repeating itself. Which could only mean one thing . . .

"Gasparilla is real," Ximena whispered. "And he's going to attack the capital."

"I knew it; I just knew it!" cried Pía. She went to throw her arms around Ximena, but at the other girl's glare, she pulled back with a sheepish blush. "Perdón. I shouldn't be happy that a pirate is going to raid our island. But you were right, Cuatreda Reale! No one could look at this much evidence and say otherwise. The admiral will simply *have* to commission an expedition to catch Gasparilla, and then everything will happen just as you said. You will become a cazadora, and I will become your archivist, and soon people will be writing scrolls about *us*."

Ximena frowned. She had made that promise to Pía when they first started working together on this research. Ximena hadn't known the first thing about navigating the archives as a young dotreda, so she'd implied that if Pía helped her to capture Gasparilla, then she would make Pía her designated archivist someday. Pía had leapt at the opportunity so quickly that she'd never questioned Ximena's motives, or whether Ximena would ever choose her over Marquesa.

It was just as well. Ximena had never *sworn* anything to Pía. She'd merely made a suggestion. The girl had run with it the rest of the way. So when the time came to clip the line that bound them together, Ximena wouldn't hesitate to do so.

But Pía's future was far from the most important thing she had to consider now. Was their map truly strong enough evidence to present to the admiral? Cazador expeditions were never commissioned on gut instinct or hunches alone. There had to be facts and strategy behind every deployment of the armada's resources. And why would anyone believe the conjecture of a candidate and an archivist in training? Especially when that candidate was a Reale, and the archivist in training was Pía Sánchez. Ximena couldn't afford to injure the professional relationship she had with the admiral. She couldn't afford to be wrong.

Still, if they waited too long, they might miss their chance. Gasparilla might attack before a proper trap could be set and disappear into the wind again before Ximena could capture him, taking her last hope of becoming a cazadora with him. She was already running out of time—Marquesa was a breath away from expulsion, and the Royal Examination wasn't too far in the distance.

So her mind turned like a ship's wheel, navigating options and outcomes.

Meanwhile, Pía chattered on, completely unaware of her partner's concerns.

"Oh, I knew we could do it. I never doubted you for a moment, Cuatreda Reale. If there was anyone who was going to be able to catch Gasparilla, it was you. With a little bit of help from me, of course, but I could never take full credit for your brilliance."

"Pía."

"We can take the map to the admiral tomorrow. Then he can take it to el ministerio—"

"Pía."

"Now that I'm thinking about it, we should sign the bottom of the scroll, that way everyone will know that we were the ones who made it—"

"Pía!"

"Yes, Cuatreda Reale?"

"I need time to think."

"Yes, of course, take all the time you need. I'll just wait here—"

"Alone."

"Oh." Pía's shoulders fell; she tugged at a strand of her hair. "Yes, naturally you need time alone. My father always said I distracted him when he was working, you know, and I realize I can be—but I'm rambling now. Very well, Cuatreda Reale. I'll just return these records to their proper places. Don't want them getting lost, right?"

She scooped the scrolls into her arms and staggered off, glancing back just once over her shoulder. But Ximena wasn't thinking about the archivist any longer. She was staring down at their map, tracing a finger over the collections of dots, as if they were constellations that would guide the ship of her future to victory.

Ximena rarely struggled with indecision. But when she did, there was only one remedy for it. So she stood up from the desk, tucked the map under her arm, and walked through aisle after aisle of bookshelves until she reached the furthest, darkest corner of the archives, where a small iron door was guarded by two archivists in training. Luckily, they were young and easily frightened—the moment they saw her, they jumped to attention and raced to open the door for her.

"If you please, Treveda Reale," one of them sputtered.

"It's *Cuatreda* Reale, idiota," the other one hissed. "Weren't you paying attention this morning?"

Rolling her good eye, Ximena pushed past them and into the room, letting the door click shut behind her.

Clearly the archivists hadn't been in this chamber for a long while—the dust was so thick that it coated her tongue, tasting of salt. But it was just as well. She loved this part of la academia above all others, and she preferred to experience it in private whenever possible. The Chamber of Founding Scrolls contained the oldest records in the archives, from when Alessandra first led the armada to conquer the archipelago and bring it under the Luzan banner. It was where the first copies of the law were housed, and, of course, where the original records on Captain Gasparilla were kept.

The chamber was so dark Ximena had to squint through the candlelight to make out the scrolls on the mahogany shelves. She ran a gloved finger across until she stopped at the section marked with a golden G. Then she pulled a scroll from the shelf and sat at the desk in the center of the room, opening it to the section she knew by heart. It began with an immaculately drawn illustration of a double-masted galleon in spidery black ink. According to eyewitness testimony, this was Gasparilla's ship, which went by the unpretentious name of *La Leyenda.*

The Legend.

"The Life and Deeds of the Infamous Pirate Captain, José Gasparilla," Ximena read aloud to herself.

Below the title sat a disorderly clump of paragraphs detailing the many, many possible versions of Gasparilla's origin story. Some words had been crossed out and others entirely blacked out with ink—proof of some poor archivist's attempt to keep a logical record.

> *José Gasparilla, also known as "Gaspar" and "El Tiburón," was allegedly born to a noble family in the south of Luza. He was a favorite among the ladies of the Luzan court, but when he spurned one lover for another, the forsaken woman accused him of stealing the queen's jewels. Unjustly faced with the gallows, Gasparilla turned pirate, commandeering a merchant vessel and renaming it* La Leyenda. *Since then, he has captured a total of* ~~thirty-seven~~ ~~forty-two~~ *fifty-five ships, and his name has been attached to raids on the Luzan cities of Novada, Chicoyo, and Sibón—before each raid, he left a note that was marked with a crimson rose and a golden G. It is rumored that he has a base somewhere in the archipelago, where he keeps a king's ransom of treasure. . . .*

Alternatively, José Gasparilla was ~~the son of a merchant~~ an orphan born in the slums of Valuza, Luza's capital. He turned pirate at the age of fourteen, after he kidnapped a nobleman's daughter and demanded that a ship and crew be given as a ransom. He named the stolen ship La Leyenda and set sail for the archipelago, where he founded the Republic of Pirates. Leaving a note marked with a crimson rose and a golden G . . .

Alternatively, José Gasparilla was a fisherman who abandoned his wife and children in search of treasure. He assembled a fleet of pirate ships . . .

And so it went, each one more ridiculous than the last. But Ximena had read all of this before. She skipped further down to the most relevant part of the story.

Driven by a hunger for personal wealth and power, Captain Gasparilla chose to ally himself with rebel pirate forces from the greater archipelago. He spearheaded the traitorous Scarlet Siege against the capital island of Valuza, stealing several thousand pounds of silver in a galleon called La Leyenda and nearly crippling the empire in its infancy (see reference above for more information on the development of the silver trade). Thankfully, however, he was killed in battle against the armada by Alessandra herself in Year 1 of the Luzan Empire, and was subsequently buried in el Cementerio de los Traidores. . . .

She dragged her finger to the sentence that would be engraved in her mind forever. The words were scrawled in a disorderly clump. The archivists must have added them to the record later, perhaps against the orders of their superiors.

The body of Captain José Gasparilla was removed from its grave by unknown agents and never seen again.

This was why Ximena came to the Chamber of Founding Scrolls: to remind herself why she was hunting this pirate in the first place. She closed her eyes, imagining herself for a moment as the great Alessandra, radiant and terrifying, rapier pointed at Captain Gasparilla's throat. She could see it all in the darkness of her mind. Like Alessandra, she would be the savior the archipelago didn't even know it needed. Today, everyone thought of her as Ximena Reale, daughter of traitors. But when Gasparilla faced the noose, they would shout her name from here to the horizon.

Ximena Reale, hero of Luza.

And if she wasn't brave enough to risk losing the admiral's favor, was she really a hero at all?

She never had a chance to answer that question. Behind her, the chamber doors suddenly flew open. Ximena leapt to her feet, unsheathing her rapier and spinning to face the intruder.

"Easy there, capitana. This face is worth a queen's ransom."

Ximena didn't lower her weapon.

"What are you doing here?" she demanded.

Dante de León smirked as if he didn't have a blade pointed at his throat. His pupils were large and dark, his eyes bloodshot. He was drunk, yet again. She fought the urge to recoil from the stench radiating from him in sickening waves.

"I could ask you the same question," he said. "All those nights when we thought you were studying or writing reports. What will people say when they hear that Ximena Reale has an obsession with the founding of the Luzan Empire?"

"It's not an obsession," replied Ximena. "I merely came to verify some information on behalf of the head archivist. I'll be back in the east wing by dinnertime."

He lifted an eyebrow. "You do know that it's nearly midnight."

Midnight? Ximena's stomach twisted. She had missed dinner and evening roll call; she would receive a disciplinary mark on her record for the first time since she was an uveda. Not the start she wanted for her cuatreda training.

But she couldn't allow Dante to gain the upper hand. He was already grinning like a cat with a mouse between its paws. So she shifted topics with her usual dexterity.

"How did you get access to this archive?"

"I might be able to answer your question more accurately without your sword at my neck, capitana."

Reluctantly, Ximena let her arm fall. But she didn't sheathe her rapier—a wise cazador would never release their weapon in their enemy's presence.

"I've never seen you in the archives before," she said.

Dante sniffed, sweeping his hair from his eyes. "I'm a de León. I have no use for studying. Besides, this place smells like dead fish. What exactly are we reading?"

"Nothing you would be interested in, I can promise you."

"I think I'll be the judge of that."

She reached out to stop him, but he stepped past her with a

dancer's elegance, bending over the desk. His brow rose a second time as he glanced between the scroll and the map she and Pía had created.

"'The Life and Deeds of the Infamous'—in the name of the law. You can't be serious, Cuatreda Reale." A laugh burst from his chest. "Gasparilla? You've spent all your time holed up in this dust pit looking for *Gasparilla?* You're either a thousand times more stupid than anyone gave you credit for, or you're terribly desperate."

"You're free to leave now, Cuatreda de León."

"But I've just begun to enjoy myself. Gasparilla!" he laughed again. "Your mother told you one too many pirate stories, no? You must behave, Ximenita, or Gasparilla will sneak into your room and gut you like a fish!"

Her fingers curled so tightly around her rapier handle that she could have bent the metal. "As I said," she said through gritted teeth, "you're free to leave."

"Why? Do I make you nervous, Cuatreda Reale?" He leaned closer, his wine-dark eyes amused. "Or perhaps you're scared of Gasparilla, and you're here to make yourself feel better."

"You never answered me. What are you doing here, and how did you get access?"

Dante sat on the edge of the desk and crossed one ankle over the other. Ximena hadn't noticed until now that he was wearing civilian clothes—an expensive black doublet and hose, likely from the best tailor in Valuza. Reaching toward his belt, he pulled out a slip of white paper and waved it over his head.

"This was found tacked to the north gate. I was instructed to bring it to the archives, which I did."

"Clearly."

"Anyway, that old sack of bones at the front desk let slip that you were in the Chamber of Old Useless Scrolls, so I thought I'd pay you a visit. There was something I was supposed to tell you, though I can't seem to remember what it was." Here he smiled again—that arrogant, white-toothed smile. "As for the second part of your rather insulting question, I'm a de León. I could access the queen's bedchamber if I wanted to."

Ximena didn't want to know anything about Dante de León and the queen's bedchamber. Instead, she reached over and pulled the paper from his hand, unfolding it carefully with her gloved fingers.

"That's empire property, you know," Dante said in a tone that indicated he couldn't care less.

Meanwhile, Ximena stood frozen. Her throat swelled shut; her lips twitched.

It couldn't be.

It must be a trick of the light.

Striding toward the lantern that sat on the desk, she tilted the paper into its dim amber glow. Yet the same symbol stared back at her—a crimson rose and a golden G.

"Where did you say this was found?" Her voice was raspy.

"The north gate. Are you feeling all right, capitana? You look like you could use a glass of strong rum."

"I don't drink," said Ximena absentmindedly, not taking her eyes off the paper.

"Ah. That explains quite a bit."

Ximena scanned the paper again. There was the rose, painted

with blood-red ink, and the golden G hovering over it. But beneath the symbol were two simple lines of hand-scrawled writing:

The honorable Captain José Gasparilla advises you to evacuate the capital of Valuza before the full moon. Those who remain forfeit their lives.

Ximena Reale had two thoughts.

The first exploded into her mind, leaving her breathless with amazement: He was real. The pirate she had spent years searching for, obsessing over, studying and analyzing and tracking—he was as real as she was. She held his note in her hand; she was reading his handwriting. More incredible still, he would be in her city within a week, just as she and Pía had predicted. The legendary Gasparilla. Hers at last.

Then the second thought went through her like a cannonball.

She had to tell the admiral.

Ximena stuffed the note in her pocket, grabbed her map, and headed for the door. They had one week to evacuate Valuza before Gasparilla arrived, and if the stories about him were true, it would take every candidate and cazador in la academia to prevent a slaughter. The high minister must be notified, and the queen warned—

"They won't believe you."

She paused with her hand around the door handle.

"The admiral already saw the note," Dante continued, strolling up to her with his hands in his pockets. "He doesn't think it's a credible threat. Do you know how many pirates have said they're going to sack Valuza in the last two hundred years? Do you know how many have actually succeeded?" His smile bent into a sneer; his eyes were suddenly sharp and lucid. "None. So it might be time to give up your delusions, capitana. You're not going to pass the Royal Examination, and you're not going to become a cazadora. Honestly, why you wouldn't want to just disappear to a deserted island with a drink in your hand instead of taking that idiotic test is beyond me."

"Because I'm not like you, Cuatreda de León."

She didn't even realize she'd spoken aloud until she saw the surprised twitch of Dante's lips. But it was too late now. The words lingered between them in the darkness.

"I'm not like you," she repeated. "I believe in things that are far larger and more important than myself. So however much I might want to give up on my *delusions*, as you call them, I won't. I can't."

For a moment, Dante was silent. His eyes moved from the top of her head to the toes of her boots. She had seen him look at girls many times before, assessing which ones would be easiest to enthrall. But this was a different kind of look, the kind one used on an enemy, sizing them up, weighing how difficult this fight was about to be. When he shrugged, she knew he had decided it wasn't worth what little effort he had to give.

"Well if you'd like to earn yourself another set of disciplinary marks, I certainly won't be the one to stop you. For now, I have a bottle of rum that is summoning me from afar. May the seas be with you, capitana."

He reached over her shoulder to open the door. She stiffened at the reek of his breath.

"Ah," he said, turning until his face hovered inches from hers. "I have just remembered what I meant to tell you. Marquesa is in prison for debauchery, pursuant to Section 431 of the code. The poor girl just can't hold her liquor."

Before Ximena could answer, Dante de León was gone, the door closed behind him.

Capítulo Tres

"I must speak to the admiral forthwith." Ximena stood at the door to the admiral's office, her glower dark enough to frighten any pirate. "This is an emergency of the highest order."

"As I said before, Treveda Reale—"

"Cuatreda Reale."

"*Cuatreda* Reale, the answer is still no. The admiral gave strict instructions that he was not to be disturbed past midnight, and as you can see," Cazadora Cecilia gestured to the clock hanging above the door, "it is currently half past twelve."

"This information is time sensitive, Cazadora Cecilia."

"Is it now? Discovered a fundamental secret of the universe, have we?"

Cazadora Cecilia, a young cazadora who already had sun-spotted skin, bleached hair, and yellowed teeth from countless deployments, stood guard outside the admiral's office each night without fail. No one, candidate or cazador, spoke to the admiral without going through her first—she was the admiral's prized first mate on every deployment. This wouldn't have been an issue in itself, if Cazadora Cecilia hadn't considered Ximena's presence at la academia to be an affront to the ideals of the Luzan Empire and an unfortunate lapse in the admiral's otherwise perfect judgment. But Ximena knew better than to waste her time convincing Cazadora Cecilia of her own worthiness. The woman was an iron wall, and the only way to get through iron walls was by battering them down.

"I'm not sure what information could possibly be so dire that you would seek to defy the admiral's orders, but whatever it is, you can leave it with me, and I will convey it to the admiral at the proper time," Cazadora Cecilia was saying. "You would do well to remember the chain of command, Cuatreda Reale. The rules exist for a reason, regardless of what your parents might have told you."

"With all due respect, Cazadora Cecilia, I don't believe either one of us is qualified to interpret this information," Ximena said. "I must speak to the admiral myself. Immediately."

"How dare you—"

"Cuatreda Reale."

The admiral stood in the doorway. He showed no signs of having been asleep—his hair was mostly groomed and oiled, his beard trimmed, and his uniform pristine. After glancing between them, he settled his shark-like stare on Ximena.

"What is this about?"

"Sir," said Ximena, immediately snapping into a salute. When the admiral acknowledged her, she continued. "I have evidence that Valuza will be attacked by the full moon. We must evacuate the city and capture the pirate as soon as possible."

The admiral's gaze narrowed. Then, after a long stretch of silence, he tipped his head.

"Come in," he said.

Ximena bowed, stepping past Cecilia to follow him into his office.

"But—but—your excellency," stammered Cecilia. "It's half past twelve, and I—"

"Thank you. That will be all, Cecilia," said the admiral.

To Ximena's delight, he shut the door in her dumbstruck face.

The admiral's office, which was housed in the southernmost turret of the west wing, was a cavernous, circular room of polished limestone. Although it was just as sparsely furnished as the rest of la academia, the domed ceiling was painted with a navigator's map of the night sky, with stars marked in white and constellations connected with shimmering gold paint. On the far wall, behind a large walnut desk, a collection of wooden clocks hung in straight, even lines, one for each of the three hundred and twenty-five islands in the archipelago. This was one of the admiral's many rules: A cazador must always know where they are, where they are going, and when they will arrive. Nothing could be left to chance. De la preparación surge la perfección.

Ximena had learned that from him.

After all, he was the one who had saved her and Marquesa. When their parents were found guilty of piracy and executed, when Elena de León and the rest of the empire would have turned their backs and left them to die on the streets of Valuza, the admiral had seen the potential in the Reale sisters. He had seen the symbol they could be for la academia, for Valuza, for the entire archipelago. Two orphaned children of pirates, redeemed and transformed into loyal servants of Luza.

It was a tale worthy of songs.

Of course, there were only two ways for candidates to be admitted to la academia. The first was by passing the entrance examination, which was offered to every thirteen-year-old Luzan child in academies across the archipelago. Only the brightest students with the highest scores were brought to Valuza for training, although patrimonios like Dante had their scores "balanced" by "additional demonstrations of merit," which really meant that their parents were ministers and la academia could not afford to alienate them.

But Ximena and Marquesa hadn't been admitted by passing the entrance examination. They had been admitted by the second and far rarer path to la academia: the caso especial. Each cazador was allowed to give out three casos especiales in their entire career to children they believed had promise for reasons that could not be tested by the exam. Most cazadores gave them to the children of powerful merchants or ministers who could help advance their careers. The admiral could have used his in any number of politically advantageous ways.

Instead, he had chosen to take a gamble. He had given both of his remaining casos especiales to Marquesa and Ximena Reale—a decision that the rest of la academia and the majority of Valuza had yet to forgive him for.

Until tonight, Ximena told herself. Soon, the entire empire would know that Ximena Reale had saved them from *La Leyenda's* cannons, and no one would second-guess her legitimacy ever again.

She could hardly contain her excitement as she waited by the admiral's desk for his signal to speak. So many hours of work, so many sleepless nights—all for this moment. Her fingers drummed against her thigh. She would start with Gasparilla's invitation, and then work her way through the map to make her case . . .

"I cannot free your sister, Ximena."

Ximena blinked, staring at the admiral as he reclined in his leather chair.

"Sir?"

"She was found at the north gate entirely incoherent. I had no choice but to imprison her for debauchery and drunkenness, pursuant to Section 431 of the code. And that doesn't even begin to address her jaunt into the city, which, as you know, is also a violation of the code."

"Yes, sir. I couldn't agree with you more," Ximena said dumbly.

"Her offenses are grievous enough to require review. She will be brought before the cazadores for an internal hearing, and if she is found guilty, she will be expelled from la academia without delay."

Panic speared her chest. Dante was right. This was real. Her sister had finally run out of chances. She would be expelled, forced to scrap through the darkest barrios of Valuza—Ximena would never see her again.

Ximena's first instinct was to argue on her sister's behalf. But this was a time for strategy, not blind desperation. If she tried to plead Marquesa's case now, she'd almost certainly lose, and likely injure her sister's relationship with the admiral further. But if she stayed the course and focused on Gasparilla, she might have a chance at becoming a cazadora. Cazadora Ximena Reale could protect her sister in a way that Cuatreda Reale could not.

So Ximena swallowed down her fear like salt water, clenched her fists at her sides, and barreled forward.

"Understood, sir," she said. "But I haven't come here to ask for my sister's freedom."

The admiral's dark brow furrowed. "Then what have you come here for?"

"As I said, sir, I have evidence that Valuza will be attacked by the pirate captain Gasparilla. We must evacuate the city as quickly as possible."

She pulled the note from her pocket and pressed it to the admiral's desk. He stared at it, unmoving.

"I thought that was simply an excuse you used in front of Cecilia," he said. "It never occurred to me that you might be serious."

Ximena's shoulders stiffened. "Sir?"

"I instructed Cuatreda de León to deliver this note to the archives myself. It's most likely a prank, or perhaps some madman's delusion."

"Sir," said Ximena. "With all due respect, I beg to differ. I have studied the history of Gasparilla extensively, and—"

"Extensively?" The admiral's eyes narrowed. "I hope you have not been neglecting your studies to chase after a ghost."

"I have proof that he isn't a ghost, sir. If I may?"

"Cuatreda Reale," the admiral said, his voice a warning.

But Ximena had not spent hours buried in the archives to give up at the first sign of resistance. She reached into her jacket and pulled out the map, unfurling it on his desk, jabbing a finger into the parchment.

"Sir, I've tracked every major pirate strike for the last four years. The latest strikes follow the same pattern that our archivists logged two hundred years ago. See? The attacks move steadily northward toward Valuza, just as they did before Gasparilla's Scarlet Siege. These pirates are growing bolder, sir. I think they hope that another Scarlet Siege is coming."

The admiral leaned over the map, his gaze roving over the parchment. The clocks above his head *tick, tick, ticked* themselves into oblivion. For all her studying in the last four years, Ximena had never quite learned to read her commander's expressions. His eyes revealed nothing; his mouth was a neutral line. So his thoughts were just as inaccessible to her now as they had ever been, and it was driving her to madness.

She didn't know how long he looked over the map. But the clock for the island of Valuza had just struck 12:45 when he said:

"I thought I taught you better than this, Ximena."

If he'd driven a rapier through her, it would have hurt less.

"This isn't a plan. It's a theory, and a loose one at that," he continued. "I couldn't commission a single cazador scout off this data, let alone the entire armada. It's a set of numbers held together by nothing but pure speculation. Gasparilla has not come back from the dead. And even if he had, and even if he were mad enough to attempt a second Scarlet Siege, he would never succeed. Valuza is completely impenetrable to enemy attacks. The empire made sure of that after the siege. In other words, Cuatreda Reale, you have wasted precious hours that you could have spent preparing for the Royal Examination. I didn't think you capable of such negligence."

"Sir, we both know I'm not going to pass the Royal Examination while Elena de León is in charge of el ministerio. Not even you have the power to override her verdict."

The admiral was one of the only people who understood her in this way. Long before he was admiral of la academia, Gabriel Pérez was a poor, orphaned boy in the southern archipelago who clawed his way to survival. One day, when armada ships visited his island, a cazador was attacked by bandits who stole his rapier and cloak. A young Gabriel Pérez followed the bandits and fought them fist to fist; he walked away with the rapier and cloak, triumphant, and returned them to the cazador. The grateful cazador granted Gabriel a caso especial on the spot. He was just ten years old. Thus began the meteoric rise of Gabriel Pérez, the greatest cazador in recent memory. Ximena had clung on to that story with a vicious hope: It didn't matter where, what, or who you came from. If you vowed to protect the law, the law would protect you.

So if anyone could understand her struggle against the patrimonio candidates and the politics of el ministerio, it was the admiral. But it wasn't as simple as that. La academia's existence was dependent on el ministerio's good will and the crown's purse. Regardless of what his personal opinion might be, the admiral would please them over Ximena every time.

"Cuatreda Reale," he said, sighing. "You are the best candidate I have ever had the pleasure of teaching. I have never once regretted giving you the caso especial because I knew from the day I met you that you would be a credit to this academy, to the empire, and to me. Please don't make me regret my choice now by sacrificing your future for a ghost story."

The disappointment in his voice was more than she could bear. "If you'll just give me a chance to explain our plan—"

"*Our* plan?"

Idiota. She wished she could rewind her words like runaway mooring lines. "Archivist Pía Sánchez helped me to create this map, sir."

"You involved an archivist in training in this?"

"Yes, sir, and I'll take full responsibility for that. But regardless, both of us believe that this is our opportunity to bring Gasparilla to justice. To make an example of him for all other pirates to see."

"Cuatreda Reale."

"We could cut him off before he attacks, blockade el ministerio and el palacio real with armada ships—"

"Cuatreda Reale," the admiral said, standing from his chair. "Your passion has clouded your judgment. I will not—indeed, I cannot—waste the time and energy of my cazadores on theories. 'The only truth is that which can be proven beyond all reasonable doubt.' You must know who I am quoting?"

Ximena lowered her eye. "Alessandra, sir. Founder of Luza and author of the law."

"Precisely." He sat once more, taking Gasparilla's note in his hand and sliding it into the drawer of his desk. "There will be no more discussion. If you choose to take any further action in this matter, I will charge you with insubordination and you will be punished accordingly. Am I understood?"

"Perfectly, sir."

"Bueno. Your access to the Maritime Archives is henceforth revoked until I restore it. And, since you weren't present for this evening's dinner and roll call, you will receive two disciplinary marks on your record."

Ximena flinched. "Can I at least visit my sister, sir?"

"Absolutely not. You are dismissed."

Her cheeks burned with humiliation. Never had she been so thoroughly humbled by a commanding officer. She knew the admiral had a kind of fondness for her, if it were possible for a man like the admiral to be fond of anything. But there was no persuading him on matters of the law. If he believed this threat to be insignificant, there was nothing she could say to convince him otherwise. So she saluted him with her fingers to her lips and turned to depart the office.

"Sir?" she said when she had reached the door.

"Yes, Cuatreda Reale?"

"Was there anyone with my sister when she was found at the north gate?"

A pause. Then the admiral said: "Cuatreda de León was with her."

"And was he charged with debauchery?"

Another pause. "No, he was not."

If she had disliked Dante de León before, she despised him now. He had coaxed Marquesa into one trap and Ximena into another, and while the Reale sisters suffered, he put his pretty silver-blond head on his pillow without worry, certain that his name would protect him as it always had. But however much Ximena was tempted to lie and cheat to exact her revenge, she was not a de León. She would defeat her enemy the only way she knew how—with honor. She would earn her way back into the admiral's favor. She would become the best cuatreda in history.

Ximena nodded. "Thank you, sir."

She turned on her heel and exited the office, ignoring the satisfied look on Cazadora Cecilia's face.

Ximena's thoughts raced as she walked through la academia's darkened hallways. While she loathed to admit it, Dante was right. No one was going to take her plan to capture Gasparilla seriously. Perhaps her research truly had been for nothing—perhaps she should have spent more time tutoring Marquesa instead of hiding in the cramped and dusty archives. Now her sister was locked in la academia's prison and the admiral thought Ximena had lost her mind.

At this rate, she would be an old woman before she could become a cazadora, if she ever became one at all.

But what if the admiral were wrong? What if Gasparilla really was preparing to attack the city? He would catch them by surprise, in a moment of weakness, and devour them all, pillaging and plundering as he pleased. What a humiliation that would be for la academia! What an affront to the law and all things good! The thought made Ximena's heart claw at her ribs. But Section 224 of the code demanded she obey her commanding officer or face charges of insubordination, and the penalty for such an offense was not simply disciplinary review—it was expulsion. So Ximena would honor the admiral. She would honor the code. She would forget about Gasparilla.

Even if that meant letting her island burn.

By the time she reached her dormitory in the treveda barracks, Ximena's shoulders were drooping with exhaustion, and the scar tissue beneath her eye patch was throbbing painfully. She fumbled in her pocket for the key, pushed it into the lock of door 38, and shuffled into the lonely darkness of her room. Feeling for a match, she lit the stub of a candle that was waiting on the dresser (Ximena always ran her candles down to nothing before she threw them out—in her opinion, there were few sins greater than wastefulness). Then she went through her usual evening routine with mechanical precision, unfastening her hair, taking off her eye patch, washing her face, changing from her uniform into a nightshirt, and turning down the bed, leaving her room spotless all the while.

At last, she tucked herself under the thin wool blankets and attempted to rest. Ximena never really slept—her thoughts always spun on endlessly on a wheel, conjuring worst-case scenarios and strategies to go with them. Tonight, she imagined all the ways Gasparilla might attack: The most obvious, of course, would be through the harbor, but no one who called themselves a pirate would attempt something so absurd, especially not with la academia just a stone's throw away. Still, Gasparilla had demonstrated that sort of boldness in the past—he might try it again. Or perhaps he would sail up the river channel through the center of the city and take his chances against the capital guards. If he could capture the palacio, then the queen would have no choice but to give him anything he wanted. . . .

On and on the wheel spun. But in her time at la academia, Ximena had become very good at putting up with her own thoughts, even if she couldn't quite ignore them. So she laid on her back and stared at the ceiling, waiting, as she always did, for morning to come.

When the bell in the courtyard had chimed five times but the sky was still dark, Ximena heard a knock outside her door.

"New cuatredas, report for training in the southeast wing by sunup!"

She scrambled out of bed, changing into her uniform and pulling on her boots. Sometime in the night, her natural Reale curls had erupted into a frenzied frizz; she slicked them down with whale oil and tied her hair at the base of her neck. Then she turned to inspect herself in the small mirror attached to the dresser, frowning. Her skin was a sickly green from lack of sleep, her lips were dry and cracked, and where her left eye should have been, a sunken hole of scarred skin remained. She didn't like to think about the story behind her missing eye. The memory was too terrible to revisit regularly. But her uniform was pristine, as always, so she strapped her eye patch over her face and her rapier to her belt with a satisfied grunt.

Ah, idiota. She'd almost forgotten: She had to pack her things and move them to the southeast wing. She pulled a cloth rucksack from under her bed and tucked her two spare uniforms, an extra pair of boots, and a jar of whale oil inside. She had nothing sentimental to take with her to the cuatreda barracks—she didn't believe in nostalgia. Reflecting on the past was for those who could afford it. So she took one last look at her dormitory, surveying the bed and the window that looked out at the sea and left it behind without another thought.

With gray light slipping through la academia's windows, Ximena hurried down the hallway and half-ran toward the southeast wing. Her rucksack bumped against her hip, her heartbeat pounded in her ears, and her nose tingled with the smell of vinegar, indicating that the servants had mopped the floors during the night. Finally, just as the sun was peeking over the horizon, she arrived in the southeast wing—two minutes early, and with Dante de León nowhere in sight. She tipped her chin up proudly. She would prove herself a cazadora yet.

A cuatreda waited at the entrance. He was short, squat, and barrel-chested, with a long dark braid falling down his back. One leg of his trousers had been trimmed at the knee, revealing a scarred stub of flesh settled into a metal boot, proof that training at la academia was just as dangerous as actual service in the armada.

"You must be Ximena Reale," the cuatreda growled. "The admiral said you would arrive first."

Ximena bowed her head, the typical salute one gave to an equal. The cuatreda offered no salute in return.

"It won't help you," he said. "Being a favorite of the admiral. You are starting with nothing. Less than nothing, as the offspring of pirates. You should know that, before we begin our cuatreda orientation."

Ximena nodded; she expected nothing less.

A moment later, footsteps echoed off the limestone walls. Two newly minted cuatredas were hurrying toward them—a droopy-eyed boy and a stringy, red-headed girl. They stopped with a salute, glancing warily at Ximena.

"Feliciano Córdoba and Elena Espinoza," said the cuatreda. "Late."

"Our apologies," said Feliciano.

"It won't happen again," said Elena.

"No," the cuatreda answered them, mouth set in a grim line. "It will not."

Then he pulled a pocket watch from his doublet, checked it, and snapped it shut again.

"It seems that the young de León is also late," he mused. "Perhaps mornings do not agree with him."

All three candidates waited in silence for what seemed like an eternity. Then, at last, Dante de León strolled down the hallway at the leisurely speed of a sea snail, his doublet untucked and his silver-blond curls dripping into his eyes. Sidling up beside them, he swept back his hair and, to Ximena's horror, clapped the cuatreda on the shoulder.

"Congratulations, Juan Carlos," he said. "I hear you might be up for the Royal Examination next month. Ready to don the Cazador Cloak, are you?"

Juan Carlos grimaced, shifting out of Dante's reach. Ximena instantly liked the other cuatreda boy more. But to Dante, that recoil was like blood in the water—his lips curled into a dangerous smirk.

"If you'd like," he continued, "I could put in a good word for you with my mother. She'd be thrilled to promote you—she loves to humiliate me with promising young talent."

Juan Carlos gave an offended snort. "There is only one way to earn your Cazador Cloak, Cuatreda de León," he replied. "First, you must rank among the top ten candidates in the cuatreda class, a feat that requires near-perfect scores in every course of study. Then, you are nominated for the Royal Examination, which is held every two years and judged by the high minister herself. Should you pass the examination, then—and only then—will you join the cazadores. It is a *fair* and *honorable* process, governed by the law."

"Fair and honorable. Is that what they teach in Luzan schools these days?" Dante drawled. "Next they're going to start telling you that el ministerio cares more about justice than silver and the queen doesn't drink herself silly at her fiestas every night."

Juan Carlos's cheeks turned a blotchy red. Dante's shot had hit its mark. "Tal vez no lo entiendas, patrimonio, because you've never had to try. But I was admitted to this academy on merit alone. I received a perfect score on my entrance examination, and I intend to receive another perfect score on the Royal Examination. I didn't accomplish that by bowing to patrimonio bribes. I don't intend to start now."

Dante only yawned. "What a thrilling testimony. Speaking of entertainment, I've heard that cuatredas can keep liquor in their rooms. Is that true, Juan Carlos?"

"Not unless they wish to spend the night in prison. Follow me, candidates."

He punctuated his sentence with a snap of his watch and led them into the southeast wing.

The cuatredas were beginning to stir—doors slammed, and footsteps echoed, candidates trickling out of their rooms and downstairs to the mess hall. As he walked, Juan Carlos talked over his shoulder, the clang of his metal boot keeping time.

"Cuatredas must pass a total of five courses: Advanced Navigation, Weaponry and Combat, Seamanship, Maritime Strategy, and, of course, Application of the Law. Your courses will meet in the rooms on either side of this hall." He pointed to his left and right. "You will train from sunup to sundown and study during your free time. The knowledge you acquire will be tested during your deployments, for which you will be drafted once every lunar cycle."

They stopped in front of a large, wooden board, where a crowd of cuatredas was gathered. Whispers buzzed among the candidates, nervous, restless, until the appearance of a cazadora in her long, black cloak silenced them. Leaning forward, they watched her pin a long piece of parchment to the board, and then waited until she disappeared down the hallway before surging forward, jostling against one another for a better view. Ximena, tall as she was, read over their heads with her eyes narrowed.

Ten names were written on the parchment:

Juan Carlos Alonso
Esteban Blanco
Carolina López
Sofía Díaz
Isabella Moreno . . .

So it continued. Juan Carlos cleared his throat and checked his pocket watch. "The candidates posted on the parchment are the top ten in the cuatreda class," he said, an edge of pride creeping into his voice. "If they hold their positions, they will take the Royal Examination that is being held next month. Do not expect to find your name on that list anytime soon. In fact, do not expect to find it at all—the vast majority of cuatredas never become cazadores. Candidates who fail the examination are demoted to the lesser naval guard, where they spend the rest of their lives patrolling harbors and taking orders from their half-wit commanders until they die of scurvy. This way, por favor."

They followed him further down the hallway, where the cuatreda barracks were housed. But Ximena couldn't help but glance back over her shoulder, staring at the board. Her name would be on it. It was not a possibility, but a certainty. She would do everything in her power to rank among the top ten cuatredas and be nominated for the Royal Examination.

Of course, capturing Gasparilla would have made that task easier.

But she shoved the thought from her mind. She must find another way to earn her Cazador Cloak, even if it meant relying on nothing but her mind, her hands, and the providence of the law.

At the far end of the hallway, Juan Carlos stopped for a second time, glancing over them with cool detachment.

"These are your rooms. You will leave your belongings here, and then depart to the mess hall for breakfast." He glanced at his watch. "It is currently seven. Your first class, Advanced Navigation, begins at seven thirty. Do *not* be late."

He took a slip of paper from his pocket, narrowed his eyes, and read: "Elena, room 428. Feliciano, room 413. Dante, room 406. Ximena, room 407."

He stuffed the paper back in his pocket and saluted them with a bow of his head. With that, he was gone, the clang of his boot echoing down the hallway.

Dante raised a brow. "¡Qué guay! We're neighbors, capitana."

Ignoring him, Ximena walked to door 407, dropped her rucksack inside the dormitory, and shut the door again. Then she turned and left for the mess hall, determined to stay as far away from Dante de León as possible. Otherwise she might end up killing him, and that would hardly be an auspicious start to her time as a cuatreda.

In the mess hall, Ximena served herself a breakfast of boiled oats and fried plantains before sitting alone at one of the square wooden tables, silent. She finished her plate in seventeen evenly sized spoonfuls and slipped out before anyone could notice her, taking the stairs up to the classrooms and stopping at the door labeled "Advanced Navigation." She glanced at the clock on the wall: 7:25 a.m.

"I expect your audience with the admiral didn't end well."

Dante leaned against the wall, eating fried plantains out of his palm. The grease dripped onto his trousers, but he didn't seem to care. He was handsome regardless of the state of his clothing, a fact that irritated Ximena even further.

"I sympathize, capitana, I truly do," he said. "Who wouldn't want to capture Gasparilla? A man who lives in defiance of the law, sailing the seas without a care in the world, bound to nothing and no one." He looked away from her. "I think that's what Captain Domínguez meant before he died. Pirates have the one thing we never will—freedom."

For the first time since Ximena had known him, Dante's voice was suddenly, strangely soft, his dark eyes glassy with a longing she didn't understand. But then he sighed, plopping a plantain onto his tongue, and whatever she had seen vanished like smoke.

"Es lo que hay," Dante said. "Stories are stories for a reason, no?"

Ximena forced herself to stay silent. It took every ounce of her willpower.

"The situation regarding your sister is an unfortunate one. Really, if I could have prevented what happened in any way, I would have done so. But you know, it's not too late to take action. My mother's office finalizes all expulsions from la academia." He wiped his oily fingers against his doublet. "Arrangements could easily be made."

Once again, Ximena said nothing. She wanted to throttle him, to toss him into a cold, dark prison cell alongside her sister so he could experience the same pain the Reale sisters felt, for once. But she couldn't allow Dante de León to lead her astray from the only chance she had left of becoming a cazadora. She couldn't break the law. Not even for Marquesa.

Dante laughed. "If nothing else, you are always a reliable source of entertainment, Cuatreda Reale. Your love for the law is truly inspiring."

When the clock struck 7:29 a.m. and a herd of cuatredas swarmed up the stairs, Dante pushed himself off the wall and strolled down the hallway. He hadn't attended a single class in person since he was promoted to treveda, and he clearly wasn't about to break his streak.

"May the seas be with you, capitana. I hear the winds are rough today," he called over his shoulder.

As Dante vanished around the corner, the classroom door opened, and the cuatredas streamed into Advanced Navigation. She forced herself to forget about Gasparilla and Dante de León as she searched for a place at the long, rectangular tables, weaving her way between the rows of unfamiliar faces. But when she went to sit, another girl intercepted her.

"Lo siento," she sneered. "This is my place."

Ximena bowed her head and continued on. She found another chair, but someone intercepted her; so she moved backward, and was intercepted again. Each time she tried, she was met with sneers, laughter, or cold indifference. At last, she seemed to find an empty chair in the back of the room, but another cuatreda nudged her out of the way and sat down before she could claim it. The boy looked up at her with grim distaste.

Juan Carlos.

"As I said, Cuatreda Reale," he growled. "You will find no welcome here."

Without another word, he turned to face the front of the room as the cazador who was teaching entered. So Ximena stood at the back of the classroom for the whole of Advanced Navigation, tall and stiff as a mast. Thankfully, with her perfect memory, she didn't have to take notes. But she watched every move Juan Carlos made, and she imagined her name on the parchment in the hallway. She saw it in black, elegant lettering: *Ximena Reale*. The cuatredas might have bested her this time.

She would not allow it to happen again.

Capítulo Cuatro

Ximena's first week as a cuatreda left her with seven bruises and a bullet wound. The bruises were accidental—the bullet wound was not.

It began during Application of Law, two days into training. Cazadora María, a sinewy, nearsighted woman who shouted as a result of her hearing loss (years of gun and cannon-fire had taken their toll on her), had just begun a lesson on the origins of the law.

"There is no greater task that rests upon a citizen than to know and fear the law," she shouted, pacing up and down the lecture hall. "A quotation from?"

"Alessandra," answered the cuatredas.

"Precisely," said Cazadora María. "Those who keep the law must never stop discovering it. A quotation from?"

"Alessandra," answered the cuatredas.

"Very good."

She turned to face the candidates, her black cloak billowing behind her.

"You have spent your lives memorizing the law. You know it as no other citizen in Luza knows it. But a cazador must never become complacent. For even after all is known, there is always more to learn. A quote from?"

"Queen Dulcinea, current sovereign of the Empire of Luza," replied the cuatredas.

The Application of Law lecture hall was furnished with seven long tables and a podium for the teaching cazador (this was usually a cazador who had decided to retire due to age or some irreparable injury). At the front of the room, carved into the limestone wall, was the law in its entirety: seven scrolls of text reduced to tiny lettering and crowned with a bust of Alessandra herself. She looked down on them all with her solemn, watchful eyes, as if daring them to violate her edicts in her presence.

Ximena stood alone at the back of the room—she had once again been denied a seat. Though she tried to focus on the lecture, two names churned in the currents of her mind, Marquesa and Gasparilla, Marquesa and Gasparilla. She wanted desperately to speak to her sister, but she was forbidden from doing so. She wanted desperately to continue her research on Gasparilla, but she was forbidden from that also. Her fingers tapped anxiously against her thigh. Ximena had always taken great pride in her ability to discipline her thoughts, but now they flew in every direction like a frightened school of fish. How could she save her sister, obey the admiral, and protect the empire all at the same time? There were no obvious answers. She had never felt more alone in all her years at la academia; she couldn't even talk to Archivist Sánchez, strange as the girl was.

But Ximena's musings were interrupted when Cazadora María shouted: "Ximena Reale, Elena Espinoza, Feliciano Córdoba!"

She immediately stood at attention; Elena and Feliciano leapt to their feet.

"We are yours to command," they said in unison.

"Approach."

They strode to the front of the lecture hall, turned on their heels, and faced the other cuatredas with their arms pinned at their sides.

"Our newest cuatredas," said Cazadora María. "You will assist in today's lesson regarding the origins of the law. First and foremost, who was the author of the law?"

"Alessandra, the poet, scientist, and philosopher," they all answered.

"And why was it written?"

They recited the story from memory. "Before the law, the archipelago was made up of hundreds of warring islands. Violence and chaos reigned supreme as people fought one another for selfish gain. Then the enlightened Alessandra, governor of the island of Valuza, saw that peace would never be possible without a common code to unite all peoples. So she established the law and spread it across the archipelago, founding the Empire of Luza. To this day, the empire remains a haven of peace and reason, standing against all those who would violate the law and its tenets."

"What are the seven tenets of the law?"

"There will be no murder, there will be no thievery, there will be no assault, there will be no kidnapping, there will be no magic of any kind, there will be no persecution, there will be no treason against the empire.

"Very good. Now recite the law, beginning to end, from memory."

There was a pause. Elena and Feliciano glanced at each other; the other cuatredas snickered in their seats. To recite all seven scrolls of the law from memory would be nearly impossible. The test was designed to humiliate them.

Cazadora María gestured toward the wall of text. "By the end of your cuatreda training, you will be expected to recite large excerpts of the law on command. It is impossible to pass the Royal Examination without such knowledge. You are dismissed; return to your seats."

But Ximena wasn't ready to wave a white flag just yet. She settled her shoulders and began: "In order to combat the vile baseness of human nature and the disastrous consequences that occur as a result, a common code is hereby established . . ."

She continued and had quoted the entire preamble of the law before Cazadora María raised a hand to stop her.

"Are you able to recite the law in its entirety?"

"Yes, señora."

Cazadora María's beady eyes narrowed. "No one has ever been able to do so in all of la academia's history. No one except the admiral."

"I strive to reflect the admiral in every way possible, señora."

Cazadora María paused, considering her. She clearly didn't know what to make of the stern-faced girl and her unwavering confidence.

"Your class ranking will be adjusted to reward your thorough appreciation of the law," Cazadora María declared at last. "You are dismissed."

Ximena saluted and retreated to the back of the lecture hall, the smallest of smiles curling her thin lips.

"Now that we have refreshed our memories," said Cazadora María to the whole class, "we will turn to tenet five of the law, which specifically addresses the issue of magic. Juan Carlos, make a seat available for Cuatreda Reale, immediately."

With a low growl, Juan Carlos slid to the left to accommodate Ximena. She sat beside him with her head held high as he glared into the side of her neck. It wouldn't be long before she stole his spot on the cuatreda ranking board. She would make sure of it.

With all due ceremony, Cazadora María opened the large scroll of the law that rested on the podium.

"Let us begin," she said. "Who can tell me why magic was banned under Alessandra's reign?"

Juan Carlos leapt to his feet, eager to regain his advantage. "Before Alessandra established the law, people throughout the archipelago practiced el idioma prohibido, the forbidden language of magical symbols that allowed them to cast powerful spells. But Alessandra realized the chaos and disruption that such magic caused, and therefore banned it under the law to restore peace to the empire."

"Quite right, Cuatreda Alonso," said Cazadora María. "El idioma prohibido was rightly forbidden from the archipelago, and all forms of magic were systematically declared unlawful. Can anyone think of a relevant example?"

Juan Carlos was first to answer again. "The first cazadores hunted down and killed all the magical monstruos in the sea."

"Es verdad. Precious few sea monsters remain in the archipelago thanks to the valor of the early cazadores. Now, let us look at the subsection that discusses how to address illegal uses of magic—"

She stopped just as quickly as she'd begun. She closed the scroll, unfurled it again. Then she looked up at the candidates with a storm of anger brewing in her eyes.

"Who is responsible for this insolence?"

The cuatredas glanced at one another in confusion.

"I asked a direct question, and I expect a direct answer. Who is responsible for this?"

When no one moved or spoke, she raised the scroll high over her head.

"I will ask once more. *Who* is responsible for this?"

Ximena gripped the edge of her table until her knuckles turned white. There, in the center of the page, was a single red rose, crowned with a golden G.

Gasparilla.

Cazadora María bent down to fish a pair of spectacles from the podium. Then, setting them over the exact center of her nose, she read aloud at her usual blistering volume.

"The honorable Captain José Gasparilla regrets to discover that you have not heeded his previous warning. Therefore, he mocks your law as you have mocked him, and he advises you once more to evacuate this city before the full moon. Those who remain forfeit their lives." She removed her spectacles with a furious flourish. "Someone in this room chose to defile a scroll of the law by posing as a known traitor to the empire, and such a crime will not be tolerated in my presence. Now, will the person who contrived this ill-advised scheme please step forward?"

Silence reigned over the classroom. Ximena felt Juan Carlos's eyes burn into the side of her neck; no doubt he suspected her of being involved, given her pirate heritage. She kept her gaze fastened on Cazadora María, refusing to flinch under his scrutiny.

Another beat of silence passed. Cazadora María scowled.

"Very well," she said. "Since no one is brave enough to come forward, I will assume that you are not, in fact, cazadores in training, but children in need of correction. Every person in this course is therefore expected to have the first tenet of the law memorized by tomorrow. If you fail in your recitation, you will be escorted to the west wing prisons, where you will spend three days reflecting on a scroll of the law to stimulate your memory."

When a candidate in the front row groaned, Cazadora María pulled herself to her full height.

"Cuatreda Alonso," she barked.

Juan Carlos stood. "I am yours to command, cazadora."

"Escort Cuatreda Arias to prison."

The girl who had groaned blanched. "Cazadora María, I meant no disrespect—"

"'When it comes to matters of the law, intent is always superseded by effect,'" boomed Cazadora María. "Who am I quoting, Cuatreda Arias?"

"Queen Dulcinea, current sovereign of the Empire of Luza," the girl answered miserably.

"Precisely." Cazadora María nodded at Juan Carlos. "Take her away."

Juan Carlos escorted the other cuatreda from the room, looking impossibly proud of himself. When they were gone, Cazadora María turned back to the other candidates.

"Given the circumstances, we shall adjourn early. You are dismissed, cuatredas."

They didn't need to be told twice. The cuatredas rushed out into the hallway, hurrying downstairs to the mess hall for a lunch of rice and stewed beans. But even as she ate, Ximena's mind was elsewhere. She couldn't help but see the crimson rose and golden G, as vivid in her mind as they had been on Cazadora María's scroll. How had the pirate managed to sabotage a document from within la academia's walls? Did he have spies planted in la academia? Or worse, among the cuatredas? She did recall a tale of Gasparilla infiltrating a city's government and bribing its officials before commencing with a raid.

She wanted to tell the admiral. . . . No. She would not disobey his instructions. This latest incident was only a continuation of the previous prank at the north gate. In fact, there was an obvious explanation for all of it: Dante de León had been there when the first note was found. He had been conspicuously absent from class when the other note was discovered. Pretending to be Gasparilla and stirring up chaos at la academia was just the kind of thing that a bored, rich, and idiotic boy would do.

There, thought Ximena, satisfied with her own logic. *All of this was an elaborate joke, and that's that.*

After lunch, the cuatredas raced back upstairs to check the updated class rankings. They crowded around the ranking board, pushing and shoving, dragging their fingers down the list of names. Ximena walked straight past them—she wouldn't be late to Seamanship just to stare at a piece of parchment.

But then someone hissed, "It's Ximena Reale, she's been moved to fifth position," bringing her to a dead halt. *Fifth position.* Her heart fluttered with a hope she knew better than to entertain. If she held her rank, she would qualify for the upcoming Royal Examination. It would be the fastest ascent of any cuatreda in history.

"Don't get too comfortable, Cuatreda Reale."

Juan Carlos stood next to her, arms crossed over his barrel of a chest.

"The higher you climb, the farther you have to fall," he said. "You're not getting anywhere close to the Royal Examination, ¿me entiendes? Not on my watch."

Ximena glanced over at him with her good eye. "Cuidado, Cuatreda Alonso. Your threats reek strongly of fear."

She turned and left him in stunned silence, taking the stairs two at a time down to the courtyard, her steps just a little lighter than before.

While the north gate opened out to the city and the rest of the island, the south gate led to la academia's docks. Ximena saluted the guards and strode down the wood-planked walkway to the designated meeting point for the Seamanship course. All around her, the sea and sky were a vast expanse of blue. Armada galleons—double-masted and square-sailed, unlike the smaller and swifter pirate sloops—creaked and groaned with the waves. There were one hundred and fifty galleons in all, each ship named for the cazador who captained it, *Padilla* and *Alma* and *Hernández* painted on their wooden hulls. Ximena imagined what her name would look like: *Reale*, in sweeping gold letters.

Once, her parents' ship had carried their name proudly across the empire. Cazadores Alejandra and Diego Reale, two young Luzans who made history at la academia when they fell in love, married, and hunted pirates across the archipelago together as a team. To Ximena and Marquesa, their parents had seemed like gods. Both sisters would wait months for their parents to return from deployment, just to hear the stories Alejandra and Diego would spin about the things they had done and seen. Sea monsters felled and pirates captured. Lives saved across the archipelago. The law upheld and protected.

So Ximena had grown up with total and complete certainty. She wanted nothing else in this life except to become a cazadora like her parents.

As la academia's bell tolled the hour, she forced herself to look at the ship now called the *Padilla*. She could still see the outline of the word underneath it. *Reale.* The paint had been scraped off and the name replaced the moment her parents were executed.

Perhaps there was some truth in Juan Carlos's words: the higher you climbed, the farther you had to fall. The Reales had been at the height of their careers when it was discovered they were selling empire secrets to multiple pirate captains. Their fall had been swift and brutal—they were arrested, tried before el ministerio, and hanged within a week. The Reale name, which had once stood for honor and valor, now meant traitor. Turncoat.

Pirate.

She thought of Marquesa, languishing in the west wing prisons. No one would be shocked at her sister's demise. They would only whisper that she was a Reale, with weak blood in her veins. They would say the same thing when Ximena failed the Royal Examination.

Unless Gasparilla—

No. No, no, no. She schooled her thoughts like an errant sail once again as the rest of the cuatredas arrived with the last toll of the bell, their faces flushed with the Luzan heat. Ximena wasn't her parents. She wasn't Marquesa. She would not be charged with insubordination, and she would restore honor the Reale name within the confines of the law.

She just had to figure out how.

"Cuatredas, form single file lines on either side of the dock."

A bearded cazador strode through the crowd of candidates: Cazador Miguel, whose broad smile and sagging belly belied the fact that he had once captured an entire fleet of pirate ships in the archipelago. He was a close friend of Admiral Pérez; they had graduated la academia in the same year, and for that he earned Ximena's automatic respect.

"Today's exercise will focus on the capture and boarding of an enemy ship. Both the *Velásquez* and the *Navarra* have been equipped with a box of silver coins. The first to subdue the opposing ship and retrieve the box will be declared today's victors. As usual, ammunition and weapons may be used to wound, but not to kill. We will debrief after the exercise has been completed. Are there any questions?"

If there were, no candidate in their right mind would voice them.

"Bueno. Juan Carlos Alonso, you will captain the *Navarra*. Isabella Moreno, you will captain the *Velásquez*. You may choose your crews at this time."

Juan Carlos and Isabella, a shrewd girl with two metal fingers, stepped forward. As they took turns choosing cuatredas for their crews, the lucky candidates moved to stand behind them, receiving positions from first mate to quartermaster. In the end, only Ximena was left, and neither captain acknowledged her existence.

"We are finished, Cazador Miguel," said Juan Carlos.

Cazador Miguel frowned. Then he approached Ximena with slow, even steps.

"What is your name, candidate?"

"Cuatreda Ximena Reale, sir."

"You have not been selected for a crew. Do you know why that is?"

Exasperation bubbled up in her chest. But she said, "No, sir."

"Then you must be automatically assigned a position." He turned to Isabella. "She will serve as a gunner on the *Velásquez*."

"But, sir—" Isabella began.

"There will be no further discussion, Cuatreda Moreno," he said. Then he turned back to Ximena. "I suggest you consider why you were not chosen today, Cuatreda Reale. A cazador must command the respect of her peers to complete an expedition successfully."

"Yes, sir," said Ximena through gritted teeth.

"Very well," said Cazador Miguel once more. "Crown or sword, Cuatreda Moreno?"

"Sword, sir," said Isabella.

Cazador Miguel took a silver coin from his pocket, flicked it into the air, and caught it against the back of his hand. An engraving of Queen Dulcinea's head glinted in the sun.

"Crown," he announced. "Cuatreda Alonso and the *Navarra* will leave the dock first. The *Velásquez* will follow behind. Cuatredas, to your positions."

"Yes, sir," came the unified reply.

The cuatredas marched to their respective ships. As they boarded the *Velásquez*, Isabella gripped Ximena by the elbow with her two metal fingers, stopping her halfway up the gangplank. She was a beautiful girl, Ximena noticed, with a high forehead and sharp cheekbones. Beauty like that didn't serve girls well at la academia. It drew attention, and attention led to envy, which turned too quickly into cutthroat competition. Ximena would have to hold her ground with Isabella Moreno—this girl was likely just as much of a fighter as she was.

"I've heard all about your exploits, Cuatreda Reale. So I thought I would remind you that *I* am the captain of this ship," Isabella said, tightening her hold. "Not you."

Ximena matched her stare for stare. "I would never usurp your authority, Captain Moreno."

Isabella paused, looking her up and down. Her blue eyes were as cold and unfeeling as the sea itself. But she must have found something that satisfied her because she dismissed Ximena with a nod of her head.

"To your position, Cuatreda Reale."

Ximena obeyed, climbing up the rest of the gangplank and onto the deck.

The *Velásquez* was one of the smallest ships in la academia's fleet, with twelve guns and room enough for a thirty- or forty-person crew. Her decks were painted with shiny black lacquer, and her sails were a snowy white—all of la academia's ships were kept in pristine condition, usually by the youngest uvedas. But although the ship was small, Ximena preferred it over a larger vessel. The *Velásquez* was built for speed, and speed was exactly what one needed when hunting pirates.

Or in this case, Juan Carlos Alonso.

"To your positions!" Isabella commanded, strolling toward the helm. They were in no rush. They could afford to let the *Navarra* have a head start before setting off in the *Velásquez*. After all, where was the fun without a chase?

"We have found the box, captain," said the cuatreda who had been named first mate. He gripped a wooden chest in his arms. "It was in your cabin."

Isabella nodded. "Stash it in the hold. Maybe in a barrel of gunpowder—they aren't likely to look there."

"As you command, captain."

He retreated with the quartermaster to the hold.

"Any minute now," Isabella muttered to herself.

Finally, when the *Navarra* was nothing more than a white dot in the blue sea, Isabella gave the order to make sail. The crew snapped to life, moving through their assigned tasks with swift precision, unfastening the mooring lines and lowering the mainsails. A gust of wind swept in from the north—just what they needed. The *Velásquez* groaned away from the dock and edged out to sea, following the *Navarra's* trail.

Meanwhile, Ximena climbed down into the hold. It was dark and cramped, with ceilings so low that she was forced to hunch over as she walked toward the *Velásquez's* cannons. The other cuatredas who had also been assigned to gunner positions glanced at her, expressions wary. No one wanted to be a gunner during Seamanship course: and the roar of cannon fire could make your eardrums burst and bleed. Worse still, a stray shot might leave you maimed or dead—one dotreda had already died that season during her first Seamanship course. It was far better to be first or second mate, quartermaster or boatswain, staying above decks and leading other crewmates into action. Captains assigned the position of gunner to those they did not like, and every candidate knew it. But Ximena wasn't going to complain. She would serve her captain just as she expected to be served herself.

"We're coming up on her tail," called a cuatreda from above decks. "It won't be long now."

"Load the guns," ordered the cuatreda who had been named master gunner, a girl who reminded Ximena distinctly of a mouse.

Ximena and the other gunners hurried and shoved bags of gunpowder down the cannons' muzzles, ramming it down flat. Then they rammed down wads of cotton cloth on top of the flattened gunpowder to ensure the cannonballs fit snuggly. Finally, they hoisted the cannonballs from their crates and loaded them.

"Guns loaded," they called when their task was complete.

The master gunner nodded, twisting her trembling fingers. Though she did her best to hide it, the poor girl looked ready to heave up her breakfast on the floor. Clearly, she had never served as a gunner before. Ximena frowned. She would never show such weakness in front of her crewmates.

The *Velásquez* heaved and slammed as it crested each wave, spraying saltwater down into the hold. At this speed, they would catch the *Navarra* before the hour was out, and the two ships would do battle. Ximena could only imagine Juan Carlos's fury when he lost to Isabella and the *Velásquez*. Perhaps he should not have been so quick to strut around like he was already a cazador.

"Enemy off the starboard bow!" came a triumphant cry.

Then Isabella's command: "Ready the guns!"

The master gunner faced them with quivering lips.

"Aim!" she shouted.

The gunners moved into their positions, four candidates to a cannon, with Ximena in charge of aiming the second starboard gun. Aiming was a subtle and perilous art: one had to take into account both the wind speed and the movement of the enemy vessel to make the shot. Squinting, Ximena took careful note of the *Navarra's* position thirty yards off, calculating the necessary angle in her mind.

"Five degrees to the north," she commanded.

The other gunners turned the cannon. Ximena squinted again.

"Two degrees more," she said.

They moved the cannon again.

"Ready!" Ximena called to the master gunner.

All together, the gunners waited in a silence strained to snapping. Waves slapped against the *Velásquez's* side; she groaned and creaked under the anticipation.

Then Isabella cried: "Fire!"

The master gunner echoed her: "Fire!"

Ximena gave the signal to her gunners, and they lit the cannon's fuse. Leaping back, they ducked and covered their ears with their hands, until the starboard cannons fired with a deafening *boom*. But the gunners' calculations must have been off: the *Navarra* sailed past unscathed, taunting them.

"Reset!" called the master gunner over the cacophony.

The gunners raced to reset the cannons and sponge them, cleaning out any char or wadding that could make them backfire. Then, on command, they reloaded the cannons and waited for further instruction.

"Aim!" cried the master gunner.

But they never got the chance. Someone at the end of the hold cried out a warning just as enemy cannon fire exploded through the *Velásquez's* side, sending seawater and splintered wood in every direction. Ximena tumbled to the floor. Her ears rang—her lungs burned—flashes danced in front of her eyes like falling stars—there was something on top of her—wood—she clawed her way out from under it. Wheezing, choking on gunpowder smoke, she staggered to her feet. There was a gaping hole in the *Velásquez's* hull. The ship was already taking on water.

Juan Carlos had forced Isabella's hand. Her crew would have to board the *Navarra* before their own ship could no longer sail.

"All hands!" Isabella's voice sounded from the deck. "Prepare to board!"

Still reeling, Ximena and the other gunners stumbled through the hold and up onto the deck. Despite the fact that the *Navarra* had nearly blown the *Velásquez* halfway out of the sea, Isabella had managed to rally the crew into an organized formation, arming them with grappling hooks, pistols, and rapiers. At the appearance of the gunners, she raised her own rapier above her head.

"The *Velásquez* will not surrender in shame," she cried. She pointed her rapier toward the *Navarra;* her blade gleamed in the sun. "Ready to board!"

"Ready!" the crew answered.

"Cast!"

Grappling hooks flew and latched onto the *Navarra's* railing, tugging the two ships so close together that their hulls scraped and splintered. From the other side, Juan Carlos's crew jeered, hurling insults like bullets. But Isabella was undeterred. She raised her rapier, gave a shrieking howl, and raced before her crew onto the *Navarra.* Ximena followed at her heels, leaping onto the deck and unsheathing her rapier in one movement.

The battle had begun.

Ximena locked blades with the first cuatreda she saw. He was a large boy, nearly as tall as she was, but he moved slowly, dragging his left leg. She dodged his first wild swipe and parried the second before swinging out a kick that sent him sprawling. She spun to catch a sideways blow from another cuatreda girl, disarming her with a stab and twist of her rapier. A third cuatreda sliced through her trousers, but she rolled out of the way before he could land a second strike, standing just in time to catch his blade against hers. He stepped forward, jabbing at her shoulder—she deflected, shoving him off balance. As he stumbled, Ximena brought her rapier in a clean cut across his thigh. He hissed, collapsing to the deck, but she strode past him without a thought. This was all part of their training. After all, if they couldn't handle a forced battle, how could they be expected to handle a real one?

A bullet streaked past Ximena's ear. She ducked, rolling again before catching herself on her feet. Then, for the space of a breath, she paused and looked over the deck. All was chaos—cuatreda fighting cuatreda, screams echoing and swords clashing and the stench of sweat mingling with salt. Still, Ximena could tell that the *Velásquez's* crew was winning. The *Navarra* hadn't been ready for such a vicious assault, and Isabella's crew had pushed them to the starboard rail in mere minutes. One by one, they dropped to their knees and raised their hands toward the sky, asking for mercy.

At any moment now, Juan Carlos would be forced to surrender. He would hand them the box of silver, and the *Velásquez* crew would be declared victorious. But where was Juan Carlos? Ximena sliced her sword along a cuatreda's arm, ignoring his screech, and surveyed the deck again. The *Navarra's* captain was nowhere to be seen.

"Cuatreda Reale!"

Isabella was locked blade to blade with a rival cuatreda. But she managed to point her chin in the direction of the *Velásquez*, and Ximena spun on her heel to catch a glimpse of a long, dark braid as it disappeared over the other ship's rail.

Juan Carlos.

"He's going after our box before we can force a surrender," Isabella cried. "Someone needs to stop him."

Ximena knew an order when she heard one. She raced to the rail, grabbed the nearest grappling hook, and swung herself over the sea to the *Velásquez*. The moment her boots hit the deck, she sprinted toward the hold. If she didn't get to the box of silver before Juan Carlos did, it wouldn't matter that her crew had performed so well. They would lose by default.

The sounds of battle faded as she moved into the belly of the *Velásquez*. The lower decks were already drowning in two inches of water from the earlier cannon strike; Ximena struggled to move as quietly as possible to the powder room, her rapier at the ready. But she couldn't help the way her boots sloshed as she crept through the hold. So she picked up her speed, hoping that she could get to the box before Juan Carlos heard her coming.

At last, she ducked beneath a low-hanging doorframe and stepped into the powder room. No sign of Juan Carlos. But how was she going to find the box? There were dozens of barrels down here, and any one of them could have the box inside. Then she saw it. The barrel in the furthest corner of the hold, with its lid tilted just slightly out of place. She raced toward it and pried open the lid, heartbeat pulsing in her ears—

Blinding pain suddenly seared through Ximena's right shoulder. She hissed through her teeth and bent forward, pressing a hand to the wound. When she pulled it away again, it was drenched with blood.

She'd been shot.

"I'm afraid I can't allow you to take that box, Cuatreda Reale."

Juan Carlos Alonso stood behind her, aiming his still-smoking pistol at Ximena. His body was a sharp line of determination. But she noticed the way his nostrils flared, the way his finger trembled around the trigger. He was desperate to win, a feeling she understood all too well.

"Do you know how long I've waited to become a cazador? How hard I've worked?" he snarled. "I didn't sacrifice my entire life just to watch some pirate's spawn take my place in the Royal Examination."

"Your crew is already surrendering, Juan Carlos," Ximena said calmly. "The *Velásquez* will be declared victorious."

"Not if I can help it."

"So what will you do? Kill me?" She raised a brow. "That would hardly help your cause."

She might sympathize with his desperation, but she would take another bullet before she sacrificed a victory. Juan Carlos knew this just as much as she did; he swore under his breath. But before he could reply, a shout from the upper deck interrupted them.

"Enemy off the starboard bow!"

Juan Carlos and Ximena exchanged startled glances. *Enemy?*

Impossible. No pirate would dare come so close to la academia, and especially not during a training exercise. Nevertheless, they both knew the protocol. So they suspended their battle over the box of silver and hurried back through the hold to report for duty on deck.

When they had crossed over to the *Navarra* again, they found their fellow cuatredas crowded against the starboard rail, whispering and pointing at something Ximena couldn't see. Juan Carlos shoved his way to the front.

"Move," he snapped. "Out of my way."

But on reaching the rail he stopped, his brow furrowed.

"What is that?" he demanded.

"We don't know, sir," replied one cuatreda. "It just appeared out of nowhere. We must have missed it during the battle."

"It isn't flying any colors," added another.

"Is anyone even onboard?" asked someone else.

Ximena strode to the rail, peering over the *Navarra's* side. In the water, no more than twenty yards off, sailed a small, single-masted sloop—and it was on fire. The flames engulfed the sloop's sails and scorched its lacquered decks, snapping and crackling furiously. Ximena could feel the heat from where she stood. Stranger still, the vessel appeared to be unmanned. There was no sign of a crew, and the tiller had been fastened to the mast by a rope to keep the sloop on course.

"Identify yourselves!" called Juan Carlos to the sloop.

There was no reply.

"Identify yourselves, or you will be fired upon!"

Once again, there was no reply.

"Wait!" cried one cuatreda. "There's something written in the flames!"

Ximena leaned forward. She hadn't noticed it before, but the flames were not random. They burned in a specific pattern of vertical and horizontal lines—a series of letters.

"You. Have. Been," she read under her breath.

She couldn't make out the last word from where she was standing, but another cuatreda read the message loud and clear:

"You. Have. Been. Warned," he said.

Warned.

Ximena gripped her rapier on instinct.

Isabella, who had also pushed her way to the rail, exchanged glances with Juan Carlos.

"Maybe they aren't pirates," she said. "Maybe they were attacked. Should we search for survivors?"

Juan Carlos stared at the ship, the muscle in his jaw throbbing, but he said nothing. They hadn't been trained to handle a situation like this. There was no protocol to follow. The boy who had been so sure of himself suddenly didn't know what to do.

"Cuatreda Alonso?" said Isabella. "Juan Carlos?"

Just as Juan Carlos opened his mouth, the sloop exploded. The cuatredas dropped to the deck as shards of wood shot out like bullets in every direction. Heat blasted over their heads and saltwater rained onto the deck. Lying on her stomach, Ximena closed her good eye and waited for the roar to die out. But when silence fell, she felt something on her face, warm and soft as silk. Ash? She reached up to catch it in her palm, turning it over.

No, not ash.

A rose petal.

"Are these . . . flowers?" said Isabella.

The cuatredas stumbled warily to their feet, palms outstretched. Hundreds of rose petals rained down overhead, red and velvety soft, settling in their hair and on their shoulders. Jaw tight, Ximena turned one over in her hand—her stomach swooped and plummeted like a frigate bird.

The petal was marked with a golden G.

Ximena curled her fist over the petal and stared at the still-flaming wreckage of the sloop. Gasparilla must have rigged the ship with gunpowder and set it on fire before sending it out to sea. If nothing else, the pirate was a brilliant showman.

"Wait," someone shouted. "I've seen this symbol before!"

"Sí, sí, in Application of Law!"

"And I saw it on the note that was posted at the north gate."

"I heard that the note was signed by the pirate Gasparilla."

"Gasparilla? But he died ages ago."

"Unless the rumors about el idioma prohibido are true."

"Someone should tell the admiral—"

Isabella unsheathed her rapier and spun to face the crowd.

"¡Basta!" she commanded. "Get a hold of yourselves! The real Gasparilla is dead and buried. This fool is clearly just an imposter who thinks he can frighten the candidates of la academia like children, and all of you are proving him right with your squealing."

She swung again, pointing her rapier at Juan Carlos's throat. He blinked at her with glazed, confused eyes.

"Act like a captain and control your crew," she said, baring her teeth, "or I'll report you for untoward conduct."

He blinked again, and then seemed to recover himself. "All hands to your positions! We make for la academia."

"All hands to the *Velásquez*," cried Isabella, leading her crew back to her ship. We'll take the dinghies to shore!

Ximena tucked the rose petal into her trouser pocket and followed Isabella. In the chaos, she had almost forgotten the pain in her shoulder, but now it sank its teeth into her with a vengeance. She pressed her bloody hand tight against the wound. Her doublet was already stained—she would have to pay for a new one out of her allowance.

"What happened to you?" Isabella demanded when they arrived at the *Velásquez*.

Ximena said nothing. Being wounded this badly during a training exercise was nothing short of shameful, and she wasn't about to admit the source of that shame to Isabella.

"Well, whatever happened, you should have it looked after in the infirmary," said Isabella. "Don't want to risk infection."

"Yes, captain," said Ximena, turning to go.

But Isabella stopped her. "Cuatreda Reale."

"Yes, captain?"

Isabella's blue eyes combed over her, and then settled back on Ximena's face. "Well done today."

Ximena nodded. Satisfied, Isabella strode back to the helm, barking orders to ready the dinghies as she went.

As they returned to la academia, Ximena struggled to remind herself of her promise to the admiral. These incidents were nothing more than a series of pranks designed to frighten la academia's candidates, just as Isabella had said. No one could successfully sack Valuza; the island was impenetrable. The idea of it was laughable.

Over and over, Ximena recited the same truths.

Yet the rose petal still burned in her pocket, and the G still glowed in her mind.

Capítulo Cinco

Ximena Reale hated the infirmary.

Stretched out on an examination bed, she waited with her spine rigid, and her hands clenched as a gray-haired nurse sponged her bare shoulder. She loathed being poked and prodded, just as she loathed lying still in nothing but a shift, exposed, vulnerable, and uniformless. To make matters worse, the nurse had propped her rapier at the end of the bed, out of Ximena's reach. She clenched her empty hands again, glancing at the clock on the wall: five o'clock. With any luck, she would be out of the infirmary within the hour.

"You're lucky, young cuatreda," the nurse said, clicking her tongue against her teeth. "The bullet went straight through. But we'll have to disinfect and stitch up the wound, and there will be no courses for you for a week. No buts!" she snapped when Ximena opened her mouth. "You will do as I say, or I will have you reported. Do I make myself clear?"

Glowering, Ximena nodded.

"Good. Now wait here a moment, and don't move. You've lost a good deal of blood."

The nurse disappeared around the corner before returning with bandages and cleansing alcohol.

"I've never heard of such a ridiculous prank," she said, clicking her tongue again. "Impersonating a traitor, blowing up sloops, and sabotaging scrolls. In my day, no sane person would have dared to do such a thing. Who will these pirates pretend to be next, I wonder? The high minister? Queen Dulcinea herself?" She paused, looking at Ximena. "We could fix that, you know. Your eye," the nurse said softly, tipping her chin at the eye patch. "Give you a nice glass one."

Many nurses had offered to fix Ximena's eye, but she had turned them all down. To others, her eye might seem hideous, a scar to heal or hide. But to Ximena, her missing eye wasn't a blight—it was a reminder. A reminder of her own strength, of her tenacity, of her ability to conquer every obstacle she faced. So when she shook her head and told the nurse that she was fine just the way she was, she meant every word of it.

"Sometimes I think you candidates have bricks for brains," said the nurse. "Would you like something for the pain at least?"

Ximena shook her head again. Stars danced in front of her eye each time she breathed, but she was not so weak as to need numbing agents.

The nurse shrugged. "Suit yourself."

Without warning, she poured cleansing alcohol over Ximena's wound. Ximena hissed with pain, biting her lip so hard that it bled. But she didn't cry out, even as the nurse threaded a needle through her skin and sewed the wound shut. A true cazador wouldn't moan over stitches.

"There now," said the nurse when she had finished. "You'll stay here for the night, just to be sure there's no infection. Food will be brought to you at eight. If you need anything, just ring the bell over the bed."

Then she was gone, shutting the door behind her.

It had been some time since Ximena had been to the infirmary; her last visit had been for a snake bite, after an unidentified culprit left a viper in her bed with a note saying, "*To our resident snake: once a pirate, always a pirate.*" So she took a moment to scan her surroundings with her usual observant precision. Housed in the southeast turret of la academia, the infirmary was a domed, circular room with four large windows and several examination beds. The beds were unoccupied at the moment, but that would likely change before the evening was through. Drunken candidates often admitted themselves to the infirmary under the guise of sickness to avoid a debauchery charge. The air was humid and tinged with cleansing alcohol, and the only sounds were Ximena's breathing and the wall clock's incessant tick, tick, ticking.

She really did hate the infirmary.

At eight o'clock exactly, the nurse returned with a bowl of rice and beans, changed Ximena's bandages, and departed again for the evening. But Ximena didn't have the stomach to eat. Instead, she eased herself up into a sitting position, wincing at the pain in her shoulder, and reached over to the bedside table where the nurse had left her folded uniform. She curled her fingers into the trouser pocket and pulled out Gasparilla's rose petal, which was already browning at the edges. She turned it over in her palm; the painted G was smudged and faded. *Gasparilla does not exist,* she reminded herself. *Gasparilla is not a threat.*

But outside the infirmary's windows, a full moon rose. It was soft and round as a pearl, suspended in the darkness over the sea and shedding cool, white light on la academia's limestone turrets. How harmless it looked, how gentle and unassuming. Yet if Gasparilla's promise was to be believed, that moon foretold their doom. He would attack Valuza before sunrise, razing the island to the ground, and most people would be sleeping when the pirate came to slit their throats. But not Ximena. She would be wide awake with an aching shoulder, stroking her rose petal to the *tick, tick, tick* of the wall clock.

"Got yourself shot, Cuatreda Reale?"

Ximena looked up to see Dante de León entering the infirmary with the nurse on his heels. His doublet was unbuttoned, his silver-blond curls sweat-slicked; dried blood crusted the corners of his lips, and his left eye was bruised black and swollen. Judging by the nurse's frown as she led him to an empty examination bed, he'd probably gotten himself punched in a cantina somewhere and wanted something for the pain.

"Who shot you?" Dante's smile was mirthless. "Not Isabella Moreno. She's as high-minded as her father, and he spends most of his time waxing poetic on the floor of el ministerio. Cuatreda Alonso, perhaps? He's the poor-and-angry-about-it type who might fire a bullet at the mentally deranged. He took a solid chunk out of your shoulder, didn't he? You'll have to miss courses, which won't help your ranking. Pobrecita."

The nurse clamped a hand to his shoulder, stopping him.

"Sit," she snapped.

He smirked at her, but sat down nonetheless.

"Here," said the nurse, dropping a frozen slab of meat into his lap. "Press that to your eye. You can stay until the swelling goes down, and then I want you out."

"Your hospitality is greatly appreciated," said Dante. "Be sure to report the incident, no? I'd like my mother to know that I had my face smashed in by the diminutive son of a fisherman."

The nurse only grunted. "If he does anything foolish, Cuatreda Reale, just ring the bell."

Ximena nodded. Then the nurse eyed them both, mumbled something under her breath, and marched out of the room.

"So," said Dante, pressing the meat to his blackened eye, "has anyone told you yet?"

Ximena stared at him.

"Ah, the silent treatment. Clearly that near-death experience sparked no epiphanies regarding your manners."

"You talk too much when you're drunk," Ximena said.

He laughed. "Yes, I suppose I do. But I'm not like you Cuatreda Reale. Without the liquor, I'd never have the courage to say the things I should."

Ximena resisted the urge to roll her good eye.

"This is where you say, 'What are the things you fear to say, Dante de León?' And I will tell you." He pointed at the bottle of cleansing liquid beside Ximena's bed. "Is that alcoholic?"

When she didn't reply, he crossed the room and grabbed the bottle, tipping it back into his mouth. Then he spit every drop of it onto the floor.

"If my mother had a drink named after her, this would be it," he said.

Then he staggered back across the room and slumped into his own bed again, crashing back into the pillows. A peaceful silence settled over the infirmary. Ximena hoped that Dante had fallen asleep, but as usual, she hoped in vain.

"My brother died today," Dante said. "I can tell you that because you don't have any friends to gossip with, and anyway I had to tell someone."

For a moment, Ximena could only hear him breathing—the uneven rise and fall of his chest. Then, he continued.

"He'd been serving as the captain of an armada galleon in the northern islands. Luza has been fighting to conquer those for years, you know. The empire is running out of silver, so they want the silver mines on the northern islands to keep Queen Dulcinea in her ballgowns and the ministers well-fed. My mother never stops talking about it. Anyway, some friend of my brother's was captured by a pirate crew, and Mateo, noblest of them all, attempted to rescue the idiot and got himself killed. So he's dead." He snapped his fingers. "Just like that."

Ximena never knew how to react in situations like this. So she forced out a stiff, cold, "I'm sorry for your loss."

"Don't be. All of it is a lie." He went silent for a moment, breathing again into the stillness. "Well, not all of it. Mateo is definitely dead. But he didn't die the way they said he did."

In spite of herself, Ximena was intrigued. "What do you mean?"

Dante didn't respond. Instead, he reached into his pocket and pulled out a folded slip of paper, tossing it across the room into her lap. She raised a curious brow, but he only waved a hand as if to say, *see for yourself*. So Ximena peeled it open with careful fingers; the paper was yellowed and crusted with a dark substance.

Blood.

It was obviously a letter, but the handwriting was such a mangled mess that she could only make out snippets of it.

> *Hermano,*
> *If you're reading this, the worst has already happened. . . .*
> *I tried to stop them but . . . thousands . . . dead . . . I know*
> *they won't let me live long enough to return home . . . I'm*
> *sending this to the only person I can trust. You.*
>
> > *Don't let this die with me.*

"They found it in his jacket pocket, addressed to me," Dante said. "I almost wish they hadn't."

She read over the letter again twice, three times.

"It doesn't make any sense," she said.

"It makes perfect sense. My brother was threatening to expose the horrors of the queen's war to conquer the northern islands. The killing. The war crimes. All of it. So the armada did what it always does to so-called traitors. It silenced him. Couldn't have the high minister's firstborn son turn his back on the empire. What would that say about the law? About truth and justice and the great cazadores who protect them?"

Ximena had no idea what he was rambling about. The campaign to conquer the northern islands of the archipelago had been going on longer than she'd been alive, and not once had she ever heard anything about war crimes committed by the cazadores. Dante was clearly delusional with the grief of his brother's death; there was nothing in that letter that was conclusive enough to suggest foul play. It wasn't even signed with Mateo's name. But she was more focused on Dante himself than on what he was saying. In four years of knowing him, she had never seen him like this. In fact, if she didn't know any better, she'd say those were tears glistening in his dark eyes.

"Now my mother expects me to become a cazador, serve the empire with honor and valor, and humbly take my brother's place as heir to the de León legacy, or she'll cut me off forever. Or worse—" His laugh was hollow with bitterness. "She'll stand aside while they silence me, too. What do you think, Cuatreda Reale? Can you see me as the future high minister of Luza? I could grow a beard, wear a cloak, righteously defend the law before el ministerio. I might even be able to convince people that I actually give two lumps for Luza or the law. Hmm? Do you think I could manage it? Or better yet, what illegal insults are flying around in that head of yours?"

Ximena wouldn't tell Dante de León what she was thinking. That she thought him a disgrace to la academia and the very idea of the cazadores, that he was the pompous, privileged son of a pompous, privileged family who never had to worry about anything in their lives. She wouldn't tell him that he would make the worst high minister in all of Luzan history. And she definitely wouldn't tell him that she didn't feel an ounce of pity for him or his dead older brother. In fact, in the darkest corner of her soul, Ximena considered the de Leóns' loss to be a kind of justice. Though it could not be found in the tenets of the law, pride was a terrible crime, and the de León family was guilty of it twenty times over.

"Why did I even bother?" Dante muttered. "As if Ximena Reale would ever believe anything but the best of her precious cazadores. Anyway, I'm sure you're thrilled to hear of my family's suffering. Most people will be when the news gets out. My mother is many things—feared, honored, respected—but beloved is not among them. And I'm the second son with a drinking problem and no ambitions whatsoever. Did I also mention that I'm remarkably self-aware?"

"Self-focused, perhaps." She didn't realize that she'd spoken her thought out loud until Dante cried out:

"She speaks! And that's quite an accusation to lay at my feet, capitana, considering your general disdain for the human race. When was the last time you cared about anything other than the almighty law?"

"If you're just going to insult me, Cuatreda de León, then I would prefer to sleep."

"Fair enough. Before you do, though, I have news you might wish to hear. Your sister is officially set to be expelled."

Ximena sat up so quickly that stars spun before her eyes. "Expelled?"

"Not surprising, I know. According to my mother's office, the girl was utterly unimpressive during her hearing. She couldn't seem to give a straight answer to any of their questions. Spent the whole time mumbling and playing with her hair. Really, it's a wonder you two are related."

But Ximena was no longer listening. All she could hear was that terrible word, booming in her mind like a drum: *expelled, expelled, expelled*. So the worst had come to pass. Marquesa would be sent away from la academia without a penny to her name, alone and disgraced, fending for herself on the capital's streets. And since Ximena could never associate with an expelled candidate, there was nothing she could do to save her sister now.

Forgive me, Marquesa. I've failed you.

"Ah," said Dante de León, watching her face. "So you *do* have a heart after all. I'm simultaneously disappointed and amused."

"My sister brought this on herself," Ximena said. Her voice wasn't her own; the words left her automatically. "The high minister was right to punish her, and it is not for me to challenge the severity of that punishment."

Though none of this would have happened if you had not tempted my sister into debauchery and left her for dead.

"Just so you know, it wasn't my fault Marquesa got caught," said Dante. "I invited her to come with us, of course, just to watch you squirm. But I never encouraged her to do the half-mad things she did. By the way, you should wear white more often." He tipped his chin at her cotton shift. "It suits you much better than black. These uniforms make everyone look like vultures."

Ximena turned away, focusing on the moon, which had risen high in the infirmary windows. In the haze of adrenaline following her injury, she had forgotten how tired she truly was. Now exhaustion crept up on her like a thief, blurring her vision and loosening the tightness in her muscles. She waited for Dante to grow bored and leave her in peace, but the boy just sat with the bloody slab of meat pressed to his eye, staring at nothing. The candlelight cast deep shadows around his eyes, turning him strangely skeletal.

"You know," he said, his voice low and rough, "I think I'm going to miss my brother."

The clock ticked on. The full moon glowed.

"I need a drink," Dante said, springing to his feet. "I would say it's been fun, but I know how much you detest liars. So farewell for now, Cuatreda Reale, and if I happen to see Marquesa, I'll let her know you said good riddance."

He had just reached the door when the deafening toll of la academia's bell rattled the infirmary walls. Over and over the sound echoed: *gong, gong, gong, gong.* Ximena gripped the edge of her sheets.

The warning signal.

In the distance, someone gave an unintelligible shout. Then someone else repeated the call, again and again, until all of la academia vibrated with the same blood-chilling cry.

"Alert, alert, all hands to your positions! We're under attack!"

Footsteps drummed past the infirmary door; candles sparked in la academia's windows; somewhere, a cannon fired. This was no drill—someone was attacking la academia. Dante turned to face Ximena.

"This wouldn't have anything to do with your friend Gasparilla, would it?"

Ximena didn't answer. Instead, she dragged herself out of bed and grabbed her uniform, hissing in pain as she pulled the black doublet over her shift. She felt the stitches in her shoulder snap—blood bloomed through the bandage—but she didn't have time to care. She shoved her legs into her trousers and reached for her rapier, strapping it to her waist.

"Where in the name of the law are you going?" Dante said.

"To my post," she said, striding toward the door.

"Not to hunt down Gasparilla?"

She paused. "The admiral gave me strict orders to ignore any future threats made by Gasparilla."

Dante de León threw back his head with laughter. "By the law, you can't make it up. They say 'jump,' and you're off the nearest cliff at top speed, no questions asked. You truly are the most loyal puppet I've ever seen."

"You wouldn't know loyalty if it slapped you across the face," Ximena said coldly. "Now step aside. I must report for duty."

"And who said I wouldn't?" he replied. "Of course I'll report for duty. I'll be in my dormitory with a bottle of liquid courage, enjoying my last night of freedom before I have to spend the rest of my life convincing my mother I'm worthier than her dead son." He gave a lopsided bow. "Wake me up if any pirates try to kill us."

Then he staggered out of the infirmary, still pressing the chunk of bloody meat to his eye. Ximena waited until she was sure he was gone before hurrying down the hallway and up the stairs to the fifth-floor armory. All candidates were expected to report for duty when la academia was attacked. Every season, they ran drills to practice firing cannons and defending against an enemy assault. But the drills were just a formality—in all of la academia's history, only one person had ever dared to fire upon it.

Gasparilla.

In the darkness of the armory, cuatredas scrambled to ready themselves with muskets, crossbows, pistols, and rapiers. Ximena strode through the chaos to grab a musket from one cabinet and a simple, sharp dagger from another. She always preferred a clean kill over violence and gore; the admiral had instilled in her the value of elegant efficiency. Strapping the dagger inside her boot and the musket against her shoulder, she followed the other cuatredas up to the sixth floor, where a wooden door opened to the battlements.

The night was as warm as freshly spilled blood. Overhead, the full moon haunted the starless sky, shining down on the cazadores as they shouted commands to the assembled candidates. It didn't take long for Ximena to find the admiral, towering over them all in his black cloak, his shark-like eyes fastened on the sea and his face a mask of grim determination.

"Hold your ground," he was saying. "La academia's walls are impenetrable. Follow my orders, and this battle will be over before sunrise. Make ready!"

Racing to their appointed cannons, the candidates loaded them with wadding and ammunition.

"Ready," they cried.

"Aim," said the admiral. "Fire!"

The candidates lit the cannons, firing at the shadowy outline of a ship that lurked offshore. Whether or not it was a pirate ship was impossible to say in the dark. But whoever it was, they were marked for death. Nobody could attack la academia and live to see the morning.

"Get down!" someone shouted.

Ximena dropped to her stomach. A cannonball blasted over the limestone battlements, narrowly missing a wide-eyed dotreda. Then, before anyone could call out another warning, a second cannonball smashed into the stone. Shards of rock sprayed in every direction—someone screamed in pain. Ximena looked over to see Juan Carlos Alonso clutching his shoulder. He'd been pierced by a chunk of limestone. Ximena crawled to his side. His eyes were wide and wild with pain; his forehead was slick with sweat.

"Don't touch me," he spat, recoiling from her.

"Hold still," she said.

Without warning him, she pulled the stone from his shoulder. He howled in pain. Then she tore off a strip of her shift, wrapped it around the wound, and tied it tight. The bandage wouldn't prevent infection, but it would do for now. As she stood to her feet, Juan Carlos watched her with an unreadable expression—he was probably wondering why the girl he'd shot just a few hours ago was helping him. Ximena only gave him a solemn nod. The code dictated that no cazador should be left behind, and she would always honor the code.

A cannonball soared past her, knocking two trevedas from the wall. Undeterred, Ximena raced to her position on the battlement, manning one of the cannons. Shouts rattled in her ears; the stench of gunpowder stung her nose. Over and over she and her team of candidates loaded, aimed, and fired on command. But it was as if the ship was bulletproof, immune—for every shot they fired, the ship returned ten more.

"What are they, immortal?" spat the cuatreda beside her, swiping blood from his lips.

"This has gone on long enough. Bring out the fire!" the admiral commanded.

Several candidates rushed forward, loading what looked like a cannonball into an iron catapult. But this was no ordinary piece of ammunition. When another candidate touched a torch to the cannonball, it burst into brilliant blue flames—one of la academia's rare and expensive fireballs. Ximena had never seen one used before. But she'd heard they could explode an enemy ship in a single burst of light.

"Make ready!" called the admiral. "Aim! Fire!"

The candidates released the catapult. Like a shooting star, the fireball streaked through the darkness toward the ship. Silence reigned for a long, terrible moment. Sweat snaked down Ximena's spine; her injured shoulder throbbed. Then came the explosion. A ring of blinding blue light erupted from the ship, beautifully fatal.

"Get down!" the admiral commanded.

The candidates ducked behind the wall, shielding their eyes. Only when darkness had returned did they stagger to their feet. Ximena squinted into the night. Nothing remained of the enemy ship but a charred mass of wood. Anyone onboard was almost certainly dead.

Seeing that the enemy had been defeated, the candidates gave a victorious cheer.

"Well done, candidates," the admiral said. "You have defended the empire well. Tonight, its people shall sleep safely under your protection. The wounded will be taken to the infirmary, and any fatalities will be handled by the nurses. In the meantime, the cazadores and I will investigate the wreckage and discover who was foolish enough to attack la academia de los cazadores." He gave a final nod. "You may return to your dormitories."

The cuatredas saluted. "We are yours to command, sir."

Ximena turned on her heel and marched with the others toward the stairs. But before they had reached the end of the battlement, a tolling bell pierced the night. The candidates paused, listening.

"Is that another warning bell?" one candidate whispered.

"It can't be."

"Must be a mistake."

They started forward again but froze at the toll of another bell.

"Where is it coming from?"

"The city?"

"The port?"

"I think it's coming from the palacio."

A third bell rang, then another, and another, until Ximena lost count of them all, until the entire capital seemed to ring with terror. She gripped the handle of her rapier.

The night was not over yet.

"Let me in! In the name of the law, let me in! I must speak to the admiral!"

Shouts from the north gate drew the candidates to the wall overlooking the courtyard. A messenger was arguing with the gate guards, but when they moved to restrain him, he wriggled out of their grasp and bolted into the center of la academia, waving and crying out.

"I must speak to the admiral!" he called. "¡Por favor, es una emergencia!"

The guards caught and pulled him back even as he continued to fight them. But Ximena's jaw tightened when she saw the standard on the messenger's chest: the royal seal. So he had come straight from the palacio itself. His news could not be good.

The admiral stepped up to the wall and looked down into the courtyard.

"Release him," he boomed. The guards obeyed. "Speak, messenger."

"Your excellency," the messenger bowed, "the city is under attack! Besieged by pirates on the river!"

"Pirates?"

"Yes, your excellency!"

"You are absolutely certain?"

"By the law, I swear it. They've already breached el ministerio and the palacio!"

Ximena sucked in a breath. They'd been tricked. While the cazadores were fighting off a single ship, a pirate crew had breached a completely undefended Valuza.

"How many ships?" the admiral called.

"Only one!"

"Does it have a name?"

"*La Leyenda*, your excellency!"

Shocked whispers flew among the candidates. Ximena waited for the admiral to silence them, to tell them that this was just another training exercise. But then, beyond la academia's walls, screams began to rise like smoke into the night. And Admiral Gabriel Pérez said nothing.

Ximena looked up at the full moon. So her predictions had come true. Valuza, the untouchable capital of the empire, was under attack.

Gasparilla had arrived.

She'd thought her opportunity to catch him was lost forever. She'd thought that Marquesa was doomed, and there was nothing she could do to save her. But now the pirate captain was at their doorstep, bringing redemption with him. Ximena had never been so grateful for disaster in her life.

Admiral Pérez turned to the cazadores. "Organize the trevedas and cuatredas into platoons and take them into the city. I want the captain and crew of *La Leyenda* dead or captured before sunrise."

"And the other candidates, sir?"

"Dotredas and uvedas will stay behind and defend la academia. Teaching cazadores will remain with them."

The cazadores began issuing platoon assignments while the admiral turned to exit the battlements. If Ximena didn't act now, she'd miss her chance to speak with him. So she shoved through the crowd, crying, "Sir! Sir!"

He turned at the sound of her voice.

"This isn't the time for conversation, Cuatreda Reale."

He didn't apologize for doubting her, though she hardly expected that he would. But he was paying attention. Ximena could work with that.

"Sir, I've studied the original Scarlet Siege extensively. I don't think this Gasparilla is here to pillage the city."

"Go on."

"In the siege, Captain Gasparilla stole several thousand pounds of silver, as everyone knows. But most people have forgotten how he did it. He didn't take silver from the treasury. He captured the queen and held her for ransom."

"You think the raid on the city is another distraction. That he will attempt to kidnap Queen Dulcinea."

"Precisely sir."

The admiral's gaze bored into hers, testing her confidence. Ximena didn't flinch.

"Who are the best cuatredas in your class?" he asked.

"Isabella Moreno and Juan Carlos Alonso," she replied without hesitation.

"Bueno. Find them and come with me. We make for the palacio forthwith."

Ximena's heart swooped toward the sky. The admiral believed her. The hunt was on.

With a salute, she raced to find Juan Carlos and Isabella. She quickly relayed what she had told the admiral; they listened without interruption.

"You're mad, Cuatreda Reale. Completely insane," Juan Carlos said when she'd finished. The bleeding from his shoulder had clotted, but he still favored the wound as he slid his rapier from its sheath.

Meanwhile, Isabella showed no hesitation. "We're in. Lead the way."

They followed her down the six flights of stairs to the courtyard, where the admiral was waiting with two other cazadores. Ximena's nose wrinkled with distaste; one of them was Cazadora Cecilia, the admiral's miserable right hand.

"Cazadora Cecilia and Cazador Ignacio will be joining us," the admiral said. "We'll keep our platoon small so we can move as swiftly as possible without drawing attention to ourselves. Cuatredas, you will follow my orders to the letter and without argument. If I or either of the cazadores fall in battle, you will leave the city immediately and return to la academia. ¿Me entienden?"

"Yes, sir," they answered.

"After me, then."

He led them out of the north gate, leaving la academia behind. It was the first time Ximena had gone beyond those limestone walls since her parents' execution. Though she tried not to show it, excitement burned in her blood—there was nothing quite like the thrill of the hunt.

"Stay close, cuatredas," the admiral called over his shoulder.

The island of Valuza was organized in a linear grid—numbered streets ran east to west, while the streets named for famous Luzans ran north to south. The grid was further divided into barrios based on the occupation of those who lived there. As they ran, Ximena and the others crossed through the Fisherman's Barrio and the Shipmaker's Barrio, before turning into the Scrollmaker's Barrio, which lined the river that sliced the island in two. Warning bells continued to chime. The bespectacled inhabitants of the Scrollmaker's Barrio leaned out of their windows, pointing at a pillar of smoke rising in the distance.

"Stay inside," the cazadores barked up at them. "Lock your doors, the city is under attack."

Bewildered, they obeyed, sealing their doors and windows shut.

At last, the cuatredas and cazadores reached the Puente de Justicia, the bridge that swept over the Río Valuza. There it was, floating in the river's black water: *La Leyenda*. It was just as fearsome as the tales described, double-masted with fifty guns, its sails dyed the blood red color of a rose and its figurehead carved in the shape of a frigate bird. Fitting, Ximena thought, for a pirate ship—frigate birds were known for stealing other creatures' prey. Its jeweled eyes sparkled in the tangerine light of the flames that licked the sky.

Flames.

Ximena's stomach twisted.

No wonder there had been smoke on the horizon. The pirates had set Valuza on fire.

"Come, Cuatreda Reale, there is no time to waste," the admiral called out.

Ximena shook herself back to reality. They raced across the bridge into the island's central quarter, the Queen's Barrio. Here, the streets widened, parks ranged over entire blocks, and the buildings were miniature palacios carved from limestone and topped with silver domes. Only families in service to the empire were allowed to live in the Queen's Barrio—ministers, scholars, and aristocrats, families like the de Leóns. It was considered the jewel of the empire, the seat of justice, order, and the law.

But in the wake of *La Leyenda*, the barrio was chaos and smoke. Pirates pillaged and plundered through the streets, smashing windows and hauling piles of silver and jewelry outside before setting the estates on fire. They were dressed in scarlet red and armed to the teeth; every one of them bore the same tattoo on their wrist, a rose and a golden G. The barrio's residents ran screaming in all directions, tripping over themselves as they fled, dragging their children behind them.

"You will not enter here! In the name of the law, you will not enter here!"

Ximena spotted an elderly minister on the doorstep of his estate. He was pointing a pistol at three pirates with a quivering arm, sweat beading on his rust-colored forehead.

"In the name of the law!" he cried again.

The pirates only laughed. "'In the name of the law, in the name of the law!'" they crowed, grinning gold-toothed grins.

With two blows, they disarmed the old man and ran a rapier through his stomach, leaving him to die as they broke down his door. Ximena stepped forward, rapier at the ready, but Isabella caught her by the arm.

"You can't save them all," the girl said. "Our objective is to protect the queen. The other cazadores will defend the people."

Ximena knew she was right. But fury churned in her stomach all the same as they followed the admiral deeper into the barrio toward the palacio real. These pirates would get the justice they deserved. She would avenge every death that happened here tonight.

Pushing through the crowd was like swimming against the current. Terrified Luzans surged past them, coughing up smoke—too many bodies—the fiery air suffocating. Thankfully, Ximena could see the grand silver dome of the palacio just ahead of them, only one street up. They were almost there.

Suddenly, something knocked her to the ground from the side. She spat out a mouthful of blood and turned her good eye on her attacker. A pirate stood over her—he must have hit her across the face with the pommel of his rapier. But before he could bring down the blade, a shot rang out, and he dropped like a stone.

The admiral stood over her with a still-smoking pistol. He offered her a hand up. She didn't thank him; it wasn't necessary. This was always how he had protected her, silently, patiently, even when she hadn't asked for his help. She loved him for it. But she wouldn't say that aloud, either. Some things weren't meant to be said.

"This way," the admiral called.

They tore down the rest of the street and arrived, finally, at the palacio real. Built in the exact center of Valuza, the palacio was the only building in the city shaped like a circle. It was intended to symbolize the unity created under the law, though it was far from a symbol of unity now: Half the palacio was engulfed in flames while marauding pirates escaped with their spoils. The magnificent central dome had been cracked by cannon fire, and the silver fragments littered the grounds like shards of moon.

Ximena swallowed; her throat was raw from smoke and ash.

It was the Scarlet Siege all over again.

She and the other cuatredas raced to keep up with the admiral and the cazadores, cutting down any pirates in their path. They had just reached the top of the palacio steps when a voice rang out, "Stop! Stop in the name of the law."

Cazador Ignacio reached behind the entrance arch and pulled out a young man who was barely Ximena's age, dressed in the uniform of a palacio guard. The boy dropped the musket he'd been holding as the cazador hoisted him high.

"Por favor," he stammered, "I mean you no harm, cazador. I thought you were a pirate."

With a grunt, Ignacio lowered him back to the ground.

"Where are the other guards?" the admiral asked.

"Gone. We received word of a threat to the queen's safety from the city's western quarters, so the majority of our forces were deployed there. But they never returned."

Cazador Ignacio swore under his breath. "This Gasparilla is quite the artist."

"Who is protecting the queen?" Cazadora Cecilia demanded.

The boy winced. "Her personal guards, cazadora. She is barricaded in her rooms with several other members of court, including—"

He stopped, lips quivering.

"Including?" the admiral urged.

"The high minister."

Cazador Ignacio swore again. The boy rambled on.

"The queen was hosting an emergency council on the war for the northern islands, so it was only natural for the high minister and the rest of the court to—"

"Have you seen a pirate who calls himself Gasparilla?"

The boy shook his head.

"Here," the admiral said, handing the boy one of his pistols. "You're going to need this."

The boy accepted it with trembling fingers. "Gracias, cazador."

The admiral's frown was grim as he pushed past him. "Don't thank me yet, boy."

Inside, the palacio was as silent and dark as a grave. But moonlight sliced through the large, glass windows, revealing evidence of the pirate attack: a blood-stained glove, a shattered mirror, candles spilled onto the floor.

"The queen's chambers are on the other side of the palacio," the admiral whispered. "Stay alert."

They followed him into the darkness. Ximena held her rapier at the ready, scanning the shadows for potential threats. She detected none. Perhaps she had been wrong, then. Perhaps Gasparilla's crew had only been interested in escaping with whatever loot they could find and ransoming the queen was of no interest to them.

When they reached a pair of mahogany doors, the admiral raised a hand to stop the small group. These must be the queen's chambers. He spoke into the keyhole, "Your majesty, this is Admiral Pérez. We have come to escort you from the palacio."

No reply.

"Queen Dulcinea, we have come to rescue you and anyone else inside your chambers."

Still, no answer. The admiral nodded to Ignacio and Cecilia, and they slammed their full weight against the doors at the same time, knocking them wide open. Then the admiral signaled for the cuatredas to follow them as they stepped into the darkened chamber.

"Your majesty," he began again, "we need you to follow us, immedia—"

He never finished. Light suddenly shattered the blackness, revealing seven pirates surrounding two dozen cowering courtiers. The guards the boy had spoken of were dead on the floor, their faces frozen in terror, their blood pooling on the tiles. Ximena scanned the captives' faces for the queen's but saw no one she recognized besides a silver-haired, stern-faced woman who might have been Dante de León's twin. So the high minister really was here.

But the queen was nowhere to be found.

"Welcome, Admiral Pérez."

One of the pirates stepped forward. There wasn't much Ximena could conclude about him, since his face was masked by a strip of fabric. But she could tell from his hands that his skin was as dark as gunpowder, and his hair, dyed a brilliant red, hung in thick locs down his back. He wore a broad-brimmed hat, ballooned trousers, and several flintlock pistols, all the same color as *La Leyenda*'s sails. On his wrist was the telltale tattoo of Gasparilla's crew: the rose and the golden G.

Ximena's jaw clenched. She recognized the theatricality, if nothing else. This must be Gasparilla. The pirate she'd spent four years searching for was standing right in front of her.

"It is a great pleasure to have you join us," he continued, his voice as low and warm as an evening tide. "Por favor, sheathe your weapons. I would rather avoid more violence if at all possible."

"Then I am afraid we shall have to disappoint you," replied the admiral, keeping his rapier pointed at Gasparilla.

"You have disappointed me several times already, admiral. I expected a challenge from the famed cazadores of Luza. Instead, my sources tell me that you called my threats insignificant. A bedtime story used to frighten children." He spread his arms. "Do I look like a bedtime story, admiral?"

"Where is the queen?" Cazadora Cecilia demanded.

"Ah," said Gasparilla. "That is another matter entirely. I shall state my terms, and you shall decide whether you wish to accept them. Does that sound fair enough to you?"

"The cazadores do not negotiate with pirates," Cazador Ignacio snarled.

"This will not require any negotiation. You will deposit a third of the silver in Luza's treasury onto my ship, and in exchange, I will return your queen to you. If the silver is not on my ship within the hour, your queen will die. These are my terms."

"And here are mine," said the admiral. "Since my code prohibits me from fighting an unarmed man, you will unsheathe your weapon, and I will strike you down where you stand."

Gasparilla laughed again; his pirates laughed along with him.

"Do so at your own risk, admiral. If you take one more step, your high minister is dead."

The cazadores froze as one of Gasparilla's pirates swept a cutlass under the high minister's chin. To her credit, the woman didn't show an ounce of fear. She held herself up as proudly as if she were standing before el ministerio.

"So, cazadores?" Gasparilla said. "What is your decision?"

The admiral stood so still that he hardly seemed to breathe. "I will make my decision when you unsheathe your weapon."

Gasparilla's arms fell. He was losing patience. Nevertheless, he unsheathed the cutlass that hung at his hip, holding it limply toward the admiral.

"Time runs as quickly as the tides, cazador. Make your choice."

For the first time, Admiral Pérez smiled. "I already have."

The next few moments passed in a blur. Cazadora Cecilia pulled four knives from her belt and sent each of them flying into the chests of Gasparilla's pirates—they dropped to the floor, senseless. Then, as the two remaining pirates raised their pistols, Admiral Pérez pulled his own from beneath his cloak, fired at the pirate holding the high minister hostage, and tossed his rapier into the chest of another. He retrieved the blade in a single, graceful movement and turned it on Gasparilla.

"Go!" he ordered the prisoners. "Evacuate the palacio immediately."

The captives wasted no time in fleeing from the room, though the high minister glanced back once over her shoulder, her eyes landing on Ximena for a moment, before she disappeared into the dark. Meanwhile, the admiral's attention never left Gasparilla.

"You are under arrest for piracy, murder, and treason," he said. "In the name of the law."

Gasparilla surveyed the room, now littered with the bodies of five guards and six pirates.

"Now *that* is what I expected of the cazadores," he said. "But alas, your efforts have been in vain. Do you have the time, young man?"

The pirate tipped his chin at Juan Carlos. The boy blinked, then reached into his pocket and opened his watch.

"Five sharp," he said.

"Then *La Leyenda* is already out to sea with your lovely Queen Dulcinea onboard."

"Why should we believe you?" the admiral said.

"Because I'm so wildly entertaining," Gasparilla replied. "And your queen's life depends on it."

The admiral dug the point of his rapier into the pirate's throat. "By the law, Gasparilla, if you harm her—"

"Gasparilla?" The pirate raised his eyebrows. "Who said I was Gasparilla?"

Ximena's rapier fell. What was the man talking about?

"Cazadora Cecilia, remove the pirate's mask," the admiral said.

Cecilia obeyed, wrenching back the strip of fabric and revealing a hooked nose, pointed beard, and yellowed, smiling teeth. Ximena could count on one hand the number of times she had seen the admiral taken by surprise. But his eyes widened with recognition as he took in the pirate's face.

"Amador," he breathed.

The pirate grinned. "So you do remember me, Gabriel. I was hoping you would." Amador turned and addressed the cazadores. "Your admiral and I were rivals during our time at la academia many years ago. Both of us were on track for the admiralty. But Gabriel gave into the empire's siren song, and I woke up from the dream."

"You sold me and my crew out to a pirate captain during our first expedition. You got ten cazadores killed," the admiral said.

"Did I? The memory is so hazy now. I thought it was twelve at least."

The admiral's lip curled with disgust. "So you threw away your career as a cazador to sail around the archipelago impersonating a traitor."

"Hardly. As I was saying before, I am Amador Gutiérrez, first mate of *La Leyenda*. José Gasparilla is my illustrious captain, and with any luck, he is several miles away with your queen in his arms."

The breath rushed out of Ximena's lungs. They had fallen for yet another ruse. Gasparilla had already escaped. He'd anticipated that the cazadores would refuse to negotiate, and now he was halfway out to sea, a dangerous advantage.

"So there is nothing to stop me from killing you and hunting your captain down like the dog he is," the admiral said, seizing Amador by the neck.

"Well," Amador gasped, "there is one thing. I'm the only one here who knows where Gasparilla is sailing to."

"We're the cazadores of Luza," Cecilia said. "We don't need your help to find out, pirate."

"With respect, señora, if you had any understanding of Gasparilla whatsoever, your capital wouldn't be in flames tonight."

He was right, and all of them knew it.

"So what do you suggest?" the admiral said.

The pirate grinned. "You ignored my captain's previous terms, so the game has officially changed. He requests that the *entirety* of the empire's vaults be delivered to a meeting location that he has disclosed only to me. There, he will exchange your queen for your silver. Simple as that."

Cazador Ignacio interrupted. "We don't negotiate—"

"Sí, sí, I know la academia's policy, and your nobility is truly inspiring. But you have two options before you, cazador. You can waste your time hunting a man who cannot be found, or you can end this with a few bars of silver." He shrugged. "To me, the choice seems clear."

The admiral studied him a moment, still holding him by the neck. "You've already betrayed me once before, pirate. I'm not inclined to trust your word again."

"I'm not asking for your trust, admiral. Only your desperation."

"Cuatreda Reale." The admiral's eyes swung to her. The anger that burned in them was foreign to her; clearly these two had more history than either of them was letting on. "Give me a reason to end this man's life and I'll do it."

Ximena understood what her commander was asking. But in all their research, she and Pía had never been able to nail down the exact location of Gasparilla's hideout. She could hazard a few guesses as to where it *might* be. But guesses weren't enough to launch the armada.

The admiral must have been able to read the hesitation in her face because he released his hold on Amador, though he kept his blade at the pirate's throat.

Amador smiled appreciatively. "The girl is smarter than she looks."

"Admiral Pérez!"

At that moment, the chamber doors flew wide open, and several cazadores swept into the room, weapons ready.

"The boy at the entrance told us where you were. Is the queen secure?"

"She has been kidnapped and is being held for ransom by Captain Gasparilla. But the high minister has been safely evacuated from the palacio." The admiral turned back to Amador. "Tonight, I will spare your life. Tomorrow, we will bring your case before el ministerio, and they will decide what is to be done about Gasparilla."

"So wise and noble. You make a fine commander, Gabriel," Amador drawled.

"Escort the pirate to prison at la academia," the admiral said as if the pirate hadn't even spoken. "If he attempts to escape, you have my permission to kill him."

As the cazadores dragged the pirate from the room, Amador's eyes met Ximena's eye, soft and slippery as an eel's. She glared back. He and his captain might have won this battle, but she would fall on her own sword before they won a second time.

Amador didn't seem to care. His lips pulled back in a grin to reveal his yellowed teeth, and a laugh rolled from his chest as he vanished into the dark.

With the room silent once more, the admiral pinched his nose between his fingers and breathed a long, deep sigh.

"The night has been long, candidates. But you have carried yourselves with honor and courage. Return to la academia and get what rest you can. The cazadores will secure the city."

"As you command, sir," they replied.

Ximena moved to depart, but the admiral's voice stopped her.

"Cuatreda Reale."

"Yes, sir?"

"Tomorrow you will accompany me to el ministerio. If my suspicions are correct, the high minister will wish to speak with you about your findings in the archives before making her decision about whether to ally ourselves with Amador."

"As you command."

Then she turned and followed the other cuatredas out of the palacio, through the city, and back to la academia. After a brief and miserable stop at the infirmary to have her shoulder stitches redone, Ximena finally arrived at her dormitory in the southeast wing and collapsed into bed without performing her usual routine. Her injured shoulder pulsed, her scarred eye itched with a vengeance, and Dante de León's snores rattled through their shared wall. There was no chance she would be able to sleep. But in spite of it all, Ximena's lips twitched into a smile. At long last, the cazadores were going after Gasparilla. And if Ximena was sure of one thing, she was sure of this:

She was going to be on that ship.

Capítulo Seis

At dawn, Ximena walked with the admiral into the city. The sea and sky were gray with ash. Entire barrios had been reduced to rubble. Luzans stumbled through the streets like specters, rummaging for belongings, crying out for loved ones. When they saw Admiral Pérez, they whispered among themselves and glared with dark, distrustful eyes. Ximena couldn't make out exactly what they were saying. But the words she did hear brought a flush of humiliation to her cheeks. *Fracaso. Failure.*

"Come to clean up your mess, admiral?"

An old woman with a bandage over one eye stepped forward. She spat in the admiral's face.

Ximena unsheathed her rapier, snarling, "You will address the admiral with respect, señora."

But the admiral pressed a hand against Ximena's good shoulder, stopping her.

"Justice will be served, señora," he said. "The cazadores take full responsibility for our failure last night. But Gasparilla will pay for what he's done to this island. I can promise you that."

"I hope you're wrong."

A girl around Marquesa's age strode to the old woman's side. A small crowd was forming around them now, and the girl must have sensed their support because her dark eyes blazed with defiance.

"I pray you never catch Gasparilla. He's our only chance to be free of you vultures. ¡Viva Gasparilla! ¡Viva la libertad!"

But before she could continue, a man old enough to be her father hobbled out of the crowd and caught her by the arm.

"Forgive my daughter and mother, Admiral Pérez. We lost my wife in the raid last night, and . . ." His voice cracked, faded away. "Forgive them. They meant no harm, truly."

"Of course," the admiral said.

With a grateful nod, the man coaxed the two women away, though they argued with him all the while. Ximena narrowed her good eye as she watched them go—she'd never heard Luzans swear loyalty to a pirate before. To do so was a death sentence, as everyone on the island knew. But perhaps they were acting out of grief rather than true allegiance. She couldn't blame them for that.

"Justice will be served," the admiral assured the crowd, "to the pirates and their sympathizers. If anyone has information on Gasparilla's whereabouts, please report it to el ministerio or the cazadores immediately."

Then he turned to Ximena, lowering his voice.

"Come, Cuatreda Reale. The high minister is not a patient woman."

No one else dared to approach them while they walked the rest of the way to el ministerio. Ximena had been to the high court a dozen times over the course of her career at la academia, but no matter how many times she visited, it still made her feel small. El ministerio's seven limestone turrets, one for each of the law's tenets, rose so high they towered over every other building in the city. Every one of its windows, doors, and archways was inlaid with silver, reflecting the empire's dominance over trade across the archipelago. Staring up at its massive entrance, Ximena was reminded of what everyone already knew: Queen Dulcinea might be the empire's sovereign, but the real power in Luza truly rested here with the high minister.

Under normal circumstances, they would have met with the guards, ministers, and archivists who processed the cases that came before el ministerio. But today, the admiral didn't even have to open the iron doors—pirates had bashed them down the night before. He and Ximena strode through the wreckage, stepping over several smashed statues and a fallen chandelier, and finally into the central chamber, where a lone attendant announced their entrance.

"Admiral Gabriel Pérez comes before el ministerio to—" he began.

A clipped voice cut him off. "Spare us the formalities, Guard. I'm the only minister in attendance and I have no patience for them."

"As you command, High Minister de León."

If the outside of el ministerio made Ximena feel small, the inside left her feeling absolutely minuscule. The ceiling soared dozens of feet overhead, finishing in a magnificent dome, and the limestone walls were stained an intimidating black. Portraits of the last several high ministers glared down at her as if they could judge her from beyond the grave. Even the ground beneath her feet was a reminder of the empire's strength, engraved with the names of every pirate successfully caught and sentenced over the last two hundred years. She could only hope that her parents' names weren't anywhere near where she stood.

This morning, the mahogany seats, which normally held the archipelago's more than three hundred ministers were empty, save for two: one in which a pug-nosed archivist took careful notes, and one high-backed chair where the high minister sat.

"I have yet to thank you for saving my life, Admiral Pérez," the high minister said, her voice filling the cavernous chamber. Though her words were congratulatory, her tone was not. "The empire owes you a great debt."

The admiral bowed low. "There is no debt, high minister. It is my duty to serve the empire."

"Naturalmente." Elena de León's gaze fell on Ximena. "Cuatreda Reale. I suppose I owe you thanks as well."

In the light of day, Ximena could observe the high minister's features more carefully. Dante truly bore a shocking resemblance to his mother. They had the same wine-dark eyes, lofty forehead, cleft chin, and aristocratic nose. But there was a hardness about her that was totally absent in Dante. Her long, gray hair was tied severely at the base of the neck, and she wore a black velvet robe and white gloves, looking as if she'd been drained of color by all her years of service. Her dour expression was a warning: Cross the high minister of Luza at your own risk. There was no point in begging her for mercy. She would show none.

Ximena recognized that look instantly. It was the sign of a woman who had been forced to claw, kill, and steal to hold her position at the top of Luza's government—a look Ximena herself had been forced to adopt throughout her own candidacy. True, the high minister's seat had been filled by a de León for the last hundred years. But that had never stopped every other notable family in Valuza from trying to seize it for themselves. So Elena de León had attended la Academia de los Cazadores. She had ranked consistently at the top of her class for all eight years of her training, graduated, and achieved equal success as a cazadora captain. Then, she had secured her position as high minister with one of the greatest captures on record.

She had turned in Alejandra and Diego Reale for treason against the empire.

Now her gaze fell on their daughter with vicious suspicion. She had never approved of the admiral's decision to offer Ximena and Marquesa casos especiales, and it was very clear she wasn't pleased that Ximena was standing before her now. But Ximena was determined to prove she was nothing like her parents. The day she betrayed the empire would be the day the tides stopped changing.

"I heard about your recent loss, high minister. My thoughts are with your family," Ximena said, hoping to win a small fraction of her favor with some carefully expressed sympathy.

Clearly, her judgment was incorrect. The high minister's gloved hands tightened on the arms of her chair; her dark glower turned darker still.

"We aren't here to discuss my son, Cuatreda Reale. We are here to discuss the cazadores' abject failure to capture the pirate who ransacked my capital, kidnapped our queen, and, according to the reports I've heard already, is now threatening to empty our treasury, too. Have I missed anything, Admiral Pérez?"

"No, your honor," the admiral replied. "But we were able to capture Gasparilla's first mate—"

"Yes, the former cazador turned pirate. Another delightful success story from la academia."

Ximena watched the admiral's jaw tighten. Without Elena de

León, his work at la academia would be impossible. The cazadores captured the pirates plaguing Luza's islands, but it was the ruthless high minister and el ministerio who tried and convicted them for their crimes. So while Elena de León looked down her nose at the admiral's ascent from poverty, and while he considered her to be a pompous and overbearing aristocrat, they tolerated each other for the sake of the law.

Just barely.

The admiral said, "Amador claims Gasparilla is willing to meet us at an undisclosed location to conduct an exchange. The contents of the empire's treasury for Queen Dulcinea."

"Ah. The pirate has a sense of humor at least."

"I think Gasparilla is long past the point of joking, your honor."

"So what is your recommendation, admiral?"

"That we do as the pirate says and exchange the ransom for the queen's safety. Then we can hunt Gasparilla separately to the best of our ability."

"To the best of your ability." The high minister's fingers drummed against the arm of her chair. "I wasn't aware la academia had changed its policy on negotiating with pirates."

"We haven't, your honor. But these are unprecedented circumstances that call for unprecedented action. I realize the ransom is high. But with all due respect, we cannot sacrifice Queen Dulcinea. The number of pirate attacks is already rising across the archipelago, and to lose our queen to a pirate . . . it would be a sign of weakness that we simply can't afford."

"I'll tell you what we can't afford, Admiral Pérez. The war for the northern archipelago has cost more silver than any other campaign in the empire's history. We've had no choice but to raise taxes, which of course the people cannot pay. So, if we don't capture the northern islands within the next year and their silver mines with them, the empire will run out of funds. I realize you are no politician, Gabriel. But surely even you are capable of understanding what that means." The high minister leaned forward in her chair. She reminded Ximena of a rapier, long, lean, and lethal. "There will be no funding for la academia or the armada. Pirate attacks will go unchecked. Rebellions will break out on every island from here to the uncharted corners of the map. Then this great empire that has survived for *two hundred years* will crumble to ash in a matter of weeks, and it will have happened on my watch. In other words, I cannot and will not authorize you to put the empire's last remaining funds on a ship and hand them off to a pirate with an ego the size of the whole archipelago.

"So here is what you are going to do, admiral," she continued. "You are going to sail to this undisclosed location as Amador instructs. But you are going to do so *without* the empire's silver aboard. When the moment for the exchange arrives, you are going to rescue the queen and capture Gasparilla and his crew so you can bring them home to be hanged for all to see. Am I making myself perfectly clear?"

Anger sparked in the admiral's shark-like eyes. "Elena—"

"You will address me by my title or not at all, admiral."

"Your honor." He spat the words out like a curse. "If Gasparilla or Amador find out the ship isn't carrying their ransom, they won't hesitate to blow us out of the water and slit the queen's throat."

"Unfortunately, that issue falls under la academia's purview, not el ministerio's. Unless you and your cazadores don't feel up to the task of doing battle with a pirate."

"I said nothing of the kind."

"Bueno. Then you will follow my orders as I've outlined."

"And you will condemn both my crew and your sovereign to death."

"Admiral Pérez." Elena de León was on her feet with all the speed of a cat. "Speak one more word in that direction and it is you I will try and hang for treason."

Silence hovered over the chamber. The only sound was the archivist's quill scratching furiously over the parchment as he noted every word of the conversation. Ximena began to wonder why the admiral had brought her here in the first place. She hadn't been asked to speak, and both the admiral and the high minister seemed to have forgotten she was there at all. Was there some secret purpose why she had to attend this battle between the great powers of the empire?

"My decision is made," the high minister declared at last, resuming her seat. "Now, to the particulars. I don't trust anyone but you to helm this mission, admiral. The crew assignments, however, I leave to your judgment. Which cazadores will go with you? You may state their names for the record."

The admiral had clearly come prepared for this question because he listed cazadores quickly and efficiently. The archivist scribbled them down one by one while the high minister listened with her usual calculating coldness. For her part, Ximena schemed in silence, trying desperately to think of ways to get her name on that list. She didn't have the advantage of being a decorated cazadora. But maybe she could offer to serve as the admiral's assistant, or even as a cabin boy. . . .

Then the admiral spoke the last two names:

"Cuatreda Ximena Reale and Archivist Pía Sánchez."

She looked up. Had the admiral really said what she thought he'd said? The high minister seemed just as confused as she was—her graying brow lifted with surprise.

"You must have misheard me, admiral. I asked you which *cazadores* would be joining your crew."

"Far from it, your honor," said the admiral. "Cuatreda Reale and Archivist Sánchez are necessary additions. They have done extensive research on Gasparilla's behavior and have even drawn up a detailed chart of affiliated pirate attacks. It would be a severe oversight on my part to leave them out of this expedition."

Ximena glanced over at the admiral, struggling to read his expression. She didn't know whether he'd added her name to the roster simply to anger the high minister after she'd superseded his authority, or because he really did care for Ximena the way she hoped he did. Not that his true motivation mattered. All that mattered was her place on the ship set to hunt down Gasparilla. She would have her chance at glory. Hope flickered to life in her chest.

Then the high minister's voice fell like a gavel.

"Absolutamente no," she said. "Candidates have no place on this expedition, let alone the daughter of previously convicted pirates. There are enough traitors at play in this mess, admiral. The last thing we need is another liability."

"Then you have a choice to make, Elena." The admiral placed special emphasis on her name. "Either we conduct this exchange my way, with the full contents of the empire's treasury in the hold of my galleon, or we do it your way and Cuatreda Reale remains onboard."

"Cuidado, admiral." Her expression darkened. "I would caution against defying me so boldly."

"I defy no one. My oath is to the empire, not to el ministerio. I am simply exercising the authority given to me under the law to protect the empire's interests."

For a moment, the high minister was silent. She had been outplayed—and as Ximena knew from personal experience, there were few things a woman like Elena hated more.

Meanwhile, Ximena's skin prickled with pride. The admiral thought she was important enough to fight for against el ministerio. It was no small thing and certainly set her above any other candidate at la academia, caso especial and pirate parents notwithstanding. Maybe she could become a cazadora and save her sister after all.

But she should have known better than to celebrate her victory before it was in hand, because just as she was imagining the Cazador Cloak around her shoulders, a smile curled across Elena de León's lips, sharp as a cutlass.

"Very well. Cuatreda Reale and Archivist Sánchez will join your crew. Should the expedition succeed, one of them will receive the Cazador Cloak."

Cazadora Ximena Reale. Adrenaline shot through her like a blast of wind in a ship's sails, and she dug her nails into the skin of her palms, unable to contain her excitement.

Then she realized what the high minister had just said.

"One of us, high minister?" she asked. "But Pía Sánchez is on the archivist track, not the cazador track—"

"Allow me to clarify. Cuatreda Dante de León will also be joining your expedition. I expect Admiral Pérez to complete an objective analysis of how you both perform, and to recommend which of you is worthy of becoming a cazador by exceptional merit."

The words drove through Ximena like a harpoon. So Elena de León truly *was* the brilliant cazadora strategist she had been trained to be. If Dante de León was part of their crew, he could claim the credit for Ximena's successes, and the high minister would be fully within her rights to name her own son cazador over Ximena. The de Leóns' shaky reputation in the wake of Mateo's death would be restored, the empire's treasury would be protected, and history would repeat itself once more: the Reales would fall so the de Leóns could rise.

Ximena knew the admiral couldn't possibly refuse to follow her orders, but her stomach plummeted nevertheless when he said, "As you command, your honor. We will depart as quickly as possible and return with Gasparilla in hand."

"I don't doubt it. And Admiral Pérez?" She stopped him as he turned to leave. "It goes without saying that if your mission fails, I will have no choice but to find any survivors guilty of treason against the empire, whether they're cazadores or not."

Ximena watched the admiral's broad shoulders tighten.

"De la preparación surge la perfección," he said. "We will not fail again."

Then he strode out of the chamber, leaving Ximena to perform a hasty salute and scramble after him.

"Insufferable woman," he was muttering to himself. "El ministerio steers this empire into the ground, and my cazadores are meant to clean up their mess. She should captain the expedition herself if she's so concerned about the outcome."

He fumed in silence all the way back to la academia; Ximena had never seen him so angry. Only when they reached the north gate did he stop, wiping a stream of sweat from his brow, and address her directly.

"I meant what I said in that chamber, Cuatreda Reale. You and

Archivist Sánchez will be essential to the success of this expedition, regardless of what the high minister might believe. So I would suggest you prepare accordingly. Go to the infirmary and have that shoulder seen to forthwith. Then you will finish out the day's courses as usual. We depart for the archipelago on my order."

"As you command," Ximena snapped into a salute. "And sir?"

"Yes?"

She wanted to thank him for supporting her against the high minister, for standing by her side when no one else would. But these were not the kinds of things that cazadores spoke aloud. So instead she said, "May I see my sister before I go?"

The admiral hesitated. He wasn't one to overrule his own orders. But today was proving to be a day of exceptions, because he nodded and said, "You may. With all the chaos of the attack, we haven't had time to deal with Marquesa properly. She is still here."

Ximena let out a breath of relief. "Thank you, sir. I understand the trust you've placed in me, and I won't disappoint you. I promise."

"I know, Cuatreda Reale."

The pride in his dark eyes sent a flash of heat racing along her skin. She turned away to avoid embarrassing herself, and headed first to the infirmary before returning to the southeast wing as if the course of her life hadn't been altered forever.

All afternoon, she forced herself to ignore the whispers and glances of the other cuatredas. No doubt they were wondering where she had been all night, where she had gone this morning, and why she had returned to la academia with the admiral. But she wouldn't give them the satisfaction of seeing her slip. She even avoided Juan Carlos and Isabella in the mess hall, though they stared at her with unabashed curiosity.

By the time the day finally came to a close, her good eye throbbed with exhaustion, her head pulsed, and the pain in her shoulder had snaked down to her hand, numbing her fingers. She finished yet another dinner of rice and beans before slipping to her dormitory unnoticed, desperate for sleep.

At least, she almost slipped into her dormitory unnoticed. Dante de León was waiting for her at the door, chewing on a piece of hardtack with his shoulder against the doorframe.

"So when are we setting sail, capitana?" He grinned.

Perhaps it was because she hadn't truly slept in more than twenty-four hours. Perhaps it was the sight of Dante's satisfied smirk as he munched on his cracker. Or perhaps it was the blow to the head she'd suffered in battle. Whatever the reason, something inside of Ximena snapped, and she swept one foot out to kick Dante's legs from under him. He landed flat on his back, his mouth open in a fishlike O of pain, while she unsheathed her rapier and pointed the blade into the hollow of his throat.

"By the law," he wheezed. "I didn't know you had it in you."

"I will say this only once. You are *never* going to become a cazador. And if you do anything to sabotage me or my efforts, I will personally report you for debauchery, code or no code."

"First of all, you've never broken a rule in your life. Second, do you honestly think I want to become a cazador? If it were up to me, I'd spend the rest of my days on an island in the archipelago, as far away from my mother as physically possible. But it's not up to me, capitana. If I don't play your little game with Gasparilla, I end up like my brother, rotting in an early grave." He swung out his arms. "So here we are."

She glared down at him. Dante de León was right—he was as

much an instrument of his mother's machinations as she was. But only one of them could become a cazador, and Ximena was determined it would be her. So however much she might want to do so, she couldn't spear Dante into the limestone floor. She lowered her rapier, reluctantly returning it to its sheath.

"Help me up?" said Dante.

Ximena didn't move.

"Fine," Dante mumbled, hoisting himself to his feet and touching the back of his silver-blond head. His fingers came away bloody. "I think you've left me concussed, capitana."

"No more than the alcohol you've drunk tonight," she said. "We depart on the admiral's orders. Buenas noches."

She strode into her room and slammed the door shut.

"You're a fool, Cuatreda Reale," Dante called from the hallway. "I've fought my mother for eighteen years. If you actually think you can win against her, you're delusional."

Lying in bed that night, she knew there was truth in Dante's words. But she wasn't going to worry about the high minister yet. For now, she would focus on the one thing she could control: capturing Gasparilla.

Capítulo Siete

"A letter for Cuatreda Reale."

Cazadora Cecilia interrupted a rather boring Advanced Navigation lecture to deliver a note from Admiral Pérez. She was obviously unhappy to be serving as messenger: her thin lips were a line of distaste, and when Ximena tried to pull the note away, she pinched it tight between her gloved fingers.

"You are very fortunate to receive the admiral's charity, pirata," the cazadora hissed. "I hope you know that."

"It isn't charity when it has been earned, señora."

Nostrils flaring, Cazadora Cecilia released the note, spun on her heel, and departed the lecture hall in a huff. Ximena broke the seal on the note and scanned its contents in a glance.

Expedition departs with the evening tide.

She glanced at the clock on the wall—two o'clock. She still had time. She turned to the teaching cazador and saluted.

"May I be excused, sir?"

The cazador waved her off. "Yes, yes, go ahead, Cuatreda Reale. Now, as I was saying about the use of an astrolabe—"

Ximena left the lecture hall as quickly as possible. She had already packed her travel bag the night before, so she hurried to her dormitory, grabbed her satchel, and then hastened toward the west wing. Any minute now, Marquesa would be expelled from la academia. But if Ximena made it to the prison before the evening tide, she might be able to see her older sister one last time. So she hurried to the first floor of the west wing, where a pair of iron doors barred the entrance to la academia's dungeons.

"Cuatreda Ximena Reale," she said, announcing herself to the cazadores standing guard. "I have come to see the prisoner Marquesa Reale."

"That prisoner has already been sentenced. Visitation is prohibited."

"I have orders from the admiral. Would you like to verify them with him?"

That, apparently, was enough.

"You may enter," the guards said.

They pulled open the iron doors, and Ximena barreled down the spiral stairs into the darkness of the prison.

La academia's prison had been built in the days of Alessandra. It was several feet below ground, and no map of it existed. To prevent captives from escaping, it had been designed as an enormous labyrinth, stretching for hundreds of yards beneath the limestone fortress. No candidate, including Ximena, was able to navigate it alone. So when she came to the bottom of the staircase, she found the one man who could help her: Teseo.

"Where is Marquesa Reale?" she demanded.

He looked up at her with eyes as glassy as pearls—he'd been blind for as long as anyone could remember. His hair hung in long, greasy strings, and the ratty cloak dripping over his back did nothing to hide the pus-filled sores spotting his wrinkled skin. Legend told that Teseo had once been an archivist, but when he fell out of favor with the high minister, she banished him to be the keeper of the labyrinth. So he'd had plenty of time to learn every twist and turn by heart.

"Your name?" he rasped.

"Cuatreda Ximena Reale."

He paused a moment, his eyes roving in his skull. Then he grabbed the torch from the wall and rasped, "This way," shuffling off into the darkness.

As Ximena followed Teseo around each bend in the labyrinth, prisoners reached their grasping hands through the bars, straining to catch Teseo by his cloak.

"Come, come, Teseo," one prisoner croaked. "Can't you give a dying man something to console him? A little wine, perhaps?"

"And who's the pretty thing you've brought with you?" another cackled.

"She'd console us better than the wine."

Teseo swung the flame of his torch toward them, and they scuttled backward like rats, laughing all the while. Ximena wrinkled her nose. It was only fitting that breakers of the law should end up in such a place. But she couldn't help but wonder what weak and sickly Marquesa had suffered during her imprisonment. Her sister wasn't built to spend her nights in a prison cell, choking on the damp and the stench of human waste. Just the thought of it turned her already unsettled stomach.

"Second cell on your left," Teseo said, interrupting her thoughts. "I will wait for you here."

"Thank you," Ximena mumbled and stepped up to the cell bars, peering through the all-consuming blackness.

"Marquesa?" she whispered. "Marquesa, it's me."

No answer. So Marquesa was shunning Ximena for abandoning her to this cursed place; that was to be expected. But she hadn't come all this way for nothing, so she gripped the bars and spoke softly, gently, into the abyss.

"I know you're angry, Marquesa," she said. "But I'm leaving tonight for the archipelago, and I won't be back for some time. I just—" The words stuck in her throat. "I just want to talk to you. To say goodbye. Nothing more."

Once again, there was no answer. The silence twisted in Ximena's heart like a rapier. Before they'd come to la academia, she and her sister had been as inseparable as the sea and sky, following so close on each other's heels that people assumed they were twins. They'd spent countless hours hunting for shells together on the beaches of Valuza, and countless more giggling about nothing over hot mugs of chocolate con queso. When Ximena's soul was aching, Marquesa was the first to know, and vice versa. So where had that version of her sister gone? It was if Ximena's memories were just words written in sand, and the waves of time had simply swept them away.

Like they'd never existed at all.

"The labyrinth will have its way," Teseo rasped. "It will turn people to the darkness, or it will bring out the darkness within them."

Ximena stepped back from the cell bars as if they'd burned her.

For years, Marquesa had mocked the law with her indolence. Now she wouldn't even deign to say goodbye to her law-abiding sister, when it was Ximena who was making the sacrifice to speak to Marquesa in the first place! Well, if that was how the game would be played, then Ximena had better places to be.

"Return me to the surface," she told Teseo. "There's no time to waste."

Teseo's lips pulled back in a toothless smile. "As you wish, Cuatreda Reale."

He shuffled ahead with his torch held before him. Ximena followed at his heels, her muscles tightened like an overdrawn sail. She didn't want to think about Marquesa anymore. She wanted to be on a ship headed for the archipelago, chasing Gasparilla over the waves. So when Teseo brought her at last to the bottom of the staircase, she went up the stairs two at a time and never looked back.

She reached the docks four minutes before the hour was up. The admiral was waiting at the foot of the gangplank. Though his eyes were tired, the rest of him appeared no worse for wear: his black cloak was clean and pressed, his doublet starched, and his boots gleamed in the afternoon sunlight.

"On time as always," he greeted her. Then his noble brow bent with concern. "Are you all right, Cuatreda Reale?"

"Never better, sir," she answered, gliding past him up the gangplank. She knew her commander wouldn't believe her—she was a notoriously terrible liar. But she couldn't talk about Marquesa right now. If she tried, she might not be able to stop the tears that were making her mangled eye itch.

"Cuatreda Reale! It's happening; it's finally happening."

As always, Pía Sánchez chose the worst possible moment to

bombard her. No sooner had Ximena's boot touched the deck than Pía was in front of her, chattering away. Her freckled skin was already blotchy from the sun, her curls a tangled nest from the salt and wind, and she could barely stand upright on the swaying deck because of the four enormous leather satchels that were strapped to her shoulders.

"I can't believe we're actually going to track down Gasparilla," Pía said. "Not that I ever doubted you, Cuatreda Reale. It all just felt so far away, but now it's happening, it's really happening, and we get to be a part of it. History in the making. I keep thinking that I'm going to wake up and everything will have been a dream—"

"Pía," Ximena said. "What's inside those bags?"

"Oh, just copies of the records on Gasparilla and the Scarlet Siege. And a history of every island in the archipelago. And a few maps. And a scroll on whale identification and mating calls. You never know what might be useful."

Ximena looked up and down at the girl. "I couldn't agree more."

"I'm just going to run down to the hold and store these records. The head archivist wasn't pleased that I took them in the first place, and he'll murder me if they're damaged on the journey. May the seas be with you, Cuatreda Reale! I've always wanted to say that."

The girl grinned, staggering over to the hold and half-falling down the steps. Ximena watched her go, wondering how, exactly, she was going to keep the archivist alive.

But that was a problem for another time, just as Marquesa was. She forced herself to focus on the vessel they would be sailing to the archipelago in: the admiral's ship, the famed *Pérez*. It was an elegant galleon with fifty guns, built for speed and maneuverability, one of the greatest vessels in la academia's fleet. Somehow, the ship reminded Ximena of the admiral himself, with its clean white sails and broad, freshly lacquered decks. The *Pérez* was true and steadfast—she could sense it in the solidity of the wood beneath her feet. It would carry them faithfully through any storms they might face.

Gong. Gong. La academia's bell rang twice to signal the hour. The admiral climbed to the helm and called out his orders.

"Prepare to make sail. We must depart before the tide turns."

"Yes, sir," came the collective reply.

Unlike most pirate hunting expeditions, which were usually crewed by candidates, the *Pérez* was crewed entirely by cazadores. They swept over the deck like birds of prey, their cloaks whipping behind them, their movements a study in practiced precision. Ximena's heart wrenched with longing. They were so dignified, so confident and bold, as if they could bend the sea itself to their will—and perhaps they could if they tried. How she longed to be among them, to feel her own black cloak sweep against her ankles, to stand as the admiral stood at the *Pérez's* helm, his eyes searching the horizon.

She tossed one mooring line to the docks and moved on to the next one. She would complete her tasks with the excellence she had been trained for—then the admiral would have no choice but to report that she was superior to Dante de León.

Where was Dante, exactly? She scanned the deck, searching for the telltale silver-blond curls and finding nothing. Perhaps he was sleeping off his drink in the hold somewhere, avoiding hard work at all costs. She could only hope the admiral had also noticed this first failure.

"Cuatreda Reale, have you seen Cuatreda de León?"

When she heard a female voice behind her, Ximena's heart plummeted. The only thing more miserable than being stuck on a ship with Dante was being stuck with first mate Cazadora Cecilia.

She turned to Cecilia. "No, señora."

Cecilia sniffed. "Insolent as always. Has anyone else seen Cuatreda de León?"

"Not to my knowledge, señora," a few cazadores replied.

"Very well. Then we leave without him. Ready to make sail, admiral," she called up the helm. Then she turned back to Ximena. "I will be watching you very closely on this expedition, Cuatreda Reale. I suggest you be on your best behavior."

"Por supuesto, señora."

But Ximena was too pleased with this recent turn of events to care about Cazadora Cecilia's vendetta against her. She'd been plotting several ways to remove Dante from the competition, but it seemed the boy had done the hard work for her. Now the high minister would have no choice but to name her cazadora if their mission to capture Gasparilla succeeded.

An auspicious start to their expedition.

The mainsails unfurled and caught the wind with a snap. While the *Pérez* heaved away from the docks, Ximena looked up at the high walls and limestone turrets of la academia. This might be the last time she ever saw them. After all, dangers abounded in the archipelago: they might fall prey to pirates, storms, or all manner of sea monsters on their journey. La academia was the closest thing she'd ever had to a home. Even Ximena, who never looked back, couldn't help but mourn the loss of it.

"Wait! Wait in the name of the law and whatever else you people like to swear by!"

Ximena looked over the starboard rail. Someone was sprinting up the dock—a boy, waving and hollering as he ran. At first, he appeared to be alone. Then a dozen men burst into view just behind him, chasing him toward the ships with everything from pistols to wooden clubs.

"We'll skin you alive, you little rat!"

"Stop or we'll shoot you and feed your bones to the fish!"

Ximena caught the gleam of silver-blond in the sunlight. Por supuesto. Dante de León had gotten himself into yet another mess. But the *Pérez* was already underway, and they wouldn't be able to turn around now. Perhaps they could simply leave him behind to face his own stupidity.

But the boy tore to the very end of the dock, grimaced, and dove headfirst into the sea. He swam frantically toward the *Pérez* as bullets shredded the water behind him.

"Help!" he called. "Help, somebody!"

"Man overboard!" cried one of the cazadores.

The crew raced to throw a line over the ship's side. Ximena's heart sank.

A moment later, the cazadores hauled a drenched Dante onto the deck of the *Pérez*. He staggered to his feet and swept his curls from his eyes, his arrogant grin already plastered onto his face.

"I am most grateful to you, cazadores," he said. "For a moment there, I thought you would leave me behind—"

"Cuatreda de León," the admiral stepped down from the helm, eyes blazing. "I am sure there must be a fascinating explanation for this."

"My apologies, sir," said Dante, bowing his head in a too-casual salute. "The fishermen were placing bets on whether Gasparilla would be caught, and I'm afraid things turned rather ugly—"

The admiral held up a hand. "I don't need to hear it. You will spend the day mopping the decks of the *Perez* and completing any other tasks the cazadores assign to you. You will receive no food for the rest of the day, and you will serve as our lookout for the duration of the week."

Dante's mouth dropped open. "But—"

"Question my orders at your peril, Cuatreda de León. I know you have grown accustomed to a certain kind of treatment, but you should know that I will judge your actions based on two things: the cazador code and the law. As long as I am in command of this ship, your family name will not be enough to win you the title of cazador. So I suggest you make yourself useful."

Dante's mouth snapped shut. Satisfied, the admiral returned to the helm, and the crew resumed their tasks. Ximena couldn't stop the smile that pulled at her lips.

"Go ahead and gloat, capitana," Dante said, shaking water out of his hair. "We both know who will be cazador at the end of our little expedition."

He shoved past her, knocking his shoulder into hers as he crossed the deck to grab a mop, which Cazadora Cecilia held out to him. His handsome face contorted in disgust. He'd never been forced to do this kind of work; he'd always managed to bribe some other poor candidate to do it for him.

"Cuatreda de León," called one cazador. "I'd like my boots polished before sundown."

"Cuatreda de León," said another. "My trousers need mending."

"Cuatreda de León, help me trim the sails."

"And when you're done with that, there's dinner to be prepared."

While the cazadores laughed, Dante grimaced again, muttering under his breath. Ximena stifled another smile. Nothing made her happier than justice being served, and justice had never been more satisfying than watching Dante de León swab the deck like a cabin boy.

As the sun drifted down toward the horizon, Valuza grew smaller and smaller until it was gone. The sea lapped gently at the ship's sides; the first stars sparkled in the twilit sky. A sailor couldn't ask for better conditions in which to undertake a voyage. If Ximena had believed in fortune or fate, she might have thought that such forces were on their side as they set out into the archipelago.

"Cuatreda Reale."

Cazadora Cecilia stood behind her.

"The admiral has requested your presence in the hold, along with Archivist Sánchez. He intends to speak to Amador to acquire our heading."

Ximena nodded and followed the first mate below deck, passing the cargo hold and the officer's quarters before arriving in the dark, musty brig, where prisoners of war and unruly crewmates were kept. There, in one of the ship's two cells, Amador sat with his back against the hull. He smiled when he saw her.

"Cuatreda Reale. Cazadora Cecilia. We meet again. Has the time come already for me to reveal our destination?"

"Indeed it has, pirate," Cazadora Cecilia snarled.

The admiral strode into the brig, Pía at his heels. He was always imposing, but even more so during deployments—there was something about being at sea that lent him an extra measure of strength.

"On your feet," he said to Amador.

"A cruel request to make of a man who spent the night in la academia's labyrinth."

"Would you rather I ask Cazadora Cecilia to hang you from the mast? Because that could easily be arranged."

Amador laughed. "As if her supreme greatness the high minister would let you. You're a dog on a leash just as much as I am, admiral."

"A dog who has the power to take your life."

"No man has that power, Gabriel. Not even you."

Still, he eased himself onto his feet, grimacing in pain. Ximena noted the bruises and blood on his hands and feet. She didn't want to know what had happened to him during his time in prison. She didn't care.

"Well?" the pirate said. "Where is my captain's silver?"

"In the hold."

Amador clicked his tongue against his teeth. "Come now, admiral. We both learned at la academia that evidence, evidence, evidence is crucial. So if you want your heading, you'll have to pay the appropriate toll."

Ximena's fingers clenched at her sides. There was no silver aboard the *Pérez*, just as the high minister had instructed. But if Amador discovered the truth, their hunt for Gasparilla would be over before it had even begun.

Strangely, the admiral didn't seem to share her panic. He just waved a hand at Cazadora Cecilia, who disappeared into the cargo hold, returning with a wooden box. Ximena recognized it immediately; it was one of the boxes they'd used in their Seamanship training exercise.

"Does this suffice?" the first mate asked as she lifted the lid.

Inside, a substantial number of silver coins sparkled. *Clever*, thought Ximena. The admiral found a way to trick Amador into thinking there was more silver on the ship without directly violating the high minister's orders, because the silver wasn't from the empire's treasury. Yet another reason he was the greatest cazador in recent memory.

Meanwhile, Amador looked vaguely disappointed.

"Bueno," he said. "A bargain is a bargain. Your heading is la Isla de las Calaveras. When we arrive, I will give you further instructions."

Ximena sucked in a breath. There were many strange islands in Luza's archipelago: islands covered in poisonous plants, islands that emerged once every dozen years, islands that glowed in the dark, and islands that housed nameless and nightmarish beasts. But Amador was pointing them to one of the strangest—la Isla de las Calaveras.

The Isle of Skulls.

"What could possibly be the purpose of sailing to such a place?" asked Cazadora Cecilia. "It's a den of lawbreakers. The calaveras use el idioma prohibido to commune with the dead. They live in direct defiance of the empire."

"Then the great cazadores of Luza will bring the light of the law to their shores," Amador drawled. "Now if you don't mind, I'd like to return to what I was doing before I was so rudely interrupted."

The pirate eased himself back to the floor of his cell, closed his eyes, and commenced ignoring their presence entirely. Clearly their conversation was at an end. The admiral motioned for Cecilia, Pía, and Ximena to follow him back to the upper deck.

"Tell me, Cuatreda Reale, Archivist Sánchez," he asked over his shoulder. "Why would Gasparilla choose that island above all the others?"

"Well," Pía chirped. "There is a myth that it was the calaveras who resurrected the original Gasparilla's body from the dead. Scroll twenty-two of the record on Gasparilla, fourth paragraph."

The admiral looked to Ximena for clarification.

"According to reports other cazadores have given, some people from the southern archipelago believe that this Gasparilla isn't an imposter. They think he's the reincarnated version of the original Gasparilla," Ximena said.

"The same man who died two hundred years ago."

"Precisely."

"So by summoning us to that island . . ." Cazadora Cecilia began.

"Gasparilla is mocking us," said the admiral.

Ximena winced. "I believe so, sir."

"By the law," he swore. "I've sailed this archipelago too long not to know a trap when I see one."

"I agree with you, sir," Cazadora Cecilia said. "But what other choice do we have?"

"None. That's what concerns me."

Ximena watched the storm of frustration spin behind the admiral's eyes.

"Cazadora Cecilia," he said at last, "I want you to keep a close eye on the prisoner. If anything seems amiss, I want to hear about it immediately."

"Yes, sir."

"We must strive to keep our destination a secret for as long as possible. The cazadores will not be pleased to know that we are visiting a colony of witches on the advice of a pirate. Am I understood?"

"Yes, sir."

"Bueno. You may all return to your duties. It's a four-day sail to the island, and I don't want to lose another hour fretting over Amador."

The admiral called out the commands that would turn the *Pérez* south. Ximena moved to help the cazadores trim the sails—and was stopped by a drawling laugh.

"Look at you, capitana. Having secret meetings with the admiral and his first mate."

Behind her, Dante leaned on the handle of his mop, his doublet unbuttoned at the neck. She deliberately avoided looking at the deep brown skin of his chest as he spoke.

"What was the meeting about, I wonder?" he said. "Surely it didn't involve the pirate in the brig. Or the *Pérez's* mysterious heading."

Ximena did nothing to confirm or deny his musings. Instead, she went about her duties as if she couldn't feel his eyes on her back, watching, waiting. She would have to be wary of Dante de León— the boy wasn't as dense as he seemed.

Truly, Ximena didn't have enough eyes to watch all the fools trying to sabotage her.

Capítulo Ocho

As the *Pérez* raced through the clear blue waters of the archipelago, Ximena fought from sunrise to sundown to maintain her advantage over Dante de León. She leapt at every task the first mate gave her, from fastening lines to cleaning the decks, and made sure to execute them all with unparalleled excellence.

But Dante didn't even seem to be trying to compete with her. For every hour she spent sweating under the vicious heat of the Luzan sun, he spent one snatching food from the kitchens and accomplishing nothing more than the bare minimum. Ximena watched him with equal parts frustration and suspicion. What kind of game was he playing?

She discovered the answer on their second day of sailing to la Isla de las Calaveras. She was perched at the *Pérez's* bow, stitching a tear in the topsail, when Cazadora Cecilia stormed across the deck toward her, hot fury boiling in her eyes.

"How dare you," the first mate seethed. "The insolence of it. I should have you lashed."

Ximena paused her stitching and looked up. "May I be of service, Cazadora Cecilia?"

"Service!" spat the cazadora. "Service, indeed! On your feet this instant, cuatreda."

Ximena dropped the sail and leapt into a salute. "As you command."

"If you confess your crime to me, your punishment will be less severe than if you don't. So I suggest you confess, Cuatreda Reale."

"Lo siento, Cazadora Cecilia, but I can't confess to a crime when I don't know what it is."

"You don't know what it is?" the first mate repeated.

Ximena shook her head.

"Then I suppose you don't recognize this, either?"

The cazadora pulled something from her pocket, and Ximena's stomach clenched. It was one of her black eye patches.

"So you do recognize it," said Cecilia. "Confess your crime, Cuatreda Reale."

"With all due respect, señora," Ximena returned, "while I recognize the eye patch, I still don't know what crime you are accusing me of."

Furious, Cecilia drew back her hand to strike Ximena across the face, but the admiral appeared over her shoulder just in time, catching her by the wrist.

"May I ask what is going on here, Cazadora Cecilia?"

Reluctantly, Cecilia dropped her hand. "I have material evidence that this cuatreda sabotaged my cabin, sir. She released several of the animals that are kept in the hold into my personal quarters, including," her nostrils flared, "two chickens, one goat, and a pig."

"And what is this evidence you have in your possession?"

Cecilia dangled the eye patch in front of his face. He took it from her and turned it over in his palm, studying it.

"Sir," Ximena said, "I swear on the law itself that I had nothing to do with this."

If she were to be found guilty of sabotaging an officer's cabin, her dream of becoming a cazadora would evaporate like smoke.

After a long moment, the admiral cleared his throat. "This evidence is insufficient to convict Cuatreda Reale of a crime."

"Insufficient?" Cecilia cried.

"Cazadora Angélica also wears an eye patch, Cecilia. It could just as easily have been her."

"But—"

"Cazadora Cecilia," said the admiral, his voice suddenly low. "We are hunting one of the most dangerous pirates alive. We have no time to waste on petty squabbles. I am sure you understand."

"Of course, admiral."

"As for you, Cuatreda Reale." He turned to face Ximena. "Are you able to prove yourself innocent of this offense?"

Ximena's mind raced, but there was nothing she could say to prove herself innocent, and she wasn't about to lie.

When he received no response, the admiral continued. "That is unfortunate," he said, and Ximena flinched at the disappointment in his voice. "You will personally clean Cazadora Cecilia's cabin, and you will join Cuatreda de León on this evening's watch."

Now it was Ximena's turn to seethe. But she saluted anyway, striding across the deck and down into the hold toward the first mate's cabin.

It was nothing short of a disaster. Chicken droppings littered the floor, a fat pink pig was nosing through Cazadora Cecilia's storage trunks, and a white-haired goat had made itself comfortable on the bunk. As it munched through the first mate's pillow, the goat glared at Ximena with black, beady eyes, as if daring her to usurp its throne. The girl stared back in disgust; she'd never hated animals more. Cleaning this mess would likely take hours, and to make matters worse, she would be the laughingstock of the ship for the rest of the day, if not the rest of the voyage.

"Well, well, this is rather childish of you, Cuatreda Reale. Are you really so jealous of the cazadores that you would sabotage one with a goat?" Dante de León leaned against the doorway. "If I were captain, I'd have you jailed for your insolence," he declared.

And that's when Ximena knew. "You did this," she said.

"Me?" he said, his face a mask of shock. "I, Dante de León, stooping to frame some pirate's spawn for sabotage? I could never be so petty, capitana."

Ximena didn't reply. She couldn't. If she tried to formulate a response, Dante might end up with a rapier through his stomach. So she stepped forward to wrangle the pig away from the storage trunks as Dante's laughter rang in her ears.

"I wish I could stay and watch," he said, "but duty calls. See you in the crow's nest, capitana. I'm sure it will be an entertaining evening."

He swaggered down the hallway, laughing all the while, leaving Ximena to scrape up chicken droppings.

That night, in the crow's nest, Ximena swore she wouldn't speak to Dante. Though she couldn't see his face—they sat back-to-back with the mast and lantern between them—she could feel the smug, cat-like satisfaction radiating from his body. It was enough to make her want to tie iron weights to his feet and drop him in the sea. That, and his constant, completely irritating whistling.

Across the sky, stars glittered like a thousand signal fires, forming patterns that Ximena had memorized many years ago as a young candidate: the crab, the serpent, the anchor, the dolphin. The sea, too, swam with starlight, heavens blending into water somewhere in the invisible distance. She closed her good eye as cool, clean air washed over her face. These were the few things that brought Ximena peace—the gentle sway of the ship, the uncomfortable stretch of her sunburned skin, the infinity of the sea and the sky . . .

"Do you feel it?"

She opened her eye, pulling herself straight. What a fool she was. She'd allowed herself to be lulled by the sea, and a mistake like that could cost the crew their lives.

"Talking isn't a violation of the code, you know," said Dante, leaning forward to look at her.

"That depends on who you're talking to and what you're talking about."

"So serious. I was only asking a question, capitana. Do you feel it? The way the sea . . ." he trailed off, fumbling for the right word. "The way it *pulls* sometimes?"

"No. I don't."

"Of course not," he drawled. "I only wondered, from the expression on your face just now. But then again, it's rather difficult to read your expressions with the eye patch. How did you lose your eye, by the way? Not that I care, but I am curious. And I need stories if I can't have alcohol."

She considered ignoring him. But she knew Dante well enough to know that if she didn't answer this question, he would only badger her with more until she caved, and there were still too many hours left before dawn to suffer through that.

"A group of trevedas cornered me after I was promoted from dotreda," she said flatly. "They heard I'd been assigned to the admiral for my first deployment, and they were less than pleased that a child of pirates had received the honor they felt they were due. So they held me down and . . ."

She trailed off, glancing back at Dante. She realized she'd never told anyone but the admiral and Marquesa this story. The boy didn't speak, but the muscle of his jaw pulsed. He appeared almost . . . vexed? Ximena didn't understand it. Dante de León had no reason to be angry about the way she was treated at la academia.

"They said they were doing me a favor," she continued. "That I would be humbled every time I looked in the mirror and remembered what I really was."

"An infuriating overachiever?"

"The daughter of traitors."

"By the law," Dante said. He turned his face away into the darkness for a moment. She watched his grip tighten on his knees. But when he looked back toward her, he was smiling again. "And I thought having the high minister for a mother was terrible. But I only have to be miserable. You have to be miserable *and* hideous at the same time."

For a breath, Ximena considered shoving Dante off the crow's nest. She could blame the fall on alcohol consumption, and no one would ever question it. But her sense of honor prevailed. She wouldn't be able to live with his murder. At least, she didn't think that she could . . .

"Don't get me wrong, the eye patch suits you," Dante said. "Black. Depressing. Slightly terrifying. Where did you get it?"

She shrugged. "Someone left several patches for me in the infirmary. I never found out who."

"I love a happy ending. Which reminds me, where *are* we heading on this little quest of ours? Some wretched den of pirates and witches?"

His haphazard guess was closer to the truth than he might have thought. But Ximena wouldn't give him a single clue about the *Pérez's* destination, and they both knew it. When another silence fell over the crow's nest, Dante bit off a chunk of hardtack he must have bribed the cook for, since the admiral had forbidden him from eating.

"He's going to betray us," he said. "Amador, I mean."

"How do you know?"

"Because I would do the same thing."

Ximena sniffed. "Is there anything in the world you care about?"

"Oh, yes," said Dante. "But I haven't drunk nearly enough alcohol to answer a question like that. And speaking of hard questions, I've been meaning to ask you: is it true?"

Knowing that he would elaborate, she didn't bother to answer his question.

"That you turned your parents in to the cazadores?"

No one had ever asked her that question before. For a long moment, she stared out into the darkness, watching the constellation of the wily serpent drift across the sky. Dante waited with unusual patience, chewing on his hardtack.

"Yes," she said quietly. "It's true."

Dante gave a low whistle. "Well, well. You've left me speechless for once, capitana." He chewed for a moment, contemplating. "Was it hard? Turning them in?"

The reflection of the moon wavered on the sea. "Yes. It was." Ximena paused, and then added, "I was a child then."

"Rather young to betray your own blood," Dante said. "A true cazadora in the making."

She turned to face him. "You can't go ten minutes without mocking me."

"Only because you make it so easy. Your beloved admiral has such a grip on your mind that you won't even consider that everything la academia has taught you might be a lie. Honestly, I know you have some brilliance lurking beneath that thick skull, Cuatreda Reale. Have you really never thought about *why* so many pirates try to rebel against the empire? That maybe the cazadores aren't—" He broke off and paused. "I'll go no further. I have no doubt you'd turn me in for treason if I did."

He was right. Ximena felt the opportunity fly from her grasp like a bird into the night. She let out a sigh of disappointment.

"The cazadores bring light to the darkness of an unlawful world," she said. "I've seen it myself."

"I'm sure you have," he said. He was smiling, but there was no humor in it. "I'm sure it looked like justice when your parents dangled from the noose. Or perhaps you don't remember it, young as you were."

Ximena turned her face up to the moon. "My memory is

perfect. I remember every detail."

That silenced him. They listened to the waves lap against the ship's hull, the mast groaning and creaking.

"It was me, by the way."

She glanced at him with her good eye.

"The eye patches. I was the one who left them for you."

"That's the most ridiculous lie I've ever heard you tell."

"It's true," he said. "Whether you believe me or not."

His smile was gone now. The lantern light flickered in a shifting wind.

"If it is true, why did you help me?"

He didn't answer at first. He only adjusted his position so they could be on the same side of the mast. She could smell the soap he'd been using to scrub all day on his uniform.

"You know, we're not as different as you think we are, capitana. People judge you for what you are, and they judge me for what I'm not."

His voice was low and even, as if he'd aged ten tears in ten minutes. She'd heard him talk this way only once before—in the infirmary, when he was telling her about his brother's death.

"We're not as different as you think," he said again. "Maybe I was just trying to make you notice it."

If they'd been dueling with rapiers, this would have been the point where he disarmed her. She looked at him, at the moonlight caught in his silver hair, trying to read his expression. Was he mocking her still? Baiting her with sentiment, only to laugh at her when she fell for it? She couldn't figure it out. She wasn't even sure why she cared enough to try.

They sat in silence for a moment until Ximena suddenly leapt to her feet. "Did you hear that? There was a splash."

"What?" Dante eased himself up, wincing. "By the law, my legs still ache from that kick you gave me."

"Silencio," she hissed.

Grabbing the lantern off its hook, she leaned out over the rail of the crow's nest, scanning the water.

"I don't see anything," said Dante. "Maybe it was a fish or a frigate bird."

"I know what I heard," Ximena replied.

Another splash. She raised the lantern again, searching for the source. And then she saw it. Something long and lithe, with green scales and pink spines that shimmered in the moonlight, disappearing beneath the water just a hundred yards off the *Pérez's* port side.

"There," she said. "There, did you see it?"

"You know, people used to tell stories in Valuza's cantinas about a terrible monstruo lurking in the archipelago."

"Sea monsters were eliminated by the first cazadores, Cuatreda de León. Their existence was a violation of the fifth tenet of the law," she spoke the words mechanically, on instinct, because they were what she had been taught for the last four years. There simply had to be another explanation for what she'd seen. Maybe it had been a large fish, or some kind of serpent.

"Law or no law, the tales remain," said Dante. "Tales of a beast with green scales and terrible wings, who can devour entire ships. People say the monster is partially blind, so it hunts by smell, latching onto the scent of its prey and pursuing it until the prey is caught or the monster itself dies of exhaustion."

"Does this monstruo have a name?"

Dante's teeth flashed in the dark. "The Ximena."

She hit him across the arm with the lantern, and he laughed.

"Come now, capitana. Since when are you afraid of sea monsters?" He studied her face in the lantern light. "This Gasparilla business has you tied up in knots."

Though half of his face was shielded by shadows, she could have sworn that he looked almost . . . concerned? No, Ximena told herself. He was probably searching for signs of weakness, and she would reveal none. Putting the lantern back on its hook, she turned away from him and sat on the opposite side of the mast.

"By the way," Dante said. "Did you manage to clean up the chicken droppings? They're notoriously difficult to get out of fabric. Not that I would know. We have servants for that kind of thing. In fact, I had this one servant as a child . . ."

She tried to focus on the whispers of the waves instead of Dante's rambling. But she couldn't quite force herself to relax, her mind conjuring up images of a sea monster attacking them while she slept. When the sun finally took pity on her and rose from the sea, Dante was still spinning a story about how he had accidentally poisoned his mother's coffee. But Ximena didn't stay to hear how the tale ended.

"Our watch is at an end, Cuatreda de León," she said. "To be perfectly clear, nothing we've said tonight changes the fact that I will do everything in my power to best you and become a cazadora."

In the dawn's light, his smile wasn't nearly as discomforting. "Naturalmente, capitana."

She paused and nodded, and then clambered down from the crow's nest and hurried into the hold, hoping to snatch a few hours of sleep before she had to report for duty. But when she took off her eye patch as she always did before sleeping, she couldn't help but pause, holding it in her palm. Then she stuffed it in her rucksack and asked the one-eyed Cazadora Angélica, who was already awake and striding down the hallway, for a new patch. Ximena didn't want any part of Dante de León obscuring her vision.

Capítulo Nueve

"Land ho!"

Just two days after Dante's trick, the call jolted Ximena from a shallow sleep. She scrambled from her bunk and into her uniform, strapping her rapier to her hip as she took the stairs to the deck. They had arrived at their destination at last. She would finally get to see la Isla de las Calaveras for herself.

From the port rail, she observed the island alongside her crewmates. It was just as she'd read about in the archive scrolls: formed from rust-colored rock, the island was almost entirely barren, boasting towering cliffs in place of trees. There seemed to be no signs of life at all, animal or human. Ximena's skin prickled. What if Dante and the admiral were right? What if they were walking straight into a trap?

"Bring the pirate to me," the admiral called out.

Two cazadores vanished belowdecks and reemerged with Amador pinned between them.

"Well, pirate?" said the admiral. "What are your instructions?"

Amador smiled. "Impatient, aren't we? The terms of the exchange are simple, admiral. You will take two boats, one for you, me, and whatever crew you can fit, and one for the silver. When we arrive, we will go to the temple of the calaveras and you will give my captain his silver, he will give you your queen, and then we can all go our separate ways. Happily ever after."

The admiral paused, as if thinking, and then said, "Very well; ready the boats—"

Amador held up a chained hand. "There's one more important detail. If any of your cazadores so much as think about raising a weapon against my captain or his crew, the queen dies."

"I'll keep that in mind," the admiral said in a tone indicating he wouldn't. "Make ready the boats and prepare to board!"

He called out the names of several crewmates before summoning Dante, Ximena, and Pía. The remaining cazadores prepared the second dinghy, loading it with several wooden crates, which Ximena could only assume were full of sawdust or some other decoy substance in place of actual silver. The sight of it brought Ximena no comfort. Gasparilla was many things, but he wasn't a fool. If he suspected they had tricked him . . .

Pía, however, was completely unaware of the concerns.

"I was reading up on the history of la Isla de las Calaveras last night, and it's absolutely fascinating, Cuatreda Reale. Apparently, before the islands were united under the empire, the calaveras were treated as holy oracles, fluent in the magical symbols of el idioma prohibido. People would travel hundreds of miles to visit the island so they could speak with their dead ancestors or receive wisdom on everything from marriage to war. Of course, after Alessandra brought enlightenment and science to the archipelago, the calaveras were discredited as cheap magicians, and el idioma prohibido was banned. But isn't that history just riveting?"

"Yes, riveting," Ximena replied, absentmindedly. She wasn't paying attention to Pía. She was watching the admiral, who had pulled Cazador Ignacio aside and was whispering something. She didn't catch the first part of what he was telling the cazador, but she did hear him say. "If we don't return within the hour, send a third dinghy after us. I don't trust Amador. He betrayed me once before. I have no doubt he'll try it again."

"Yes, sir," Cazador Ignacio responded.

Then the admiral gave the final order to depart, and Ximena dragged Pía along with her to the boats.

Before long, they were rowing toward the island. The admiral stood at the head of the dinghy, hat tipped down to shield his eyes from the sun as he surveyed the cliffs. They were even taller than the turrets of el ministerio.

"If he makes us climb those rocks, I'll swim back to the ship," Dante muttered as he dragged his oar through the water.

"There will be no climbing today, Cuatreda de León," the admiral answered without turning around. "Steer to port. The temple lies deep within the island. The only way to access it is through those caves."

He pointed toward the base of the cliffs. Ximena squinted her good eye to make out several small holes in the orange rock. She didn't know what sounded worse, climbing a perilously high cliff or rowing into pitch-black caves. But it seemed they didn't have a choice in the matter. So the cazadores obeyed their commander and rowed toward the caves.

Meanwhile, Amador whistled to himself, picking dirt from

under his nails. Ximena's warning instinct flared. A pirate at ease was never a good sign.

"Shall I regale you all with a story as you row?" Amador said.

"Please do," Dante said.

"Silence, pirate," Cazadora Cecilia spat.

Amador grinned. "It's an entertaining tale, I promise. Once there was a man who visited the Isle of Skulls. He told the calaveras that he wished to ask his ancestors for wisdom. You see, he'd been betrothed to a girl he did not love. So one of the calaveras, a girl they called Zabel, helped him connect with the ghosts of his people through el idioma prohibido, and the man received his answer."

"What was it?" Pía asked.

Cazadora Cecilia said, "Don't listen to him, girl."

"They told him he'd already met the girl he was going to marry, but she wasn't his betrothed. Naturally, the man was confused. Who was this girl he'd supposedly met? He asked his ancestors over and over again for many days, and the longer he stayed on the island, the more he learned about the calaveras and their ways, and the more in love he fell with Zabel, the calavera who'd helped him. Eventually, he asked his ancestors if she was the one they spoke of, and his ancestors told him yes."

"Amador." The admiral's voice was a threat, low and severe. "That's enough."

"But I've just arrived at the twist, admiral! Because, my friends, this man was not just any man. He was a cazador. And with all the secrets he had learned from Zabel, he led a raid into the sacred temple of la Isla de las Calaveras, capturing and killing nearly everyone inside for practicing magic and associating with pirates."

"That's a sad ending," Pía said.

"True stories are always sad. Don't you agree, Gabriel?"

The admiral only said, "We enter the temple from the second cavern to the left."

Ximena didn't understand why her commander's shoulders were so tense or why the pirate was grinning like a shark that had tasted blood, until Pía leaned over to whisper in her ear, "I just remembered where I've heard that story before. Scroll thirty-five on Admiral Gabriel Pérez, paragraph two. He led a raid on la Isla de las Calaveras on the high minister's orders many years ago, when he was still only a cazador. Amador was his first mate then. He betrayed the admiral shortly after that."

Ximena watched the admiral as they rowed. What did it matter if he had employed deception to carry out the high minister's orders? Thousands of cazadores had done it before him, and thousands would do it after. Besides, el idioma prohibido was explicitly against the law. There was a reason Alessandra had banned magic; it led to nothing but chaos and disorder wherever it was practiced. By all measures, then, the admiral was entirely justified in his actions. She would stand by him as he had stood by her.

They continued to row until the caverns were above them. Up close, the caves were far larger than they had appeared from a distance. It was almost as if some creature had burrowed its way into the rock, boring holes for the sea and its passengers to slip through. Pía nudged Ximena, gesturing for her to look up. Strange paintings covered the ceiling, faces that might have been human, if not for the black voids that burned in place of their eyes.

"Is that what they look like?" whispered Pía. "The skull people?"

Ximena didn't know. She'd never met a calavera herself. She'd only read about the witches who painted themselves like skulls, and if they looked as frightening in reality as they did in the paintings, she wasn't sure she wanted to meet one now.

Thankfully, their journey through the cavern was short. The dinghies emerged into a lagoon surrounded on all sides by rock. The cliffs blocked the wind from entering the cove, so a tomb-like silence settled over the water, which was blacker than ink. Ximena couldn't tell whether it was a few feet deep or bottomless.

"The temple of the calaveras."

Amador's voice shattered the silence. The pirate tipped his chin toward the far end of the lagoon. There, several columns, arches, and two stone doors had been carved out of the rock, artistry rivaling any building on the capital of Valuza.

"Hand carved over a hundred years ago," he said. "Impenetrable to pirates and cazadores alike. Unless, of course, you know someone on the inside. To the doors, if you please."

"I'm not sending my crew inside," the admiral said. "Gasparilla will meet us here, or not at all."

"Would you like your queen to die, admiral? Then by all means stay here."

The muscle in the admiral's jaw worked. Finally, he growled, "Do as he says."

They obeyed him, steering the dinghies to the doors, which were carved with elaborate, geometric patterns of skulls and flowers. Pía gazed up at the temple in awe, Dante with something between boredom and skepticism. Only Ximena gripped her rapier. She'd been worried about Gasparilla before, but now she wondered what else waited for them inside the calaveras' den, and whether or not they'd survive it.

"Whatever you do," the admiral instructed, "keep your weapons sheathed until absolutely necessary. The calaveras are not fond of cazadores. They'll look for any excuse to attack us."

"With good reason," Amador said. "But if you're ready for all the horrors of the dead, then allow me to do the honors." He raised his voice to a shout. "I am Amador Gutiérrez, accompanied by the cazadores of Luza."

Silence answered them. Ximena's heart picked up its pace when she realized they were trapped in a walled enclosure with only one exit. If they were ambushed, their odds of escape were slim to none.

"We could just open the door," Dante drawled.

"We could," Amador acknowledged. "And trigger the release of several dozen poison-tipped arrows."

Dante shrugged. "Better than floating around here."

Suddenly, there was a hiss like shifting sand, and the stone door eased open to reveal a cavernous darkness. The cazadores turned to the admiral expectantly; his face was creased in a solemn frown.

"Forward," he said.

So they dipped their oars into the water, pushing the dinghies further into the darkness. They were barely inside the temple before the doors eased shut behind them with a thud. Ximena swallowed hard, wondering if that had been the last time they would see the Luzan sun.

"Should we continue, admiral?" asked Cazadora Cecilia. "We can't see a thing."

"Forward," was all the admiral said.

"I always knew that man would be the death of me," Dante muttered.

Perhaps it was the word *death* that summoned them, because it was then that Ximena heard it: the rattle of bones and the throbbing hum of a guitar. Not a song she'd ever heard before, but a song she'd somehow always known, beating in time with her heart. Where was it coming from? The water—it was coming from the water. Maybe she could find it, if she stepped out of the boat, if she swam down . . .

"Cuatreda Reale!"

Pía seized her by the wrist, shattering her thoughts.

"What—what happened?" Ximena said.

"You almost fell in the water," the archivist squeaked.

"So you hear it, too?" Dante's voice was soft and hazy in the darkness. "The music?"

In response, Pía let out a shriek. Ximena turned instinctively toward the threat—and found herself face-to-face with a skeleton. No, a woman painted like a skeleton. Her skin glowed the brilliant white of bones and her eyes blazed an unnatural amber, but she was breathing, alive.

A calavera, grinning at her with sharp teeth.

Another shout, this time from Cazadora Cecilia. A second calavera dangled in front of their dinghy, its amber eyes glinting, and a third appeared soon after, then a fourth, then a fifth, until they had the cazadores surrounded.

"Hold your ground," the admiral called out. "Raise no weapons."

But the calaveras didn't seem to care whether or not they had weapons. They seized the sides of the boats with their bony hands, dragging the dinghies through the water at twice the speed of the oars. Every instinct in Ximena's body told her to unsheathe her rapier and cut their attackers down. But she couldn't disobey the admiral's orders. So she gripped her seat and clamped her good eye shut as the calaveras hauled them deeper into the darkness.

As they traveled, the music grew louder, stranger, its melody running as wild as a riptide. Ximena was so lost in the sound that she didn't know how long they had been moving, until they arrived at a cavern as large as a city square, covered in more painted designs. It was a rookery of rock and bone: Calaveras hung from the individual carved chambers like spiders, hissing, their eyes fastened on the cazadores. There were dozens of them, maybe more. The cazadores were completely outnumbered.

This time, Ximena couldn't stop herself from reaching for her sword—but froze when she felt Dante's fingers against her hand.

"Not yet," he whispered, and she knew he was right. She couldn't put the entire crew at risk for one moment of rashness.

In the center of the cavern, on a platform of stone, calaveras danced to the discordant music, snapping wooden castanets out of time. The women twirled in ruffled dresses of spectacular color, gold hoops in their ears and flower wreaths in their hair. They looked like wraiths in the torchlight—no, not torchlight. The strange symbols painted on the walls were glowing, eyes and skulls and flowers burning the brilliant blue of the hottest flame. *El idioma prohibido*. The language of magic. Ximena had never seen it performed before, but it was just as unnerving as the archive scrolls had warned. Unnatural, blood-chilling, and . . .

"¡Qué bonito!" Pía breathed.

"The Dance of the Dead," said Amador. "A ritual performed to honor those who have passed on, or to call down a curse on the living."

"Which version is this?" Dante asked.

Amador didn't answer. He only stood and said, "Calaveras, I, Amador Gutiérrez, present you with the cazadores of Luza. They've come to speak with Gasparilla."

All at once, the music stopped. Dozens of pairs of amber eyes fixed themselves on the cazadores, watching, waiting. Ximena searched for any sign of the legendary pirate captain. She found none.

Suddenly, the calaveras began to step aside one by one, revealing a small woman in a violet dress and veil. She walked slowly and silently to the edge of the platform, her feet making no sound against the rock. She lifted her veil, revealing two eyes as violet as her dress, burning like twin stars, burning with—

Hatred. She looked down on the cazadores as if they were beasts, abominations who didn't deserve life.

"Zabel." The word fell from the admiral's lips like shattering glass.

"I prayed every night for this day to come," the woman replied. Her voice was as high and lilting as the music had been. "Now my prayers have been answered. Isn't that what you always told me, Gabriel? From preparation comes perfection. Vengeance belongs to those who wait."

Ximena glanced over at Dante. If a warning bell had been buzzing in her mind before, now it was blaring. Something was wrong.

Terribly wrong.

The admiral swung to face Amador. "You have ten seconds to explain yourself, pirate. We've done everything you've asked, and now I'm tired of your games. Where is Gasparilla?"

"That depends, admiral. Where is your silver?"

"On that boat, as you instructed."

"Oh honestly, Gabriel," Amador said, rolling his eyes. "Don't insult my intelligence again. We both know there was never any silver in those crates. Your high minister isn't the type to give up the contents of her treasury just like that. However—" He leapt onto the stone platform so quickly that the cazadores didn't have time to stop him. "She might be persuaded by the brutal murder of her admiral."

It all suddenly snapped into place in Ximena's mind. Gasparilla had anticipated their attempt to trick him. So he'd led the admiral straight into the clutches of the vengeful calaveras, knowing that when news of his death reached Valuza, the high minister would have no choice but to meet Gasparilla's demands. The treasury would be bankrupt.

And the empire would fall.

The calaveras let out a gleeful hiss.

The admiral unsheathed his rapier and yelled, "Row! ¡Rápido, rápido! ¡Ándale, ándale!"

The cazadores picked up their oars, rowing as fast as they could away from the platform. But the calaveras were already swarming down the cavern walls toward them, their hissing loud in Ximena's ears. They were never going to make it out of the temple alive.

She heard a shout next to her—two calaveras had seized Dante by the arms and dragged him into the water. He kicked and writhed, but their grip was firm. They hoisted him onto the stone platform before Ximena had time to fight back.

"Man overboard!" she cried.

"There's no time," the admiral barked as he sliced a calavera from the air. "We have to row for the exit."

"But sir—"

"That's an order, Ximena!"

She froze. It would be all too easy. She could abandon Dante to an almost certain death and blame it on a direct order from the admiral. She wouldn't have to compete for the title of cazadora; she wouldn't have to worry about the de León family haunting her steps for the rest of her days.

Yet the cazador code burned in her mind: *no cazador shall be left behind.*

So Ximena Reale did the unthinkable—she dove into the water to save Dante de León.

Someday, her honor was going to be the end of her.

When she surfaced again, she caught one last glimpse of the cazadores before they disappeared into the tunnel, the calaveras right behind them. She swam the rest of the way to the stone platform, where Zabel and Amador stood.

"This one isn't even a cazador," the witch was saying. "He's a minnow, and I asked for the shark."

"So kill him while you wait," Amador replied. "Your people will bring you the admiral's head on a spike soon enough."

Ximena didn't need to hear anymore. She hauled herself up onto the platform, unsheathing her rapier as soon as she had her footing.

"You will release him, or I will strike you down where you stand."

Slowly, Zabel turned her violet stare to Ximena.

"Of course Gabriel would escape and leave children behind to take his punishment." She waved a hand to the calaveras holding Dante. "Kill them quickly, without suffering. The boy first and then the girl."

"Go, Ximena," Dante gasped as they wrenched him to the floor. "Run."

Ximena stepped forward, heart drumming. "I won't let you kill him."

Zabel's brow lifted into her veil. "This boy means so much to you that you would risk your life to save his?"

"He means nothing to me," Ximena said. "But my code demands I stay by his side until the end."

"Just as I must stay by yours, Cuatreda Reale!"

Ximena turned to find Pía scrambling onto the rock, soaked to the skin and shivering.

Zabel studied them both. This close, Ximena could see that the witch was old enough to be her mother, the paint around her eyes barely concealing the wrinkles creasing her skin. But something had replaced the hatred in her eyes now, something guarded and calculating, as if she were trying to solve a particularly difficult puzzle.

"You're not like the other cazadores I've met," she said, "though you wear the uniform of la academia. What is your name, girl?"

"Ximena Reale."

Zabel's painted lips tightened. "Reale," she said. "Your family name?"

"Yes."

What the calavera made of this was impossible to say. Her painted expression didn't change when she said, "Their courage has earned them their lives. Sell them to the pirates. I have no further use for them."

The calaveras released Dante, shoving him toward Ximena.

"Idiota," he said as he stumbled into her. "I told you to go."

"I had no choice."

"There is always a choice, capitana."

Before she could reply, something sharp pierced the side of Ximena's neck—she winced, reaching up to touch the wounded area, but found that she couldn't lift her arm. In fact, she couldn't move her legs, or keep her eyes open, and she was slumping to the floor, into a darkness as warm and gentle as the ocean waves.

Capítulo Diez

"I knew it! I knew you were still alive. Dante was worried—"

"I most certainly was not."

"But I told him it wasn't possible, that Ximena Reale couldn't be vanquished by a poison dart."

"Did you just use the word *vanquished* in casual conversation?"

"Given the context, Cuatreda de León, it's quite a fitting application—"

"Quiet," groaned Ximena. "Both of you."

She sat up slowly, waiting for her spiraling vision to settle back into place before looking around. They were obviously in the hold of a ship: it was cramped, slimy, and dark, with seawater leaking in from the sides and the ceiling, and the stench was unbearable, a disgusting mixture of urine and mold.

"Where are we?" she muttered. Her head pounded with a vengeance; her shoulder throbbed from her gunshot wound. "How long have I been asleep?"

Dante licked his cracked lips. "We're on the *Delfín*, the pirate sloop captained by Catarina Salazar."

The name was familiar, but Ximena was in too much pain to place it. Thankfully, though, she had Pía to jolt her memory.

"Captain Salazar is one of the most prolific and vicious pirates on record," Pía said. "The cazadores have destroyed her ships twice, but each time, she has managed to survive and reestablish herself. She also has a particular taste for the theatrical. There are multiple accounts of her dining with the greatest governors in the archipelago, seducing them with her beauty and her silver tongue, and stealing the very knives from their tables before they realized what was happening."

"Oh, and to answer your other question," added Dante, "you've been out for three days."

"What?" Ximena struggled to get to her feet. "Three days?"

They had lost precious time, time they could have spent trying to escape and signal for the cazadores. They couldn't afford to waste a moment more. But when she moved forward, something yanked her back to the floor, sending her vision spiraling again. She hadn't even noticed that her wrists and ankles were in shackles—all three of them had been chained to the *Delfín's* hull.

"Valiant effort, capitana," said Dante. "But it's no use. If there were a way to escape, I'm sure those poor fools would have tried it long ago."

She looked in the direction he was pointing. Chained to the opposite wall were several men and women who wore the signature blue uniforms of the Luzan Naval Guard. But they were far from being trained soldiers now: they were stretched on their sides, moaning in pain, their eyes bloodshot and yellowed from scurvy, their bones poking through their skin. Ximena recoiled with horror.

"From what I've gathered, Salazar likes to pick on smaller navy patrols," Dante said, anticipating her thoughts. "She keeps her captives alive and ransoms them back to the nearest island governor for an easy payday. Occasionally, though, she uses them for entertainment."

"Entertainment?"

"Indeed. Yesterday, the captain had one of the sailors strung upside-down from the mast and burned alive. She told us about it in great detail."

Ximena winced. She hadn't survived this long to die that way.

"We have to escape," she hissed.

"And how do you suggest we do that?"

She didn't know. She sat back against the hull, trying in vain to ignore the navy sailors' groans so she could think.

"Well, while you come up with a brilliant plan to get us out of here, capitana, I'm going to get some sleep. I don't want to look like that," he tipped his head to the navy sailors, "when I pass on to the next life."

She bristled. "After I sacrificed myself to save you—"

"Nobody asked you to save me," he interrupted her.

Only now did Ximena notice how tired he looked: his eyes were shadowed, his jaw lined with bruises, and a hideous scab snaked down from his left ear to his chin. He'd even been stripped of his uniform, left with nothing but a thin shirt and baggy trousers.

"And I still don't know why you did it," he continued. "Though I assume it's just your natural idiocy shining through. Either way, I need sleep, and I'm tired of talking to you."

Mumbling to himself, he curled onto his side with his back to her and Pía and was snoring within minutes, though whether he was truly asleep or just trying to irritate Ximena was hard to say. But she quickly forgot about the snores when she saw Dante's back. Beneath the sheer linen shirt, his skin was shredded and scabbed, a mottled mess of blood and tissue. Her stomach turned. She knew those marks as any sailor would.

"He got himself whipped," Pía whispered, her voice small and soft. "When they brought us aboard, they stripped us of our uniforms and gave us these shirts to wear instead. But when they tried to take your uniform, Dante fought them. So they tied him to the mast and lashed him. Ten times." She shivered. "I keep hearing his screams in my head."

Ximena looked back at Dante. Why in the name of the law would he do something so stupid? She had seen too many things over the last few days that could not be explained: legendary pirates returning, witches dancing for the dead, Dante getting himself lashed for her sake. She suddenly longed for the days before Gasparilla's attack, when her life had been simple, clear, ordered—when all she had to worry about was wrangling Marquesa, avoiding Dante de León, and devoting herself to the law.

But she didn't have time to feel sorry for herself. She had to figure out their escape plan before the *Delfín* arrived at its destination—or before Captain Salazar discovered that she had captured the high minister's son.

They could attempt to organize a mutiny. But looking at the navy sailors, Ximena doubted any of them were strong enough to stand and hold a weapon, let alone fight with one. Perhaps they could take Salazar hostage. But the pirate wouldn't be likely to enter the hold unguarded . . .

"What is that?"

Pía's voice broke through her thoughts. The girl had her face pressed to a crack in the ship's hull. She waved Ximena to her side, pointing toward something in the distance. Ximena strained against her chains to look, but she saw nothing except sea and sky.

"You should rest, Pía," Ximena sighed. "People hallucinate when they're exhausted."

"I know I saw something," the archivist insisted. "A fish or a snake, with bright green scales."

Ximena froze. "What did it look like?"

"I only saw it for a moment. But it had green scales, and pink spines along its back, the color of clam bellies."

Ximena's pulse pounded in her ears. Could it be the same beast she and Dante had spotted from the crow's nest that night?

"Pía," she asked carefully, "is it possible that sea monsters are not actually extinct as we'd like to believe?"

Pía's brow crinkled in thought. "There are no *official* records of a recent monstruo attack. But there have been a few unexplainable shipwrecks reported in the last handful of years."

Ximena didn't want to believe that the empire was wrong in any respect. But she couldn't deny the possibility that there was a gap in their records, or that some monstruos still lurked in the deep.

"If such a monstruo were to exist, how would it track its prey?" she asked.

"Well, according to the bestiary scrolls, most sea monsters had horrible eyesight, so they hunted by smell instead."

Ximena recalled her conversation with Dante in the crow's nest. *The monster is partially blind, so it hunts by smell, latching onto the scent of its prey and pursuing it until the prey is caught or the monster itself dies of exhaustion.* Leave it to Dante de León to spin a story around a grain of truth. Apparently one of the monstruos *had* survived, and somehow, it had tracked the candidates here by smell. If it attacked the ship, the pirates would be completely unprepared. The *Delfín* would sink. . . .

A plan began to form in Ximena's mind: a ludicrous plan, but a plan nonetheless. If they could somehow lure the monster into attacking the pirate ship, they could escape in the chaos, giving the navy sailors a chance to flee at the same time. Of course, they had no way to unlock the sailors' chains, and even if they did escape, they would be stranded in the middle of the ocean with nowhere to go. But it was better than being burned alive or worse.

"Pía we need to wake Dante up and—"

But before she could finish, a door at the end of the hold banged open, revealing a middle-aged woman in black high-heeled boots. Ximena didn't need an introduction to know who she was: Catarina Salazar, captain of the *Delfín*. She was just as beautiful as Pía had warned, lithe and sleek as the dolphins her ship was named for, her almond eyes dark, her curving lips painted scarlet, her black braided hair shimmering down her back.

"At last," the pirate said with a grin. "Our little cazadora is awake! I hope you enjoyed your rest, tesoro."

Ximena glared at her in silence. Unperturbed, Salazar sauntered across the room, stopping to bend down in front of her face. She studied Ximena as a fish studies a worm.

"Have we met before?"

"If we had, you'd be in prison," said Ximena.

"And yet," said Salazar, "there's something familiar about you." She caught Ximena by the chin with surprising force, tilting her face upward against her will. "Ah, yes. I have it now. You are the spitting image of Alejandra Reale. And if my memory serves, which it usually does, Alejandra and Diego had two daughters."

"The Reales were hanged for their crimes, as you will be."

"Yes, you sound just like her. How Alejandra would roll over in her grave if she knew her precious daughter had become a pirate hunter!" Laughing, she released her hold on Ximena's chin. "I suppose you think me a heartless killer. A murderer, a thief. The scourge of the great Luzan Empire."

"I don't *think* you are. I *know* it."

"Do you now?" The amusement in Salazar's eyes suddenly darkened, making Ximena's heart lurch against her ribs. "And what would you say if I told you that every coin I steal is delivered into the pockets of peasants across the archipelago? People your empire has trampled and forgotten?"

"I'd say that you're a liar, as well as a murderer and a thief," Ximena replied through gritted teeth.

"So certain. So stern. I wonder what it would take . . ." Salazar allowed the words to linger in the reeking air. Then she smiled, straightened up, and gave a sharp clap. "I propose a game. My men are bored, and you, young cazadores, are just what they require."

Three men entered the hold behind her. Two of them unlocked Ximena and Pía from their chains, hauling them up with a force that made Pía squeak, while the third woke Dante up with a kick to his bleeding back. Dante groaned as they dragged him to his feet, his bleary eyes finding Ximena's.

"Why do I get the feeling this is your fault, capitana?"

She didn't look at him. She couldn't. If Salazar found out who Dante really was, she would surely hold the boy for ransom, and Ximena wouldn't be responsible for putting the empire in further jeopardy. Thankfully, though, Salazar had already jumped to quite a different conclusion.

"Ah, yes," the pirate said. "I'd almost forgotten about this star-crossed romance. Two young cazadores, so deeply in love that they would risk their lives to save each other from the calaveras."

Her men laughed. She leaned down into Ximena's face, still smiling. She wore a perfume that smelled of oranges, but Ximena couldn't help but notice the blood crusted under her fingernails.

"We're going to have fun, you and me," the pirate said. "I can promise you that." She turned to her men. "Take them above decks."

The pirates hauled the candidates out of the hold. Blinking against the sun, Ximena looked around and assessed their enemy: there were more than fifty pirates on deck, wiry men with tattooed arms and cutlasses at their hips. They hurled insults and slurs as the candidates were tied to the mast, Ximena pinned between Dante and Pía, the rope chafing her ribs. Salazar raised a hand to silence the chaos.

"So," she asked the candidates. "Which of you would like to go first?"

"That depends on whether or not your game involves liquor," replied Dante.

"Sadly not," said Salazar. "But it does involve something much better. Ever heard of keelhauling, little cazadores?"

Ximena stiffened as Pía let out the smallest squeak. Keelhauling was against la academia's code, and with good reason. When a sailor was keelhauled, they were dragged beneath a ship from bow to stern, tugged by a rope tied around their waist. Most victims died by drowning, unless they bled out from being shredded against the sharp barnacles on the ship's hull.

"I see that you have," said Salazar, grinning. "So I'll ask you again. Which of you will be going first?"

"I will." The archivist's lips were trembling, but she met the pirate stare for stare. "You may do what you like to me, as long as you leave my friends unharmed."

"Well, well. The girl is braver than she looks! But will you not step in for her, boy?" she said to Dante. "Or will you stand by and watch the girl suffer?"

Dante opened his mouth to reply, but Pía interrupted him.

"I refuse Cuatreda de León's help," she said. "I've accepted my fate, and I don't require assistance."

"Cuatreda de León," the pirate repeated. Her smile was like the flash of a knife. "Any relation to the high minister, young cazador?"

Ximena's throat tightened with alarm. "I'll go," she cried. "You may keelhaul me first."

"Wonderful." The pirate clapped her hands, successfully distracted. "Lace her up, gentlemen."

"No!" Pía cried.

"Ximena," Dante hissed. "Wait, please, don't do this."

Ximena ignored him. If she didn't distract the pirates, they would no doubt discover Dante's true identity. Plus, the only way to lure the monster to the *Delfín* was to act as human bait. So, whether she liked it or not, she had to save Dante de León a second time.

The pirates untied Ximena from the mast and wrapped a rope around her waist. Then they led her to the bow of the ship, where the frothy sea waited several feet below. Salazar leaned over her shoulder.

"The key," she said, "is to take a breath just before you hit the water. Then you might have enough air to survive the ordeal." She turned to her men. "Don't kill her, understand? I need to get my money's worth when I sell her off to the governor."

"Yes, captain," they growled.

She grinned and waved her hand. "Off she goes, then."

Laughing, the pirates grabbed Ximena by her shoulders and tossed her off the bow. She barely had time to take a breath before she plunged down into the deep, cold water. She only hoped the oxygen she had would be enough.

Opening her good eye underwater, Ximena could see straight down to the seafloor. The water was clear and blue, stretching on for miles in every direction—there was no sign of a green-scaled monster.

That was all she managed to notice before she felt a brutal tug at her waist, dragging her beneath the *Delfín's* hull, squeezing the air from her lungs. Her back slammed hard against the wood, and stars burst in front of her eye as the barnacles raked at her skin. It took everything she had not to breathe out, and closing her eye again, she struggled not to panic. *They won't kill me*, she told herself. *In another moment, I'll be back on deck with Dante and Pía, as if nothing happened.*

But the moment stretched on and on, and her lungs burned for air. When she slammed against the hull again, she saw more stars from the pain. How much longer would she have to endure? The ship's shadow seemed to go on forever. Perhaps the pirates would kill her after all. What was one captive to them, when they had so many?

Her lungs heaved. Her legs spasmed. Four faces swirled in her mind as her vision began to fade. She saw the admiral, his eyes dark and filled with judgment; she saw Marquesa, smiling and holding her frigate bird to her chest. Then, strangest of all, she saw her parents. It had been years since Ximena had dreamed of them, but she saw them now as clearly as the day they'd died. Mamá's eyes were a warm hazel like Marquesa's, while Papá was tall and lean like Ximena, his Reale curls blowing wildly across his face. They were trying to say something, their mouths moving in unison, but Ximena could only make out the first three words: *mira la verdad*. Then her lips opened, and she felt her chest cave in . . . and the world went black.

"Idiots. I told you not to kill her."

"We'll get her back, captain, just a moment."

Something heavy pressed against Ximena's torso. Then she was coughing up seawater, gripping the deck of the *Delfín*. *Alive*. The thought was like a heartbeat. *Alive, alive, alive*. But another thought soon followed it: *failure*.

The monster hadn't attacked the ship.

"Did you enjoy your trip, little cazadora?" came Salazar's voice. "The barnacles took a piece of you, by the looks of it. Now, let's see if your friends are as lucky as you are. Strap her to the mast and fetch the boy."

Two pirates hauled Ximena from the stern and lashed her to the mast once more—the wood felt like fire against her raw skin. Beside her, Pía fussed and fretted.

"Are you all right, Cuatreda Reale?" the archivist whispered, worry in her voice. "Oh, you're bleeding! You should have let me go in your place, now you might die from infection—"

"Enough, Pía," Ximena wheezed. "I've lived through worse."

"Any tips for survival, capitana?" Dante joked as the pirates untied him. Though his smile was teasing, his eyes betrayed his fear.

"Don't die," Ximena rasped.

"Good advice," he said. "Inspired and succinct."

The pirates took him to the bow, where they wrapped the rope tight around his waist and picked him up by his shoulders.

"Any last words?" Salazar asked.

Dante opened his mouth—and a violent roar shook the deck. The pirates dropped Dante and frantically drew their cutlasses, searching for the source, but there was nothing except sea and sky.

Salazar barked a laugh.

"Spineless cowards," she crowed. "Quaking in our boots, are we? Trembling at a boy's theatrics? You're a disgrace to the word pirate. Now toss the little cazador overboard before I have you all whipped."

As the crew hoisted Dante into the air again, a shadow fell over the *Delfín's* deck. Ximena squinted upward to see two massive wings blocking out the sun. A second roar shook the mast. She smiled.

The monstruo had arrived.

It looked just as Dante had described it: a long, lithe serpent covered in green scales and pink spines, with a head like a gull's and two feathered wings. When it swooped down toward the ship, it gave another terrible shriek, flicking its tail to release a dozen knife-like barbs. The pirates howled in pain as the barbs found their targets; their skin began to bubble and boil, melting away onto the deck. *Poison*, Ximena thought. The monster's barbs were poisonous.

Pía gasped. "It's a solbara. According to paragraph seven of the bestiary scrolls, the first cazadores hunted and killed them all in the early days of the empire."

"Well, apparently they didn't do a particularly good job of it," Dante drawled.

"What does solbara mean?" Ximena asked.

Pía's eyes were wide with terror as she whispered, "Ship wrecker."

So the ship was marked for destruction.

Perfecto.

When the pirate holding Dante captive took two barbs to the throat and dropped his sword, Dante snatched it and cut himself loose. Then he raced across the deck and freed Ximena and Pía.

"So the moral of this story," he said, "is that I was right, capitana."

Ximena rolled her good eye. She wasn't nearly desperate enough to acknowledge that Dante's cantina tales were accurate. She grabbed a cutlass off a dead pirate and tossed a second to Pía, who promptly dropped it and had to scramble to pick it up.

"We have to get off this ship," Ximena said. "Now!"

"Really, capitana? What gave you that idea? The snake-bird trying to kill us, or the pirates trying to sell us like cattle?"

"It's called a solbara," said Pía. "Not a snake-bird."

"I'll remember that next time I invite one to dinner," said Dante.

"There's a dinghy off the port side," Ximena interrupted them. "Cut it down and get away as fast as you can. I'll catch up with you."

"Catch up with us?" Pía squeaked. "We can't leave you behind, Cuatreda Reale!"

"For once, I agree with the archivist," said Dante. He ducked to dodge a rain of poison barbs, then swept his hair from his eyes. "I didn't get myself whipped just to watch the snake-bird use you as a toothpick."

Ximena growled with frustration. They didn't have time to argue.

"Pía, please," she said. "Ayúdame."

Fear flickered behind the archivist's eyes. But the girl was nothing if not loyal, so she nodded her agreement, grabbed Dante by the sleeve, and pulled the boy across the deck even as he shouted his objections.

Ximena didn't stay to watch them go. Instead, she raced up to the bow, where Salazar was shouting desperate orders to her men. She needed the captain's keys if she was going to free the navy sailors in the hull before the solbara sank the ship. So she came up behind Salazar and pointed her cutlass at the pirate's back.

"Your keys," she said. "Now."

The pirate turned, unsheathing her sword and smiling. "How about another game, little cazadora? Take my keys off my cold, dead corpse, or don't take them at all."

"As you wish."

Ximena lunged to stab at her chest, but the movement made her injured shoulders flare with sudden, blinding pain, so her blade swung wide. Captain Salazar parried, driving her back with a cut at her neck. The pirate fought with a brute force that Ximena hadn't prepared for—blow after blow pushed her across the deck, with pirates shouting and dying all around her. Grimacing, she barely blocked Salazar's slice toward her arm, and then jumped to avoid a cutlass to the legs. But when she attempted to dodge another swing, she lost her balance on the pitching deck and tumbled to the floor, cutlass skidding from her hand. Salazar pressed her blade to her throat.

"Bad luck, little cazadora," she said. "It seems I'll be keeping my keys."

She raised her cutlass above her head—and a poison barb pierced her chest. She froze, clutching at the wound. Her mouth opened and shut around words she couldn't quite speak. Then she sagged to the deck, dead, the barb still sizzling between her ribs.

Ximena didn't waste any time. She scrambled to her feet and grabbed the keys from Salazar's waist, then bolted across the deck and down into the brig. She tossed the keys to the nearest navy sailor.

"Hurry," she barked. "Free yourselves. The monster is going to sink the ship."

The solbara's shriek emphasized her point. The first navy sailor fumbled to unlock his shackles, then passed the keys to a younger girl, who unlocked her own and passed them on.

"Gracias, cazadora," the girl rasped.

Ximena didn't have time to correct her. "May the seas be with you," she whispered, before hurrying out into the light.

Above decks, the *Delfín* was a floating graveyard. Salazar's crew had been annihilated, their bodies strewn across the ship, riddled with poisonous barbs. Overhead, the solbara released another screech before swooping down with its claws extended and snapping the mainmast in two like mere a twig. Ximena had seconds to move, or she would be crushed. So she dropped her cutlass and threw herself over the *Delfín*'s side, diving into the sea.

When she'd surfaced again, she caught sight of Pía and Dante about fifty yards off. She swam as fast as she could manage toward the dinghy and let Dante pull her up into the boat.

"You seem to have the gift of immortality, capitana," he said. "How am I supposed to be promoted to cazador if you won't get yourself killed by a sea monster?"

But Ximena wasn't listening. She was watching as the navy sailors threw themselves into the sea, paddling out of the way as the *Delfín* sank, shredded by the solbara's claws. As Dante and Pía began to row, she wondered if she had just condemned those sailors to death. Then she buried the thought and picked up an oar. *If your neck is always craned over your shoulder*, Alessandra had once said, *your feet will forget how to walk.*

"Cuatreda Reale?" Pía's voice was high and tight. "Why is the solbara following us?"

Ximena's jaw clenched. The monster had abandoned the wreck of the *Delfín* and was flying straight toward them, its mouth open in a screech.

It won't stop until it has found its prey.

"Because it has our scents," said Dante. "Now would be a good time to row."

They pulled their oars through the water with all the strength they could muster, but Ximena knew it was no use. There was nowhere to hide, nowhere to run, and the solbara wouldn't give up until it had devoured them.

Suddenly, the monster gave a deafening howl—a harpoon had pierced its left wing.

"Where did that come from?" Ximena said, bewildered.

"I don't—" Pía started as a second harpoon sliced through the sky to spear the monster's right wing.

"Who cares?" said Dante, rowing even faster than before. "When you spend enough time in Valuza's cantinas, you learn not to question when someone gives you a way out of a bad situation."

Screeching, the solbara careened down into the water with a huge splash, the waves rocking their dinghy. A third harpoon sank into its skull, and the beast's lifeless body sank beneath the waves, disappearing in a flash of green scales.

"How—" Ximena began, until a voice boomed out over the water:

"Care to explain why a solbara was hunting you, cazadores?"

Capítulo Once

Apparently, Ximena had gone mad. She scanned the sea with her good eye, but there was nothing except water in every direction. She must have imagined the voice that had called out over the sea. But if she had imagined it, so had Dante and Pía, because they looked just as confused as she felt.

"Up here, cazadores."

There was the voice again. An enormous shadow descended over them as the candidates tilted their necks back to look upward. Over their heads floated a small sloop, its hull painted a spectacular purple, its sails fanned out to catch the wind. A dark-haired woman leaned over the side, smiling. Ximena's shoulders immediately relaxed. She would recognize that purple paint anywhere in the archipelago.

"Are you the merchants of Bezucár?" she called out.

"As you say," the sailor replied.

The smallest of laughs burst unbidden from Ximena's chest. Dante raised his fist with a whoop.

Pía grinned from ear to ear as she recited from memory, "Scroll seven on islands of the archipelago, paragraph fifty-eight. The merchants of Bezucár trade their goods in sloops that can travel through water and sky, depending on the orientation of their special sails, which are made from a very rare fabric only woven on the island of Bezucár itself. But more important, the merchants are longtime allies of Luza's cazadores, often supplying deployments with extra provisions in exchange for the armada's protection."

"Just so," the merchant said. "May I ask how you got yourselves into this mess?"

Ximena explained that they were from la academia, and they had been captured by pirates and separated from their crew. She didn't mention Gasparilla's name, as some details were better left out until absolutely necessary.

"Then those men are in service to the empire as well?" asked the woman, pointing toward the navy sailors treading water just ahead of them.

Ximena nodded. The woman disappeared from the rail for a moment. Then a long rope ladder tumbled down to the dinghy from the sloop.

"Climb up, cazadores," called the woman. "We have no time to lose."

Without hesitation, Ximena reached for Pía and steered her toward the rope ladder.

"Cuatreda Reale," Pía squeaked. "What are you doing?"

"Boosting you up," said Ximena.

Gulping, Pía squeezed her eyes shut and began climbing hand over hand up the ladder. Ximena turned to Dante.

"You next," she ordered.

But Dante didn't move. He was watching Pía's ascent, one hand shielding his eyes from the sun.

"Tell me you're not afraid of heights," Ximena said.

"I'm not," he said. "I just think we're trusting these people too easily. Who knows what could be waiting for us up there? The whole crew might be cannibals, for all we know."

Ximena lifted a brow. "You're afraid of heights."

"Fear is healthy, capitana," he snapped. "It keeps you from doing stupid things like jumping out of a dinghy to save someone you hate."

"Climb the ladder."

Dante tossed his head like a disgruntled cat. "Fine. But when we end up roasted over a spit, don't blame me."

Though he did his best to hide it, Ximena noticed the way his hands trembled as he climbed up the ladder. She stored that piece of information in her brain for future use.

When the merchants dragged her over the ship's rail, Ximena let out a sigh of relief. The sloop was small, with triangular sails and about a forty-person crew, all of them dressed in fine, patterned silks. The dark-haired woman who'd spoken before stood in front of them all, her posture squared with a captain's confidence. Her tanned face was creased and weatherworn, but her eyes were warm as hazelnuts, lacking a pirate's hardness. She wore purple trousers embroidered with white flowers—the signature pattern of la Isla Bezucár.

"Welcome, cazadores, to the *Flora*," said the woman. "I am Captain Marisol Giraldo of la Isla Bezucár. We are honored to have you aboard."

Ximena bowed at the waist. "I am Cuatreda Ximena Reale, and this is Cuatreda Dante de León and Archivist Pía Sánchez. We are—"

Ximena was cut off suddenly as something slammed into the deck. She turned to see several merchants carrying knives and the feathered wings of the felled solbara—they must have trimmed them from the carcass.

"We've been tracking the beast for some time now," explained Captain Marisol. "The feathers of the solbara can be sold for a great price in the Luzan markets. It's a good thing we were close by, cazadores. Few people have experienced a solbara attack and lived to tell of it."

"We owe you our lives, Captain Marisol," said Pía.

The woman nodded. Gratitude and hospitality were highly valued among the merchants of Bezucár.

"Now," she said. "Let's see what we can do about your unfortunate friends."

She called commands to her crew, and they hurried to obey her. With a sudden creak, the *Flora's* sails angled themselves to the south, steering the sloop toward the navy sailors who were still swimming below. The crew lowered several rope ladders over the ship's side.

"It's all right, amigos," called Captain Marisol to the navy sailors. "We've come to rescue you."

The navy sailors eyed the sloop with something between confusion, suspicion, and fear. Who knows what they had seen during their time on the *Delfín*; they probably thought this was a trap. So Ximena leaned out over the water, waving them up.

"Climb," she said. "You're safe now."

The sight of Ximena seemed to convince them. One by one, they hauled themselves up from the water and onto the sloop, until there were several dozen shivering sailors clustered on the *Flora's* deck.

"Take them to the hold," ordered Captain Marisol. "Give them water, food, and fresh clothes, and find them a place to sleep. Sunset is almost upon us."

"Yes, captain," the crew answered, herding the sailors toward the hold.

Ximena offered a tight-lipped smile as they passed. It had been risky to go back and save the sailors, but it had been worth it in the end. In fact, her heroism on the *Delfín* just might earn her that Cazador Cloak. . . .

Then she remembered. They had failed to capture Gasparilla. The admiral was gone, likely dead. Even if some of the *Pérez*'s crew had survived the calaveras, which would be a miracle, they would have no idea where to find Ximena, Dante, and Pía. So Gasparilla was still at large, and Ximena was stranded in the middle of the sea with no way to find him before he destroyed the empire. The adrenaline of captivity and escape had kept these thoughts at bay, but now they surged in her mind like a raging tide, robbing the air from her lungs.

"Speaking of food . . ."

Ximena felt more than saw Captain Marisol grip her arm. But somehow she found herself staring into the captain's warm, gentle eyes, and her breathing was slowing, her heart rate falling back to neutral. The merchant squeezed her hand, a silent encouragement. They were safe for now. The rest would come in time.

"You must be half-starved," the captain continued. "We shall have a feast in honor of the young candidates. No arguments," she added when Ximena began to refuse. "If there is one thing you must know about the people of Bezucár, there is nothing we love more than music, friends, and good food."

At the mention of food, Dante licked his lips. "So you're not cannibals, after all. I think I might like the merchants of Bezucár."

Captain Marisol grinned. "I never said what would be on the menu, Cuatreda de León."

Dante's smile fell, and the captain laughed.

"My crew will take you to the hold and give you everything you require. When you return, we will feast until sunrise."

"You have our thanks, captain," Ximena said.

They followed one of the merchant sailors down into the hold, where they were shown to two cabins, one for Ximena and Pía and the other for Dante.

"These cabins are usually occupied, but we're two men short on this voyage," said the merchant, a bald man with pierced ears. "You may stay here for the night. There are clothes in the chests, so you can wear anything you like. Another crew member will be down to tend to any wounds in short order."

Dante frowned. "I'll tend to my own wounds, thank you very much."

At the merchant's offended expression, Pía leapt to the rescue.

"Forgive him, sir," she said. "He was hit very hard over the head during the attack, and he hasn't been himself since."

The man nodded. The girls thanked him profusely and waited until he had turned the corner before glaring at Dante. But the boy only shrugged.

"Never reveal a weakness if you can help it," he said. "I think some queen said that."

Then he stepped into his cabin and shut the door, locking it behind him.

"You know, both of you are a bit like the solbara," Pía said. When

Ximena glanced sidelong at her, her cheeks broke out in scarlet splotches. "Perdón, I meant no disrespect. You're not sea monsters. Far from it. It's just that, well, the solbara has those impenetrable scales, like armor. And you and Dante wear your scales. You won't let anyone see what's underneath. Entonces . . . on second thought, I'll just go inside now."

She scuttled into the cabin, leaving Ximena alone. For a long moment, Ximena stared at Dante's door. Then she shook her head and followed the other girl into the cabin. She was nothing like Dante de León, whatever the archivist said.

In the cabin, Pía changed into a shirt and trousers, which were much too large for her, while Ximena pulled out the closest thing she could find to a cuatreda uniform, a brown chaqueta and pants. But she struggled in vain to tame her hair—the keelhauling had washed the whale oil out of her curls, and now they reared up with a vengeance, almost as wild as Pía's. She was already on her fifth attempt to tie them back when Pía tapped on her shoulder.

"May I?"

She was holding a long blue headscarf. At Ximena's nod of approval, she stepped behind her and wrapped the scarf across her forehead, pinning the curls back. Strange. No one had touched Ximena's hair since her mother had died. The memory returned with a force that took her breath away: her mother's fingers buried in her curls, wrestling them into a braid each night as she told stories of the cazadores and their exploits. Like Ximena, her mother wasn't a gentle woman by nature, but her conviction was as steadying as a strong wind. Ximena realized that she had never allowed herself to dwell on how much she missed her mother's reassurance. Perhaps it was because she knew that if she *did* dwell on it, it would unlock something deep and dark inside her, a door she wouldn't have the strength to close.

"There," declared Pía, summoning her back to the present. "You look beautiful, Cuatreda Reale."

Ximena stiffened. She'd been called many things in her life, but never that. Before she had a chance to collect her thoughts, they heard a knock at their door, and an older woman with a leather bag shuffled into the room.

"May I address any injuries?"

Ximena nodded gratefully, pulling aside her shift to reveal the gashes from the barnacles. The woman's eyebrows rose.

"The pirates gave you a warm welcome, I see."

She reached into her bag and pulled out a vial of ointment. Ximena tried her best not to flinch while the woman massaged the oil into her skin; it burned with a cool heat against her shoulders and back. After several minutes, the merchant sailor stepped back, satisfied.

"Leave the oil on under your clothes and reapply every few hours," she said. "If you need help, just ask the captain to send for me."

"Gracias," Ximena whispered. She couldn't remember the last time she had been treated with such kindness.

The woman turned her attention to Pía next, tending to the wounds on her wrists left behind by Salazar's chains. Then she retreated from the cabin and closed the door, leaving them alone once more.

"I wish I could be like you."

Ximena turned to see Pía perched on one of the bunks. She was fiddling with the edge of her trousers.

"You face the world with such courage. Calaveras, monstruos, pirates. Like you're not even afraid." She looked up, eyes large and liquid. "Are you afraid, Cuatreda Reale?"

Ximena stared back, unsure of what to say.

"Sí," she said slowly. "Sometimes, I am afraid."

"What are you afraid of?"

She wished Pía would stop asking so many questions. Thankfully, the archivist rambled on as she usually did.

"I'm afraid of letting other people down. That's why I came to la academia, you know. For my father and little brothers. My father works hard, but he's only a blacksmith, and with taxes being what they are . . . an archivist's salary would pay for my family twice over. Otherwise my father will have to send my brothers off to fight for the northern islands. You don't have to buy food for dead war heroes after all." She swiped her nose across her sleeve; her eyes were pink and puffy with tears. "That's why I'm so grateful to you, Cuatreda Reale. I knew I'd become an archivist if I had you on my side. I write to my brothers about you all the time, you know, telling them how incredible you are. You're nothing short of a Sánchez family legend."

Ximena's stomach twisted with guilt. In all the years she'd known Pía, she'd never once asked the girl about her life outside of la academia. She hadn't even thought about it. But Pía had a family, just as she did. One that depended on her for their survival. An image flashed behind her eyes: Marquesa, her Reale curls wild, her hazel eyes vulnerable. Ximena knew all too well what it was like to fight and kill and struggle to protect the people you loved most. Perhaps she had been too quick to dismiss Pía as small-minded and weak; the girl must have some strength in her, if she could carry the burdens of her family so bravely.

"Birds," Ximena said before she could think about it. "I've always hated birds. And I don't like storms."

Pía's brow furrowed. "That's all?"

"Is that not enough?"

Pía looked at her for a moment, and then sighed. "We should go, Cuatreda Reale. They'll miss us at the feast."

Silently, Ximena watched Pía go out the cabin door. She couldn't shake the feeling that she had just failed a test.

So her mood was stormy when she arrived on the *Flora's* upper deck. But the merchant crew was already celebrating around a long wooden table covered with food: roasted pig and fresh fish, sliced mangoes and tres leches cake. They talked and laughed in the lantern light, sipping from wooden tankards of fruit wine. Dante and Pía were squeezed onto a bench between the merchants. Overhead, newly born stars blinked against the gauzy, twilight sky, while ocean waves crashed several feet below. It would be night soon.

Meanwhile, Ximena stood stiff and frowning at the edge of the deck. These kinds of excesses would never have been allowed at la academia. They were luxuries that belonged to the residents of the Queen's Barrio, not candidates in training. Though honor demanded that she act the part of polite guest, she wouldn't allow herself to be lured in by the merchants' decadence, as Dante and Pía had already done. She would eat, drink, and then disappear belowdecks before anyone could miss her.

"Don't worry, capitana. Interacting with other humans isn't known to have any life-threatening side effects." Dante appeared at her side, chewing on a mouthful of roast pig. "I'm just telling you that," he said, "because you look scared out of your mind."

"The code forbids candidates from indulging in excess of any kind."

"And you find this excessive?"

Her silence was answer enough. Dante threw back his head with laughter.

"By the law, capitana, you need to get out more."

"Is there a problem, young cuatredas?"

Captain Marisol was descending from the helm, a bemused smile on her face.

"Nothing serious, captain," said Dante. "It's just that Cuatreda Reale suffers from a terrible fear of feasts."

"A fear of feasts."

"Yes," said Dante. "And dancing and music and anything that isn't as dark and miserable as an academia uniform."

"Well," said the captain, a grin creeping across her lips. "There is only one way to solve that." She gave a sharp whistle and the table fell silent. "Find a place for Cuatreda Reale and serve her a plate of food. Gustavo!"

The bald man who had escorted them to their cabins stood from his bench. "¿Sí, capitana?"

"I think it's time for a little music, no?"

He nodded. "As you wish."

Someone dragged Ximena to a bench while someone else pressed a dinner plate into her hand, piled high with pork and mangoes. The large table was dragged to the starboard rail, clearing the center of the deck, while Gustavo reemerged from the hold with a guitar in his hand. The *Flora's* crew gathered around him as he took his seat on an overturned barrel and strummed an open chord.

"What shall I play?" he asked.

The crew called out suggestions, but Gustavo didn't seem pleased by them. Then Pía crept up to him and whispered something in his ear before bolting away, her cheeks flaring red.

"Claro," said Gustavo, his voice rumbling in his chest. "Yes, that is precisely it."

He tuned his strings, closed his eyes, and began. It was a song Ximena had never heard before, driven by a pulsing beat she could feel in her ribs. The crew gave a collective shout of approval and took to the center of the deck, splitting into pairs and dancing, their hips swaying, their boots drumming. Gustavo's fingers flew over the frets of the guitar, picking the notes with elegant precision. He carved a trail and the merchants followed. The music was in their limbs, their eyes, their lungs.

In spite of herself, Ximena found her foot *tap, tap, tapping* against the deck. She watched as the dancers' shadows mingled and blended on the floor, their features cast into relief by the lanterns, their laughter rising like smoke toward the stars. She picked a slice of mango from her plate and placed it on her tongue. The juice coated her teeth, achingly sweet. All the while, she could hear the sea below, whispering, murmuring—calling her.

Was this what her life might have been like if her parents had lived? The thought had never crossed her mind in all of her years at la academia. But here, watching the *Flora's* crew and smelling the salt air, she couldn't help but wonder. Would she and Marquesa have danced on a deck under the stars, teasing each other and stealing mango slices when no one was looking? Would their mother have played the guitar while their father sang, spinning songs into the night? Would they have known *this*—this feeling that bubbled up in Ximena's chest—this warmth that spread down to her toes—this thing she had no name for?

No, thought Ximena. *There can be no joy outside the law.* Why was she even thinking about these things when she should have been planning the next steps to find their missing crew and catch Gasparilla? She swallowed and pushed her plate aside. The mango juice suddenly tasted bitter in her mouth.

"There's that look again. You must be the only person in the world who is immune to music, capitana." Dante sat down beside her.

Ximena refused to glance at him.

"I think Pía has had too much wine," said Dante.

She glanced up to see Pía twirling in the center of the deck, her head thrown back in laughter, her hips shifting awkwardly to the beat. Ximena's lips twitched. If the archivist could have seen herself in that moment, she would've died of embarrassment.

"In fact, I think I've had too much wine. I suppose you'll report us for debauchery, no?" Dante snapped his fingers. "In one night, my bid for cazador goes up in flames. What would my mother say?"

Then he laughed, knowing full well that she wouldn't report either of them, however much she might want to. Still, Ximena didn't look at him. Her parents' faces swam before her, and her sister's voice echoed in her ears. Their ghosts danced through the haze of music and lantern light. They haunted her in the dark.

Suddenly, she felt something warm against her hand. She looked up, startled, to find Dante sitting inches away, his fingers pressed over hers. His silver-blond curls dripped down into his eyes like liquid moonlight; his eyes were dark and teasing.

"Dance with me," he said.

She blinked. "I think you're right—you've had too much wine."

"One dance," he said. "That's all."

"No," Ximena said, pulling her hand away.

But Dante only grinned at her, his teeth flashing in the darkness. "What's the matter, capitana? You face the solbara unafraid, but you're terrified to dance with a fellow cuatreda? And you see yourself as a future cazadora."

As usual, Dante knew just what to say to make her hands clench and her jaw tighten.

"Surely you do *know* how to dance," he said.

"Yes, I know how to dance."

"Then prove it."

"Fine," she snapped. "One dance. Then you will leave me alone for the rest of the evening."

His grin sharpened. "As you wish, capitana. May I?"

He stood, holding out a hand; Ximena paused. But when she saw the dare in his eyes, she clamped her fingers over his, holding tight so that her fingers didn't shake. Dante only laughed. "Easy there, capitana. It's a dance, not torture."

Aren't they the same thing? Ximena thought miserably. Dante must have read her thoughts on her face, because he laughed again, steering them toward the center of the deck.

"Pía," he called, "pick a song for us."

"Absolutamente, Cuatreda de León—"

The archivist's eyes shot wide when she saw their hands joined together. But she did as Dante asked, leaning over and whispering in Gustavo's ear. The bald man grinned and began to play a song with a melody like ocean waves, warm but biting of salt.

"Why do I get the feeling that you're going to kill me for this?" Dante asked.

"Murder is against the tenets of the law."

"How unfortunate for you."

Ximena recognized the music immediately. At least it was a dance she knew, so she wouldn't have to embarrass herself in front of the *Flora's* entire crew. It began with the two partners circling one another, walking with slow, even steps to the beat of the music. Dante's steps had cat-like precision—too precise for someone who claimed to be drunk. How much of Dante de León was a performance?

"You're thinking too much, capitana," he said.

"And you don't think enough."

"Relax. You're dancing under the stars with a handsome partner and incredible music. Enjoy it while it lasts. Gasparilla and all your other cares will keep until tomorrow."

Dante caught her hand to twirl her around, switching their direction. They stepped faster now, two steps for every count of the music, their heels clicking against the wood. In the truest form of the dance, Ximena should be swaying her hips. But she was a candidate of la academia and a future cazadora, not a dancing girl. She'd rather drown than debase herself in such a manner.

"I think we might have found something you aren't good at, Cuatreda Reale," Dante said. "What kind of wooden pole taught you to dance?"

"My mother," she answered. But when Dante's eyes darkened with something dangerously like sympathy, she suddenly wished she hadn't.

"We must pick up where she left off, then," he said. "Your turn, capitana."

When the melody shifted, Dante stopped in place, brow lifted in a challenge. She bristled; if he wanted her to prove herself, then she would. So she began her orbit around him, stepping and spinning, stepping and spinning, until the stars and lanterns were nothing but a blur of light. Her boots pounded the deck, the deck tilted under her feet, and the guitar sang in her ears. Later, she blamed the music for what she did—a song played in time with the whisper of the sea was more powerful than any enchantment. But her arms rose against her will, curling over her head, and she twisted her wrists just as her mother had taught her. For a moment, she almost felt like the young woman she was, a woman who might have liked dancing in another life. A girl who might not have cared what people thought of her, who might have caught the flash of a boy's smile out of the corner of her eye and dared to smile back.

She was stopped by Dante's hand, catching her by the wrist.

He stared at her for a moment. "Not bad," he said. "Now my turn."

He twirled her once, released her, and stepped back. Ximena stood in place as he stepped and spun around her, his eyes fixed on hers even as his shoulders turned away. The intensity of his gaze made her want to reach for her rapier, to run or look away, but to do so would have been a sign of weakness. So she stared back, and his answering grin flashed white in the dark. She couldn't deny that he was a good dancer; he moved with an unusual grace for his size, his limbs as fluid as the sea. In fact, Dante de León might have been built for dancing, for the moment of freedom found in music and rhythm and moonlight. She wanted to hate him for it, but somehow, she almost envied him.

Dante knew how to live.

She only knew how to survive.

He wound his circles tighter and tighter until he was standing in front of her again, silver-blond curls catching the light of the crescent moon.

"Together," he said.

They began their final circle around each other, spinning closer, closer, until the last chord rang out from Gustavo's guitar. Ximena stopped just a breath away from Dante de León; she could see the sweat glistening on his brow, her reflection in his wine-dark eyes. She was so busy studying his features that she barely noticed that he'd reached behind her, tugging on a strand of her hair.

"Hermosa," he said softly.

She blinked. She must have misheard him. Perhaps it was the music still ringing in her ears, or the way Dante was looking at her now, the same way he had stared up at the ladder to the *Flora*. Terrified. Determined.

"We don't have to go back," he said.

She looked at him, confused. "What do you mean?"

"We don't have to go back. We could stay here, with the merchants. Everyone will think we've been killed by the calaveras with the rest of the crew. No one would come looking for us."

Her eye narrowed. "What are you implying, Cuatreda de León?"

Gustavo began another song; the merchants laughed and danced; but Dante wasn't paying attention. His jaw was set with unnerving focus.

"We can forget about the cazadores," he continued. "The cazadores, Gasparilla, the law, all of it. Think about it, capitana. We've spent every day of our lives doing what *they* say, what *they* want. We don't even exist outside of la academia. What if we take the chance we've been given? Sail the seas and never look back? We could go anywhere in the archipelago, do anything we want. We'd never have to bow to their orders again."

"What you're proposing would be treason against the empire," said Ximena, her voice low and cold.

"And what has the empire ever done for us? They killed my brother for trying to expose the truth about the armada and the cazadores. They killed your parents for the same."

She shook her head. "My parents died because they chose selfish gain over the greater good. The law—"

"Don't talk to me about the law. All it has ever done is wreak havoc and misery on everything it touches."

Just like that, the string that bound them snapped. Ximena turned and headed for the hold.

"There is truly no end to your arrogance," she said over her shoulder.

"*My* arrogance?" he said, following her. "Ximena Reale is going to lecture *me* on arrogance?"

Bristling, she spun toward him again. "You mock and belittle people who have dedicated their lives to the law. You call us mindless, soulless puppets, and all the while, you spend your days moving from one bottle of liquor to the next, squandering your wealth, disgracing your family, and trying desperately to drown the truth."

"And what truth would that be?"

"That you're a coward."

"Am I now?"

"Yes," she seethed. "You say the empire is corrupt. You say the law is evil and the cazadores persecute people across the archipelago. You say that you're trapped by your mother and your family's legacy. You have so many things to *say*, Dante, but have you *done* anything about it? No. Because you're a coward. You always have been, and you always will be."

For the first time that evening, Dante's eyes burned hot with anger. He stepped toward Ximena and pulled himself to his full height, matching her glare for glare.

"You know what?" he said, his voice low and firm. "You're right. I am a coward. I'll never be half the man my brother was, and I know it, and I drink it away every chance I get. But you, capitana, are worse than I'll ever be because you're just as much of a coward, yet you absolutely refuse to admit it."

"How dare you—"

"Open your eyes, Ximena! The empire is falling. My mother has overplayed her hand to conquer those miserable northern islands, and the empire is rotting from the inside, overspending and overtaxing its way into oblivion. Gasparilla is just a symptom of the disease. The people of the archipelago didn't want the cazadores two hundred years ago, and they certainly don't want them now. So they'll cheer Gasparilla on while he brings the empire to its knees and hangs every one of us cazador vultures from the mast of *La Leyenda*. And you know what? I don't blame them. In fact, I agree with them! ¡Viva Gasparilla! ¡Viva la libertad!"

Ximena gasped, a bolt of shock fired through her chest. She knew Dante hated the law, but she hadn't realized just how much. The drink must have loosened his tongue.

"By the law, you still look at me with murder in your eyes," he continued. "All that intelligence, all that skill, gone to waste. You won't even consider the truth about the law, about your noble Admiral Pérez," he snarled the name, "because you're scared to death.

You're terrified, because without the law, without the cazadores, you have absolutely nothing."

If she'd had a weapon, she would have unsheathed it. She settled for stepping forward until she was an inch away from him.

"You are despicable, Dante de León," she said.

"Yes I know," he replied, looking into her eyes. "I would hate you, too, if I didn't want to kiss you so badly."

She moved to slap him; he caught her by the wrist, tugging her closer. His nose brushed against hers. She could smell the salt on his skin and the mangoes on his breath.

"No te preocupes, capitana," he said, his voice rough as sand. "It's as you say, no? I'm too much of a coward to do anything but wish."

She wrenched her hand away.

"When we find the admiral and return to the *Pérez*, because I will ensure that we will, I am reporting you for treason against the Empire of Luza and recommending you for expulsion."

"Perfecto. My offer stands nonetheless. If you change your mind, and I hope that you will, I'll be waiting."

"If I change my mind," she replied, "you have my permission to shoot me."

Ximena turned and marched to her cabin, slamming the door shut. Her heart pounded like an execution drum, and her thoughts were a whirlpool, spiraling out of control. In the last two weeks, she had faced pirates, witches, monstruos, and a keelhauling, yet her courage had never failed her. But ten minutes with Dante de León, and she was shaking from head to foot, her fingers fumbling with the strap of her eye patch, struggling to unbutton her chaqueta. She had never despised any one person with so much force in her life. It robbed her of air, of focus, of peace.

No. She would not allow it. She needed all her wits about her if she was going to hunt down Gasparilla and save the empire. Dante de León only had as much power over her as she gave him, and she would surrender none.

So as she lay in her bunk that night, she didn't hear the ghost of a guitar in her ears, and she didn't dream of a boy with hair like moonlight.

Capítulo Doce

The following morning, Captain Marisol summoned the candidates to her cabin, where she served them steaming cups of hot chocolate and cornmeal arepas. Normally this would have been Ximena's favorite meal, but today she didn't have the stomach for it. She was too busy ignoring Dante, just as he was occupied with ignoring Ximena. Meanwhile, Pía glanced nervously between them, fidgeting in place and munching anxiously on an arepa until the captain broke the silence.

"Todo bien, young candidates?" the captain said. She looked official enough sitting at her desk with several maps spread before her, but her feet were bare against the colored carpets on the floor, a common tradition among Bezucár merchants. "I heard there was an argument outside the hold last night."

"Everything is fine, captain. But we appreciate your concern," Ximena replied. She could tell that the merchant captain wasn't the slightest bit fooled by her attempt to cover up Dante's disgrace. But mercifully, she seemed to decide to leave well enough alone, and deftly switched subjects.

"And I trust that you've been well treated since arriving on the *Flora*?"

"Yes, captain. Muchas gracias."

"I'm glad to hear it. Now that you've rested, we must undertake the task of reuniting you with your crew. Do you have any idea where they might be headed?"

"No, captain. All we can hope for is that they escaped alive from la Isla de las Calaveras."

"May the seas be with them," she murmured, almost as a prayer. "In their absence, this is what I propose. The *Flora* is in need of supplies and repairs, so we're sailing for la Isla Verde to the south. You are welcome to stay aboard until we make berth and then you can disembark on the island. Perhaps the navy sailors will also find a home there."

It was a reasonable enough plan. La Isla Verde was a highly trafficked stop for vessels in need of supplies. And if they were lucky, they might run into the *Pérez* at the island's shipyard. And the quicker they found the *Pérez*, the faster they could hunt down Gasparilla.

"Your hospitality is unparalleled, captain," Ximena said. "Once again, we find ourselves in your debt."

"I'm always happy to serve the cazadores and their allies in any way I can. Without them, Bezucár's merchants would have been bankrupted by pirates twenty times over. It is we who are in your debt."

Ximena chose that moment to cut a glare at Dante. *¡A ver!* she wanted to scream. The law protected the people of Luza. Nothing and no one could convince her otherwise.

"We'll arrive at la Isla Verde within the week," said Captain Marisol, rising to her feet. "Until that time, please consider the *Flora* your home. Archivist Sánchez." Her lips curled into a smile. "You may take the pitcher of chocolate if you'd like."

Over the course of the meeting, Pía had finished five cups of chocolate and seven arepas. Now the captain of the Bezucár merchants offered the entire silver pitcher to her as a parting gift. The poor girl flushed to her ears, muttered her thanks, and shuffled forward to accept the pitcher before racing from the room. Captain Marisol's laughter followed them out into the hallway as they exited the cabin.

"What happens if we don't find the cazadores on la Isla Verde?" Pía asked, skipping to keep up with Ximena's long stride.

"Then we return to la academia in defeat," answered Dante. "Isn't that right, capitana?"

"No one is going anywhere in defeat," Ximena said firmly. "We're going to find them."

They simply had no other choice.

"Vessel off the port stern!"

Later in the afternoon, however, that call from the Bezucár lookout disrupted their plans. Ximena stopped loosening the mainsail, squinting to spot a small black dot on the horizon. It was still too far away to tell what kind of ship it was, or which flag it was flying. She could only hope it wasn't a pirate sloop. After all, there was a reason the merchants of Bezucár had such a close relationship with the cazadores: Without the armada's protection, they were vulnerable to attack from pirates along their shipping routes. The merchants didn't stand a chance against a full-blown enemy onslaught.

Captain Marisol's voice rung out over the deck. "Are they friend or foe?"

There was a pause as the lookout peered through his telescope. "They're not flying a standard, captain!"

Ximena glanced at Dante and Pía, who also stood frozen in the middle of their tasks. Their uneasy expressions mirrored her own. The candidates knew all too well that only one kind of vessel would be sailing the archipelago without a flag.

A pirate ship.

Captain Marisol's eyes were grim as she called out, "All hands on deck! Release the mainsail. We'll outrun these fools while we have the advantage of distance."

The crew raced to carry out her orders, but Ximena knew it was no use. The *Flora* lacked the heavy artillery necessary to face a pirate crew. If the merchants were forced into direct combat, they were as good as sunk.

"Wait!" the lookout's cry sliced through their panic. "They're running up a flag now."

Another pause. The entire crew seemed to hold its breath, while Ximena's heart drummed beneath her ribs.

Then the lookout cried: "It's an armada ship, captain! The cazadores are here!"

A deafening cheer rose up from the merchants of Bezucár. The air rushed out of Ximena's lungs. *Thank the law and all its tenets.* The cazadores had found them first.

"Captain!" the lookout spoke again after several minutes. "They're signaling us to stop."

"Then we will obey their order. Bring the ship down to the sea," she answered.

Ximena, Dante, and Pía watched in awe as the merchants worked the lines to slowly, carefully tilt the sails into an upright position. The *Flora* descended from the sky like a seabird, gliding into the water and sending it up into a spray. Ximena stumbled at the sudden jolt, caught herself against the rail, and swiped the salt out of her eye to get a better look at the swiftly approaching ship. She wondered which of the armada galleons had decided to stop them.

"Captain," the lookout shouted suddenly. "That's not just any cazador ship. It's the *Pérez*."

This time, not even Ximena restrained herself from giving a whoop of joy. In fact, something like a laugh even left her lips when she saw Pía jump with excitement and throw her arms around Dante's neck. The boy was so startled that he tripped over his own feet and sent them both crashing into a barrel.

Ximena had no idea how the admiral had managed to find them. She'd ask for the explanation later. All she cared about now was that he was mercifully, miraculously alive, and he was on his way to rescue them.

She counted the seconds as the *Pérez* neared them, until she heard one of the cazadores shout, "Buenos días, merchants of Bezucár. We are searching for three candidates of la Academia de los Cazadores who were recently taken captive by Catarina Salazar. Have you heard news of the *Delfín* in the last few days?"

"Unfortunately not, cazadora," Captain Marisol answered. "However, I do have those very same candidates aboard my ship, and they are very eager to be reunited with their crewmates."

Within moments, the cazadores of the *Pérez* were onboard the *Flora*, sweeping over the deck in their long black cloaks, thanking Captain Marisol for her bravery. Ximena searched the crowd for the admiral, heart skipping. She had to see him. She had to know he was really alive.

At last, she caught sight of him stepping down from the boarding ramp. He looked older, somehow, far older than his thirty-odd years, and for the first time, Ximena noticed that his dark hair was streaked with gray. But when his eyes found Ximena's, they were filled with the same steadfastness and certainty that had always been there. She pushed through the other cazadores until she stood before him.

"Cuatreda Reale," he said.

"Admiral," she said, pressing two trembling fingers to her lips in salute. "I'm pleased to report that although we were captured by the pirate ship *Delfín*, we were able to secure our escape with the help of the Bezucár merchants. Unfortunately, I must also report an incident of treason that took place . . ."

As she went through her systematic chronicle of everything that had occurred since their separation from the *Pérez*, the admiral listened in silence. When she had completed her report, he said, "Are you quite finished, Cuatreda Reale?"

"Yes, captain."

She lowered her head, waiting for him to admonish her for racing back into the cave after Dante, for her recklessness and lack of foresight. She wasn't even going to argue with him; she knew she deserved every scolding he could give.

So she certainly didn't expect him to pull her against his chest, wrapping his arms around her.

"Thank the law," he said into her hair. "I feared you were dead, or worse."

The words she might have said died in her throat. She couldn't remember the last time she'd been embraced this way—before her parents' deaths, perhaps. It was as if she'd been dropped into a pool of freezing water. She couldn't move, couldn't breathe.

But the longer he held her, the more the tension in her body unraveled, until her stiffened spine relaxed, and she found herself hugging him back. The admiral was here. She didn't have to fight off the evils of this world alone. Gabriel Pérez had searched the seas to find her; he'd battled calaveras and pirates to come to her rescue. Marquesa and her parents had failed her time and time again. But the admiral never had. That was the truth his arms around her promised: he would always fight for her.

Always.

"Now," he said, stepping back, "tell me more about this incident of treason you mentioned."

Grateful for the sudden restoration of order, Ximena straightened her uniform and opened her mouth to tell the captain of Dante's planned desertion and traitorous rant against the empire. But before she could speak, the boy in question appeared at her side.

"I never thought I'd say this, but it's good to see you, admiral," Dante said, grinning. "Had you come any later, we might have been pickings for the gulls. How did you find us, anyway?"

"One of my cazadores caught Amador escaping from la Isla de las Calaveras," the admiral replied. "When we questioned him, he revealed that he'd sold you to Catarina Salazar. But by the time we chased down the *Delfín*, it was nothing but a pile of wreckage."

"Yes, we were attacked by one of the monstruos the empire insists do not exist," Dante supplied helpfully.

The admiral only focused on Ximena. "We knew it was likely you had perished in the wreck. But we also knew that if by some miracle you *had* survived, you would make for la Isla Verde. So we were sailing there when we happened upon the *Flora*."

"Isn't that a lovely tale of cazador heroism," said Dante, and Ximena glowered at the sarcasm in his tone. "As for Cuatreda Reale's accusations, I can't deny them. But I can tell you that I'd drunk a significant amount of Bezucár wine when I spoke of treason," he winked at Ximena, "and one's tongue always goes astray under such circumstances."

The admiral glanced between them. "Do you deny his version of events, Cuatreda Reale?"

Ximena's teeth ground together. Dante only smiled, looking as innocent as a child. He'd found the loophole once again, and he knew that Ximena wouldn't lie just to see him punished. So she had no choice but to say, "What Cuatreda de León says is true."

"Very well then. However, do not mistake my mercy for leniency, Dante de León," the admiral added, turning his shark-like glare on Dante. "You will be punished for your unseemly conduct the moment we return to the *Pérez*. For now, though, I must speak with the Bezucár captain."

"I'll join you, sir," said Dante. "I'd like to pay my respects to Captain Marisol as well. After all, she saved us from a snake-bird *and* threw us the finest feast I've been to in years. Have you ever encountered a solbara, admiral? The stench of their breath is enough to make a grown man weep . . ."

With that, they were gone, leaving Ximena to fume in silence. How did Dante always escape the consequences of his actions? And why did Ximena's heart clench when the boy threw another wink over his shoulder at her? She remembered his nose brushing hers after their dance on the *Flora*, his lips hovering just above—

Basta, Ximena. What in the name of the law was she thinking? With a scowl, she hurried to join Pía and the other cazadores. Dante wouldn't prevent her from doing her duty.

When the deck had been cleared, the cazadores readied themselves to depart the *Flora*. Ximena and Pía bowed low to Captain Marisol, thanking her for her hospitality.

"Are you still taking the navy sailors to la Isla Verde, captain?" asked Pía.

"Yes," said Captain Marisol. "There they can heal and reunite with one of the naval guard's patrols."

Pía smiled. "So justice will be done."

"Yes, archivist," said Captain Marisol, smiling back. "Even in the darkest storms, justice shines like the sun."

So the candidates took their leave of the Bezucár merchants, clambering aboard the *Pérez*. Ximena watched as the *Flora* took flight again; it soared up through the blue until it was nothing but a spot over the sea. The time for rest had passed.

Now the hunt for Gasparilla would begin again.

Capítulo Trece

"We need to find Gasparilla's hideout."

Ximena, Pía, the admiral, and Cazadora Cecilia gathered at the *Pérez*'s helm. Amador was in the captain's cabin below, but before they could interrogate him, they needed a plan. One to finish this hunt once and for all.

"Right now, Gasparilla thinks we died at the hands of the calaveras," the admiral continued. "He'll be focused on getting his ransom from the high minister, which means his attention will already be diverted elsewhere. So, I say we attack him at the very source of his power while we have the advantage of surprise."

"Sir, with all due respect, Amador is never going to give up the location of his captain's hideout," Cecilia said. "You know what these radicals are like. They'd rather cut out their own tongue than turn on their leader."

"Es verdad. But everyone has their price, Cazadora Cecilia. Even Amador Gutiérrez."

Here he turned to Ximena and Pía.

"Candidates," he said. "I need any information you can give me on Amador's pirate activity since he deserted la academia. Close contacts, potential vices, secrets he might not want exposed. If you think it might be even remotely important, I need to know about it."

"Oh, oh, wait a moment!" Pía cried. "I think I have just the thing!" The archivist scampered down from the helm, returning a moment later with her arms full of scrolls. "The record on Amador is incredibly thorough," she said. "I was reading it over just before we visited the calaveras. He has been connected to at least one pirate attack per year, like clockwork. But do you know what else shows up like clockwork?"

She unraveled one of the scrolls, pointing to a section of the parchment.

"Summer of the Year 225," she read aloud. "Amador Gutiérrez reported at the site of the attack on la Isla Verde's harbor. Winter of the Year 225. Nothing to report. Summer of the Year 226. Amador Gutiérrez seen at the attacks on la Isla de los Monos and la Isla Blanca. Winter of the Year 226. Nothing to report."

Cazadora Cecilia crossed her arms over her chest. "I don't follow, archivist."

Ximena froze and stared at Pía.

"He disappears from the record every year at the same time," Ximena said under her breath. "Just like . . ."

Pía's eyes were soft with sympathy when she nodded. "Yes, Cuatreda Reale. Just like your parents."

Ximena's fingers tapped anxiously against her thigh. Her parents had behaved the same way when they were cazadores. They had served in the armada for the majority of the year, of course. But during the winter season, when the archipelago's seas were roughest, they requested leave to stay home with their daughters. So Ximena knew there was only one reason why a pirate would vanish from the scrutiny of the cazadores with such regulated frequency.

Amador must have a family. One he cared enough about to abandon pirating once a year.

"Archivist Sánchez," said the admiral. "That is nothing short of brilliant."

Pía's cheeks broke out in splotches. "G—gracias, señor. I live to serve."

"Vengan conmigo, candidates. There is no time to lose."

They followed the admiral down to the captain's cabin, where Amador waited in chains with Dante standing guard.

"Amador Gutiérrez, you will give us the location of Gasparilla's hideout before the hour is up," the admiral said as he took his seat at his desk. "No lies. No traps."

"And why would I do that, admiral?" The pirate lifted a brow. "You have no leverage over me. You can keep me in chains or torture me as you cazadores love to do. But I'm not going to surrender my captain's hideout. If such a place even exists, of course, which I can neither confirm nor deny."

The admiral drummed his fingers against the arm of his chair in a steady, measured beat. "You know, it isn't common for pirates to have a family. Given the dangerous nature of pillaging and plundering, most captains prefer their crew to remain unattached. I've met only a handful of pirates with husbands or wives on land, and fewer still with children."

"Is there a point to this speech, admiral?" Amador drawled, seemingly bored.

"Leverage, pirate. That is the point."

He leaned forward in his chair. Ximena had watched the admiral conduct a handful of interrogations before. He was like a shark, circling his prey slowly, carefully, before darting in for the kill.

"Allow me to be straightforward, old friend. We know you have a family, and more important, we also know their location. So unless you would like the cazadores of Luza to pay them a visit, which would end rather unfortunately given their association with a known pirate, then I suggest you give me the coordinates I've asked for. Now."

In the brief time she'd known him, Ximena had never seen the pirate's confident amusement slip. But the admiral's words were a bullet shattering glass. Amador's smile crumpled, his eyes dilating like a wounded animal's.

"Liar," he hissed.

The admiral shrugged. "Maybe so. But are you willing to take that chance? You know me well enough to know that I will never show mercy to traitors against this empire. Anyone who has aided and abetted your activity will be arrested, tried, and hanged as if they committed piracy themselves. So in the end, the choice is yours. Your family, or Gasparilla."

Ximena could feel Dante's eyes on her neck, could sense his treasonous thoughts: *A ver, capitana. Look at what your precious cazadores are willing to do.* The offer was brutal, that much was true. But Admiral Pérez was the wisest man she knew. Surely he understood the law and its tenets better than she ever could. Didn't he?

"La Tormenta."

Amador's voice dragged Ximena back to the present. The admiral leaned over the desk, his eyes narrowed and glittering.

"¿Qué dijiste?"

"La Tormenta," Pía echoed. "Scroll seven on the islands of the archipelago, paragraph fifty-four. It's a terrible storm that never dies at the southernmost edge of the sea. No one has ever managed to breach it. Over a thousand ships have sunk in the attempt."

"The girl speaks the truth," Amador said, his confident drawl replaced by a weary, defeated sigh. "You must sail through la Tormenta if you are to find Gasparilla's base. It's a week's sail from here if the wind blows in your favor. I'll give you the coordinates as you requested."

"Of course. A storm no ship has ever breached," the admiral said. "Your family's safety must mean very little to you for you to tell such tales, pirate."

"This is no tale," Amador snapped. "La Tormenta is the barrier that protects Gasparilla's hideout. You must pass through it if you wish to find your queen."

The admiral's eyes cut to Ximena. "Cuatreda Reale?"

"Es posible," she said. "There are stories from Alessandra's time that tell of the original *La Leyenda* passing through a great hurricane. Perhaps they were referring to la Tormenta."

For a long moment, the admiral stared down Amador, weighing the truth of his words. But he must have seen something that satisfied him because he stood up and said to Cazadora Cecilia: "Get the coordinates. We set course for la Tormenta without delay."

"Yes, sir."

"Cuatreda de León," the admiral added, "escort the prisoner to the brig and ensure he is watched at all times. If he attempts to escape, the guards have my permission to kill him on sight."

"As you command," said Dante.

The boy dragged Amador to the cabin doors, but before they

left, the pirate stopped and looked back over his shoulder. It was the same look Ximena had seen in Zabel's eyes, in Catarina Salazar's glare: hatred, pure and dark.

"Gabriel," he said. "I have your word that my wife and daughter won't be harmed."

The admiral looked up and stared at Amador for a moment. "I swear it."

"Then if you wish to survive la Tormenta, you must sail straight into it. Those who stray from the course will meet a terrible end."

The admiral nodded. "I'll take that under advisement, pirate."

With that, Dante led Amador out of the room, Pía and Cazadora Cecilia trailing after them. Ximena, however, lingered in front of the admiral's desk. She couldn't speak without permission, so she waited for him to acknowledge her, questions circling in her mind like a school of fish.

"Out with it, Cuatreda Reale." The admiral looked up, studying her. "Something is troubling you."

Ximena hesitated. She'd just managed to heal her fragile relationship with the admiral. She didn't want to say anything that would risk severing that bond. But he *had* asked, and his noble face was open and not unkind.

"Captain Salazar said something strange to me before the solbara killed her. She insisted that everything she stole was given to the slums. To the people the empire has forgotten."

"Not a particularly creative justification," the admiral replied, almost dismissively. "Many pirates believe they are crusaders fighting back against their Luzan oppressors. Of course, what they say doesn't change what they fundamentally are—lawbreakers. If Captain Salazar truly cared about the people of Luza, then she would have helped them in a law-abiding way, as the cazadores are trained to do. So I wouldn't give her another moment of thought, Ximena. Her mind was weak, corrupted by greed. She didn't understand the importance of the law for the archipelago's security."

"Of course. You're right, sir, as always." She paused, taking a breath.

"But there's something else?" The captain's lip curled in a half-smile; he knew her too well.

Ximena exhaled, squaring her shoulders. "If we *had* actually known where Amador's family was, and if he'd refused to give up the coordinates to Gasparilla's base . . ."

The admiral let out a low laugh. "That is quite a few ifs, Cuatreda Reale."

"I realize that, sir. But I suppose what I'm asking is . . ." She hesitated again, searching for the right words. "Would you really have had them executed for Amador's crimes?"

The admiral's expression grew serious again; the muscle in his jaw flexed. "Yes. Is that all?"

Ximena nodded. "Yes, sir."

He studied her a moment longer, and then nodded back. "Then you may go. And try to get some rest, Cuatreda Reale. You'll need your strength for when we face la Tormenta. It's true, what the archivist says—too many ships have been sunk by its fury."

"As you command, captain," she replied.

Justice must be done, Ximena told herself as she left the cabin. *By any means necessary.* She knew that. She'd always known that. Perhaps the admiral was right, and she was simply overtired. It was the only logical explanation for why she couldn't shut out the image of Amador's wife and daughter swinging from the gallows, or why she couldn't seem to forget Catarina Salazar's sneer of judgment. *How your mother would roll over in her grave if she knew her precious daughter had become a pirate hunter!*

As Ximena climbed down into the hold, the exhaustion she'd stifled for so long suddenly threatened to drown her: her legs swayed underneath her, and her eyelids drooped against her will. So when she heard a *thump* from Cazadora Cecilia's cabin, she assumed she was hallucinating. She had just seen the first mate moments ago giving orders at the helm—she couldn't possibly be in her cabin.

But then Ximena heard another *thump*, and she paused in the hallway, her senses alert. This was no hallucination. Someone was in Cazadora Cecilia's cabin, and they were rifling through her belongings. Unsheathing her rapier, Ximena stepped softly toward the door, which was opened just enough to allow her to peek through the hinges.

As she peered into the room, her tightened jaw fell slack. Standing in front of a small, round mirror was Dante, and he was holding Cazadora Cecilia's spare cloak. She watched in shock as he wrapped the fabric around his broad shoulders and breathed in, studying himself in the glass, his eyes somber and his mouth stern. A thought jumped unbidden to her mind: *He looks like a cazador.* His head had that distinctly noble tilt, his body that telltale confidence of unshakable courage. Yet there was something else in his face Ximena didn't recognize—something soft, aching.

Almost like . . . longing.

She had called him a coward before, and she'd meant it. Dante de León had never pursued his convictions in the entire time she'd known him. But was it possible that some small, long-buried part of him didn't want to be that person? That he secretly longed to become the man his brother had been, with courage enough to defy their mother even if it meant certain death?

His eyes suddenly caught hers in the mirror. "Have you taken up spying now, capitana?" he asked coolly.

Startled, she stumbled back from the door. She considered striding off down the hallway as if nothing had happened, but she knew he would make her pay for it later. So she stepped into the cabin, sheathing her rapier.

"I should report you for intruding on an officer's private quarters," she said.

"Feel free. But I'm here on Cazadora Cecilia's orders. She asked me to fetch her compass." He reached into his pocket, pulling out a round, silver instrument. "So really it is *you* who are intruding, Cuatreda Reale."

Ximena looked him up and down. "You're wearing her cloak."

"Indeed," said Dante.

When he didn't elaborate, she scowled. "You have no explanation to give for your behavior?"

"None whatsoever. Haven't you ever done something just because you wanted to, Ximena?"

Her throat constricted at the sound of her name. He said it with a note of challenge that made her want to unsheathe her rapier again.

"Do you want to try it on?" he said.

"Absolutely not."

He shrugged, sweeping the cloak from his shoulders and folding it. "Your loss."

"I thought you said I looked like a vulture in black," she said.

"Did I? Well, I've told worse lies." He paused his folding. His curls fell into his eyes, concealing his expression. "Do you believe people can change, Ximena? That they can become something other than what they are?"

Her name again. When had he started using it so liberally? She shook her head.

"No. I don't."

"Not even if they've been inspired to do the right thing? Not even if they have some . . ." He searched for the word. "Some powerful incentive to chart a new course?"

"Second chances are an open door to evil," she quoted.

"Ah, yes. My mother has such a way with words."

"People pretend to be reformed when it is advantageous to them," Ximena continued. "Haven't you noticed that pirates only repent when they face the gallows?"

"Perhaps because they weren't given the chance to repent beforehand."

"Or perhaps it's because they don't deserve that chance."

Ximena watched as his fingers tightened around the black cloth. Then, with all the elegance of a cat, he closed the distance between them, sweeping his hair out of his eyes, which were as large and dark as new moons.

"Perhaps," he said, "I will force you to reevaluate your theory."

She grit her teeth, furious at the restless fluttering in her ribs. "Not likely."

"You're very sure of yourself."

"I'm the only thing I can be sure of, besides the law."

Dante laughed. "There is only one thing I love more than proving you wrong."

"And that is?"

She refused to look away from him, and so they stood in the

center of the cabin, glaring each other into the ground. Then, before she could react, he unfolded the cloak with a snap and swept it around her shoulders. She froze just as she had done when the admiral had embraced her. She should have pushed Dante off and told him to remove the cloak from her shoulders forthwith, but she couldn't. Not when he was this close. Not when he was looking at her as if he'd never seen her before in his life. Not when she didn't want him to look away. . . .

"Never mind," he announced at last. "It looked better on me."

And just like that, the spell was broken. She wriggled out of the cloak and folded it neatly into a square. No, people couldn't change—Dante de León and his self-satisfied grin were proof of it. He was just toying with her again, and unfortunately, she had let him win this round.

"I should bring Cazadora Cecilia her compass," he said. "I wish you a pleasant rest of your evening, Cuatreda Reale."

But before Dante could depart, Cazadora Cecilia herself entered the cabin, nostrils flaring with irritation.

"Would you care to explain what you're doing with my cloak, Cuatreda Reale?"

Ximena snapped to attention. "Forgive me—"

"I am entirely to blame, Cazadora Cecilia," said Dante. "I was searching for your compass and asked Cuatreda Reale for her assistance. She was merely holding the cloak out of the way so I could complete my search more effectively."

Cecilia sniffed, glancing between them with narrowed eyes. Whether she believed him or not was impossible to tell.

"Give me the cloak and the compass," she said, holding out her hand.

They obeyed, and Cecilia slid them back into the trunk. Then she turned to face the two candidates once more.

"Out," she said. "You'll scrub the entire upper deck before the sun sets, or I'll report you both to the admiral without hesitation."

"As you command," they said.

Before the cazadora could change her mind, they hurried into the hallway and up the stairs to the deck. Dante winked at Ximena as he tossed her a mop.

"How was that for noble?" he asked.

"Nobility does not boast," she quoted.

"I don't recognize that one. Who said it?"

"Ximena Reale."

He laughed, curls tumbling away from his face and catching the rose of the twilight. Try as she might, Ximena couldn't help but smile to herself as she dipped the mop in a bucket of water. Together, they washed the deck in a silence that, if not exactly companionable, at least didn't result in bloodshed.

Meanwhile, the cazadores set the *Pérez* on its southward course. Ximena knew it would only take them a week to reach la Tormenta. But then again, any amount of time was too long. If word about the admiral's alleged death had already reached the high minister, it was possible that she'd already sent Gasparilla his ransom, putting the empire in a dangerously vulnerable position. They had to get to Gasparilla before all the empire's silver did, otherwise . . .

"We'll catch him."

Dante's voice cut through her thoughts. How had he read her mind so perfectly?

"If anyone can find a pirate who can't be found," he said, "it's you, capitana."

She straightened up, looking at him, trying to gauge his sincerity. But there was no malice in his face—he wore the same steady expression he'd worn in Cecilia's cabin. So she acknowledged him with a nod, and they returned to work.

And as the sun began to slip down beneath the waves, she pretended not to notice Dante's brilliant smile, or the way his eyes followed the swish of her mop.

Capítulo Catorce

The further south they traveled, the wilder the sea became. Waves scratched and clawed at the ship's side, hungrier here than they were near Valuza and the central archipelago—the first rumblings of la Tormenta. Ximena tried to ignore their ravenous churning as she worked.

But the sea is a hard thing to ignore.

Just two days into their weeklong journey, the admiral gave the sudden order to drop anchor in the middle of the water. The *Pérez* stalled, groaning as the anchor tugged against its hull.

"Cuatreda Reale!"

The captain summoned her to the helm, where she found Dante, Pía, and Cecilia huddled around a map.

"Is something wrong?" she asked.

"Not yet," said the admiral, his expression grave. "But there will be, if we're not careful."

Pía pointed to a spot on the map. Ximena stepped forward, squinting to make out the faded lettering.

"La serpiente de la muerte. The snake of death," Pía read aloud. "Have you heard of it?"

Ximena and Dante shook their heads.

"Scroll eight of—"

"By the law, skip the introduction, archivist," Cecilia snapped.

"Of course, my apologies, Cazadora Cecilia. La serpiente has been the bane of sailors in the southern archipelago for centuries. The water here is shallow enough to strand a ship half our size. But the worst part is, there's no completely accurate map of the channels that are sailable. So it can only be navigated by those who have already crossed it before."

"Fine, then we'll sail around it," said the first mate.

"You could, cazadora, but that would take a few weeks, at least."

"A few weeks!" cried Dante and Ximena.

Pía winced. "I suppose we could try our luck and sail through the channels blindly. But if we're stranded, there's little hope of rescue. Most crews stranded in la serpiente die of dehydration within days."

"We have no other choice, then," said the admiral. "We'll chart a course through la serpiente. Archivist, you're familiar with the maps, are you not? However inaccurate they might be?"

"Yes, sir, I am."

"Then you will give directions to the crew to the best of your ability and guide us to the other side."

Pía blanched. "B—but sir, I'm not a cazadora in training. Perhaps this task is better left to Cuatreda Reale, or one of the crew—"

"We don't have time to pass your knowledge along to the cazadores. And while you may be an archivist, you are still under my command, señorita. So you will obey my orders without argument."

Pía cut a panicked look to Ximena. She remembered what the archivist had confessed to her on the *Flora*, about how terrified she was of failing the people around her. So she offered the girl what she hoped was an encouraging nod. Pía set her shoulders, letting out a shaky breath.

"Weigh anchor, lower the sails." Her voice came out in a high-pitched squeak. "If we're going to survive, we must be able to maneuver as carefully as possible, without the influence of wind."

"Cuatredas, to your positions," said the admiral.

With a salute, Dante and Ximena returned to the deck. They joined the cazadores in drawing up the anchor and lowering the sails, reducing the *Pérez's* speed to a crawl as they inched forward into the channel.

"Five degrees to starboard," Pía called from where she was bent over the map.

Cazadora Cecilia turned the rudder.

"Seven degrees to port."

Slowly, carefully, they eased through one thin channel after another, slipping through the emerald waters in near silence. As Pía worked, Ximena felt the smallest flicker of pride flare to life in her chest. It reminded her of when Marquesa passed her very first archivist training exam. Her sister hadn't cared about the result, just as she hadn't cared about anything else related to the cazadores, but Ximena had insisted they celebrate with a cup of chocolate from the mess hall. It was the first and last time she'd felt any hope about Marquesa's progress at la academia. Now, Ximena found herself wishing she had a sister like Pía. A sister who cared about la academia and the empire as much as she did. A sister she could be proud of.

Suddenly, a cry from the crow's nest stopped the *Perez's* progress in its tracks.

"Man overboard! Man overboard!"

Ximena peered over the starboard rail. Just off the *Pérez's* bow, a galleon was stranded on a sandbar, its hull snapped in two. *A shipwreck.* But what drew Ximena's attention was the strange man who stood on top of it, shouting and waving a rifle above his head.

"This is my ship, you mangy dogs!" he cried. "And I won't let you have it so long as I breathe!"

Maybe dehydration had driven the man mad, just as Pía had warned them about—he seemed to be shouting at no one, and he was wearing a fine silk coat and a silver wig, as if he were at a ball rather than standing on a shipwreck in the middle of the sea. But when the *Pérez* drew closer, Ximena could make out the dark outlines of small, skinny bodies carrying harpoons, knives, and fishing nets. She gripped the edge of the rail, suddenly furious. She'd seen this kind of incident once before, when she was on deployment with the admiral: wreckers, thieves who watched for sinking ships and pillaged their remains.

When the man fired his rifle into the sky, the urchins scattered.

"That's right, you filthy rats!" he cried. "Crawl back to your master!"

But when he reached into his pocket for more ammunition, his eyes widened. He must have run out of bullets. The wreckers—they couldn't be more than children, Ximena realized—sneered, sensing their advantage. They clambered back toward the helm, preparing to kill the shipwreck survivor and steal whatever was left on his ship.

"Drop your weapons," the admiral boomed from the helm. "Or I shall order my crew to fire upon you."

The wreckers froze when they spotted the cazador ship. They clearly didn't have the same reckless courage as their pirate cousins, because they abandoned their mark without ceremony, leaping into makeshift wooden skiffs and rowing away.

"Bring the survivor aboard," ordered Admiral Pérez when they'd gone.

"But sir," said Cazadora Cecilia. "We don't have time to—"

"The code is the code. We don't abandon shipwreck survivors."

Cecilia's nostrils flared, but she couldn't disobey a direct order. "As you command."

Ximena watched as several cazadores lowered a dinghy into the water and rowed out to the wreck. Cazadora Cecilia tried her best to coax the man into the boat, but the survivor shook his head adamantly.

"A captain doesn't abandon his ship!" he cried.

The admiral sighed. "Then we shall go to him. Cuatreda de León, gather food and supplies. We'll prepare a second boat."

Armed with a crate of provisions, the admiral, Ximena, and Dante, rowed out to the wreck. The man appeared even stranger up close: his aging face was painted white and his cheeks were pink with blush powder, but his teeth were nothing but rotting stumps, black and hideous when he smiled.

"Arturo thanks you, cazadores," he said. "Though he would not have asked for your help, because he otherwise despises cazadores, he is grateful for this unexpected kindness."

"Arturo?" said Dante. "Who is Arturo?"

"Why, that is me," said the man. "Captain Arturo Padilla of *La Princessa*, and the only survivor of this terrible wreck."

A weary sigh escaped the admiral's chest. "Padilla. The Gentleman Pirate," he said. "I might have known."

"So you have heard of me?"

"I've heard of your disastrous attempts at pirating. Two dozen failed raids, four sunken ships, and two years spent in a pit in the jungle after being captured by Captain Salvador Domínguez."

"Yes," said the Gentleman Pirate, his smile sagging. "Arturo has struggled through many failures. But this time will be different, you will see! Arturo Padilla will not abandon his ship. He will die before he does."

"That much is true at least," Dante mumbled.

The admiral gestured to the sunken *Princessa*. "How long has it been since the wreck?"

Arturo unfolded one finger at a time, scrunched his brow, then counted again. "Four weeks and three days. Or maybe three days and four weeks. It is difficult to tell."

"How have you survived so long?"

Arturo shrugged. "Rum and hardtack. The food, thankfully, was spared. It is only those wreckers that plague me, Thiago's little *ratas*."

The admiral didn't bother to ask him who Thiago was.

"Where is the rest of your crew?"

"The rats took them!" cried Arturo in dismay. "One by one, they took them. Arturo hasn't seen them in many days. Many days and many nights."

"He's mad," Dante muttered.

Ximena was inclined to agree. But when the pirate's glassy gaze settled on her, his eyes suddenly sharpened, and he pointed a trembling finger at her face.

"A ghost. A ghost," he said, falling to his knees and clutching his rifle. "Her spirit sails the seas yet!"

"I'm just as real as you are, pirate," said Ximena flatly.

Arturo crawled forward, peering down at her. "Your name, ghost. What is your name?"

"I am Cuatreda Ximena Reale."

"Ximena Reale," he repeated. "Daughter of Diego and Alejandra?"

"As you say."

"So you are not a ghost."

"Not to my knowledge."

He bent his head, his body falling slack, and for a moment Ximena wondered if he'd fallen unconscious. But then the pirate's shoulders shook in a great, heaving sob.

"Seas be merciful," he cried. "Their daughter lives!"

While Arturo cried, the admiral watched unamused.

"I would normally have you arrested for your crimes, pirate. But it seems your fate is prison enough. Return to the ship. We don't have time for any more distractions today."

He motioned for Dante and Ximena to row the dinghy back to the *Pérez*, but a cry from another cazador stopped them.

"Sir! Enemy off the port bow!"

Ximena swiveled to see the outline of a dozen small skiffs on the horizon—the wreckers had returned, this time in force.

"Arm yourselves," the admiral called to the *Pérez*. "If it comes to a fight, so be it."

The cazadores lined up with their rifles at the ready, aiming toward the skiffs as they approached. The boats were packed with wreckers—wiry, brown-skinned boys with their ribs and teeth bared, their eyes sharp with hunger.

"Do what you like to me, Thiago," Arturo declared. "You will not take my ship!"

He jabbed his rifle toward the first of the boats, where a dark-haired boy stood with a harpoon in his fist. Well, not a boy, exactly—as the boats neared, Ximena saw that he was the oldest of the wreckers, with a young man's stubble darkening his jaw. His clothes were rags, his hair was dreadlocked, and his skin was brown as leather from the sun, but he gazed at them with an air of command, as if he were a prince over his small tribe of sea rats.

"It's not your ship we want," he answered, pointing the tip of his harpoon toward the *Pérez*. "It's theirs."

Arturo blinked. Then he threw back his head in the strangest laugh Ximena had ever heard, a sound like a screeching gull.

"Do you know what that is, you fool? It's a cazador galleon. You won't get your hands on a splinter before they've strung you up from the mast."

Thiago shrugged. "I'll take my chances."

"Listen to him, boy," said the admiral. "If you raise your weapons against my crew, you won't survive the battle that follows."

Ximena knew her commander would make good on his threat. Any altercation with the wreckers would end in a bloodbath. But judging from the look in Thiago's eyes, the boys weren't about to go home empty-handed. Her mind spun through available options before landing on the only one that wouldn't result in a massacre.

"Wait," she said. "I propose a deal."

Thiago's eyes turned to her; she was startled to see they were as blue as the sky. "What can you offer me?"

She looked to the admiral, who gave her the smallest of nods.

"You know your way through la serpiente," she said.

Thiago's blue eyes narrowed. "Yes."

"Then we can make a trade. You guide us through the channels, and you can have the pirate's ship."

Arturo squawked. "Señorita Reale—"

"Not good enough," said Thiago. "We can take the ship ourselves."

"True enough," Ximena answered. "But I'm offering you your lives, along with a ship full of treasure. I suggest you take what you can get."

"Señorita Reale, Arturo must protest—"

"Well?" she demanded. "Do you accept?"

For a moment, Thiago considered, turning his harpoon in his hands. Then he said, "Give us the pirate and you have a deal."

"Done," said Ximena, ignoring Arturo's howl of fury.

Thiago smiled. "Follow us, then, cazadores."

Two cazadores seized Arturo, dragging him into their dinghy as he kicked and screamed that he would rather drown than leave his ship behind. When they were all safely returned to the *Pérez*, the admiral gave the order to weigh anchor once more, and they followed behind the wreckers' skiffs into the channel.

As it turned out, Thiago was true to his word—he guided them through la serpiente with ease, though he glanced back over his shoulder now and again, as if considering whether he could still take the cazador ship.

In the meantime, Ximena stood guard by Arturo, who sat

cross-legged on the deck with his wig sliding down into his eyes, tied to the mast. She did her best to ignore the way he was staring at her, but it was hard to look away from a man so ridiculous.

"Are you sure you are not a ghost?" he asked, gazing up at Ximena.

"Quite sure."

"Can you be sure you're not a ghost? After all, how does one prove these things?"

Ximena rolled her eye. They could not be rid of this pirate fast enough.

"It is strange to Arturo, to see their child on a ship of vultures," Arturo said. "Don't you know who your parents were, querida?"

"Yes," Ximena snapped. How long would she be haunted by her family's legacy? "Alejandra and Diego Reale, notorious pirates."

"*Heroes*," he corrected. "That is what they were. Heroes, worthy of legend. What kind of lies have these people told you?"

She looked away from him. He was a madman, and these were a madman's ravings, unworthy of her time or attention.

The pirate huffed. "To the depths with the cazadores," he said. "The Reales were heroes, querida, and Arturo will not hear a word against them. They snuck information to pirate crews about the armada's whereabouts from the inside, so those crews could snatch back the silver the empire had been stealing from the islands for centuries. They even used their leave from the armada to sack empire ships themselves. ¿Me entiendes? Your parents were single-handedly responsible for putting coins back into the pockets of the archipelago's people. That is how I met them, you know." He leaned down to pick at his teeth with one hand, examined the results, and flicked them away. "They led the raid against my house themselves. I was Minister Padilla then, terribly important, stupidly wealthy. When they asked me to surrender my family silver, I asked them why, and do you know what they told Arturo?"

In spite of herself, Ximena glanced back at the pirate. His bloodshot eyes were glazed as he lost himself in the memory.

"They said, 'That silver was bought with blood, and one of those forks could feed an entire pueblo.' I'd never thought of such a thing before, but somehow, I believed they were right. So I gave them the silver and my jewels and my candlesticks and my portraits, and the very next day I commissioned a pirate ship of my own. The magnificent *Princessa*, sailing under the command of Captain Arturo Padilla, Gentleman Pirate. Que descanse en paz."

His eyes welled up with tears again.

"The Reales fought against the empire's tyranny with their dying breaths," he said. "Of course, I'm sure they would have told you all of this themselves in time. But they must have thought they could protect you by keeping you in the dark."

Ximena searched the pirate's face. For what, she didn't quite know. His words echoed in her mind: *heroes*. It was a word she'd never heard alongside her parents' names. Traitors, yes. Liars, thieves, and villains, certainly. But never heroes. She hardly knew what to make of it. Had her parents truly turned pirate to help the people of Luza? Had they died fighting for what they believed was justice?

"My parents were criminals," she said, half to herself. "They wanted nothing but silver and glory."

"Yes, there are some like that," Arturo agreed with a curl of his lip. "Fools like Trinidad Ruiz or Benito de Soto, disgraces to the title of pirate. But most believe what your parents believed—that we must fight for our liberty, for a better world. For a world without the law."

"Cuatreda Reale."

Ximena turned to find the admiral standing behind her, his expression stern.

"We've hit open water. Release the pirate over to the wreckers."

She moved to untie the pirate's bindings. Arturo didn't resist when she guided him to the rail and pushed him into the dinghy, and he didn't make a sound when she and Dante rowed toward the wreckers, stopping before Thiago's boat. He only watched her with a strange kind of reverence in his eyes, as if she were about to save his life rather than condemn it. It made her inexplicably nauseous.

"I hate Thiago Torres," the pirate said as Dante hauled him to his feet. "I would rather spend ten more years in Domínguez's pit than spend ten minutes with his rats."

"But we are so much nicer to look at," said Thiago, earning a laugh from the wreckers behind him.

"Here," Ximena said. "Take him."

She shoved Arturo from her boat to Thiago's, and the pirate stumbled into the waiting arms of the wreckers. They sneered down at him, teeth bared, like a pack of starving dogs.

"What will you do with him?" The question left her mouth before she could stop it.

Thiago's blue eyes settled on her. "What does it matter to you?"

She had no answer for that. "Our deal is done. Go, before my commanding officer changes his mind."

"Farewell then, Ximena Reale." Arturo gave her a black-toothed smile. "It was fated that we should meet, and I pray we meet again, in this life or the next."

Thiago gave the order to depart, and the wreckers rowed their skiffs back into la serpiente, their thin arms powered with a desperate strength.

"¡Recuerda!" Arturo shouted as the skiffs faded into shadows in the distance. "Remember the fork!"

Ximena stared after him, feeling as if she had lost something terribly important, something that she just might regret losing.

"Care to explain, capitana?" Dante asked.

"We should get back," she replied, picking up an oar.

For once, he didn't try to spar with her. He just nodded, and they rowed back to the *Pérez* in silence, though Dante's smile suggested he might have overheard more of her conversation with the Gentleman Pirate than he let on.

Back on the *Pérez*, the cazadores were preparing to set off once more, hoisting the dormant sails to catch the wind. Pía was at Ximena's side in a moment, chattering away.

"You were magnificent, Cuatreda Reale! A spectacular negotiation, practically flawless. In fact, it brings to mind a particular ship log, in which the Cazador Simón . . ."

Ximena agreed aloud, but she wasn't really listening. In her mind, she heard Arturo say that same word, over and over again: *heroes*. She knew better than to believe the tales of a pirate. She shouldn't allow her thoughts to linger on them any longer than she'd already had.

"We sail for la tormenta." The admiral's voice boomed over the deck. "All hands to your positions."

"As you command," the cazadores replied.

So Ximena did what she did best: she focused on the task at hand, shoving all thoughts of the Gentleman Pirate into the furthest corner of her mind, where they would rot away to nothing. She buried the Reale ghosts, and she told herself they would not rise again.

Incredibly, she almost believed it.

Capítulo Quince

They drove deeper into the roiling sea. The *Pérez* pitched and rolled with the waves, leaving Pía nauseous, Ximena anxious, and Dante irritable. In fact, the entire crew was wound up as tight as a winch, the cazadores pausing in their tasks to gaze up at the blackened clouds and mutter to themselves about the ships la Tormenta had claimed.

Two days after leaving la serpiente behind, the *Pérez* sailed into rain so thick that the cazadores couldn't see more than a yard in front of them. They certainly couldn't see the rocks lurking beneath the water, but when Ximena heard the sharp snap of fracturing wood, she knew what had happened.

"Rocks, sir!" she shouted to the upper deck.

"Head below and inspect the damage," came the admiral's reply.

After several minutes, a cazador shouted up from the hold: "She's taking on water, sir. We can bail her out for a day or so, but she can't sail much longer than that."

Ximena's heart plummeted. They couldn't afford another delay.

Every hour lost was an hour Gasparilla gained.

The admiral swiped the rain from his brow. "We make for la Isla Rosa. It's the closest island to our current position. We can reach the harbor before the day is out."

"Sir," said Cazadora Cecilia, "we'll lose valuable time if we stop for repairs. And you know what kind of island it is—"

"The *Pérez* will never survive la Tormenta in this condition, and the shipbuilders of la Isla Rosa are some of the best in the empire. If we're going to survive the storm, we must make it to the harbor."

Cecilia pursed her lips disapprovingly, but relayed his orders to the crew nevertheless.

As the cuatredas grabbed their buckets and splashed down into the hold, the water was already as high as their ankles, cold and biting. The cazador who had been sent belowdecks led them to a hole the size of a cannonball, which had been torn in the hull.

"Do the best you can, cuatredas," he said. "We must hope that it will be enough."

As she bailed, Ximena struggled to quell her anxiousness. These repairs would cost them precious time, time that Gasparilla could only use to his advantage. What if he had already received his ransom from the high minister? What if he was spending the empire's silver in some far-off city, laughing over a tankard of ale about the foolish cazadores who had tried to stop him? Then Ximena would never become a cazadora, Marquesa would truly be lost forever, and the empire itself would—

She started at the touch of a hand on her shoulder. Pía stood behind her, looking even smaller and paler than usual.

"Are you all right, Cuatreda Reale?" she asked. "I know you hate storms. If you'd like, I can take over your duties so you can rest. I'm sure I won't be as efficient as you are, but I've spent most of my time watching the cazadores, and I think I can manage to—"

"Failure," said Ximena.

Pía blinked. "I'm not sure I understand—"

"You asked me once what I feared. That is my answer. And right now, there is a very good chance that our ship is going to sink, Gasparilla is going to get away with his crimes, and I'm never going to become a cazadora."

For a long moment, Pía said nothing. Then she gave the slightest of smiles.

"Don't worry, Cuatreda Reale. I won't let you fail alone."

She took Dante's bucket, waving the boy away, and for the next several hours the two girls bailed side by side. The archivist didn't quit even when she lost her footing and splashed down into the water, soaking herself from head to foot; she merely grimaced and staggered up, taking her place beside Ximena once more, shivering but silent. Watching the girl from the corner of her good eye, Ximena wondered if she'd been too quick to dismiss the idea of friendship. Perhaps it was more than a useless distraction after all.

Mercifully, they were released from their task when a cry rang out:

"Land ho! La Isla Rosa off the port bow!"

Ximena, Pía, and Dante climbed up to the deck.

"For an island named after a flower, la Isla Rosa is stunningly dismal," Dante said.

Ximena glowered at it from the deck: It was a clump of grayish-brown rocks shaped like a crescent moon in the middle of the sea. A small harbor sat at the center, and at the furthest end glimmered a constellation of amber lights—a pueblo, Ximena assumed. The *Pérez* limped toward it like a wounded animal, groaning and swollen with water, until at last the admiral gave the order to drop the anchor.

"To the boats," he said. "We'll stay in the city until the hull is repaired."

"What about Amador?" Cazadora Cecilia asked.

"We'll leave him in the brig until tomorrow when we leave," the admiral replied.

Ximena couldn't help but notice the way Cazadora Cecilia flinched. The last time she had seen the first mate so skittish was before they had visited the calaveras. What kind of people lived on la Isla Rosa, exactly?

"Pirate sympathizers."

The admiral gave Ximena her answer as they rowed toward the island. He stood at the prow of the dinghy with his back to them.

"The people of Isla Rosa believe pirates to be their saviors, great heroes of justice and truth. La academia attempted to resolve the issue many years ago, but the sympathizers flourished in spite of our efforts."

"Efforts?" Pía asked through chattering teeth.

"The cazadores cleansed the island." Dante pulled back on his oar; the rain slicked his curls tight to his skin. "Came in the night and arrested them in droves. Killed whoever fought back. Men, women, and children."

"Cuatreda de Leòn—" Cazadora Cecilia began, her tone a warning.

"You were entrusted with that mission, sir, if I recall correctly." Though Dante's drawl was light, his eyes drove into the admiral's back, cold as knives. "Defending the law by ridding the island of its sympathizer infestation. Of course, no one ever found out what truly happened on la Isla Rosa. My mother saw to that."

The admiral was silent for a moment. Ximena waited for him to explain himself, to denounce the story as false and tell Dante that he had no right to speak in such a manner to a commanding officer. Instead, the admiral merely said, "We did what was necessary. In the name of the law."

Even Dante seemed surprised at that—he shot Ximena a look. *I told you so.* But she was too preoccupied to acknowledge him. Had the cazadores truly arrested and killed the citizens of la Isla Rosa? It was a direct violation of the law's foundational tenets. *There shall be no murder. There shall be no persecution.* Ximena watched the admiral's shoulders, the tightness that didn't go away, the way his fingers drummed against the pommel of his rapier. He had almost certainly been to this place before and was dreading whatever awaited him here now.

No, she told herself. Gabriel Pérez was the epitome of heroism, honor, and truth. He was everything she wished to be and more. He was the family she'd never really had, the only person she'd ever allowed herself to love besides Marquesa.

The crew was silent as they rowed up to the harbor docks. Rain continued to pelt down in cold, heavy sheets, and the waves snarled and rolled while the cazadores disembarked. Though Dante offered her a hand up, Ximena refused it, stumbling onto the dock herself.

"Who goes there?" A woman strode toward them, her lantern held high over her head. Though Ximena couldn't make out her features in the darkness, she heard the fury in her voice.

"Who goes there, I say?" the woman called again. "No one is allowed on these docks past curfew—"

She stopped at the sight of the Luzan emblem on the cazadores' chests.

"No cazadores allowed here. I suggest you leave immediately before I summon the watch."

Ximena spotted the flash of silver coins in the admiral's palm. "We'll be gone before morning," he replied.

For a moment, the woman hesitated. Then her hand shot out, and she took the coins and quickly shoved them in the pocket of her skirt.

"See that you are."

The admiral tipped his head, moving past her.

"Watch your step, though, cazador," the woman called after him. "Your silver won't protect you here."

The streets of la Isla Rosa were narrow and crooked, lit only by a few flickering lanterns. The limestone buildings leaned into one another like toppled dominoes; the air reeked of fish and sewage. As they walked, Ximena glanced up to see several pairs of eyes watching them from the windows—but the moment they noticed her looking, their shutters slammed shut. Perhaps they'd made a mistake in coming to la Isla Rosa after all.

Admiral Pérez finally stopped in front of a blue, wooden door, knocking against it with his fist. Ximena glanced up at the sign that hung overhead: El Pez Volador. The Flying Fish.

A click. Then an old man poked his hooked nose through a slit in the door.

"State your business," he croaked.

"We're travelers in need of lodging," said the admiral.

The old man's eyes drifted down to the admiral's uniform, then widened—before the captain had time to move, the old man spat into his eye.

"Vultures," he hissed. "You'll have no lodging from me."

And with that, he banged the door shut.

The admiral wiped his face with the edge of his cloak, stoic as ever. "This way," he said.

They tried three more inns with the same result—one innkeeper even tossed a bucket of fish bones at them on their way out. By the time the city's clocktower chimed midnight, they were soaked to the skin and starving, no closer to finding shelter than when they had started.

"Sir," said Cazadora Cecilia, "perhaps we can have the ship repaired on another island—"

"We can't afford the delay," the admiral said.

"But if the innkeepers won't let us stay the night, I highly doubt the shipbuilders—" Cecilia started.

"We cannot afford the delay, Cecilia."

"And even if we do find somewhere to stay, someone would likely kill us in our sleep—"

"You shouldn't be so quick to judge us, cazadores," a female voice called out from the darkness.

Swords sang through the night as the crew spun with their weapons drawn to face a small, elderly woman in an apron. Her smile flashed through the darkness.

"We're not as inhospitable as we might seem," she said. Her voice was like the hiss of the sea on rock. "My husband and I are the innkeepers of El Pez Volador. We can offer you lodging in our storehouse, if it suits you."

Slowly, the admiral lowered his sword. "We thank you for your kindness. We'll pay you in full."

"No need," replied the old woman. "Consider it a debt repaid."

Without further explanation, she turned and ambled off into

the darkness. The admiral motioned for the crew to follow. Ximena gripped the hilt of her rapier. The innkeeper hadn't greeted them kindly before. What if his wife was leading them into a trap?

"Afraid of abuelas in aprons, capitana?" Dante whispered.

"Sharks are also fish," said Ximena, quoting an old Luzan idiom. "You would know that, Cuatreda de León, if you hadn't skipped our marine science course as an uveda."

Dante laughed. Then he pointed after the woman with his rapier. "Do you know her?"

"How in the name of the law would I know her?"

"Couldn't say. But she hasn't stopped looking at you since she appeared."

It was true. The old woman continued to glance back over her shoulder every few steps, her beady eyes fastening on Ximena before drifting back to the street ahead. Once again, Ximena's skin prickled. Something was definitely not right.

The old woman led them into an alley behind El Pez Volador and opened a round, blue door. The cazadores followed, wary, weapons held ahead of them.

"Here we are, cazadores. You may stay here for the night, so long as you are gone before sunrise."

The admiral nodded. "Muchas gracias, señora."

The old woman's eyes latched meaningfully onto Ximena. It reminded the girl vaguely of the way Captain Salazar and the Gentleman Pirate had looked at her. Was it possible the woman recognized her somehow?

But all she said was, "I pray you find the help you seek." Then she bowed and retreated, closing the door behind her.

With the strange woman gone, Ximena finally relaxed. She

sheathed her rapier and took a moment to observe their surroundings. The storehouse was hardly more than a shack, packed with several barrels of ale and crates of salted fish. Water leaked in through cracks in the ceiling, but it was warmer and drier than la Isla Rosa's streets, so it would have to do.

"Stay here, and stay quiet," the admiral said. "I'm going to meet with the shipbuilders. If I don't return before dawn, leave without me."

"Sir, is it wise to go alone—" Cazadora Cecilia began.

"That's a direct order, Cecilia."

She lowered her gaze. "As you command, sir."

Rapier in hand, Admiral Pérez tipped down his hat and stepped out into the night. Ximena heard the words of the dock keeper in her mind: *Watch your step, cazador. Your silver won't protect you here.*

"Well then," said Dante, "we might as well make ourselves comfortable, no?"

He shook the water from his curls and reclined on the dusty floor, leaning his back against an ale barrel. The crew followed suit, settling in the dirt, tipping their hats down over their eyes and pulling their cloaks around their shoulders.

But Ximena had no intention of sleeping—how could she rest while their captain was in danger? Dante de León must have sensed her indecision, because he opened one eye and smiled sardonically.

"Such loyalty. If only he deserved it."

"He's one of the best men I've ever known," replied Ximena without hesitation.

For the briefest of moments, Dante's smile slipped. "That is unfortunate indeed. In more ways than one."

The boy must have been more tired than he looked, because he was asleep within moments, snores rattling from his chest. Pía settled beside him, and before long she too was asleep, curled into his shoulder, her matted curls tucked under his chin.

Ximena's throat tightened; Marquesa's face rose unbidden in her mind. Her sister had slept with her like that when they were children. They had whispered together under the bedsheets until their father caught them, giggling when he tickled them into submission.

Where was Marquesa now? Was she sleeping in a shack like this one, wasting slowly away from illness? Was she begging on the streets of Valuza just to avoid starvation? Ximena struggled to shove those images from her head, but Marquesa's hazel eyes seemed to burn in the dark, like twin moons of judgment.

"Can't sleep, Cuatreda Reale?"

Cazadora Cecilia stood across from her, frowning.

"I rarely sleep," Ximena answered. "And usually not well."

"Then we have two things in common."

"Two things, Cazadora Cecilia?"

"My mother was a pirate, Cuatreda Reale. And I also sleep quite rarely."

At first, Ximena was too stunned to speak. Cazadora Cecilia—Gabriel's prized first mate—was the daughter of a pirate.

"You were the admiral's first caso especial," Ximena whispered. She didn't know how she hadn't figured it out before. "Before my sister and me."

"Indeed," Cecilia confirmed. "I am his great triumph. A traitor's daughter turned loyal servant of the empire, a testament to the law's providence."

The cazadora eased herself to the floor, her back to a wooden barrel. Ximena had never seen her look so tired. Her face was drawn and haggard, her usual sharpness dulled to a blunt edge.

"I realize that I have been . . . firm with you, since the beginning of our acquaintance." The cazadora spoke as if each word caused her physical pain. "Part of it was motivated by jealousy, I suppose. You are the admiral's shiny new toy, and I am his forgotten relic. But that is not the only reason I behaved as I did. As you know, Cuatreda Reale, nothing comes easily to people like us. Not even with the admiral's favor. So we must be strong enough to fight for what we want against all odds. I only wanted to make you stronger. To force you to fight."

Ximena studied her in the dim light. She had no particular love for the *Pérez's* first mate—the woman had made her life more difficult than it ever needed to be—but she respected anyone who was strong enough to triumph over impossible odds. So she said, "Gracias, Cazadora Cecilia."

The cazadora gave an uncomfortable nod, clearing her throat. "You take first watch. Wake me in an hour."

A dozen more questions flooded into Ximena's mind. How had Cecilia kept her secret for so long? How had she passed the Royal Examination? Did the high minister know about her history? But Cazadora Cecilia's eyes were already closed, and whether she was sleeping or not, Ximena knew she wouldn't be pleased if someone interrupted her rest.

So Ximena watched over the *Pérez's* sleeping crew, until the sound of creaking wood jolted her out of her thoughts.

"Señorita Reale!"

Ximena leapt to her feet, searching for the intruder. But there was no one in the storehouse. The rest of the crew still slept soundly, undisturbed, and there was no other noise except for Dante's terrible snoring.

"¡Aquí arriba!"

She looked up. A boy no older than ten peered down at her through a hole in the roof, brown cheeks bunched in a smile.

"You should be more careful with your belongings," the boy said. He dangled something in the air—her rapier.

"If you want it back, you'll have to catch me," he said.

And then he was gone, just as quickly as he'd come. Ximena froze. She couldn't leave her post. But she also couldn't wake Cazadora Cecilia and confess she'd been pickpocketed by a pirate child. If she was quick, however, she could find the boy and return to the storehouse before anyone noticed she was gone. So with that, she opened the door and raced out into the storming night.

The boy wasn't very adept at covering his tracks. Ximena followed him through la Isla Rosa's winding streets, sprinting between the domino houses and piles of fish bones. Eventually, the boy seemed to tire of running. He stopped, grinning, the stolen rapier glinting in his hand, and slipped through the entrance of a ramshackle building. When she saw the sign above the door, Ximena stopped.

El Pez Volador.

What kind of trickery was this?

But she was Ximena Reale, a would-be cazadora. She wouldn't be defied by a pirate urchin. Bristling and soaked once again, she burst through the inn's door.

"Where is the thief who stole my rapier?"

The inn clearly doubled as a cantina—men and women of la Isla Rosa sat huddled around wooden tables with mugs of wine and bowls of fish stew. But at the sight of a drenched and furious Ximena, they fell silent, staring, mugs halfway to their lips.

"Turn the thief over to me," Ximena said, "and no harm will come to any of you."

A man pointed to the back of the room, where she spotted the boy in the arms of an old woman. *The same woman who led us to the storehouse*, Ximena realized. The boy handed the woman the rapier and kissed her cheek.

"What took you so long, Tito?" the woman said.

He shrugged. "It's more fun that way."

She clicked her tongue against her teeth, though it did little to hide her amusement. "Well done, cariño. Now go to sleep with your brothers."

"Yes, Abuela."

The boy grinned at Ximena one last time before scampering up the staircase.

"Welcome, daughter of pirates," said the old woman. "My apologies for the deception, but I could think of no better way to bring you here."

"What?" Ximena felt as if all the air had been sucked from her lungs. "How—but—"

"I recognized you the moment I saw you, querida. I was watching from the window when my husband turned you and the cazadores away the first time." The old woman smiled her eerie smile. "You look so much like them; you could be a ghost."

Whispers darted around the cantina—*Alejandra and Diego Reale, daughters, two of them, alive!*—while Ximena stood in shock for the second time that evening.

"Why have you brought me here?" she demanded. "What do you want with me and my crew?"

The old woman's smile faded. "Querida, there's no need to pretend here. You're with your people. You're home."

Ximena glanced around the room once more. How had she not seen it before? The fabrics stained red and tangerine, the unkempt hair and blackened teeth.

The tattoos of a crimson rose on every forearm.

Pirates. The whole cantina was full of pirates, or at the very least pirate sympathizers.

She'd never wanted her rapier so badly in her life.

"My home is la Academia de los Cazadores," she snapped, panic rising into her throat. "You will return my rapier, or I will have no choice but to administer justice."

"So you're not a captive of the cazadores?"

"No, by the law. I'm a cuatreda."

A gasp escaped from the old woman's chest, and she stumbled into an empty chair. The innkeeper, summoned by his wife's cry, rushed out from the kitchen.

"Estefanía!" he said, shuffling to her side. Then he caught sight of Ximena, and the worry in his eyes hardened. "I told you not to bring that girl here. She is nothing but trouble!"

"She's *their* daughter," said Estefanía.

"In name only."

"Blood runs deep, Carlos."

Ximena could feel every eye in the cantina on her neck. If she stayed a moment longer, she wouldn't make it out of El Pez Volador alive.

"My weapon, innkeeper!" she said.

Carlos huffed. "She can't be their daughter. She's obviously as dense as sand."

His wife waved him off. "Come closer, querida," she said. "Talk with me for a moment. Then I promise to return your weapon."

Ximena and the innkeeper exchanged glances. Neither, it seemed, wanted to move. But Estefanía glared at them both, and Carlos edged to the kitchen as Ximena stepped closer, taking the seat opposite the old woman.

"There now. Let's start again, shall we? What are you called, querida?" asked the old woman.

"Ximena."

"Ah. A warrior's name. You're hunting Gasparilla, I expect?"

Ximena stayed silent.

"And how did you come to be with the cazadores?"

"That's my business."

"Very well. Let's try a more basic question. Do you know where you are, Ximena?"

"I don't have time—"

"You're in the birthplace of your parents. In a manner of speaking, that is," said Estefanía.

More lies. Her parents had grown up on Valuza, not la Isla Rosa. But Estefanía appeared unperturbed by Ximena's glower.

"Long ago," she continued, "Alejandra and Diego Reale were two of the most feared cazadores in the archipelago. So naturally they were assigned to a special raid under the young and ambitious Cazador Gabriel Pérez. The raid on la Isla Rosa."

She had a storyteller's voice, and despite Ximena's better judgment, she found herself leaning closer.

"But they weren't hardened like the other cazadores. They watched the massacre of our people in horror, even begged Cazador Gabriel to show mercy. He refused. So the men, women, and children of la Isla Rosa perished at the hands of the cazadores that night. My son among them."

She nodded at the stairs the boy had taken. He must be her dead son's child, then.

"That night, Alejandra and Diego Reale ended up in this very cantina. They cried to me and my husband to forgive them, for the deaths of our son and our neighbors. I told them that we would not forgive them. Not unless they spent the rest of their lives atoning for what they had done."

"So they turned pirate," Ximena breathed.

"Just so."

The floor seemed to tilt beneath Ximena's feet like a ship in a storm. She'd never known why her parents had turned pirate; she'd never even thought to ask. What did their reasoning matter to her when the outcome was already fixed? But now the words had been spoken aloud.

And there was no running from them.

The old woman's eyes bored into hers.

"You don't have to do this, Ximena. You don't have to fight against Gasparilla. He's the last hope these islands have for freedom. For liberation from the empire's clutches, once and for all."

Ximena's lip curled. Liberation was a generous word for treason.

"What would you have me do?" she said. "Turn traitor like my parents?"

"Exactamente." Estefanía reached across the table for Ximena's hand; the girl yanked it away. But the woman continued, undeterred. "Stop the cazadores. Fight for the right side. You're the daughter of two brilliant pirates, querida. That legacy is yours to claim, if you choose it. So fight with us. Stand for the people of Luza. ¡Viva

Gasparilla! ¡Viva la libertad!"

The rest of the cantina echoed her: "¡Viva Gasparilla! ¡Viva la libertad!"

Several images flashed through Ximena's mind in quick succession. She saw Arturo and Catarina Salazar, the admiration in their eyes when they spoke of her parents. She saw the cazadores storming la Isla Rosa, slaughtering people as they went. She saw Dante de León, his hatred when he spoke of the law.

What if this woman is right? What if they're all right? a voice whispered from the shadows of her thoughts. *What if I have been wrong about pirates all along?*

"Ah, there it is," Estefanía said. "The Reale blood. It's still inside of you, I can feel it."

"No," Ximena said aloud. She staggered to her feet so quickly that her chair smashed to the floor. Her hands trembled at her sides. "No, that's quite enough. I've listened to your story. Now my end of the bargain is fulfilled, and you will give me my weapon as promised. Mi espada, por favor."

The old woman inhaled as if Ximena had shot her.

"You have made your decision then."

"There was no decision to be made. I am a candidate of la academia, and I will soon become a cazadora. My one purpose in life is to capture Gasparilla and save the empire from ruin."

Estefanía's eyes were misty with tears.

"Very well then," she said.

She slid Ximena's rapier across the table. Ximena slid it into its sheath; but somehow, it didn't feel like a victory.

"Because you've shown me kindness," Ximena said, "I won't tell the cazadores about your alliance with Gasparilla. But if you value your lives, you will stay out of our way until we depart the island in the morning."

"As you wish," said Estefanía. "May the seas be with you, Ximena Reale."

No cazador in their right mind would return such a blessing from a pirate sympathizer. But as she looked into Estefanía's face, Ximena found herself nodding and saying, "And with you, señora."

Then she strode out of El Pez Volador and back to the storehouse, trying desperately to calm her shaking hands.

"Where have you been, Cuatreda Reale?"

She stopped. The admiral stood in front of the storehouse door, his arms crossed over his chest, his expression stern.

"Sir—"

"I gave you a direct order to stay put. Instead, I find that you've spent the night in a cantina with pirate sympathizers."

"My actions were inexcusable, captain. But a thief stole my weapon, so I went into the cantina to retrieve it."

The admiral eyed her in the darkness. She'd seen him question many pirates in the past, but he had never turned that power against her before.

"What did the innkeepers have to say?"

"Nothing of consequence."

"Ximena," said the admiral. "You're skilled at many things but lying is not one of them."

She swallowed. "They said they knew my parents. That I could claim their legacy and fight against the empire."

"And what did you say?"

"I refused, of course. They returned my weapon, and I left," Ximena said. "I told them nothing else."

"And yet your face says something quite different, Cuatreda Reale. Don't—"

"Have you ever doubted?" She didn't know where those words came from. But once they escaped, they couldn't be stopped. "Have you ever wondered whether the law was truly just?"

"Many times," said the admiral. "A good cazador is not without doubt. But a great cazador overcomes that doubt with belief."

"Do they also persecute innocents? Do they arrest and kill those who only wish to care for people in need? We're taught from birth that the law brought peace to the warring islands of the archipelago. But what if the islands didn't *want* the law? What if they would be better off the way they were before Alessandra arrived?"

"Cuatreda Reale—"

"Sir, these people don't want to be part of the empire, yet the empire refuses to allow them to leave, because without their silver, the entire system collapses. Por favor, sir," Ximena said, hating how small she sounded. "Explain it to me. I know the law better than anyone, and I can't name a single part of it that allows that kind of abuse."

"The law is a contract, Cuatreda Reale," the admiral said. "The empire brings peace to everyone under its protection, but it comes at a price. The people of Luza understand that."

"Is that what you told yourself before you had them arrested and killed?"

A cold breeze swept in from the sea. The only sound was the rain falling in the street.

"Ximena." The admiral's face was inscrutable. "I've known you since you were barely strong enough to hold a sword. I've watched you grow into the sharpest candidate la academia has ever seen.

You," he said, voice cracking just slightly, "are like blood to me. For that reason alone, I won't arrest you for the words you just spoke."

Then he pulled himself to his full height and assumed the tone of a commander, glowering down his twice-broken nose. "For your disobedience and insubordination, you will spend the rest of the journey cleaning the crew's bunks. You will be deprived of all meals for one day, and you will take first watch every night. Is that understood?"

Ximena couldn't even believe what she had done. She opened her mouth to apologize, to tell him that she hadn't meant a single word, that her emotions had gotten the better of her. But the words clumped together with a sob in her throat, and all she could manage was a whispered, "As you command, admiral."

As she slunk past him, she wondered if he would ever trust her again, or if she'd just lost one of the few people who truly loved her.

Capítulo Dieciséis

Silence. It was more unnerving than all the witches, sea monsters, and pirates they'd faced combined.

With their ship repaired, they set sail, away from la Isla Rosa. The sea was stormy, the wind wild, but the *Pérez* faced no other obstacles, no other enemies or threats. Even the islands they passed were small, rocky, and uninhabited, graced only by a handful of nesting frigate birds. It made Ximena so restless that she took on double the work she usually did, spending every waking moment racing around the ship, trimming lines or swabbing the deck. She was almost thankful for the admiral's punishment. At least it gave her something to do besides think about the fact he hadn't spoken to her in days.

She was especially grateful for the excuse to spend the next two nights in the crow's nest by herself instead of trying to sleep. She dreaded the nightmares that lurked in the corners of her mind. But when pure exhaustion forced her to rest for an hour or two in her cabin, they sunk their teeth into her with vicious cruelty. She

dreamed of storms and drowning, of blood and children screaming. Then there would be a sound like a gunshot, and she would jolt
awake with a shout, swiping tears from her cheeks.

Each time, Pía watched her in silence, her large eyes gleaming in
the dark. Then she'd creep over from her bed without a word, tuck-
ing herself into Ximena's back, her face pressed against her shoulder.
Ximena stiffened, rigid as wood, and considered telling Pía to leave
her alone. But she never did. After all, it was only when Pía's snores
rumbled against her spine that Ximena could finally rest.

Loyal as she was, Pía never asked Ximena to explain her behavior. But Dante wasn't nearly as tactful.

"You're not sleeping," he said, cornering her one day after breakfast.

"Since when is my sleep your business, Cuatreda de León?"

"Since you forgot to wash the breakfast dishes even though the
task was assigned to you. You never forget anything, capitana." He
wrinkled his nose. "Also, those dark circles under your eye make you
look like a corpse."

She pushed past him, glowering.

"And . . . I heard you scream."

The sudden softness in his voice disarmed her more than she
cared to admit.

"The walls are thin, capitana." His boots clicked against the deck
behind her as he stepped closer. "Having nightmares?"

"I have duties to attend to—"

"Is it the admiral? Things have seemed a bit frigid between you
two, though I can't say I'm angry about that. Or perhaps it's la Tormenta that's keeping you up at night? You aren't afraid of storms, are
you, Cuatreda Reale?"

"A cazador knows no fear," she said. "Now if you'll excuse me."

She strode off down the hallway, not looking back. She didn't like Dante's newfound ability to read her thoughts.

At last, after a long week of sailing, they heard the cry from the crow's nest—*hurricane off the starboard bow!*—and Ximena raced with the rest of the crew to the upper deck, pushing her way to the rail to catch a glimpse of the storm. The deck pitched and rolled under her feet; the wind gusted against the sails and the waves tore at the ship's side with white and frenzied claws. Beside her, Pía gripped the rail to keep her balance.

"There it is," the little archivist said, her face a deathly shade of white. "No turning back now."

La Tormenta loomed before them in all its terrible glory. Ximena's stomach dropped into her boots. It was far, far worse than anything she had ever imagined: a wide wall of black clouds stretching for miles, flickering with lightning, so dark and thick that she couldn't see beyond it.

"I suppose there are worse ways to die," Dante quipped. He'd appeared at her side without her noticing. "Far better to drown under the bone-crushing weight of the sea than to face the noose."

"Bone-crushing weight?" Pía squeaked.

"Naturalmente. And that's to say nothing of your lungs slowly collapsing and filling with water."

Pía's eyes widened with fear; her breath came fast and shallow. Ximena squeezed her shoulder to reassure her, glaring at Dante. He had decency enough to look chagrined.

"No temas, Pía," he said. "At least we'll be with you when you go."

The archivist nodded vaguely to herself, gripping the rail so tight that her knuckles went white.

"Cazadores!"

They turned to face the helm, where the admiral was standing. Though he avoided looking at Ximena, his face betrayed no fear, no hesitation—in fact, his eyes burned with something like excitement, catching the flash of lightning.

"We sail straight into the heart of la Tormenta. I know you've heard the storm leaves no survivors, that it's impossible to break through to the other side. But we are the cazadores of Luza!"

The crew's cheer merged with the thunder.

"Water and wind will not best us," the admiral said. "We will survive this storm and we will catch Gasparilla, or by the law, we'll die trying. To your positions!"

Jolted into action, the crew hurried to their posts, pulling in the jib and fastening the mainsail. So the *Pérez* ripped through the roaring sea toward la Tormenta, closer and closer to their doom.

"Hold your positions," called the admiral.

La Tormenta was twenty yards away now, then ten yards, then five yards. Ximena sucked in a breath—Dante's hand, which had eased up toward hers, closed around her fingers.

"Steady, capitana," he murmured.

She nodded. They would survive this. They hadn't crossed the entire archipelago to fail now. She counted down the seconds: *diez . . . nueve . . . ocho . . .*

Then the *Pérez* broke through the wall of the storm with a shattering crash, and the sky went dark. Lightning cracked through the clouds like a whip; thunder shook the wooden decks; the wind shrieked around them with an otherworldly fury, whipping the sea into waves as tall as la academia's turrets. Dante's grip tightened around Ximena's hand—a wave was already barreling toward the *Pérez*, ready to devour them.

"Hold fast," Cazadora Cecilia shouted through the gale.

The *Pérez* swooped up the wall of water like a bird; Ximena's stomach plummeted as the ship lifted. By the law, they weren't going to make it. They were tipping too far, too fast, and they were going to plunge to a watery death below. She gripped onto the line she was holding and squeezed her eye shut. But at the very crest of the wave, the *Pérez* tilted forward just far enough to slip down the other side, crashing back to the sea.

"Stay the course!" cried the admiral. "Fasten the mainsheet!"

They hurried to follow his commands, reigning in the runaway sails. Their only chance at survival was maintaining their current course. If they strayed too far in either direction and lost their chance to break through the storm, the *Pérez* would join the thousands of ships buried in la Tormenta's waters.

Cazadora Cecilia called again for the crew to hold their positions as a monstrous wave approached. It caught the *Pérez* by the hull and hoisted it up into the air, so high Ximena felt they might fly, before tossing them back into the sea. Water engulfed the deck with a roar—Ximena lost her footing, tumbling to her knees. Dante grabbed her ankle just before she slid overboard.

"¿Estás bien?" he demanded.

"Yes, yes, I'm fine. Where is Pía?"

Dante looked over his shoulder, searching for the archivist, but the girl was nowhere to be found. He turned back to Ximena with worry in his eyes and shook his head. Her lungs constricted.

"Man overboard!"

The cry from the crow's nest was faint, but she heard it, none-theless. Ximena scrambled to the rail, slipping and sliding over the sea-slicked wood, and scanned the roiling water until she caught sight of a small clump of red hair sinking beneath the waves.

"Man overboard!" she screamed. "Pía's in the water!"

The cazadores lurched into action. But as they organized them-selves into their proper positions, Pía drifted further and further into the darkness. Ximena's heart drummed—they didn't have time to coordinate a rescue.

"Just tell them I'm going after her," she called to Dante.

"Ximena, no. Please—"

Whatever he tried to say next was lost to the wind. She fumbled her way back to the mast and grabbed a coil of rope, fastening it first to the wood and then to her waist. She would dive into the sea and drag Pía back herself. But just as she began to run, she glimpsed a flash of silver-blond curls disappearing over the rail.

Dante?

"Man overboard!" She raced to the rail, searching for any sign of him. "Two candidates in the water!"

Thunder rattled the clouds; the *Pérez* climbed another towering wave, crashing back to the sea again and sending a spray of water over the deck. Ximena cursed Dante and his lack of common sense. Why on earth would he throw himself off the side of the ship with no way to return to it?

"Dante!" she shouted into the darkness, praying, for the first time in her life, that he was somehow alive.

Then, as the *Pérez* tilted up the side of a wave yet again, she saw him. He was fighting against the current with Pía in his arms, struggling to stay afloat, gasping for air.

"Rope!" he cried. "Rope!"

Without hesitation, Ximena untied the rope from her waist and hurled it into the sea. It landed ten yards from Dante's reach. He swam toward it and gripped it in the hand that wasn't holding Pía.

"¡Ayúdenme!" Ximena shouted to the cazadores, who raced to her aid, forming a line to haul Dante and Pía up from the sea.

The two soaked candidates collapsed on the deck, choking and heaving. When one of the cazadores tried to help him up, Dante batted her hand away and stumbled to his feet, sweeping his curls out of his eyes. His grin caught the white-hot glare of a lightning bolt.

"Saved you the effort, capitana," he said. "You all right there, Pía?"

Pía offered him a weak smile through her shivering, but Dante didn't see it. He was looking at Ximena, who was looking back at him, standing stock-still on the deck, wind whipping her hair into a frenzy of curls. She couldn't believe he was alive. She couldn't believe he'd risked his life for a girl he hardly knew. She couldn't believe that in his soaking-wet tunic and trousers, with his hair dripping into his eyes, he looked more like a cazador than he ever had. His shoulders were broad and firm; his eyes flashed with courage; and his smile knew no fear. Where was the boy who tormented her in la academia? Who was this strange young man who had replaced him?

It's only temporary, she thought to herself. *If we survive this storm, he'll slip right back into his old ways, as people usually do, and this night will be forgotten.* Yet he didn't shift his gaze from hers, and she couldn't drag her eye from his.

The moment lasted as long as a thunderclap. Then it was over. Dante hauled Pía to her feet, the cazadores rushed back to their positions, and the *Pérez* caught another monstrous wave.

This time, however, the ship didn't pass up and over the other side of the crest. Instead, it tilted further and further backward, until Ximena couldn't hold her balance on the deck. She slipped, crashing into Dante and Pía, her feet scrambling for purchase.

"Hold onto me!" Dante cried.

She grabbed his right hand as he caught hold of the rail with his left; Pía gripped Ximena by the waist so tightly that it choked the air from her lungs. Still, the ship tipped backward, the black wall of water towering over them as thunder rolled.

Ximena knew in an instant: the *Pérez* was going to sink.

"Captain!" she cried. "Orders?"

For the first time in days, the admiral's eyes found hers. There was something in his face she'd never seen before. It took her a moment to recognize it, but when she did, her throat swelled shut. *Fear.*

The admiral was afraid.

Then he gave the order she never thought he would give—one that only comes when all was lost.

"Abandon ship! Save yourselves!"

The cazadores stared at their captain, wide-eyed. They couldn't abandon the *Pérez*—it wasn't in their blood. Besides, the odds of surviving such a storm in the water were slim. But the cazadores were obedient to their core. So one by one, they reluctantly dove into the roiling sea, disappearing beneath the waves.

"Go, Ximena, Pía," Dante said. "You have to jump."

Despite the chaos around them, the boy's eyes were steady, calm. If Dante de León could be that self-possessed, certainly Ximena could find the courage to jump overboard. So she released her grip on his hand. She breathed once, twice. Then she dove, hurtling down until she hit the cold, dark water.

Immediately, the sea fought to drown her, tossing her back and forth, tearing at her hair, her arms and legs, until she couldn't tell which direction was up or down. Her lungs burned; her muscles twisted and screamed. But Ximena couldn't allow la Tormenta to claim her—not without a struggle. So she began to swim, pulling herself forward until she broke the surface with a gasp.

But before she could take another breath, a wave slammed her down again, filling her lungs with saltwater. Her ears rang; her head pounded; she struggled back toward the air, resurfacing and swiping the salt from her eyes. The *Pérez* was nowhere to be seen. In fact, she couldn't see anything at all—the sea and sky were as black as tar. She frantically looked around and saw she was alone. Completely and entirely alone in a storm that never died. When the next wave shoved her down, she could almost hear the sea mocking her.

Idiot girl.

You thought you could best me.

I who cannot be bested.

She was so very tired. It would be easy to relax into the darkness. To close her eyes and never open them again. And the sea sang in its soothing whisper:

It's all right, Ximena.

Sleep now, Ximena.

Then it grew louder, more insistent.

Ximena.

Ximena.

XIMENA.

The sound of her name pulled her to the surface for a third time.

But that last call had not come from the sea. Someone was shouting for her; she was sure of it. She turned, searching for the source, but found none.

"Ximena! Ximena!"

She spun toward the sound again and began to swim, lifting arm over arm with all of the strength left in her body. She dove beneath the oncoming waves and gasped for air between blows. She didn't know who was calling her. She didn't have to know. Whoever it was, they were the only thing she had left in a world of endless night, so she swam toward them as she would swim toward a lifeline.

But another wave caught her by surprise, slamming the air from her chest, and Ximena could fight no more. She sagged down beneath the water, vision blurring, hearing lost. Still, the voice called to her: *Ximena, Ximena.*

I'm sorry, she told the voice. *I can't come, I'm sorry.*

And she allowed the sea to carry her down, down, down . . .

Capítulo Diecisiete

Suddenly, and without any warning, the storm ceased. Ximena burst to the surface, swallowing air in heaving gulps. All around her, the sea was blue and flat and calm—only the black clouds in the distance gave away that la Tormenta had ever happened. They'd made it to the other side of the storm.

Or Ximena had, at least. Where was the rest of the crew? She tried to call for the admiral, but she couldn't push the words out from her salt-burned throat. Squinting her good eye against the sun, she scanned the horizon for wreckage, for bodies, for anything human. An island, about a hundred yards to the south, sat small and green against the vastness of the sky. Was that Gasparilla's hideout? Perhaps she could swim to it before nightfall. Then she could come up with a plan for finding the others.

But the sound of her name interrupted her efforts.

"Ximena! Ximena, over here!"

She turned to find Dante waving an arm above his head, several yards off, with Pía clutched against his side. Then she realized: it was *his* voice that had called out to her in the darkness. His voice that had dragged her up from oblivion.

He can never know, she swore to herself. If Dante found out that he'd summoned her back from the brink of death, he would be absolutely insufferable. But she didn't have time to think about such things now. They had to find their crew. So she shoved aside her restless thoughts and swam toward the surviving candidates.

"Cuatreda Reale!"

Pía left Dante's side to bury her face in Ximena's neck.

"I thought—I thought you were—"

Pía's voice crumbled into sobs. Ximena held her as they treaded water. Did the archivist truly care about her that much? The thought sent a bolt of panic through Ximena's body. It was a terrible responsibility, to live for someone else. She wasn't sure she was ready for it.

"Ximena," Dante said softly.

Ximena looked up to find Dante's eyes fastened on her. His doublet was torn, his shoulder bleeding, his lips cracked and blue, but his stare was just as fierce as it had been on the *Pérez*. Ximena's stomach flopped and writhed like a fish on land. She knew he wanted to say something, but she also knew that she didn't want to hear it, that once he spoke it—whatever *it* was—into existence, there would be no way for her to ignore it again.

Then, mercifully, another voice called out, "Cuatreda Reale!"

Ximena turned to see the admiral swimming toward them with Cazadora Cecilia close behind. A bedraggled Amador paddled after them—the pirate must have escaped from the brig before the *Pérez* went under. He had truly unlocked the secret to immortality.

"Felicidades, cazadores," he said wryly. "You made it to Gasparilla's hideout."

So Ximena's guess had been correct. The island was the pirate captain's base. But how in the name of the law did *La Leyenda* pass in and out of la Tormenta without sinking?

"Not all of us shun el idioma prohibido," Amador said, anticipating her thoughts. "Pirates have been using it for centuries, and my captain has a particular fondness for it."

"Did no one else survive?" the admiral cut the pirate off.

Ximena shook her head. "The storm must have taken them."

"By the law," Cazadora Cecilia breathed.

"Then we make for the island," the admiral said gravely. "We can shelter there and plan our next steps."

"Impossible," said Amador. "A reef circles this side of the island, infested by sharks."

"Then what do you suggest, pirate?"

"I suggest you follow me. This island is my home, after all."

"And why should we trust you?" Cecilia said.

"Because you have no other choice, cazadora, if you don't wish to be food for the sharks."

He swam ahead of them toward the island. The candidates exchanged glances—they weren't exactly eager to trust the pirate again.

"Vamos, candidates," said the admiral. "We'll follow the pirate until we reach the island. Then we'll track down Gasparilla."

"Oh, yes, I'm sure this won't end badly," Dante muttered.

Ximena didn't like it either. But she obeyed the admiral's orders, forcing her tired arms to pull her through the sea.

After what felt like hours—dragging an exhausted Pía along made their progress painfully slow—they'd swum halfway around the island, wading into the shallow waters of a mangrove forest.

A bolt of longing shot through Ximena's chest at the sight of the waxy green leaves and finger-like roots reaching down deep into the water. Before her parents' deaths, she and Marquesa had spent hours wading and climbing through the mangrove forests on the south side of Valuza. They were just pretending to be cazadores then; the fish that swam beneath the trees were their pirate prey. Then, when the sun had set, her parents would cook whatever tiny fish the girls had caught, showering them with praise as if they'd brought home the feast of a century. The memory made Ximena's chest ache. She usually prided herself on her ability to never dwell on the past. But in her pain and tiredness, she couldn't fight off this one moment of weakness. She missed her sister. She missed her parents. She missed her family.

"This way, cazadores," said Amador. "We have to cut through the trees to reach the island."

Warily, they followed after him, clambering through the mangroves' roots, ducking beneath the low-hanging branches. They were all too weary and grief-stricken to talk. So the only sounds were the squawks of the gulls and the gentle lapping of the sea, until Dante broke the silence with a yelp.

"What is that?" he demanded, pointing to the water.

Amador smiled. "A mangrove snake. Their venom could kill seven grown men in mere seconds."

Ximena rolled her good eye. "Mangrove snakes eat small fish and birds. They're completely harmless."

Dante had barely exhaled when Amador spoke up again.

"On second thought, that might have been a coral serpent. It's difficult to tell them apart."

Dante looked at Ximena. "Are they harmless, too?"

She shook her head. "Extremely deadly."

"Bueno," Dante drawled. "Then if it's not too late, I'd prefer to face the sharks."

"That can be arranged."

The voice didn't belong to Amador. Ximena spun to find three dinghies floating behind them, loaded with two dozen armed crew she didn't recognize. But she did recognize the crest painted on their boats: a crimson rose and a golden G.

The cazadores hadn't found Gasparilla.

It seemed Gasparilla had found them.

Dante turned on Amador. "You led us into a trap. Again."

Amador shrugged. "Honestly, how was I to know Gasparilla sends patrols to this part of the island? I'm only his first mate."

"It seems you did something right for once, Amador."

The new voice spoke again: It came from a short, bald woman dressed in brilliant yellow linen and armed with several flintlock pistols. Her lips were pierced with silver rings. She wore the usual tattoo of a rose and golden G on her left wrist, identical to Amador's.

"A handful of shipwrecked cazadores," she said. Her eyes, as green as palm leaves, surveyed them with growing satisfaction. "Qué fortuito."

"Not just any cazadores, my dear Canaria," Amador replied. "That is the great Admiral Gabriel Pérez himself, recently believed to be dead, and *that*," he tilted his head toward Dante, "is the high minister's only remaining son."

"Then this is a very special occasion indeed." La Canaria's ringed lips turned up in a smile. "We've met each other once before, admiral, many years ago. Do you remember?"

She tipped her chin up to reveal a hideous scar curving across the hollow of her throat like a crescent moon.

"Your sword was sharp," she said. "But not sharp enough."

She waved to her crew, and several arms reached down to haul the cazadores up into the dinghies. Ximena struggled against them, but two pirates pinned her down and tied her hands behind her back with thick, coarse rope. The others were swiftly restrained in the same manner.

"Where are you taking us, pirate?" the admiral growled.

"To the captain, of course."

"And what does he plan to do with us?" rasped Cecilia.

La Canaria pursed her pierced lips. "I'm not sure you want to know the answer to that, cazadora."

The pirates laughed. Huddled next to Dante, Pía began to shake.

As the dinghies steered deeper into the mangrove forest toward the island, Ximena surveyed their captors. There were at least two dozen pirates, all of them armed with pistols and rapiers. If she could somehow get hold of a weapon, she could cut her own bonds and attempt to free the others before they reached Gasparilla's hideout . . .

Beside her, Dante coughed, throwing a pointed look over his shoulder. She followed his gaze, catching a glimpse of a small silver knife between his palms. Her heartbeat stuttered again—he'd swiped a knife from one of the pirates when they'd tied him down.

By the law, she thought. Why hadn't she thought of that?

Dante only winked, and then tucked the blade out of sight. She knew what he was thinking without him speaking it aloud. They had to wait for the right moment to strike. They had to wait until they'd seen Gasparilla.

The dinghies continued to weave through the dark and grasping mangrove trees until they reached a rotting wooden dock. La Canaria leapt from the leading boat.

"This is our stop, cazadores. Blindfold them," she added to the crew before striding down the dock, her yellow clothes fluttering like feathers in the wind.

Dante's defiant smirk was the last thing Ximena saw before a pirate pulled a strip of reeking fabric over her eye, blinding her to the world. She tried to count how many steps they took but she lost track somewhere around eight hundred and fifty-two—she suspected that Gasparilla's crew might be walking in circles to confuse them.

"Where are they taking us, Cuatreda Reale?" Pía whispered from somewhere beside her. "Why haven't they killed us yet?"

"The captain likes his prisoners alive enough to scream," offered la Canaria. "Now move along. The next person to speak loses their hand at the wrist."

After traveling for several more minutes, they came to a stop, and Ximena heard la Canaria whisper something unintelligible. Then there was a groan like the creaking of a ship, a waft of sea salt and mildew, and the sunlight was suddenly extinguished. Someone stripped away the fabric from Ximena's eyes; she blinked into a darkness so complete, she couldn't see a thing.

"Welcome, cazadores, to la República de los Piratas," said la Canaria. "We are so very glad to have you with us."

The blood thundered in her ears; her heart squeezed behind her ribs. *At last.* This was it. The Republic of Pirates.

Several torches leapt to life, and Ximena Reale found herself standing in Gasparilla's hideout. Except it wasn't at all what she'd expected. It was a city made from the wreckage of sunken ships, fractured masts and hulls glued into a labyrinth of wooden tunnels. *Casualties of la Tormenta, no doubt*, Ximena thought. Hundreds of tiny apartments were built into the walls, porthole windows glowing amber with candlelight, and curious inhabitants leaned over the balconies to sneer down at the cazadores as the pirates paraded them down the central street.

"Los buitres," someone called out from above. "Scum of the seas."

When Ximena looked up to find the source, something smashed against the side of her face—an egg, runny and warm, the broken shell scraping her skin. More projectiles followed, tossed by children and adults alike, along with every insult available in the Luzan language.

Yet, for all its hideousness, there was something *alive* about this place that bothered Ximena, like an itch she couldn't reach. The whole structure groaned and creaked, swaying to its own rhythm, as if its walls were a ribcage of wood, as if the city itself had lungs and a heart. Guitars sang through open windows; a shot rang out as a rogue pistol fired; colorful strips of fabric, cut from tattered sails, swooped down over their heads; and the air was tinged with spices and metal, dangerous and sweet. Against her will, Ximena's heart began to pound as it had when she'd looked out at a distant horizon. She could feel it. The pull of the sea.

The pull of . . . *freedom*.

Dante felt it too. She could see it in his face, the longing, the hunger. It unsettled her. But the knowledge of their mutual feeling was not nearly as disconcerting as the look he gave her when he caught her staring. It was a look of shock, recognition, and, far worse, hope.

."Walk." La Canaria shoved Ximena's good shoulder, pushing her forward. "The captain doesn't like to be kept waiting."

After journeying down several long tunnels, they stopped again in front of a large, wooden wall. A dead end.

"La corte de Gasparilla," La Canaria said grandly. "Gasparilla's court. Do not speak unless you are spoken to, cazadores. ¿Me entienden?"

She didn't wait for them to answer. Instead, she rapped her knuckles once, twice, three times against the wooden wall, and then stood back with her hands on her hips, waiting.

Dante cleared his throat. "Is the wall supposed to do something?"

"Did you not hear my instructions?" la Canaria said.

"Well, you've spoken to me now. So what does the magical wall do?"

"You'll find out soon enough."

"Look, if we're going to wait in a rat-infested tunnel with pirates who haven't bathed in weeks, I'd like to know why—"

A terrible groan shook the tunnel, cutting Dante short. Then, slowly, the wall began to turn inward, giving way to an explosion of light and sound on the other side. Ximena sucked in a breath. "A hidden door."

"Your captain certainly has a talent for theatrics," Dante said.

La Canaria delivered a swift blow across the side of his face. He staggered back, spitting a mouthful of blood to the ground.

"Your name won't protect you here, boy," she said. "Test me again, and I will not be so kind."

As they stepped through the doorway, Ximena looked around in awe. Gasparilla's court was, in fact, a sunken galleon that had been hollowed out and flipped upside down. The slopped ceiling above their heads was the galleon's wooden hull, and the beam that ran from one end of the room to the other was obviously the ship's keel.

But this wasn't just any galleon, Ximena realized. Though the color was faded, she could tell that the wood was still stained with old lacquer. Black lacquer. Her stomach twisted. Gasparilla had built his hideout from a cazador ship.

At the sight of the cazadores, the pirates of Gasparilla's court let out a thundering cheer. Ximena had never seen so many pirates in one place. They were drinking rum at long wooden tables; they were playing dominoes on overturned barrels; they were leering down from the gallows that loomed large in the center of the court, fitted with several nooses. But Ximena's eye was drawn to the chair at the far end of the chamber, the one engraved with the telltale rose and golden G—the chair that was currently empty.

He isn't here. Her stomach plummeted to her boots. *Gasparilla isn't here.*

"Well, well." La Canaria leapt atop the gallows. "It seems the captain is late. Qué desafortunado."

Snickering rumbled through the hall.

"But the cazadores have come all this way, braving la Tormenta itself to see our fabled court. It would be rude of us to force them to wait for our host, would it not?"

"¡Por supuesto!" cried the pirates.

"Shall we commence with the trial, then?"

Another cheer shook the walls, a guitarist struck up a gleeful tune, and Ximena felt someone yank at her wrists, dragging her up to the gallows platform.

"Release me at once, pirate filth, or I'll—" she began, which earned her a hard slap across the face. She swallowed her own blood.

"Hospitable, aren't they?" Dante said as they shoved him under the noose beside her. "It makes dying here just a bit more bearable."

"Oh! What's this?"

La Canaria stepped behind Dante, plucking out the hidden knife, twirling it between her thumb and forefinger. At his stunned expression, she threw back her head and laughed.

"It's a good thing you're the son of the high minister because you would make a terrible pirate, querido."

"Canaria, you can't sentence me!" Amador wriggled like a worm on a hook between two burly pirates. They pushed him beneath a noose, fastening his hands behind his back. "I'm a member of Gasparilla's crew, exempt from the penalties applied to—"

"An exception has been made," said la Canaria.

"Exception? Under whose authority?"

La Canaria cocked her head and grinned. "Mine. If I'm not mistaken, Amador, the captain tasked *you* with killing the admiral the first time, a task you failed to complete. So I've taken it upon myself to rid him of your presence. I think I'd make a wonderful first mate, no?"

Amador spat at her feet. She ignored him, taking a pistol from her belt and firing a shot into the ceiling.

"Silencio in the court, if you please!" she crowed.

"What crimes are we accused of?" the admiral demanded as the pirates hauled him under a noose.

Without answering, the pirates hoisted Pía and Cecilia onto the platform, laughing at Pía's shrieks. The poor archivist thrashed and twisted, her eyes wild with terror.

"What crimes are we accused of?" Admiral Pérez boomed again. "You will answer me, pirates, if there is any conscience left in you. No one in Luza is executed without a fair trial in accordance with the law."

"What crimes?" La Canaria echoed him. "What crimes, he asks us!"

The pirates laughed again. La Canaria spread her arms wide, addressing the whole of Gasparilla's court.

"Shall we inform the cazadores of their crimes, in accordance with the law?"

A third cheer. La Canaria's answering grin was feral.

"Cazadores of Luza," she crowed. "You stand accused of murder, persecution, assault, theft, trespassing, not drinking nearly enough liquor, and being a thorn in the side of every self-respecting pirate in the empire, along with many other crimes that we have not the time nor the breath to mention. Are we all in agreement?"

The resounding cheer condemned them.

"Then I hereby pronounce their sentence: the cazadores will be hanged by the neck until they are dead."

"Last words, last words!" called a pirate who'd been playing dominoes.

La Canaria shook her head. "Overruled. Last words are always disappointing. Hang them," she instructed the pirates on the platform, who obliged her without hesitation, slipping the nooses over their heads.

"No honor among thieves, then," snarled the admiral.

"Honor? Who are you to talk of honor, admiral, while you wear that seal on your cloak?" La Canaria tipped her chin at the admiral's chest. "You've only been given the same sentence as the thousands of people you've captured and hanged. If that isn't fair, it is certainly poetic."

She waved a hand, and her crew tightened the remaining nooses around Pía and Cecilia's necks. One pirate stepped up to the lever as the guitarist played a resounding minor chord. Pía shivered, squeezing her eyes shut.

"Pía," Ximena said. "Pía, look at me."

The archivist opened one eye.

"You're going to be all right," Ximena said. "I promise."

Pía's chin trembled when she smiled.

"I trust you, Cuatreda Reale."

Beside them, Dante cleared his throat.

"Ximena, if we're really going to die, there is something I need to say."

"Not now."

"But there might not be another time."

La Canaria held three fingers above her head, and then dropped the first. "¡Tres!"

"I just need to tell you—"

"Don't," said Ximena.

"¡Dos!" la Canaria called.

Dante's dark eyes found hers. "But I—"

"¡Uno!"

As the guitarist strummed a triumphant chord, the pirate pulled the lever, and the trapdoors fell open beneath their feet.

Capítulo Dieciocho

Ximena hadn't thought very much about dying. Her mind, governed by logic as it was, couldn't conceive of what death would be like. It seemed too abstract a concept: fading into some white and terrible light, disintegrating beneath the sea, leaving the world behind. So she felt no fear as the trapdoors opened, only a slight twinge of frustration. *This is how it ends*, she thought. *Ximena Reale, hanged by pirates. I'll be the laughingstock of la academia.*

La Canaria was right, she supposed. There was something poetic about this death, even if she wasn't one to appreciate poetry. She wondered if the pirates she'd captured had been afraid before the noose snapped their necks. Or had they too been surprised, caught off guard by the sudden appearance of the inevitable?

And since when did she care what pirates felt?

Her final thoughts were for Marquesa. She prayed that her sister would forgive her for her failures. She prayed she was safe.

Then Ximena Reale waited for death as patiently as she might wait for a strong wind at the start of a voyage.

But death never came. When Ximena opened her eye, the noose was still tight around her neck, and her boots were resting on a wooden box just below the trapdoor opening. She blinked, confused, and looked around.

Laughter erupted through Gasparilla's court. La Canaria crouched down before the cazadores and grinned, her piercings glittering in the torchlight.

"Did we frighten you, cazadores?" she said. "How inhospitable of us. But you see, we don't plan on dispatching you so easily."

Six pirates leapt onto the platform, cutting them down from the nooses and closing the trapdoors. Ximena felt a sword slice through her bindings, freeing her hands. Then la Canaria dropped a handful of swords in the center of the gallows platform with a clatter.

"Let's make this interesting, shall we? One of you will be lucky enough to leave this island alive. But to win such an opportunity, you must eliminate your companions in combat. Ready?" She didn't wait for an answer. "Begin!"

The small group stared at the gleaming swords. Then they looked at one another, expressions wary. Ximena's eye flitted to Dante—if anyone was going to betray the group to save themselves, it would be him. But the boy didn't move. He simply stood, curls tumbling into his eyes, licking his cracked and bleeding lips. Perhaps he had some courage in him, after all.

But where was Amador? Ximena glanced sidelong to where the pirate should have been and found nothing except an empty noose. He'd abandoned them to die once again. Her jaw tightened. In truth, she shouldn't be surprised. It was not as if the pirate owed them any loyalty after the admiral had threatened his family.

"How noble," crowed la Canaria. "The cazadores have proven

their righteousness once again. Maybe it's time to complicate our little game."

The flick of her wrist was so quick that Ximena almost missed it. La Canaria's rapier sank into Cecilia's chest with a sound like tearing fabric. Someone shrieked—probably Pía—and the admiral moved to catch his fellow cazadora as she fell, mouth open, to the platform. Blood pooled around her, gleaming in the lantern light.

The great Cazadora Cecilia was dead.

Ximena's breath caught in her throat. It wasn't possible. Cecilia couldn't be dead—there were so many questions Ximena hadn't asked her, so many stories she'd yet to hear from the only other descendant of pirates at la academia.

Fury bubbled up like bile in her chest. The pirates would pay for this.

Ximena slid her boot under one of the rapiers on the floor, kicked it up into the air, and caught it one-handed.

"I think it's time we change the rules, pirate."

The chamber buzzed with the sound of steel as a hundred pirates unsheathed their swords. A shot rang out; Dante launched himself at la Canaria; the admiral abandoned Cecilia's corpse, grabbing a sword. But just as the battle began, a voice shouted over the cacophony.

"¡Basta! Basta, you fools, or the captain will have your heads!"

The pirates lowered their weapons, stepping aside to reveal Amador standing at the foot of Gasparilla's chair.

La Canaria threw back her head and laughed. "You're like an insect that will not die, Amador Gutiérrez."

"I have an excellent sense of self-preservation," the pirate replied. "The captain orders you to leave the cazadores alive. For now."

La Canaria bared her teeth. "And who gave you permission to speak for the captain?"

"I did."

A figure emerged from the shadows behind Gasparilla's throne—a pirate dressed in a long red coat and knee-high boots, his long hair braided down his back and gold-trimmed hat tipped down over his eyes, concealing his face. His fingers were bejeweled with half a dozen rings; his sword was a gleaming silver rapier; and around his waist he wore a leather belt fitted with a large, gold buckle, which bore the image of a rose. Ximena's rapier nearly clattered to the ground. He was here. The man she'd been hunting for four long years.

Gasparilla.

The pirate captain relaxed into his seat, one leg crossed over the other. When he spoke, his voice was barely more than a rasp.

"Would you defy my orders, Canaria?"

La Canaria sheathed her sword, the hungry light in her eyes extinguished.

"Never, captain," she answered. "I was only—"

"And yet you would kill my first mate and my prisoners." Gasparilla's rings clicked against the arms of his chair. "One might call that an act of mutiny."

"It was a joke, captain, a mere—"

The captain silenced her with a single raised finger. A chill raced down Ximena's spine. What kind of power did this man have, that he could bend people to his will without a word?

"Amador," rasped Gasparilla.

The pirate stepped forward. "Yes, sir."

"Escort the canary to her cage. She'll be tried for her actions tomorrow."

Amador's lips curled into a smile. "Yes, sir."

Two pirates grasped la Canaria by the arms. Her green eyes widened as they tugged her off the platform and into the shadows.

"Captain," she cried, her voice high and strangled. "Captain, por favor, it was a joke! I would never betray you, never!"

But Gasparilla said nothing. He didn't even turn to look as la Canaria was dragged away to her doom, his rings still clicking against the arms of his chair. When the pirates had disappeared, he turned his head slowly, mechanically, toward Amador.

"Bring the prisoners to my chambers."

"As you wish, captain."

"And Amador?"

"Yes?"

"Well done. You'll be rewarded."

Amador tipped his head. "I am ever at your service, captain."

Another two pirates seized Ximena from behind, wrenching the sword from her hand. They hauled her off the platform, across the court, and through a small wooden door behind Gasparilla's throne. But before Ximena could take in her new surroundings, someone dealt a kick to the backs of her knees, leveling her.

"May the seas be with you, cazadores," the pirates sneered. "You'll need all the luck you can get."

Their laughter ricocheted off the walls as the chamber door slammed shut, leaving the group alone.

"Well, that was exciting," said Dante. "We should get ourselves hanged more often."

Glaring at him, Ximena eased herself to her feet. The chamber was dimly lit and sparsely furnished, with nothing but a desk, a chair, several candles, and a bookshelf against the far wall. Perhaps this was where Gasparilla had written his notes to la academia; perhaps he'd smiled to himself at this very desk, thinking of the chaos that would ensue. But it was not the furniture that captured Ximena's attention—it was the smell. The reeking stench of a hundred rotting roses, steaming up from the half-dead flowers strewn across the floor.

"He's slightly less terrifying than I thought he would be," Dante said. "Gasparilla, I mean."

"Then I am sorry to disappoint you, Dante de León."

Ximena flinched, instinctually reaching toward her waist for a sword that was not there.

"No need to fear me, Ximena Reale. I have no desire to kill you."

"Forgive me if I don't believe you," she replied.

A rasping laugh. "I'm not in the habit of forgiving cazadores."

Gasparilla stepped from the shadows at the other end of the chamber, hat tipped low, boots clicking against the wood. Slowly, as if he had all the time in the world, he settled into the chair and took a sip of wine from a golden goblet on the desk.

"You have established quite the kingdom for yourself, pirate," the admiral growled.

"Not a kingdom, cazador. A democracy. An island ruled by its own people, subject to their will."

"A very noble description of chaos."

"If you call freedom chaos, that is your choice," he shrugged. "My island offers a refuge to those who want no part of your empire. We're all equal here."

"So you are a philosopher as well as a pirate."

"I don't expect you to understand, cazador. To you, liberty is a threat. To me, it's as essential as breathing."

Ximena glanced at Dante, who was watching the pirate captain with a dangerous level of interest.

"Unfortunately for you, your empire has yet to meet my demands," Gasparilla continued. "But perhaps having Admiral Pérez and the high minister's son in my possession will encourage them in the right direction. So here are my terms, cazadores. I will release Cuatreda Reale and the little archivist. They will bear my message to the high minister, informing her that if she does not deliver my ransom within three days' time, her queen, her son, and her admiral will perish."

Ximena knew then there was no way to win this game. Gasparilla held all the cards: If he received the full contents of the treasury, the empire would crumble in an instant. If he killed the queen, the admiral, and Dante, the empire would also die, torn apart by pirate attacks and rebellion across the archipelago.

The pirate had outplayed them one last time.

Gasparilla rapped his ringed fingers twice against the arms of his chair, and the chamber door opened. Three pirates stepped inside with their weapons at the ready.

"Escort Cuatreda Reale and the archivist to the docks," said Gasparilla. "Amador will set sail with them with the morning tide."

But as the pirates moved to seize the candidates, the admiral said, "You might want to reconsider your terms, Gasparilla."

The pirate captain tilted his head. "And why is that, great admiral?"

"Because the armada is waiting just beyond la Tormenta, and they will destroy you so completely that no trace of the great pirate Gasparilla will be left."

Ximena glanced at him. What in the name of the law was he doing?

"That is a fool's bluff, cazador," said Gasparilla, his rasp low, dangerous. "And you are no fool."

"Neither are you. So you must know that it's not in my nature to bluff."

"Captain!"

Amador burst into the room, his brow slick with sweat.

"The cazadores!" he said. "There's a whole fleet of them just outside the Black Wall. We have two scouts to swear by it."

Pía gasped, and the admiral's eyes glittered with triumph. So they'd never been alone after all—the admiral must have sent word to la academia without telling the crew. Ximena could have danced with joy.

Meanwhile, Gasparilla sat as still as a statue. Then, slowly, he stood from his chair, finishing his wine in one last gulp.

"Ready *La Leyenda*," he said. "We'll meet the cazadores in battle."

Amador hesitated. "Captain—"

"Are you my first mate or not?" said Gasparilla.

The pirate hesitated, and then nodded, hurrying out of the chamber.

"One ship against a dozen? Slim odds, captain," said the admiral.

"My favorite kind," answered Gasparilla, though his rasp was noticeably thin. He nodded to the three pirates still waiting against the wall. "Lock them up."

Ximena glanced at Dante and then at the admiral. Only one option remained, and they knew it. So when the pirates approached, all three of them spun on their heels, kicking the legs out from under their captors and snatching their swords as they fell. Then they turned their blades on the captain at his desk.

"I believe," said Ximena, "that your odds just became significantly worse."

Gasparilla unsheathed his sword. "Then I shall endeavor to defy them."

Ximena launched herself at Gasparilla just as the chamber door banged open and pirates appeared. But Ximena didn't turn around to assess the new threat—Dante, Pía, and the admiral could handle a few drunken pirates. She'd been waiting for this moment for a long time. She was going to finish Gasparilla herself.

Her sword clashed against the pirate's with all the fierceness of a battle cry. The captain parried, shoving her off as he stepped around the desk. They matched each other blow for blow; Ximena had never fought so hard to stay on the offensive. In fact, she'd never fought a pirate with such impeccable technique, such natural skill.

"You fight well," the captain said. "Have you ever considered following in your parents' footsteps? Turning pirate?"

"I'd rather feed myself to the sharks," Ximena growled.

"I'm not sure I believe you."

If his observation was intended to throw her off balance, it worked. Her next slice fell an inch too far to the left, and the pirate laughed, pressed his back against the wall—and disappeared. Ximena stopped, breathing hard.

Another spinning wall.

She glanced over her shoulder. The chamber was a tangle of bodies and swords, Dante, the admiral, and Pía battling against Gasparilla's crew. Ximena knew they didn't have long before the sheer number of attackers overwhelmed them. But she would have to trust them to defend themselves—she couldn't allow Gasparilla to escape.

"Go!" the admiral called out as he ran his rapier through one pirate's stomach. "Go, Ximena!"

That settled it. She took a breath and hurled herself at the wall, tumbling as it spun and dumped her on the ground of a darkened tunnel. The air was thicker here, warm and humid, reeking of rot.

Somewhere, water *drip, drip, dripped* down to the floor. There was no sign of Gasparilla.

"You say you're loathe to turn pirate. But I think you secretly crave it. The sea. The freedom."

Ximena looked around. Gasparilla's voice slipped through the blackness like a night wind. She fought the urge to shiver and stumbled to her feet, holding her rapier in front of her.

"I didn't take you for a coward, Gasparilla," she said. "Come out and face me."

"You're a deft actor. You know just what to say and when to say it. Of the law, by the law, for the law." The mockery oozed from his voice like tar. "But we both know whose blood runs in your veins. We both know what you really are."

Ximena gripped the handle of her rapier. "You don't know anything about me."

"I know much more than you think."

A flash of a red cloak. Ximena turned, slicing her sword downward—and missed. Gasparilla slipped easily past her with another rasping laugh.

"This way, little cazadora, this way."

The creaking groan of wood signaled another spinning wall. She didn't have time to guess, so she hurried toward the wall on the right, crashing through it as it rotated.

Another tunnel, darker than the last. She could hardly see her sword in front of her face now. She walked slowly, carefully, her good eye roving for a glimmer of scarlet.

"You're a daughter of the Reales." Gasparilla's voice was here, there, everywhere. "How can you slaughter your own kind in the name of the law?"

"Pirates are not my kind," she said.

"Is that Ximena speaking? Or la academia?"

"What do you care?"

"It isn't too late, you know. You aren't one of them yet. Until you wear that cloak, the choice is yours to make."

"Come out, cobarde," Ximena snapped. "Or do I frighten you so terribly?"

A red cloak—a golden buckle. Gasparilla stepped into a sliver of light that leaked through the ceiling, his rapier gleaming.

"Join me, Ximena. Serve in my crew. Live here in my republic. We can bring freedom to the people of the Luzan Empire together." Then, softer, "I have no desire to spill Reale blood."

And for the smallest of moments, Ximena hesitated. The part of her that doubted—that still thought about what Dante had said—whispered for her to accept, to leave the cazadores and the empire behind. But that longing was swiftly devoured by the iron jaws of duty, honor, and worse, fear. Because who was Ximena Reale without the cazadores and the law?

No one.

"You'll have to kill me first."

A sigh. "As you wish."

Ximena barely had time to raise her rapier before Gasparilla brought the first blow down on her head. But she regained balance quickly and pressed forward, feigning a stab at his stomach and then bringing her blade in an arc toward his head. He dodged with a swirl of his cloak; she hissed when his sword caught the side of her arm, drawing blood.

"Is that the best you can do?" she snarled.

Gasparilla answered with another blow to her side. Another slice came, and then another, until Ximena had no choice but to back up into the wall. He was too fast, too smooth, evading each of her counterattacks as if he were swatting a particularly pesky mosquito. Though she managed to block a stab heading toward her stomach, the blow that followed knocked her sword from her hand, and she found herself pinned to the wood with Gasparilla's sword at her neck.

"Farewell, Ximena Reale. Forgive me," said the pirate who did not deal in forgiveness.

In that moment, Ximena's mind ran mechanically through a dozen potential strategies and their respective outcomes. But only one seemed likely to save her life. So she saw her chance to defeat Captain Gasparilla, and she seized it without a second thought.

Gritting her teeth, she leaned backward into the wall, which spun out from underneath them, and she and the pirate dropped with a thud to the floor of another tunnel. Gasparilla's sword clattered out of his hand—Ximena caught it and pressed it to the pirate's throat, breathing hard.

Now, she thought, *let's find out who you really are.*

Wearing one of her rare grins, Ximena gripped the brim of the pirate's hat, tore it from his head—

And froze. A chill fired down her spine, and the breath left her lungs in a strangled gasp. So her good eye had failed her at last. She couldn't be seeing what she thought she was seeing. She couldn't be staring into a face she knew better than her own. A face with her mother's eyes, and her father's chin.

"Marquesa?" she choked.

Gasparilla stared back with all the boldness of a legendary pirate and grinned. "Hello, sister."

Capítulo Diecinueve

The night Ximena betrayed her parents to the cazadores, it was storming. She tried to ignore it—the roar of thunder, the crack of lightning. But all she could think about were great sea monsters in the clouds, clawing and snapping their jaws, and finally she could bear it no longer.

"¡Mamá!" she screamed. "¡Mamá, Mamá!"

For a moment, there was nothing but silence, and Ximena feared that her mother hadn't heard her. But candlelight soon bathed the hallway, and Alejandra Reale appeared at the bedroom door.

"This storm is a rough one, no? I expect all of Valuza is awake tonight."

She moved to the side of Ximena's bed, taking her in her arms. Ximena curled into her mother's chest, breathing hard, flinching with each crack of thunder. She knew she was too old to be acting this way, but she was too frightened to care. Usually, she had to fight her fear of storms alone— her parents sailed with the armada half the year, and though they were supposed to spend the other half at home with their family, lately they had been absent more often than they were here. Papá said it was because they were investing in some new merchant venture. Whatever the reason, it made Ximena treasure every moment she spent in her mother's arms.

Alejandra's laugh was like the rocking of a ship, gentle and familiar. "Are you going to hide all night, mija?"

Ximena nodded. Alejandra laughed again.

"Look at me," she said.

Ximena felt a hand under her chin, coaxing her face upward. Trembling, she blinked into her mother's face, studying her slightly crooked nose, her broad jaw, her weathered skin, and her eyes, which were soft and green as seaweed. Alejandra reminded Ximena of a ship's mast—steady and firm, bending but never breaking in the wind.

"There we are," her mother said. "My brave girl. Shall I tell you a story, like I did when you were small?"

"Don't start without me!"

Marquesa swung into the room at her usual breakneck speed, wild curls flying behind her, and flung herself onto the bed.

"Ven, Ximena," she said, tugging on her sister's hand. Her smile was almost as wicked as the glint in her eye. "We can act it out while Mamá tells it."

This was the sisters' favorite game. When they weren't swapping secrets or practicing in the courtyard with their swords, they spent every free hour they had creating elaborate theatrical productions out of their mother's stories. Between Ximena's precision and Marquesa's flair for the dramatic, they made the perfect team. At least that's what Papá said when they forced him to watch their shows.

"Fine," Ximena said to her sister. "As long as you play the villain this time. I'm tired of being the evil pirate and horrible king."

"But you're so good at it! And we both know you'd make a terrible damsel in distress."

"I might be better at it if you would ever let me try—"

"How about I tell you a story with no villain or damsels at all?" Alejandra cut in.

The sisters turned their heads as one. It wasn't often that their mother told a tale they'd never heard before.

"What kind of story would that be?" Ximena asked.

"Would you like to find out?"

Glancing at each other, they nodded. Alejandra settled back into the bed pillows with a contented sigh.

"Well then," she said. "Our story begins on a night like this one, in a cantina full of sailors just arrived from the sea. A young, foolish man—we shall call him Lorenzo—was bragging to all who would listen about the day he'd bested a cazador in a duel. The cazador had challenged him, he said, and he'd responded in kind, defeating him so thoroughly that the pirate hunter had begged for mercy. As he told the story, the cantina's patrons clapped and cheered, praising the young man and his bravery. 'May the seas be full of Lorenzos!' they said, raising a toast.

"I like this already," said Marquesa, leaping from the bed. She snatched up the wooden practice swords from the corner of the room and tossed one to Ximena. "You play Lorenzo. I'll be the cazador."

Before Ximena could argue, her mother continued, "Of course, they didn't know that the very same cazador who Lorenzo claimed to have bested was also in the cantina that night. When the young man had finished his boasting, the pirate hunter stood from his table in the shadows, crossing the floor with long even steps."

Marquesa mirrored the movement, sword outstretched before her, chin tipped high, as Alejandra spoke the dialogue:

"'We remember that story very differently, hermano,' the cazador said in a voice like sharpened steel."

"The cantina fell silent as all eyes turned to the very pale and terrified Lorenzo.

"'Who are you?' the young man said.

"'I am the captain you claim to have killed,' the cazador answered. 'And I challenge you to a duel.'

"Though his hands trembled at his sides, Lorenzo had no choice. So he said: 'I accept your challenge. We will meet here in a fortnight.' The cazador bowed his head in acknowledgment and left the cantina without another word.

"That night, the young man stumbled home in a rage and told his family about the scheduled duel. His mother swooned; his father sobbed with fear. But Lorenzo also had a sister, and she was as brave as she was beautiful."

"Oh, never mind," Marquesa interrupted. "You can be the cazador, Ximena, and I'll play the sister."

"Every time," Ximena muttered.

"She'd trained for many years in the art of combat," Alejandra went on, "becoming the greatest swordswoman in Valuza. So, when she heard of her brother's plight, she decided she would disguise herself and take his place in the duel against the pirate.

"The fortnight was up soon, and Lorenzo's time was up. While the family was still kissing their son goodbye, the young woman donned her brother's cloak and headed for the cantina, where she found the cazador waiting with a sizable crowd behind him.

"'Let us see if you can kill me twice, hermano,' the pirate said.

"The girl couldn't reply without revealing her true identity. So she bowed her head, drew her sword, and the duel began. Everyone who watched it gasped in amazement—they'd never seen such skill, such grace. It was as if the combatants were dancing rather than dueling to the death."

"On guard, cazadora!" Marquesa cried, launching herself at Ximena with her wooden blade at the ready. Their father had taught them well in the art of swordsmanship. They exchanged blows until sweat beaded on their brows; they were as serious as they would be with real weapons.

Meanwhile, Alejandra narrated over them. "The fight was a long one; the girl had never faced a better match. But when her patience had run out, she disarmed her opponent with a twist of her wrist, and the cazador stood in shock as his sword sailed into the crowd."

Reluctantly, Ximena allowed Marquesa to disarm her. Her older sister gave a shout of triumph when the sword clattered to the floor. Thunder rolled again—but Ximena hardly noticed it. She wasn't half as afraid of storms when her sister was near.

Alejandra continued the story over the noise.

"'Do you have any last requests before I kill you?' the young woman asked, lowering her voice to disguise her identity.

"The cazador nodded. 'Take off your hood,' he said, 'so I may look on the face of the man who has bested me before I die.'

"She knew she could not refuse, so she pulled back her hood, revealing herself to be Lorenzo's sister.

"When the cazador realized the boy he'd been fighting was a woman, he knew what he must do. He fell to one knee, held out his hand, and asked the girl to marry him."

Marquesa dropped to one knee; Ximena could hardly stop herself from gagging as she took her sister's hand. They waited for their mother to finish the tale. But she didn't. Alejandra was strangely silent, gazing out the window into the black night.

"So? Did the girl say yes?" Marquesa asked.

"She did," Alejandra said, turning back to them. "And they sailed the seas together for the rest of their days."

Ximena frowned. "I don't think she should have said yes."

"And why is that, mi vida?"

"Because she was a better fighter than he was. What did she need to marry him for?"

"Sometimes we need people in ways we don't expect," her mother said. "Now, why don't we go downstairs and make some hot chocolate?"

Nodding, Ximena and Marquesa followed her down the stairs to the kitchen. The ceramic tiles were cold against Ximena's bare feet, but her mother's skin was warm. Each time lightning struck, or thunder rolled, Alejandra took Ximena's hand and squeezed her fingers to remind her she was still there.

"Here we are," Alejandra said when they arrived at the kitchens. "Cook is asleep, so we have the stove to ourselves. Get your mugs and have a seat."

"I'll get extra candles," Marquesa declared before scampering out of the room.

Ximena padded over to the cabinet beneath the window, where the glasses were stored. She grabbed her favorite red mug and sat on the stool by the counter, watching as her mother poured the milk and chocolate into a pot and stirred it, the steam glazing her face.

"Do I smell chocolate?"

Ximena turned to find her father leaning against the doorframe, his arms crossed over his chest and his expression decidedly grim. Diego Reale was a tall man with a sailor's lean build and long, curly hair that he tied at the base of his neck. He was missing his pinky finger on his right hand, and a scar sliced through his left eyebrow—from a cantina fight or a pirate's sword or a shark, depending on what kind of mood he was in.

"No one told me your mother was making chocolate," he said.

"Because if we told you, you would drink it all," said Alejandra over her shoulder.

"You wound me, amor," said Diego, his frown slipping into a crooked grin. "I would only drink most of it. What are we celebrating this evening?"

"Your daughter's bravery."

"Ah," said Diego. "That is worth celebrating, since my daughter is the bravest girl in all of Luza."

He kissed the top of Ximena's head, his beard scratching her skin, and she smiled back at him. The bravest girl in all of Luza. Her Papá had been telling her so since she could walk. But somehow, she couldn't quite force herself to believe it.

"Grab your father a mug, mija," said Alejandra. "The smallest one you can find."

Ximena hopped off her stool to get another mug from the cabinet. When she returned, her mother poured the steaming chocolate into the cups, and then dropped a block of cold cheese into each one. Ximena, as always, sipped too early—she yelped when the liquid scorched her tongue.

"Patience makes a man richer than gold," said her mother.

"But it isn't nearly as fun," said Diego.

Alejandra smacked him over the head; he grinned at Ximena and winked.

"¿Mamá? ¿Papá?"

Marquesa stood in the doorway, candles in her hands. Ximena almost didn't recognize her. She looked so much older than she had just a moment ago, her wild smile dampened and her eyes dark with a knowing that made Ximena's blood run cold.

"There's someone at the door," Marquesa said.

Their parents exchanged a glance.

"I'll be right back," said Diego, his tone suddenly serious. He kissed Alejandra's cheek and strode from the room toward the front hallway.

"Come and sit, Marquesa," said their mother. "I'll make you a cup . . ."

Ximena couldn't hear what Alejandra said next. This happened more and more frequently now: she would catch her parents and Marquesa chattering together in furtive whispers when they thought no one was watching, and when Ximena asked what they were talking about, they told her that she would learn, someday, when she was older.

Well, Ximena didn't want to wait until she was older. So when Alejandra turned back toward the stove, she slipped off her stool, tiptoeing after her father.

She found him by the front door, talking softly with a burly man who was missing a hand. Though it was dark, she recognized the sailor as the Reales' first mate, Lionel.

"We need you at the docks," Lionel was saying.

"It's the middle of the night, Lionel."

"I realize that, captain, and I wouldn't have come if it weren't urgent—"

"Where is the rest of the crew?"

Lionel hesitated. "Off duty, captain."

"In the cantina, you mean."

"Yes, captain. But there's someone at the docks who has requested to speak with you and the señora."

"It can wait until tomorrow—"

"It's a pirate, captain."

Thunder rolled overhead, shaking the walls.

"Give me a half hour. We'll meet you at the docks."

Lionel bowed his head. "Muchas gracias, capitán."

The first mate exited the house, leaving her father alone in the darkness of the hallway. A rumbling sigh escaped Diego Reale's chest; he rubbed his beard, the muscles in his jaw flexing. Ximena had never seen her father look so tired. It distracted her enough that when her father turned, she didn't try to hide. She simply stared at him, biting her lip.

"If you're going to spy," her father said, his voice rough, "you must not get caught."

"Where are you going, Papá?"

"Just to the docks, amor," he said. "But only for a little while. Send for your mother, will you? We must leave before the hour is out."

"But—"

"No questions, mija." Her father very rarely snapped at her, so when he did, it stunned her to silence. "Please."

Ximena nodded and hurried back to the kitchen to fetch her mother. Alejandra followed her to the front door, accepting the coat Diego held out to her and sliding her feet into old leather boots. Marquesa watched with tired eyes, still holding her cup of chocolate.

"Go back to sleep now, my loves," she said, kissing the top of Ximena's head. "We'll be home by dawn. Don't tell anyone else where we've gone, all right?"

"Marquesa," said Diego, "if anything happens, my rapier is beside my bed. Understand?"

"Yes, Papá," said Marquesa.

"Good. And save me some chocolate, no?"

The Reale sisters nodded. Diego opened the door, and Alejandra smiled over her shoulder as they stepped out into the rain—that smile burned itself in Ximena's memory, never to be erased.

The silence was broken by Marquesa's yawn. "I'm going back to bed," she said. "Are you coming?"

"In a minute," Ximena said. She didn't want to tell her sister that she was still too frightened to sleep with the storm howling outside.

But of course Marquesa always observed more than she expected. "If you're scared," she said, "I can stay awake, and we can play draughts."

Ximena was tempted to take her sister up on the offer, until she saw the way Marquesa's eyelids drooped. Her cheeks burned. Her fear had already kept her sister up too late tonight.

"Está bien," Ximena said. "I'm fine. Really."

Marquesa eyed her for a moment. But she must have decided it was better not to push the issue, because she pressed a kiss to Ximena's forehead, whispering, "Buenas noches, hermana," and padded back up the stairs.

Ximena returned to the kitchen and sat on her stool, holding her mug between her palms. The bravest girl in all of Luza. She repeated Diego's words under her breath as another lightning bolt flashed in the distance. The clock chimed eleven, and then midnight. Thunder rattled the walls—she flinched, and then scowled at herself. It didn't matter what her father called her. She was still here, cowering in the kitchen like a child.

She put her mug down, pushing it away. She was Ximena Reale. The daughter of Alejandra and Diego Reale. She was no coward. So she stood up, and strode back toward the stairs, head held high. She'd go back to sleep, and she would shut out the noise of the wind and rain. Then, in the morning, when her parents returned home, they would smile and praise her for her courage.

Which is exactly what would have happened if the cazadores had not broken into the house.

She was walking up the stairs when they burst through the front door, rapiers drawn, black cloaks dripping water. There were ten in total, all of them tall and dark and menacing—the emblem of the Luzan sun gleamed on their chests. The tallest of them, a young man who looked vaguely familiar, stared down at Ximena and frowned. She stared back, barely breathing, unable to move.

"Search the house. I want them alive."

"Yes, sir," answered the cazadores, striding off in groups of two.

Before Ximena could run or cry out, the young cazador had her by the arm and was kneeling down before her.

"You're the Reales' daughter?" he said.

She nodded, not knowing what else to do.

"What is your name?"

"Ximena," she squeaked.

The cazador suddenly smiled—he didn't look nearly as frightening when he smiled. In fact, Marquesa would have called him handsome, with his sharp jaw and strong teeth.

"Ximena," he repeated. "I have a cousin by that name. And where are your parents, Ximena?"

"I—I can't tell you that."

"I'm afraid you must. We need to speak with them."

For all twelve years of her short life, Ximena had been taught to respect and fear the cazadores. She'd learned two centuries of academia history at school; she'd spent hours studying the design of armada galleons. She'd proudly watched her parents receive medals for valor and courage from el ministerio, waiting for the day when she could become the next Reale to enter la academia.

But as much as she adored the cazadores, her mother had also given her a direct order: don't tell anyone where we've gone. What if her parents were in the middle of a secret plot to catch a pirate? Ximena wouldn't be the reason her parents' mission failed. So while part of her wanted to answer this handsome cazador, the other part recoiled at his touch, and she pulled away, backing slowly up the stairs.

"Lo siento," she said. "No puedo."

"Do you know who your parents are, Ximena?"

She stared at him, confused. Everyone in Valuza knew who her parents were.

"Alejandra and Diego Reale, cazadores of Luza."

"Not cazadores anymore," said the man. "Pirates."

Now she laughed, high and nervous. "Señor, I think you must be mistaken."

But the cazador's eyes gleamed with a certainty that did not waver. "I'm not mistaken, Ximena. Your parents are Alejandra and Diego Reale, traitors against the empire."

"No es posible—"

"I swear by the law itself. Your parents have been engaging in pirate activities while on leave from their service in the armada."

"No. My parents have spent their entire lives fighting pirates. They're the most honorable cazadores sailing the archipelago."

"If you're right, then they have nothing to fear from me," the cazador replied. "Either way, Ximena, it's your duty as a future cazadora to tell me where your parents are."

"Capitán!"

The cazador looked up. Several of his men stood at the top of the stairs—one of them held her father's sword, and the other held Marquesa, who was struggling desperately to free herself.

"There is no one in the house except the girls and an old cook. No sign of the Reales."

The cazador swore under his breath. Then he turned his attention back to Ximena, his lips tilting once again into a smile.

"You want to do right by the law, Ximena. I can see it in your eyes," he said. "Tell me where your parents went."

"Run, Ximena!" Marquesa cried. "Get Mamá and Papá!"

Ximena glanced up at the door. If she pulled her hand from the cazador's grip, she could escape and find her parents at the docks. But what if he was right? What if her parents really were pirates, traitors against the empire? An image sprung to her mind, her father and mother, grinning wildly and clutching bloody swords. She squeezed her eyes shut. She told herself that she didn't believe it, that the cazador had been sent here to tempt her into betraying her parents. But his terms weren't unreasonable. Her parents had nothing to fear from the law if they were truly innocent. And the cazador's eyes were so kind, his voice so gentle.

So when she opened her mouth again, she said:

"You won't hurt them?"

"I give you my word that your Mamá and Papá will be dealt with fairly and in accordance with the law," said the handsome cazador. He took her trembling hands in his. "Now tell me. Where are your parents?"

"¡No les digas nada!" cried Marquesa. "Please, hermana, you don't understand, it's not what you—"

A cazador covered her mouth with his gloved hand, silencing her.

Ximena swallowed. "At the docks. They left a few hours ago."

"Gracias, Ximena. You are the bravest girl in all of Luza."

The cazador didn't notice when Ximena flinched. Instead, he stood and sheathed his rapier, dark eyes alight.

"Head to the docks and arrest the Reales. Don't harm them if at all possible."

"As you command," said the cazadores.

The man holding Marquesa stepped forward. "¿Y las niñas? What should we do with them?"

A new voice interrupted before he could answer.

"I'm impressed, Cazador Gabriel. You've certainly lived up to your reputation."

Cazador Gabriel Pérez bowed as a woman stepped into the house, her black cloak dripping rain. She was around Alejandra's age. The gray streaks in her hair couldn't dull the severity of her beauty. Ximena recognized her before the cazador even spoke her name.

"Minister de León," he said. "We've located the Reales and plan to arrest them forthwith."

The woman's lips turned up just slightly. "Well done. The Reales always were a plague on this empire. Now we can finally be cured of them."

She surveyed the hallway like a commander over a battlefield, victory in her eyes. Her eyes fell briefly on Ximena; her nostrils flared with disgust. "I will testify to your success myself before el ministerio. And who knows? When they name me high minister, I might just consider you for admiral of la academia."

He bowed again. "It would be an honor, Minister de León."

"You can dispose of the girls," Elena added. Her nose crinkled in disgust. "The empire has no further use for them."

Cazador Gabriel looked first at Ximena and then at Marquesa. His expression was inscrutable as he studied them with his shark-like eyes.

"I'd like to grant them my remaining casos especiales," he said suddenly.

"I beg your pardon?"

The cazador turned his gaze on the black-cloaked woman. "There can be no greater testament to the power of the law than transforming its worst enemies into its most loyal defenders," he said carefully. "I don't think we should underestimate the power of such a conversion, Minister de León."

To Ximena, the words meant nothing. But Elena must have understood because her expression turned black as the storm outside. "I hardly think—"

"Take them to la academia," Cazador Gabriel said. "Ensure they are well treated."

Two cazadores stepped forward to carry out their captain's orders. But a third cazador appeared from the next room, stopping them; he was holding Diego's sword.

"It belongs to the Reales, sir. Shall I confiscate it?"

Cazador Gabriel turned the blade over in his hands, inspecting it.

"I think," he finally said, "that this belongs to you."

He handed the rapier to Marquesa. She accepted it, tears streaming down her cheeks, just before the cazadores dragged them out into the street. Ximena went quietly and without argument; she didn't say a word as they walked through Valuza's barrios. But Marquesa kicked and screamed, shouting for Alejandra and Diego, for Lionel the first mate, and even for their cook.

Somewhere in the chaos of wind and rain, Marquesa's eyes locked on Ximena's. They were wide and wild, like a sea creature after it has been harpooned from behind. Now, all these years later, Ximena understood.

Those eyes never forgot.

And they never forgave.

Capítulo Veinte

It was their father's sword that Ximena now held to her sister's neck. Marquesa must have kept it all these years, without her knowledge.

"How—why—"

The questions clotted in Ximena's throat. She didn't understand. Her sister couldn't be Gasparilla. Marquesa had been a student at la academia for the last four years. A poor student, yes, but a student, nonetheless. There was no way she could have run away to pillage and plunder the archipelago while no one was looking.

Was there?

And how had Marquesa escaped la academia's prison? The labyrinth was impenetrable; no one had ever breached it. Perhaps someone had helped her from the inside? But that didn't explain how the girl had assumed the name of a legendary pirate, established a republic, and ransacked the capital itself.

Quiet, timid, easily persuaded Marquesa.

Ximena's mind reeled like an unanchored ship. None of it made any sense. How had she not seen this coming? How had she missed her own sister turning pirate?

"Are you going to kill me, Ximena?" The rasp had fallen away from Marquesa's voice, and her tone was as hard and cold as steel. "It would be easier if you did. You'd be hailed a hero, I'm sure, and you wouldn't have to suffer the humiliation of having another pirate in the family."

Heart pounding, Ximena knew her sister was right. It would be easier to simply kill Marquesa and tell the cazadores that Gasparilla had perished during their duel in the tunnels. She had killed many pirates before—what was one more?

But this was not just any pirate.

This was Marquesa.

"No," Ximena whispered.

She stood up, keeping the point of their father's rapier at Marquesa's throat. Though she tried to hide it, her arm shook so badly she almost lost her grip on the handle.

"Then what *are* you going to do, hermana?" asked Marquesa. "Arrest me? Or perhaps you're going to let me escape and redeem yourself after betraying our parents so long ago." Marquesa studied her sister's face, hazel eyes narrowed. Their mother's eyes. "Perhaps my little sister has a heart after all."

"How could you do this?" Ximena said. She hated how small she sounded, like a child raging at the unfairness of the world. "After everything we lost, after everything I sacrificed?"

"I could ask you the same question," Marquesa replied. "How can you continue to hunt our people? To kill for an empire that only wants power and silver?"

"Says the pirate who lives for just that."

"So you despise me." There was no anger in Marquesa's voice.

Only the disappointment that comes with something long expected. "Then make your choice, hermana. Who are you willing to die for?"

Ximena weighed her options. She could allow Marquesa to escape. She could claim that Gasparilla had bested her in a fight and disappeared into the tunnels, never to be seen again. No one would blame her, since the pirate had managed to evade capture for so many years and had escaped from great cazadores before. No one would ever discover the truth.

But Ximena would know. It would haunt her each time she closed her eyes, the knowledge that she had betrayed the empire and the law she held so dear. It would eat her alive, like a parasite, consuming her thoughts and dreams until it drove her mad. Though she might sail away, become a cazadora, and wear the emblem of the Luzan sun on her chest, part of her would remain here, in this darkness, with her sister's eyes daring her toward mercy. And she would despise herself for her weakness.

"Captain Gasparilla, otherwise known as Marquesa Reale," said Ximena, "I charge you with piracy and treason against the Empire of Luza. You will be arrested and brought to la Academia de los Cazadores, where you will be imprisoned until you can be tried by el ministerio and sentenced accordingly."

At first, Marquesa didn't react. Then she nodded, her frown so like their father's that Ximena's stomach wrenched. "So be it."

"Captain!"

Amador stepped through a spinning wall. A dozen pirates waited at his heels, weapons drawn, holding a bedraggled Dante, Pía, and admiral between them.

"Cuatreda Reale, you're alive!" Pía cried.

"Have I gone blind," said Dante, "or is that your sister?"

She didn't answer him. Instead, she wrenched Marquesa to her feet, still holding the rapier blade to her sister's throat.

"Tell your crew to release my companions and escort us through la Tormenta in *La Leyenda*," she growled in Marquesa's ear. "Now."

Marquesa said nothing, her jaw set in defiance.

"Now," Ximena snapped. "Or on our parents' graves, I will kill you."

"Ready *La Leyenda*, Amador," Marquesa said. "Take us to the armada."

"And release the queen," Ximena added.

Marquesa snarled, and through gritted teeth, said, "And release the queen."

Amador glanced between them, hesitating. "But captain—"

"Fathoms below, Amador, don't make me repeat it," Marquesa snapped. "Do as my sister says."

Amador muttered something to two members of his crew, who vanished into the darkness. When they returned, they were dragging someone between them, a small, almost childlike woman so bruised and covered in dirt that Ximena didn't recognize her until she lifted her head. Any Luzan would have known those features— they were stamped on the back of every silver coin, the curved nose, regal forehead, and disapproving lips.

"Your majesty," she breathed.

In response, Queen Dulcinea of Luza gave a wheezing cough. Weeks in a pirate prison had clearly taken their toll.

"Cazadores," she whispered. "What in the name of the law took you so long?"

Before the hour was out, they were on board *La Leyenda*, floating in front of the towering clouds of la Tormenta. Amador manned the helm while Ximena stood beside him, keeping Marquesa pinned in her grasp.

"Well?" Ximena demanded. "Take us through the storm, pirate."

Amador glanced one last time at Marquesa, who nodded without a word. So her first mate pulled a black chip of coal from his pocket, bent down to the deck, and drew a lidless eye surrounded by a circle. Then he gave the order to steer *La Leyenda* forward, straight into the storm's fury.

Ximena braced herself for the howling winds and roaring seas that had destroyed the *Pérez*, but they never came. Gasparilla's ship passed through the storm as smoothly as a sword through sand, black clouds raging on all sides but never touching them. At Ximena's confused frown, Amador sniffed.

"El ojo del huracán," he said. "An old charm from el idioma prohibido."

The forbidden language of magic. Ximena's stomach lurched. She'd just inadvertently broken the law by allowing the pirates to use el idioma under her watch. But it was too late now. Amador was already wiping the symbol away, sneering at her obvious discomfort.

At last, the black clouds gave way to a flaming sunset, and the armada came into view. Ximena had never been so grateful to see the Luzan crest in her life.

"Run up the white flag," she said.

Marquesa shrugged. "We don't have a white flag."

Scowling, Ximena tore a strip from the bottom of her own shirt, handing it to Amador.

"Run it up," she said. "Or it's you we'll hoist up the mast."

"You sound more like a pirate every day," said Amador, but he did as she said, giving the fabric to one of his crew who raised it like a proper standard.

At the sight of the flag, a great cheer erupted through the cazador fleet. Gunshots rang out, cannons fired.

"Te lo dije, Ximena."

The admiral joined her at the rail. Clearly he'd decided to forget about their argument on la Isla Rosa now that she'd captured Gasparilla—his dark eyes glowed with pride.

"A great cazador turns doubt into belief," he continued. "I knew you were strong enough to do what needed to be done."

Only then did it occur to her that her quest was over. She'd captured the infamous Captain Gasparilla, just as she'd always dreamed of doing. The high minister would have no choice but to name her a cazadora now. After all, this was nothing short of the greatest victory in la academia's history.

So why didn't it feel like one?

The cazadores wasted no time in surrounding *La Leyenda*, sliding several wooden boarding ramps across the sea so Ximena and the others could climb across with their pirate prisoners in tow. They arrived on la academia's *Santiago* to the deafening roar of applause. But the moment the cazadores saw the queen, they fell abruptly silent, dropping to their knees.

"Your majesty," they said.

"Oh, please, there's no need for all that," the queen said, waving them up. If she knew how ridiculous she looked standing on the deck of a ship in a shredded, dirty ballgown, she didn't give it away. She lifted her small chin proudly. "Admiral Pérez?"

The admiral stepped forward. "Yes, your majesty."

"I assume you are responsible for my rescue. You have my thanks, although you were miserably slow."

"Actually, your majesty, that honor belongs to Cuatreda Reale. She captured Gasparilla almost singlehandedly."

"Really?" The queen looked Ximena up and down. Her expression was vaguely curious, like a bird that has just noticed a potentially interesting insect. "Well then. I shall have to relay that information to the high minister. Cuatreda Reale," she added, addressing the crew, "has successfully captured the most notorious pirate in the archipelago and saved our empire from almost certain doom. She will be honored in kind in the name of the law."

"In the name of the law," the cazadores called back.

"Now, I'm sure you're all as thoroughly exhausted as I am, so why don't we skip the rest of the formalities and weigh anchor, or whatever you sailors like to say."

The admiral saluted. "As you command, your majesty. Candidates, you may go belowdecks."

Ximena started. She couldn't rest now. She had to talk to her sister, interrogate Amador, find out the truth of how Marquesa had become Gasparilla—

The admiral pressed a hand to her good shoulder. "Cuidado, Cuatreda Reale. If you speak to Marquesa before the trial, people will talk. Your bid for cazadora will be tainted by association," he said under his breath. "I suggest you go below and rest while you can."

She hadn't thought of that—in the rush of adrenaline and shock, she hadn't been thinking at all. But the admiral was right. Even with the queen's vote of favor on her side, the high minister would still be looking for reasons to deny Ximena her cloak, so it wouldn't be wise to give her any. She nodded and muttered a quiet, "Yes, sir," following Dante and Pía belowdecks.

"I can't believe this, Cuatreda Reale. Your own sister!" Pía whispered. "How do you think she did it? I suppose she could have snuck out of la academia like Dante used to do. No offense, Cuatreda de León . . .

Ximena could feel Dante watching her as the archivist rambled on. She knew he probably had many things to say, none of which she wanted to hear. So before he could tease her or ask any questions, Ximena locked herself in the closest cabin and flopped back onto the bunk. She wasn't ready to talk to anyone about Marquesa, let alone Dante de León.

The journey back to la academia seemed to take twice as long as the voyage there. The admiral continued to refuse Ximena's requests to talk to Marquesa before the trial, and Ximena couldn't sleep, eat, drink, or think while her sister was in the brig just below her feet. So the minutes seemed like hours, and the days felt like weeks.

In reality, it was just over a fortnight before the *Santiago* pulled into la academia's docks, welcomed by the cheers of a hundred candidates. When Ximena disembarked, they watched her with a mixture of awe and suspicion: the admiral had sent word about Gasparilla's capture, along with the pirate's true identity. She knew some people would assume she had helped her sister just as her parents had helped pirate captains before they were caught.

In fact, Ximena had hardly stepped onshore before someone spat at her feet.

"Pirate lover." It was Juan Carlos Alonso, his teeth bared in a snarl. "Tell me, Cuatreda Reale, did you give your sister the keys to Valuza yourself? Or did you just cheer her on while she burned our island to the ground?"

"I'd watch your tongue if I were you." Dante stepped between them, dark eyes blazing. "You're addressing a hero of the empire."

Ximena rallied her usual stoicism and looked the offending candidate in the eye.

"Buenos días, Cuatreda Alonso," she said. "I assume I may still call you cuatreda, since you aren't wearing a Cazador Cloak. Were you not nominated for the Royal Examination while I was away? A pity. Maybe next year."

Then she strode past him without looking back. Nothing she did would ever be good enough for people like Juan Carlos Alonso. She'd always be Ximena Reale, daughter of pirates.

And now sister to Gasparilla.

The thought made her face burn with shame.

When they reached the end of the dock, Pía turned to Ximena and saluted. "It has been an honor to sail with you, Cuatreda Reale. A true honor. In fact, it might be the greatest accomplishment of my life. The other archivists will never believe me, you know, when I tell them the stories—"

"Our relationship is at an end."

Pía blinked. "What?"

Ximena pulled herself to her full height. She was on track to become a cazadora now. She needed an archivist at her side who wouldn't be questioned, who wasn't quite so . . . strange. After all, people already thought her blood was tainted by piracy. She couldn't afford to associate herself with another outcast. So whatever friendship she and Pía had shared while at sea was dead. The girl must learn to accept it, or she'd cause Ximena more trouble than she was worth.

"You have served the empire well, but the mission to capture Gasparilla is complete. Therefore, our relationship is at an end, Archivist Sánchez," she said. "You may return to the Maritime Archives."

Pía blanched. "But—but we're a team, Cuatreda Reale. We've talked about it for years. Catching pirates in the name of the law. Together."

"I made no promises to that effect, archivist. Now if you'll excuse me, I must return to my dormitory before the victory celebrations tonight."

Ximena almost lost her nerve at the look in Pia's eyes: the girl seemed so suddenly, painfully lost, as if she'd been marooned on an island and left to die.

Pía's tears fell down her cheeks. "Yes. Right, por supuesto. No promises were made. You know, my father is always telling me that I jump to conclusions. Foolish Pía. I've done it again, haven't I? Well then. May the seas be with you, Cuatreda Reale, Cuatreda de León."

"And with you, Pía," Dante said quietly, empathy in his voice.

The archivist bowed. With one last glance over her shoulder, eyes swollen with tears, she shuffled toward la academia, disappearing through the south gate.

"Your kindness is astounding, Cuatreda Reale," Dante said darkly.

"I didn't ask for your opinion, Cuatreda de León," Ximena replied. "Farewell. I'll see you at the celebrations tonight."

The admiral had ordered la academia to prepare the festivities for their arrival: A feast in the evening and a parade the next morning. All to celebrate the capture of Gasparilla.

Her sister.

Ximena struggled to hide her nausea as she crossed la academia's courtyard and entered the cuatreda wing. She told herself she was grateful to be home, that she'd never felt more at peace than she did when she was within these limestone walls. But when she reached her dormitory, she threw up in the wash bin, twice.

By the law, Ximena. You've fought dozens of pirates before. You'll kill more before you die. Pull yourself together.

She straightened her uniform, eye patch, and cuatreda pins, and slicked down her hair with whale oil. By the time she stepped out into the hallway again, her hands were no longer trembling, and her boots clicked against the stone with the determined precision of a loaded cannon. She had worked for this moment for four years. She wasn't going to let anything take it away from her.

That evening, the inhabitants of la academia gathered in the central courtyard, where several long feasting tables had been set up on the grass. A guitarist played Luza's anthem as the cazadores and candidates laughed, talked, and ate—the admiral would usually frown on such extravagance, but the capture of Gasparilla was apparently worth the lapse in decorum. Ximena had been placed at the high table, which would have been a privilege if it didn't mean having to sit next to Dante all night.

"Are you enjoying the feast, capitana?"

"Yes," she said.

"The food is excellent, no?"

"Yes."

"Especially the roast. Perfectly seasoned."

"Yes."

"I'm not sure you're entitled to an opinion, capitana. You haven't touched a thing on your plate."

Ximena's jaw clenched. "I'm not hungry."

"After a fortnight of sailing with nothing but pork rinds and hardtack?"

She didn't answer him. When he fell silent, she thought he might have grown bored enough to bother someone else. But then she heard him shift in his seat and felt his breath against her ear.

"It's not too late, you know."

She tried to ignore him. She tried to imagine that he was a fly buzzing by her ear, to focus her attention on the feast. But somehow, she still found herself asking, "Too late for what?"

"To save Marquesa."

His words hit her like a block of lead.

"I'll pretend, for both our sakes, that I didn't hear that, Cuatreda de León," she said.

"So we're back to titles. Well then, Cuatreda Reale, you have two more days before your sister is hanged in this very courtyard. If you put that brilliant mind of yours to work, you might be able to concoct some way to change her fate—with my help, of course."

She gripped the arms of her chair. "Once again, you're suggesting treason."

"I'm suggesting sense," Dante returned. "If you don't wish to see it that's your choice."

Ximena stood up. "Excuse me, Admiral Pérez," she said. "May I have your permission to return to the dormitories?"

The admiral's brow furrowed. "Granted. But Cuatreda Reale—"

"Thank you, sir," she said. She saluted him and turned on her heel, hurrying away from the courtyard as fast as she could manage with any degree of dignity. She'd just reached the door to her dormitory when she heard a second pair of footsteps behind her.

"I don't wish to speak to you," she said over her shoulder.

"You can't run away from this, Ximena."

She bristled. Who was Dante de León to lecture her on running away, when he'd spent the majority of his life trying to escape responsibility?

"You can save your sister's life, or you can watch the law destroy the only family you have left," he said, striding up to her. "But you can't just bury yourself in your room and make this disappear."

"Leave me be," she snapped, fumbling with her key. Her fingers were shaking again, and though she hoped Dante wouldn't notice, she knew he already had.

"You called me a coward that night on the *Flora*. And you know what? I've heard those words in my head every night since, because you were right. I am a coward, and I have been for most of my life. But I'm tired of the person I am. I want to be *more*."

"I'm so glad you've had this epiphany."

"Listen to me, capitana. This is our chance. The empire is already eroding. It won't take much to push the islands into outright rebellion, but Gasparilla has to be there to lead them. We have to set your sister free. Don't you see? This is our one shot at sabotaging the empire from the inside. Just like your parents did."

She turned on him. "You dare—"

"Yes, I dare. Someone has to, or you're going to condemn your sister to death and regret it for the rest of your life."

"It's the punishment she deserves."

"By the law!" he cried, dragging his fingers through his hair in exasperation. "You can't believe that. I know you don't believe that. You saw the same things I saw on that voyage, Ximena. You saw what the cazadores have done. You heard about the crimes they've committed."

"I do believe it, Cuatreda de León," she said. "I've spent four years studying and serving the law. It's the compass behind every decision I've ever made. So if my sister wants to turn pirate and throw away the life we fought so hard for, then she can hang with every other pirate who's done the same."

He laughed, an empty sound. "You know, I don't think I've ever met anyone as infuriating as you are. And that's saying something, considering I was raised by my mother."

Ximena wrenched her door open. "I'm going to bed. The admiral needs me first thing tomorrow morning—"

"Oh, yes, the admiral. The man who swindled you into getting your parents hanged."

As always, he'd found just the right bruise to poke.

"You are dangerously out of line, Cuatreda de León. And he didn't *swindle* me. I knew exactly what I was doing."

"You were a child, Ximena. Anyone with half a brain could tell that he used you."

"Maybe so. But I'd do it again without hesit—"

"Don't. I can't listen to you say it again. I can't." His breathing came hard and fast, as if he'd been running, and his muscles were coiled with frustration. "So there's nothing I can say to change your mind. Nothing I can do."

"Correct."

His wine-dark eyes dragged over her once, calculating. Then he stepped forward with the catlike speed that always caught her by surprise, making her stumble back into the doorframe, reaching for her rapier. She would have unsheathed it if he hadn't been so close, close enough to hear his heart drumming, the rhythm of it strange and familiar all at once. She couldn't tell who was more terrified in that moment—her or Dante.

"Si te dijera que te quiero," he breathed. "¿Sería suficiente?"

The words buried themselves beneath her ribs, a killing blow.

If I told you that I love you, would it be enough?

But Ximena Reale was tired of games. She'd played them with Marquesa, with Amador, with Pía, and even with the admiral; she had absolutely no desire to play another round against Dante de León.

"Say it then," she dared him. "Dime que me quieres."

She knew long before it left her lips that it was a challenge he couldn't meet. But a small part of her cracked nonetheless when his eyes cut away from her.

"Well, capitana," he said. "I suppose we both have something to regret."

Then he strode down the hallway, abandoning her in the cold, lonely moonlight.

Capítulo Veintiuno

Needless to say, Ximena slept little that night, and began the next morning so thoroughly exhausted, she wanted nothing more than to lock herself in her dormitory and never leave it again. But she didn't have that luxury—a cazador knocked on her door at dawn, instructing her to be ready by six o'clock. So she oiled her hair, fixed her eye patch, and hurried downstairs to join the cazadores for the parade. She found them ready and in formation, golden suns gleaming on their chests.

"Good morning, Cuatreda Reale," said the admiral as she approached. "Are you well?"

She forced a smile. "Never better."

He eyed her for a moment longer before nodding and turning back to the cazadores to give them their orders. The parade would travel through the city and end at el ministerio, where the admiral, Ximena, and Dante were expected to give a full report of their expedition before the high minister. In the afternoon, Gasparilla would be tried before the jury of ministers—and tomorrow, she would hang.

You saw what the cazadores have done. The crimes they've committed.

She grit her teeth. Dante de León would be the end of her.

They marched through the gates of la academia in two neat rows. Dante said nothing as they walked, so she did her best to act as if he weren't there, as if she couldn't hear his voice in her mind over and over:

I suppose we both have something to regret.

Marching through the city, the cazadores were met with thundering cheers. Luzans leaned out their windows and crowded into the streets, tossing golden ribbons and handfuls of dried rice onto the cazadores' heads. They chanted the admiral's name, of course. But it was their next cheer that took Ximena by surprise:

"Ximena! Ximena! Ximena! Hero of Luza, bane of pirates!"

They didn't seem to care that Gasparilla was her sister—they only cared that the pirate who'd ravaged their empire was caught, and the girl in front of them was responsible for his capture.

As a child training in la academia, Ximena had dreamed of this moment—she'd told herself that the pain, loneliness, and toil would be worth it when people finally recognized her greatness. So she straightened her shoulders and waved to the crowd. She would enjoy every second of her name echoing through the capital's streets. In fact, she would revel in it.

What did Dante de León know about justice, anyway?

Nothing.

Nothing at all.

The parade came to a stop on el ministerio's doorstep. During their voyage, a brand-new set of doors had been installed to replace

the pair destroyed by Gasparilla, and a single phrase was embla-
zoned in the iron.

LA LEY ES ETERNA.

"The law is eternal," Ximena read aloud.

Just a few weeks ago, she would have treasured that phrase like
a prayer.

So why did it feel like a threat now?

"Bienvenidos," an attendant said, opening the doors and waving her, Dante, and the admiral inside. "The high minister is
expecting you."

Together they followed the attendant into the great chamber,
where Elena de León presided over all three hundred and twenty-
five ministers of Luza, a flock of black robes and white gloves.

"Admiral Pérez," the high minister boomed. "Cuatreda Reale,
Cuatreda de León. We owe you a debt of gratitude for your valor
and bravery in this quest. You have successfully captured the pirate
Gasparilla and restored Queen Dulcinea to her throne, pulling the
empire back from the brink of extinction."

The ministers erupted into applause.

"Such a victory must come with a tale to match," the high minister continued. "You may give your full report, Admiral Pérez."

The admiral stepped forward, bowed, and began his story. He
spoke of their encounter with the witches and their capture by the
pirates; he recounted Amador's betrayals and the sinking of the
Pérez. At last, he came to the tale of the pirates' republic and Gasparilla's capture, explaining how Marquesa came to be known as
the legendary pirate. He hadn't allowed Ximena to interrogate the

pirate herself, instead tasking a small group of cazadores with the challenge.

"It was Amador Gutiérrez who first introduced Marquesa Reale to piracy," he told the ministers. "He was captured and imprisoned three years ago along with fifty other pirate sailors captained by Catarina Salazar. Marquesa was also serving out a short sentence at that time, a debauchery charge in her dotreda years. While in their cells, Marquesa told him of her pirate ancestry as a daughter of the Reales and struck a bargain with him. She would help him escape from prison upon her release, as long as he helped turn her into the most lethal pirate to sail the archipelago. The fulfillment of Alejandra Reale's final words: ¡Viva Gasparilla! ¡Viva la libertad!" Here the admiral paused. "She wished to become Captain Gasparilla."

Ximena's heart climbed up into her throat. She knew what no one else in this room knew: that her mother's dying cry was what had ignited her own desire to hunt Gasparilla. Yet somehow, those same words had turned her older sister to piracy. Two paths from the same origin. One sister a pirate, the other a pirate hunter.

It was enough to make her nauseous.

Meanwhile, the ministers leaned forward in their seats, starving for the admiral's next words. The nerve of these fools, to sit there with their pompous airs in their ridiculous robes, treating Gasparilla's capture like a bedtime story. Once again, Ximena heard Dante in her mind:

You saw what the cazadores have done. The crimes they've committed.

Yes, some part of her answered. *And here are the tyrants behind the orders.*

"For the next three years, Marquesa Reale snuck out of la academia at intervals under the guise of drinking with Dante de León and his compatriots. But in reality, she and Amador were taking turns raiding and pillaging, building the legend of Gasparilla's return. Eventually, the rumors had spread so widely that Marquesa was able to approach the pirates' court. She persuaded them that she alone was capable of finishing what her parents had started. She alone could lead them in destroying the Empire of Luza from the inside, just as Gasparilla had done two centuries ago during the Scarlet Siege."

"So the fools elected a girl as their leader?" Elena de León interrupted, earning laughter from the surrounding ministers. "They must have been quite desperate."

"Desperate enough to ransack the palacio, kidnap the queen, and kill anyone who stood in their way." When Dante de León raised his eyes, they burned like the Luzan sun. "Hardly a laughing matter, Mother."

The high minister's smile thinned. "As you say, Cuatreda de León. Have you anything else to report, admiral?"

"That is the end of my tale, high minister."

"Then we shall commence with the second part of this meeting: the naming of a new cazador."

She waved to the attendant, who brought forward a Cazador Cloak. Ximena's heart began to pound. She and Dante kneeled before the high minister's dais; she struggled to calm her rapid breathing.

"When your name is called, please rise to accept the Cazador Cloak," said Elena de León.

Ximena squeezed her good eye shut. *Breathe in, breathe out. Breathe in, breathe out.*

"Dante de León."

Her stomach plummeted as she opened her eye and turned to Dante. She should have known. So long as Elena de León sat in the high minister's seat, she would never become a cazadora.

"Mother." Dante stood up. "There's been a mistake."

The high minister's gaze sharpened. "Are you questioning my judgment, Cuatreda de León?"

"Yes," he answered. "In fact, I'm overruling it. I refuse to accept the Cazador Cloak."

A disconcerted grumbling traveled among the ministers. It seemed there would be more history made today—no one had ever refused the title of cazador. But the high minister only sat forward in her seat.

"Perhaps you need time to think, Cuatreda de León. You have had a long journey—"

"I don't need time to think," said Dante. "Cuatreda Reale is responsible for the capture of Gasparilla. Not me. And I won't dishonor that cloak by wearing it because my mother is the high minister of Luza," he added. "If I ever wear it at all."

"Then you would defy a direct order from your high minister."

"Happily." His voice was sharp and cold as a rapier's edge. "My brother used his last breaths to defy you, Mother, and if there's any honor left in me, I'll go to my grave beside him."

He'd gone too far. The high minister stood up, her mask of calm slipping to reveal a black and terrible rage—her hands trembled, her lips twitched, and her eyes boiled with a bitterness so deep that it seeped from her in waves.

But Elena de León was nothing if not a politician. So she reined in her temper just as quickly as she lost it, sitting back in her chair with another paper-thin smile.

"Very well then. Ximena Reale, on the recommendation of your mentors and peers, I invite you to accept the Cazador Cloak and join the ranks of la academia's finest cazadores. Please prepare to take the cazador oath."

Ximena froze as the attendant walked toward her. He wrapped the cloak around her shoulders; it fell heavy and warm against her back.

"Repeat after me," said the high minister. "I, Ximena Reale, do solemnly swear."

Ximena's mouth moved of its own accord. "I, Ximena Reale, do solemnly swear."

"To uphold, treasure, and protect the law and its tenets."

"To uphold, treasure, and protect the law and its tenets."

"Protecting my queen and her subjects alike."

"Protecting my queen and her subjects alike."

"From this moment forward until the last breath I take."

"From this moment forward," Ximena finished, "until the last breath I take."

"Rise, Cazadora Ximena Reale. May you bring the light of Luza to the furthest corners of the empire, and may the seas be with you."

The ministers burst into a round of thunderous applause. Dante joined them, his expression inscrutable. Meanwhile, Ximena stood up, the weight of her cloak pressing down on her shoulders. *Cazadora Ximena Reale.* After years of dreaming and studying and training, she'd done it. Her past would no longer bind her. She would no longer be Ximena Reale, daughter of traitors, but a cazadora, protector of Luza, bane of pirates.

Yet the cloak sat heavy on her shoulders, as if it might drag her to the bottom of the sea and drown her.

"Well done, Ximena."

She felt the admiral's hand on her back and turned to embrace him.

"There has never been a candidate more deserving," he said. "I knew from the moment I met you that you'd make a brilliant cazadora."

"I owe it all to you," she replied, stepping back.

"And to think none of this would have happened if I hadn't gone to your family's house that night," he said. "The law works in mysterious ways."

No, none of this would have happened, Ximena thought. *My sister would not have been captured, and my parents would not be dead.*

Aloud, she said: "It does indeed, sir."

They were interrupted by the high minister's gavel.

"The pirate known as Gasparilla will be tried before this court at noon. If found guilty, she will hang at sunset tomorrow. Admiral Pérez and Cazadora Ximena Reale are dismissed. Cuatreda de León," she said, "meet me in my office."

Dante gave her a mock salute. "As you command, Mother."

He followed his mother out of the chamber with his usual swagger. Ximena could only imagine what the high minister wanted with him—after all, the boy had just embarrassed her in front of el ministerio. But she didn't have time to think about Dante for long, because Luza's ministers surrounded her, shaking her hand and offering her congratulations.

"What was it like, my dear? The Republic of Pirates?" one minister asked.

"Did they truly try to hang you?"

"Is Gasparilla good with a sword?" asked another.

Ximena blinked, unsure of what to say. "Well—I—you see—"

"Cazadora Ximena must return to her training," said the admiral, stepping in front of her. "I'm sure you'll see her again at one of the high minister's balls."

Then he took her by the arm and led her out of the chamber. A pair of horses waited for them in the street, each branded with the Luzan sun. As they mounted, Ximena thanked the admiral for rescuing her, but he only laughed.

"You'll soon discover, Ximena, that a good cazador is equal parts sailor and politician. Since we serve at the queen's pleasure, we must also put up with her minions."

He smiled to let her know he was joking, and she blinked at him, startled. She'd never heard the admiral joke before. But perhaps he behaved differently around his fellow cazadores—and now, she was one of them.

Upon their return to la academia, the admiral instructed her to pack her things and meet him at the southwest wing before high noon. The wing forbidden to all but the cazadores. She was finally going to see it.

Candidates scampered out of her way as she walked. "Excuse me, Cazadora Ximena," they said. "My apologies, Cazadora Ximena." She couldn't help but tip her chin high with pride. They couldn't mock her now. She was their superior, as terrifying in her black cloak as the older cazadores had seemed in theirs.

But at what cost?

She packed her things just as she'd done when she'd been promoted to cuatreda a few months earlier. When she was finished, she stepped back out into the hallway, only to bump into Dante.

"You should use the eye you have left," he muttered.

He stormed past her into his room, slamming the door behind him. So his talk with his mother hadn't gone well. She thought about asking him what had happened but stopped herself. It would be better for them both to maintain the distance they'd established.

The hallway clock chimed. She glanced up: twelve o'clock. Marquesa's trial was likely just beginning. Within the hour, she would be condemned for piracy and sentenced to hang. But Ximena was also late to meet the admiral, so she hurried around the corner and down the two flights of stairs to the courtyard, where she found him waiting.

"Shall we?" he said.

They crossed the courtyard to the southwest wing. What would it be like? She'd heard so many stories. Candidates claiming to have snuck inside said there were no dormitories since the cazadores never slept, or the walls were painted with silver from smelted pirate treasure. Of course, she knew those tales were ridiculous exaggerations. But that didn't stop her from trying to guess what waited beyond those doors.

"Are you ready?" the admiral asked, grasping the iron handles on the door.

She took a breath. Then nodded. "As I'll ever be, sir."

"Then welcome, Cazadora Ximena, to the southwest wing."

The doors opened, and Ximena's breath caught in her throat. The great hall of the southwest wing was one magnificent training ground—hundreds of cazadores sparred against one another in perfect rows, rapiers flashing, black cloaks swirling behind them. Beneath their feet, the floor seemed to tip and groan.

"It's rigged to move like the deck of a ship," the admiral explained.

"We have to stay in practice, no?"

Grunts and the clashing of blades bounced off the limestone dome overhead, sounding to Ximena like the sweetest kind of music. Then a whistle blew, and the cazadores stopped, relaxing out of their fighting stances to clap one another on the back and wipe the sweat from their brows.

"The cazadores train for six hours a day when they're not assigned to a mission," the admiral said. "You'll join us in our exercises when the trial is over."

He motioned for her to follow, and they moved down the hallway to a second, smaller chamber, where several dozen archivists fluttered around an impossibly tall wooden board with slips of paper tacked to it.

"Reports of piracy are posted here," he said. "If a threat is deemed worthy, a senior cazador brings it to me for approval and commissioning. All expeditions begin here."

They took a flight of stairs below ground, where they paused before the iron door of a vault. The admiral gave instructions to the guards who stood outside, and they nodded, working together to crank the wheel that would open the lock. Ximena stifled a gasp. Inside the vault gleamed more treasure than she had ever seen in her life: coins, jewels, goblets, and crowns, glittering in silver heaps so high, they could have been buildings.

"And every expedition ends here," the admiral said. "All treasure seized from pirate sloops is processed here before it is moved to the empire's vaults."

So Luzans across the archipelago struggled and starved while the empire spent this silver on a pointless war. Ximena's stomach twisted, first at the revelation and then at the stench of something burning. When she asked the admiral where the smell was coming from, he laughed.

"I hardly notice it anymore," he said. "It comes from the furnace below us. Only the head archivist goes down there."

"What for?"

"To dispose of unnecessary records."

"Unnecessary records?" Ximena had never heard of such a thing. The archivists saved everything from hardtack recipes to astronomical charts.

"Texts written by pirate sympathizers," said the admiral. "There's no sense in filing them in the archives and treating them as truth."

"Right," said Ximena. "Of course."

Marquesa's face appeared in her mind, just as clearly as if she'd been standing there. Her sister had been right—the empire had been lying to them all along.

The smell of burning paper followed Ximena long after she'd left it behind.

She followed the admiral up two flights of stairs, arriving at a long hallway lined with doors. He walked her to a door already labeled with her name, unlocked it with a key from his pocket, and waved her inside.

"Your chambers, Cazadora Ximena," he said. She still wasn't used to seeing a smile on his face. "There are many more things to see, but for now, unpack your things and come downstairs to the mess hall for lunch. If you need anything, I'll be in my office on the fourth floor."

"Thank you, sir."

"Believe me, Ximena, the pleasure is mine."

With a bow of his head—the salute given to an equal—he strode down the hallway, disappearing around the corner. Ximena watched him go, wondering when she'd stopped feeling safe in his presence.

Ximena's new dormitory was larger than her previous ones had been, though still appropriately austere, furnished with a bed, a dresser, a vanity, and a small leather chair. A spare cazador uniform was waiting for her on the bed, but there was a package next to it that she didn't recognize. She unraveled the linen wrappings to discover the most spectacular rapier she had ever seen. Its handle was pure gold and studded with rubies, its blade clearly formed by a master craftsman. She would have recognized this sword anywhere.

Gasparilla's sword.

Her father's sword.

There was a note pinned to the side:

> *I know you will redeem this blade for the pursuit of justice and honor. May it serve you well, Cazadora Ximena, and may the seas be with you.*
>
> Admiral Gabriel Pérez

She sat on the bed with the note in her hands, reading those two lines over and over again. Then she crumpled the paper in her fist and tossed it into the wash basin. She didn't look at it again as she unpacked her belongings and tried on her new uniform, and it sat abandoned when she left the room a few hours later, heading toward the mess hall.

Ximena had never felt as small as she did while standing in the doorway of the cazador mess hall. The cazadores sat at long, wooden tables, washing roasted pork down with goblets of wine, swapping stories with the confidence of seasoned sailors. She might have been a child in a costume by comparison—her boots seemed too big for her feet, her hat too large for her head, her rapier too heavy at her waist. Thankfully, the admiral spotted her across the room before she could lose her nerve and run.

"Come, Ximena," he said.

She tried and failed to ignore the stares that followed her as she crossed the room. Thank the law that the admiral made it a practice to eat with his subordinates, otherwise she would have been completely alone.

"Cazadora Martina was just asking about your battle with Catarina Salazar," the admiral said when she sat down. He nodded at the cazadora sitting across from him, a younger woman with startling blue eyes. "I was telling her about the way you jumped out with your rapier, threatening to cut down the pirate where she stood."

"With courage like that, it's no wonder you became a cazadora so quickly," said Martina with a smile. "The admiral says you're the youngest cazadora in history."

"If my admiral says so, I won't argue," said Ximena.

"Humble, too," said Martina. She winked at the admiral. "You've trained her well."

"A teacher is only as good as his student."

Martina nodded toward Ximena's waist. "Is that Gasparilla's sword?"

"Yes," Ximena replied. "A generous gift from the admiral."

"A fine gift."

An edge slipped into the cazadora's voice, an edge Ximena recognized after many years of battling the candidates of la academia. Envy.

"Tell me, Ximena," Martina finished her wine and leaned

forward. "Is it true that Gasparilla is your sister?"

Ximena choked on her food. Before she could formulate an answer, an archivist burst into the mess hall, carrying a notice above her head.

"El ministerio has spoken!" she cried. "Gasparilla is sentenced to hang!"

The cazadores leapt up with a roar of triumph. Only Ximena remained sitting, staring at her plate, unable to move. She could hardly judge the cazadores for their reaction—how many times had she herself gloried in the execution of a pirate? But her heart pounded at a breakneck pace, and something roiled and twisted in her stomach, clawing at her insides. It was that Reale instinct that was never wrong, screaming, *this is not justice!*

She tried to ignore it. She tried to raise her head and join the cazadores' cheers. But her voice stuck in her throat, and the words died on her tongue.

You saw what the cazadores have done. The crimes they've committed.

Oh yes, the admiral. The man who swindled you into getting your parents hanged.

She didn't even realize that Admiral Pérez was speaking to her until he called her by name.

"Ximena," he said. "Did you hear that? Gasparilla will hang by sunset tomorrow."

She nodded slowly, and then pushed her plate away and stood up. "If you'll both excuse me," she said, "I've just realized I forgot something in my old dormitory."

The admiral's noble brow furrowed. "Ximena—"

"Gracias, admiral," she said. "For everything."

She'd walked a few paces away from the table when the admiral called her name again, stopping her.

"Ximena," he said. "Cuidado."

His eyes were as sharp and knowing as a shark's, and his voice was a warning, the kind he gave to wayward cabin boys.

She bowed her head in salute. "As you command, sir."

Then she strode out of the mess hall, one hand gripping the handle of her rapier to keep her fingers from trembling.

That evening found Ximena lying flat on her bed, polishing her rapier and trying to ignore the fireworks that boomed in the city. All of Valuza would be celebrating tonight. Luzans would raise their glasses and toast to the cazadores, praising the pirate hunters for their bravery and cunning. Tomorrow, there would be feasts and parties to mark Gasparilla's death, and by the end of the month, news of the pirate's demise would reach the furthest corners of the empire. A celebration to end all celebrations.

No doubt the cazadores would question Ximena's lack of participation in the festivities. But for once, she couldn't bring herself to care what they thought. She polished the blade of her rapier, polished it again, then polished it a third time before setting it aside in its sheath. Her good eye lingered on it: her father's sword. Gasparilla's sword. She wondered if it had a name. Perhaps she could give it one. After a moment's consideration, she settled on a suitable enough title.

Venganza.

Vengeance.

She slid her eye patch off her head and smoothed the fabric with her thumb. She didn't try to fall asleep—her mind was turning at hurricane speed. In fact, she didn't even notice when the sun rose and bathed her room in golden light, but when a cazador knocked on her door to inform her that the admiral was waiting, she eased herself out of bed to oil her hair and replace her eye patch. She scrutinized herself in the mirror for a long moment. Though her cheeks were pale green and dark circles clung to her eyes, she looked every inch a cazadora, and that was all that mattered.

She met the admiral at the end of the hall. Dressed in his finest uniform, he greeted her with another fond smile.

"This is a historic day, Ximena," he said.

"Indeed, sir."

"Are you feeling well? You look as if you haven't slept in months."

"It was a long day, sir."

"Of course." His eyes traveled over her face. "Are you certain—"

"They're expecting us in the courtyard, sir."

His brow pinched. "So they are."

Without another word, they traveled down the stairs and stepped out into the courtyard. The whole of la academia had been assembled—candidates and cazadores alike stood in neat, black rows, all facing the gallows platform. Even the high minister had deigned to join them, presiding over the proceedings from the gallows, her expression unreadable. The sun burned hot; the wind was fair; the air tasted of salt.

A fine day for an execution, if such a thing can be determined.

Ximena followed the admiral to the front row of cazadores. They saluted him and when he acknowledged them with a nod, they stepped back into their places. The drummers struck up their fatal beat—*boom ba-boom, boom ba-boom.*

"Bring out the prisoner," the admiral said.

The doors to the west wing swung wide. Two cazadores emerged, holding Gasparilla between them, and marched through the rows of people to the gallows. They pushed the pirate up onto the platform and saluted the admiral. The drums continued their steady pounding.

When she saw her sister, Ximena fought the urge to gasp. Weeks in cazador custody hadn't done Marquesa any favors—her cheeks were sunken, her clothes bedraggled, her jaw bruised. But in spite of her sufferings, the pirate's eyes blazed. She surveyed the assembled crowd with defiant certainty, as if they were standing in Gasparilla's court, rather than the courtyard of la academia.

"Marquesa Reale," boomed the admiral. "Otherwise known as the pirate Gasparilla. You have been found guilty of treason, piracy, murder, and assault, among other crimes. Therefore, you have been sentenced to hang by the neck until you are dead. Do you wish to repent of your crimes before this sentence is carried out?"

Marquesa raised her head. "¡Viva Gasparilla!" was all she said. "¡Viva la libertad!"

For a moment, silence reigned. Marquesa's gaze found Ximena's, but Ximena was the first to look away. After all, this was the punishment her sister deserved. Treason demanded nothing less than death, and the law must be upheld.

The admiral gave the signal to the candidate at the end of the platform, who placed her hands around the lever and pulled. Marquesa's blazing eyes widened with a sudden swell of fear. Then the trapdoor opened, and there was a bone-chilling snap. Ximena's good eye drifted down to her feet as a great cheer shook the limestone walls of la academia.

Gasparilla was dead.

Capítulo Veintidós

Ximena sat straight up in bed, her forehead slick with sweat. She fumbled for her sword, but it was too dark to see anything, and the moon was new and black, offering no light.

Night. It was still night. The sun hadn't risen yet, so Gasparilla hadn't been executed, and everything she had just seen, heard, and felt had been nothing more than a dream. Her exhaustion must have overpowered her thoughts and dragged her down into sleep. An anxious laugh burst from her chest.

"Get a hold of yourself, Ximena," she mumbled as she willed her breathing to slow back down. This entire situation was chipping away at her sanity; if she wasn't careful, she'd go insane.

She needed to move. So she wrenched the sheets back, climbed out of bed, and paced back and forth in her dormitory. *I'll do what I've always done,* she lied to herself. She would strangle her fear and doubt through sheer force of will.

So she walked around her room another twenty-two times, whispering the law under her breath, reminding herself that preparation leads to perfection. This was just another test. She would rise to the challenge like the cazadora she was, and she would emerge on the other side of it even stronger than she had been before.

But then she saw the noose around Marquesa's neck again, as vividly as she'd seen it in her nightmare. She heard the final roll of the execution drum, felt it in the hollow of her ribs. *By the law.* She swept the wash bin off her vanity, smashing it to the floor. Ximena had been a fighter long enough to know when she was losing. And she was losing tonight, badly.

She crossed the room fifty-two more times, each turn like the cut of a rapier blade. Still the truth was unavoidable. She couldn't condemn her sister to die. She had simply seen too much, heard too much, and it had shattered the illusion of la academia forever. No matter how hard she tried to escape it, Ximena came to the same conclusion that her parents had before her: if she spent the rest of her life as a cazadora, hunting people in the name of an empire she no longer believed in, it would destroy her from the inside out.

That left only one option.

She had to save Gasparilla.

She stopped in the center of the room. A plan was beginning to take shape in her mind. But she shoved it away, scowling to herself. *Absolutamente no.* No one in their right mind would attempt such a thing. Still, the idea returned to her with all the patience of a tide, over and over. It was the only choice that made any sense, though it didn't make sense at all. Once again she had the strangest urge to laugh. She was a fool—worse than a fool—for considering this. But after several more minutes of pacing, she took up Venganza, strapped it to her waist, and strode out of the room. She'd made her decision.

Now it was time to follow through.

The hallways of la academia were dark and silent, no sign of any other candidates. So as she turned the corner into the cuatreda wing, Ximena reached behind her head and untied her hair from its usual ponytail, digging her fingers into her scalp to resurrect her oiled-down curls. She'd spent the last four years stifling whatever Reale blood still dwelled in her.

Tonight, it would burn untamed.

It didn't take her long to reach the cuatreda dormitories, coming to a stop before an all too familiar door. Ximena hesitated again. If she had any sense left, she would march straight back to the cazador dormitories, where she'd wait for the sun to rise and her sister to be executed.

But then she remembered her dream. She remembered Marquesa's eyes, wide with fear, and the sickening snap of bone. She saw her sister's body swinging in the wind, lifeless—just like their parents so many years ago.

Ximena inhaled, exhaled. Then, before she could change her mind, she raised a fist and gave two precise knocks.

For a long moment, no one answered. She scowled, her courage slipping, and turned to go—but the door opened, and leaning against the frame was Dante de León, his face unshaven and haggard.

"Are you here to gloat?" he said. "Because if you are, I'm really not in the mood—"

"I need your help to break Marquesa out of prison."

Dante blinked once, twice. "I'm sorry, I think I've had too much rum this evening. Did you just say you want to break your sister out of prison?"

With a huff, she strode past him into the room, motioning for him to shut the door. He obeyed, locking it behind him.

"Now," he said, crossing his arms over his chest, "would you care to explain what this sudden passion for illegal activity is all about?"

"My sister will be hanged tomorrow, and I need your help to break her out of the labyrinth before that happens."

He stared at her, his dark eyes roving over her face. Only then did she notice that his right eye was blackened by a fresh bruise.

"What happened?" she demanded.

"Ah, this?" He touched it with his fingers and winced. "My mother's gavel is heavier than it looks. She wasn't pleased with my little display at el ministerio, as you might expect. But our talk went surprisingly well—she threatened to disown me if I ever humiliated her in public again, and then she said she wished I'd died in my brother's place. She can be very charming when she wants to be. But back to your family crisis. You wish to break your sister out of the labyrinth?"

"Yes."

His eyes narrowed. "You realize what this means. If we're caught, we'll be convicted of treason and hanged."

"Yes."

"You will almost certainly lose your Cazador Cloak."

"I know."

"Which I sacrificed my dignity to give you."

"You didn't—"

"You're turning pirate, Ximena." A challenge burned in his eyes. "There's no going back after this."

She flinched at the word "pirate," but steeled herself and straightened her shoulders. "I know."

The smile on Dante's lips was anything but harmless.

"Well then, capitana," he said. "We need to find ourselves some gunpowder."

Dante may not have inherited his brother's talent for strategy, but he'd spent ten years sneaking out of la academia to drink and dance in the city's cantinas and was therefore surprisingly well-versed on the subject of escapes. So they made quite the team as they planned Marquesa's rescue, huddled over a candle on the dormitory floor and testing idea after idea until they'd nailed down every last detail.

"It's time," Dante declared when the hall clock struck five. "But before we go—"

He opened the top drawer of his dresser, reached all the way to the back, and pushed. There was a popping sound—a hidden extension, carrying a bottle of rum and glasses. He poured liquor for both of them and passed a glass to Ximena.

"A drink to treason," he said.

Ximena hesitated. But it wasn't like she could turn back now. So she tossed the rum down her throat, coughing and sputtering at the burn. Dante laughed.

"If someone had told me Ximena Reale would be drinking rum in my room someday, I would've called them mad."

"I'm starting to think I'm the one who's mad," she said. "But maybe that's not such a bad thing."

"Couldn't have said it better myself, capitana."

She hadn't realized they were standing so close together, but when she looked up at him, she could count the flecks of gold in his eyes and trace the yellow outline of his bruise. Maybe it was the rum addling her brain, but she heard the question he'd asked her the night before: *if I told you I love you, would that be enough?*

She'd said no, and she'd been telling the truth—but it wasn't the whole truth. It wouldn't have been enough for Dante to say he loved her.

But it wouldn't have been nothing, either.

Ximena almost pitied the boy. He'd given his heart to someone who didn't know how to hold it, who couldn't hold it without running away in terror. For even though Ximena Reale was skilled at many things, from swordplay to sailing to capturing mythical pirates, she didn't know the first thing about love.

"We should go," she said then.

"You're right," he replied, but he didn't move.

She cleared her throat. "It's almost daylight."

"How very observant of you. Is your hair different? I swear your hair is different."

"Yes," she said. "It's different."

"Hmm," he hummed. "It suits you. And you don't smell like whale oil, for once. Here." He pulled a slip of paper from his pocket and pressed it to her palm; she noticed that he took care not to touch her. "Read it when the time is right. When you're safe."

"Are you so confident that we'll succeed?"

"You're Ximena Reale," he said, grinning. "You'll succeed or die trying. Then you can read my note in the afterlife."

"Oh, yes, I'd love to occupy my time in the afterlife with insipid love poems by Dante de León."

He winked. "Don't be so swift to underestimate my poetic abilities."

"I've known you for four years. If you're a poet, then I am Queen Dulcinea."

He laughed. "To the labyrinth then, mi reina?"

"Not yet," she answered. "There's something I have to do first."

As the first tendrils of sunlight peeked through the window, Ximena left Dante's dormitory and hurried toward the very place she had started this journey: the Maritime Archives.

When she pushed through the iron doors, the archives were empty. The rolling ladders, usually whirring back and forth along the shelves, waited silently in place; dust settled on the scrolls, undisturbed. It was too early for most archivists to be at work—but Ximena wasn't looking for most archivists.

"Pía," she whispered into the shelves.

The faint rustle of parchment was the only reply that greeted her.

"Pía, I need to talk to you."

Somewhere, a clock chimed. Still there was no sign of the archivist.

"Por favor," Ximena said. "One moment. Then I'll leave, and you'll never have to speak to me again."

"Buenos días, Cazadora Ximena."

Pía stood behind her, eyes bloodshot, cheeks splotchy. The sight speared Ximena's heart. Clearly she had hurt Pia even more deeply than she'd thought.

"How can I be of service?" the girl asked. "Would you like to read the record of Gasparilla's trial? It was just delivered last night."

"No, Pía. I lost the right to ask you for help the moment I betrayed your trust," Ximena said. "That's not what I'm here for. I'm here to beg your forgiveness."

"And why should I give it to you?"

Ximena had seen Pía scared. But she had never seen her angry. Tears pooled in the archivist's eyes. Her small hands were clenched at her sides.

"You *used* me," Pía said. "Just like my father uses me to keep a roof over our family's head. Just like the admiral uses me to punish people who don't deserve it."

"I know," Ximena said softly.

"I don't need you, you know. I might not be able to fight with a sword like you do, or command people's respect. But I'm just as intelligent as you are, and I'm strong, too, in my own way. I wouldn't be standing here if I wasn't."

"I know, Pía."

"So why should I forgive you?"

"You shouldn't." Perhaps the archivist's tears were contagious. Ximena swiped a hand under her eye patch. "I certainly don't deserve it. But I—I never knew what a friend was before you, Pía. So I won't tell you not to hate me. But I won't stop loving you, either."

Pía tugged at her hair, falling uncharacteristically quiet.

"I'm sorry," Ximena said again. "More than you'll ever know. But I'll leave you now, as promised. Farewell. May the seas be with you."

With that, she turned to go. She'd said what she'd come to say. Now she would just have to find her way in the world without the archivist at her side.

It was one thing to turn your nose up at friendship when you'd never had it. It was quite another to walk into loneliness after being loved. So tears tracked down Ximena's cheeks and caught on the collar of her Cazador Cloak. She'd broken too many things over the last few days, and the shards of her life were sharp, drawing blood.

Then something slammed into her from behind. Two arms circled her waist; a small face pressed between her shoulders.

"I love you too, Ximena Reale."

Ximena stiffened at the archivist's touch. But soon she found herself turning around, holding the other girl close, burying her face in a mound of red curls. She didn't know who started laughing first, her or Pía. It didn't matter anyway. All that mattered was that they were together again, and by some miracle, Ximena hadn't lost the only true friend she'd ever had.

"So what are you going to do with that gunpowder at your hip?" Pía finally asked, pulling away. "Yes, I noticed it. I'm assuming this has something to do with Cuatreda de León?"

Ximena shook her head. "It's too dangerous, Pía. You've faced death one too many times on my behalf. I refuse to watch you do it again."

"I thought we'd established that I'm allowed to do what I like with my life, Ximena." Pía grinned. "Don't you think I want to be part of the mission to rescue the great Captain Gasparilla?"

"Our odds are terrible."

"I wouldn't expect anything less."

Ximena nodded, took a deep breath, and began to explain the ridiculous plot she and Dante had concocted piece by piece, and when she'd finished, Pía gave a decisive nod.

"You're right. That is a horrible idea. Hand me the gunpowder."

Ximena handed her the pouch.

"Now," said Pía, strapping it to her hip. "Let's commit treason."

"As you command, archivist."

Together, she and Pía raced out of the archives to la academia's labyrinth. They stopped before the pair of guards who waited in front of the entrance.

"I must speak with Teseo, immediately," Ximena told the guards, keeping their mission vague. She could only hope her voice didn't sound as shaky as she felt.

Thankfully, the guards didn't question her.

"Of course, Cazadora Ximena," they said, opening the doors.

With a nod of thanks, the girls ran as fast as they could down the spiral staircase. They found Teseo dozing against the wall with his hands folded, corpse-like, over his chest. Ximena nudged him with her boot; he woke up with a wheezing cough.

"Take me to Gasparilla," she commanded.

"No one is allowed to see the captain, cazadora," he rasped. "On direct orders from the admiral."

She unsheathed her rapier and held it to his throat.

"Don't test my patience, Teseo. Take me to Gasparilla, or I'll gut you like a fish."

He paused a moment, testing her willingness to kill him. Then he grabbed his torch off the wall.

"This way," he rasped, shuffling into the darkness.

The two girls followed behind him. Ximena's fingers beat anxiously against her leg. She prayed that Pía would remember to open the gunpowder pouch, and that Teseo wouldn't hear the powder hissing down to the floor as they walked. *Curse Dante and his half-mad ideas.* In all likelihood, she and Pía were walking directly into the arms of death.

Deeper into the darkness they wove, ignoring the grasping hands of the prisoners, until the blackness was so thick that Ximena could no longer see inside the cells. She didn't know how long they walked before Teseo stopped, holding up his torch.

"Here," he rasped, waving it toward the cell in front of them.

Only then did Ximena realize they had arrived at the very center of the labyrinth—the cell was a dead end, the terrible heart of the maze. The admiral had certainly done his best to ensure that

Gasparilla would not escape.

But he hadn't counted on Ximena Reale turning pirate.

"Gracias, Teseo," she said. "I apologize for this."

She unsheathed her rapier and slammed the pommel into his skull. He dropped like a crate of lead, but not before she caught his torch and held it in the darkness.

"Marquesa," she hissed. "Marquesa, please, we don't have much time."

"Ximena?"

Marquesa stepped into the light, her hazel eyes glinting. She still wore Gasparilla's scarlet clothes, but they were blackened with grime and soot, and her cheeks bore the marks of a recent beating. She glanced from Ximena to Teseo's crumpled body.

"This is unexpected," she said.

"To say the least," Ximena replied. She bent down to search Teseo's body—he always carried the master key to all the labyrinth's cells. At last, she found it, hanging from a chain around his neck. She yanked it until it came free.

"You're going to help me escape?" Marquesa asked.

"We both are," chirped Pía.

"Why?"

Ximena slid the key into the cell door and turned it until she heard a click. "Hurry, before Teseo wakes."

The door opened, and Marquesa stepped outside, blinking in the torchlight.

"Why are you doing this?" she asked. She looked her sister up and down, taking in the cazador uniform. "You're a cazadora now. You have everything you've ever worked for, everything you've dreamed of. Why would you throw it all away for a pirate?"

Ximena squared her shoulders. No matter how loud the fear screamed in her mind, no matter how many doubts still rattled in her skull, she wouldn't back down now. Not after coming so far.

"I'm sorry, Marquesa. For everything. And I know that words will never be enough to pay for the things I've done, for the people I've—" she paused, swallowing against the tightness in her throat. "The people I've hurt. Nothing I can say will ever change the past. But if you'll let me, I plan to spend the rest of my life fighting to redeem it. To honor our parents' legacy." Ximena held her hand out to her. "All I ask," she finished, "is that you trust me to help you escape."

Marquesa glared at her in silence. Under such cold scrutiny, Ximena's courage wavered, and her hand began to fall—until Marquesa's fingers caught hers, the pirate's warm, calloused skin so like their mother's.

"Forgiveness is given," Marquesa said. "Not earned."

Then, for the first time in years, Ximena found herself in her sister's arms. The sensation was so strange, like a dream come to life; she could scarcely believe it was real. She'd prepared herself for a fight, with words or swords or some combination of the two. How could Marquesa hold her as if nothing had happened? Could she truly be forgiven so easily?

"Marquesa," she began, "I—"

"Do you know how many nights I prayed for this moment?" the pirate rasped. "How many times I hoped, wondering if you would ever open your eyes and see the truth? If I'd known all it would take was the threat of my execution, I would've gotten myself caught much sooner."

"Don't say that," Ximena breathed. "Don't even think it."

Marquesa only squeezed her tighter. "Please believe that I didn't want to lie to you, Ximena. When we were children, Mamá and Papá told me the truth about who they were, but they insisted you were too young to keep such a terrible secret. So they swore me to total silence and left you in the dark. Then when I became Gasparilla, I had to lie to you all over again, because I knew you would despise me if I told you the truth, and I couldn't . . ."

Ximena nodded. She didn't have to hear the words she already knew, the words that had brought her to the labyrinth: *I couldn't lose you.*

The empire had already destroyed half the Reale family. They weren't going to destroy what was left.

Not if Ximena could help it.

She held her sister close for one more moment, and then pulled away. And if Marquesa Reale's eyes sparkled with tears, it must have been a trick of the shadows, because Gasparilla the pirate did not cry.

"Now we must go," Ximena said, "before Teseo wakes up."

"It's no use," said Marquesa. "I was only able to escape the first time with the help of my crew. There's no way out without a guide."

Ximena smiled. "That, hermana, is why we brought one."

She tilted Teseo's torch down to the floor. The gunpowder Pía had poured at their feet sparked, and the charge ran ahead into the shadows, fizzing and popping as it went.

"Dante de León helped you with this plan," Marquesa drawled. "I'd bet my life on it."

"That's a story for another time. For now, we run," said Ximena, tugging her sister by the hand.

Sprinting past the prison cells, they followed the trail of

gunpowder around one corner, then another, and another, working their way out from the center of the labyrinth. Ximena ignored the shouts of the prisoners who begged to be set free—she was too focused on their goal. But Marquesa couldn't distance herself so easily.

"Give me the key," she said.

"Marquesa—"

"If you give me the key, I'm responsible for whatever happens, not you. Besides, it'll be a good distraction for the cazadores."

Grimacing, Ximena tossed the key over her shoulder. Marquesa handed it to the closest prisoner as they ran.

"Free yourself, then the others," she ordered.

The prisoner let out a delighted cry and the girls raced around the corner, leaving the chaos to unfold behind them. They turned down two more tunnels before arriving at Teseo's post; Ximena dropped the torch and put it out with a stomp.

"Up the stairs," she said.

They climbed as quickly as they could and emerged into the cold, gray dawn of la academia. Dante was already there waiting for them; the guards lay unconscious at his feet.

"Must have been something in the wine," he said with a shrug. Then he tipped his head to Marquesa. "Glad to see you're still alive, Gasparilla. Just so you know, the gunpowder was my idea, and I'm incredibly handsome. The poets need to get the details right when they write their songs about us."

"You're also insufferable and completely full of yourself," Ximena said. "To the docks, everyone."

They tore through la academia's hallways, headed for the south gate. Ximena's stomach dropped when a bell rang out behind them—the guards must have woken up and sounded the alarm. If they were lucky, they'd have mere minutes before the whole of la academia descended on them like vultures.

Ximena pulled Marquesa behind the closest corner, and then peered carefully into the hallway to see Juan Carlos Alonso and several cuatredas striding toward them, torches raised. She was already calculating their odds of outrunning the patrol when she felt a hand around her wrist. It was Dante, his wine-dark eyes serious.

"Go."

She shook her head. "But—"

"Go, Ximena. I'll distract them."

Ximena knew there was nothing Dante de León wanted more than to run away from la academia, commandeer a pirate ship, and never look back. Yet here he was, sacrificing that dream for her sake. She didn't understand it. She'd been so certain that there wasn't the faintest glimmer of courage in him. Yet he must have found it, because standing in place of the boy she'd hated was a man she didn't know, one who possessed all the command of his namesake.

De León.

Of the lion.

And perhaps her senses had departed with her love for the law, but she trusted him. She knew he wouldn't betray them to the cazadores. She didn't know how she knew it, but she did. In fact, some small, selfish part of her wanted to refuse his offer, to ask him to come with her and leave la Academia de los Cazadores for good.

But the look in Dante's eyes told her that he'd already made up his mind. Around the corner, she could hear the cazadores shouting—another moment of delay and they'd be spotted.

"I would have followed you to the horizon, capitana," Dante said.

Then he took her face in his hands and kissed her. The air flew from her lungs; her mind went suddenly blank. He tasted like treason and stolen silver, like cheating death by a fraction of an inch. Ximena Reale had lived all her life in blacks and whites. Now her entire world burned in vivid, blinding color, and it was more than she could feel, so bright it was almost painful. But if this was what color felt like, she decided it was worth the pain. So she held onto Dante with all her determined stubbornness, because she never let go of the things she wanted, not while she could help it. He grinned against her lips like a pirate.

"Go, capitana," he said, pushing her away. "Before they find you."

Ximena was not sentimental by nature. She left things behind without a second thought. But as she turned the corner, she glanced back over her shoulder at Dante, and she caught the flash of his teeth and the wink of his eye. Then he was gone, and Ximena couldn't help but wonder whether that was the last time she'd ever see him.

"Juan Carlos!" she heard Dante say. "Thank the law you're here. I tried to stop them, but the pirates beat me back. They went down that corridor—if you hurry, you'll catch them."

Meanwhile, Pía and the Reale sisters fled down the stairs and out the doors to la academia's courtyard. They sprinted toward the south gate in the crisp morning air as the alarm bell rang a second time. *Faster, faster*, Ximena thought. They were running out of time.

The two guards posted at the entrance spotted them and raised their swords.

"Stop, in the name of the law!"

But Ximena sliced the first across the arm and knocked him unconscious, while Marquesa somehow managed to kill the second with his own weapon. The pirate captain tied the guard's sword to her own belt and kept running; Ximena followed her, forcing herself not to look at the dead man's face. She had to remember that cazadores were her enemies now, not her brothers and sisters in arms.

Their boots pounded like a war drum against la academia's wooden dock. They tore past the smaller sloops, then slowed when they reached the galleons. Ximena knew exactly what ship they needed—the *Delgado*, the second fastest in the armada after the sunken Pérez. It towered above them in the pale morning light, its masts spearing the sky.

If they were going to outrun the cazadores, they needed to steal the admiral's ship.

Ximena clambered aboard the galleon ahead of Marquesa and moved to unfasten the mooring lines.

"Pía, hoist the sails!" she cried. "Marquesa, tie the helm off."

Marquesa raised a quizzical brow but followed orders nonetheless. While Pía loosened the mainsails, she climbed to the upper deck, tying the wheel in place with a spare line.

Still, the alarm bell rang, and shouts echoed from la academia.

Ximena gave the order to make sail and the *Delgado* heaved forward, easing out into the harbor. A stray wind blew saltwater into her face, and she breathed deep, steadying herself. The day was clear, the wind fair, the sea calm.

A fine day to commit treason.

But the cazadores had spotted the *Delgado* from the battlements, and they were already readying their cannons, prepared to sink their prize galleon to prevent Gasparilla's escape. Someone shouted the order to fire, and a cannonball struck the *Delgado's* side before the ship could make it more than a few hundred yards into the harbor.

"Reload!" came the order. "Ready! Aim! Fire!"

Several more shots hurtled from la academia's battlements; one of them shattered the *Delgado's* first mast. But the cazadores were not finished yet. As the *Delgado* limped further toward open water, they rolled a catapult to the wall. Ximena knew in an instant.

They were going to launch a fireball.

"Don't look back, and don't stop!" she called out.

In another rare instance of obedience, Marquesa did as she was told. The *Delgado* edged closer and closer to the sea, closer and closer to freedom, moving at less than half its usual speed.

But no ship had ever escaped the cazadores' fireballs, and the *Delgado* wouldn't be the first.

With a groan and snap, the catapult fired, sending the charge hurtling through the air toward the galleon. It smashed into the *Delgado's* side, burying itself in the hull—and then it exploded. A spectacular ring of light erupted from the ship as it shattered, shards of wood flying across the water. The cazadores ducked behind the walls to avoid the debris. Then, when the roar had faded to silence, they stood again, taking inventory of the decimated *Delgado*. Blue flames rose from the ship's carcass and into the dull, gray morning. There were no signs of survivors. Only one conclusion could be drawn.

Gasparilla was finally dead.

The cazadores let out a howl of victory, clapping and cheering from the battlements. They'd sunk the *Delgado*, and the dread pirate was no more.

Capítulo Veintitrés

But the Reales were not onboard the *Delgado*. They were on the once-captured *La Leyenda*, sailing south with the wind to their backs, just as Ximena and Dante had planned.

"How did you know?" Pía asked when Ximena joined her and Marquesa at the helm. "How did you know they wouldn't notice us?"

Ximena leaned against the rail, gazing out at the wreckage of the *Delgado*. "Because we were trained to think like them," she said. "If we could focus their attention on the admiral's galleon, we knew they'd miss *La Leyenda* as she escaped out the side of the harbor. The cazadores are notoriously single-minded. But however blind they might be, they're not fools. It won't be long before they spot us. Let out the jib, we need to pick up the wind once we hit open water."

Marquesa crossed her arms over her chest. "Which of us is the captain here? I think I'll be giving the orders, thank you very much."

"And which of us saved the other from the depths of la academia's labyrinth?"

"Hmm, fair enough," said Marquesa, the ghost of a smile on

her lips. "Perhaps a joint captaincy, then? We can sail *La Leyenda* together under the name of Gasparilla. No one will know the difference."

It seemed a fine enough plan to Ximena. After all, there was no hope of returning to la academia now—the admiral would discover the truth of her involvement in Gasparilla's escape before the day was out, and he would send every ship in the armada to capture them. Her cazadora title would be revoked; her belongings confiscated; her name and likeness would appear on wanted posters throughout the empire. Everywhere she went, she'd be hunted like an animal, unable to stop, unable to rest. She would forever be known as Ximena Reale, the cazadora who turned pirate.

But she had the deck of *La Leyenda* beneath her feet and the spray of the sea in her face. She had the Luzan sun beating down on her neck and the wind in her untamed curls. She had her sister at the helm, her father's sword at her belt, and her good eye to see by. In fact, for the first time in her life, she could choose where she wanted to go and how she wanted to live, free from the shackles of the law. Until the day they fed her to the noose, that would be enough.

That would be enough for Ximena Reale, the cazadora who became Gasparilla.

"Shall we chart a course for la república, Captain Gasparilla?" said Marquesa.

Ximena's lips turned up just slightly. "We shall, Captain Gasparilla."

"Very well then. But first, there is something we must do."

She swept downstairs to the captain's cabin with Ximena and Pía at her heels, throwing open the doors to reveal a large chamber with a desk, bed, bookshelf, and wardrobe, all painted Gasparilla red.

While Ximena waited, Marquesa crossed the cabin to the wardrobe.

"Here we are," she declared, tossing several garments at Ximena and Pía's feet. "Put these on."

After a moment's hesitation, Pía changed into a shirt and trousers as red as her hair. Ximena laughed. Perhaps they could make a pirate out of the little archivist yet. Then she replaced her own cazador uniform with a scarlet shirt, jeweled belt, and puffed pants. Marquesa grinned her approval, holding out a small, round mirror.

"A ver," she said. "Now you can call yourself a pirate."

Ximena blinked in shock. She didn't recognize the girl in the mirror. Her curls exploded in every direction, barely restrained by a red bandana; her patched eye seemed strangely menacing; and the red set off her usually sallow skin, making her look dangerous and terrible and, somehow, more like herself than she'd ever been.

"Black was never your color," Marquesa said.

"I look like—"

"Father," her sister agreed. "I always thought you looked like him the most."

"We'll make them proud," Ximena said softly.

Marquesa gripped her hand and squeezed it. "That we will. And you can start by giving me my sword back."

"Not likely," said Ximena.

"It was mine first."

"And I stole it."

Marquesa bared her teeth in something between a smile and a snarl. "Filthy pirate," she said. "Fine then. If you get the sword, I get the helm."

She exited the cabin, closing the door behind her. It occurred to Ximena that she didn't truly know her sister. All their lives she'd assumed Marquesa to be as mild and meek as a mouse, afraid of her own shadow, never speaking above a whisper—and in that time her sister had become a pirate whose name was feared across the empire. But Ximena wasn't one for making the same mistakes twice. She had an entire voyage to discover her sister's secrets. She wouldn't underestimate her again.

For now, though, Ximena bent down to gather up her Cazador Cloak. She held it gingerly in her arms, the remains of a dead dream. Then she fished for the note, which she knew was hidden in a pocket on the left side; she laid the cloak on the bed as she unfolded the paper, glancing over its contents.

Capitana,

I've discovered that I'm very bad at writing letters. I've written this one ten times, and it still doesn't say what I want it to say, because I never can find the words when it comes to you. So unfortunately, this is the best I can do: forgive me. Forgive me that I didn't say what I should have said long ago. You deserved to hear it, and I was a coward and a fool to stay silent. But you've always made me wish I was more than the man I am, which is why I'm writing this free of all alcoholic influences, a decision I'm still questioning whether or not I regret. Anyway, to the point. There is nothing in this world I love more than you.

May the seas be with you, Ximena.

~ D

"Ximena? Is everything all right?"

Pía was watching her with knitted brows, but Ximena couldn't answer just yet. She read the letter over again, then a third time, and a fourth. Though her expression didn't change, and her body didn't move, her heart drummed a lopsided beat, stumbling over itself. Once again, Dante de León had succeeded in taking her by surprise. She could only hope that he wouldn't be among the cazadores when they came after *La Leyenda*—she realized that she might have a rather difficult time killing him.

Ximena glanced over his words once last time, even though she'd already committed them to her perfect memory. Then she tore the paper into shreds, folded the scraps into her discarded uniform, and tossed the entire bundle out the cabin window and into the sea, watching as it sank below the waves. Cazadora Ximena was dead and buried.

Any ties she had to Dante de León must be buried with her.

"You won't be alone, Ximena," said Pía behind her. "If we fail, we do so together."

"You should be careful what you promise, Pía," said Ximena. "What if failure means walking a very, very high plank?"

Pía swallowed. "Then I'll do my best not to scream."

Though Ximena laughed and the archivist laughed with her, they both knew Pía had meant what she said, and Ximena was grateful for it. Such things didn't always have to be said aloud.

Just then, the alarm bells of la academia rang out in the distance, and shouts echoed over the water. The cazadores had finally spotted them. Ximena and Pía raced out of the cabin and up to the helm, looking out over the water to watch the cazadores board their ships. Though *La Leyenda* was nearly a half mile ahead, la academia's fleet was swift, deadly. It would be quite the challenge to evade them as far as la Tormenta.

Marquesa, Ximena, and Pía exchanged glances. Their lips bent up into smiles as sharp as rapier blades. A challenge indeed.

So the pirate ship that should not have existed sailed on to the horizon, vanishing in a gleam of gold and scarlet.

Epílogo

"Cuatreda de León. She's expecting you."

An attendant met Dante at the entrance to el ministerio. Only a day had passed since *La Leyenda's* disappearance, but the high minister had wasted no time in summoning her son to the capital. At first, he'd declined her invitation, sending the attendant back to el ministerio with a letter that simply said: *Gracias, but I'd rather feed myself to the sharks than talk to you, high minister.* But his mother had responded by sending two armed guards to escort him out of la academia, so he'd had no choice but to obey her orders.

Of course, that didn't mean he had to be happy about it.

When Dante scowled, the little attendant flinched, anxiously rubbing his beak-like nose.

"I should hope she's expecting me," Dante replied, "since she's the one who requested my presence in the middle of the day."

"I apologize for the inconvenience, sir. If you will follow me," the attendant spluttered, opening the doors and waving the young man through.

With a long sigh of frustration, Dante strolled into the center of the great chamber as if it were a ballroom. He smiled up at the waiting ministers and winked at his mother.

"Buenas tardes, damas y caballeros," he said. "I wish I could say I was glad to be back. But I'm sure I don't have to tell you how dull these meetings are."

"Cuatreda de León," his mother boomed, interrupting him. "Do you know why you're here?"

"To entertain you all with my dashing good looks and riveting wit?"

One of the ministers chuckled, but stopped when she received a deadly glare from Elena de León. The high minister continued, "Where were you yesterday evening, Cuatreda de León?"

"In my dormitory, high minister."

"And was there anyone with you?"

"Yes, high minister. A bottle of Luza's finest rum."

Another ripple of laughter, this time mixed with disapproving murmurs. The high minister slammed her gavel down.

"Order, if you please," she said. "I will ask you more directly, Cuatreda de León. What do you know about the escape of Ximena and Marquesa Reale?"

Dante's answering smile was placid. "Nothing whatsoever."

"Are you certain?"

"As the law," said Dante.

His mother sat back in her chair, fingers tight around her gavel. "We have received reports from la academia's guards that you were seen outside the labyrinth prior to the pirate's escape. Do you have any explanation for that?"

"Ah, yes," Dante sighed. "We were having a drink, and the poor idiots couldn't hold their liquor. I can't help it if the world's greatest pirate decided to break out of jail the moment they fell unconscious."

The high minister's eyes narrowed to slits. "There have been other reports. Testimonies suggesting that you might have had . . . *particular* inclinations toward ex-Cazadora Ximena."

Dante barked a laugh. "Inclinations? For the daughter of pirates? Where on earth have you been getting your information, high minister?"

"Apparently from a most unreliable source. Bring the prisoner forward."

Two guards entered the chamber; the ministers gasped. In their grasp was Admiral Pérez, who held his head high in spite of the chains around his wrists.

"Admiral Pérez," boomed Elena de León, "were you responsible for the training of ex-Cazadora Ximena Reale?"

"Yes, High Minister de León," he answered.

"Did you recommend that she be awarded the title of cazadora?"

"Yes, High Minister de León."

"Did you suspect that she might harbor sympathies toward the pirate Gasparilla?"

"Yes, High Minister de León, I did for a short period of time. But I never thought that those sympathies would translate—"

"So you concealed relevant information from el ministerio."

"I didn't believe it to be—"

"Admiral Gabriel Pérez, el ministerio finds you guilty of treason against the Empire of Luza. Are there any opposed?"

No one dared to raise their hands.

"Mother—" Dante interjected, but the high minister banged her gavel, silencing him.

"It is done. The admiral will be taken to la academia, where he will be hanged by the neck until he is dead. You may strip him of his cloak and escort him out."

Before Dante could protest, the attendant stepped forward to take the admiral's cloak from his shoulders with trembling fingers. Admiral Pérez didn't struggle; he simply stood there, his eyes glazed, staring straight ahead. Then guards dragged him from the chamber and the doors slammed shut behind them, as if the admiral had never existed at all.

The high minister trained her eyes on her son like a shark that has tasted blood.

"Now I will ask you again, Cuatreda de León," she said. "What do you know of the Reales' escape?"

Dante ground his teeth. "Nothing."

"Are you willing to swear it?"

"On my brother's grave."

She leaned forward. "Are you willing to prove your loyalty to el ministerio, to the queen, and to the empire?"

"If I must."

His mother's smile was as smooth and cold as the limestone walls. "Very well. Bring the admiral's cloak forward."

The attendant shuffled over, the cloak draped over his arms.

"Dante de León," the high minister said, "on the recommendation of your mentors and peers, I invite you to accept the Cazador Cloak and join the ranks of la academia's finest cazadores. Please prepare to take the cazador oath."

Though he fought to show no emotion, Dante's face visibly paled.

"Really, high minister," he said, "I'm not sure this is necessary—"

"Kneel and repeat after me," said the high minister. "I, Dante de León."

"High minister—"

"I, Dante de León."

"Mother—"

"Repeat after me, cuatreda, or you will be hanged before sundown."

Dante swallowed, squared his broad shoulders, and kneeled. "I, Dante de León."

"Do solemnly swear."

"Do solemnly swear."

"To uphold, treasure, and protect the law and its tenets."

"To uphold, treasure, and protect the law and its tenets."

"Protecting my queen and her subjects alike."

"Protecting my queen and her subjects alike."

"From this moment forward until the last breath I take."

"From this moment forward—"

He paused, his tongue suddenly dry. But at his mother's piercing glare, he continued, "Until the last breath I take."

The high minister's lips curled up in satisfaction. "Rise, Cazador Dante de León. May you bring the light of Luza to the furthest corners of the empire, and may the seas be with you."

Dante hardly heard the applause that rose from Luza's ministers. He was still kneeling, his head bowed, silver-blond curls concealing his expression.

"Rise, cazador," the high minister commanded again, "and accept your first commission."

Dante looked up and stood slowly. Anyone who didn't know him might have assumed that he was elated—his face was wreathed in a gleaming smile, and his dark eyes glittered like gold coins at the bottom of the sea. But the high minister of Luza knew her son better than she knew herself. And she knew that the look on his face was one of unadulterated fury.

"What is my commission, high minister?" asked Cazador Dante.

The applause faded as the ministers awaited her answer. Elena de León sat back in her chair, turning her gavel over in her hands.

"You're going to capture Gasparilla," she said. "And you're going to kill Ximena Reale."

Acknowledgments

Capitana began as a solo expedition, just me, my laptop, and an unholy amount of cafecitos. But if there is anything I've learned through the fabled Publishing Process, it is that no pirate ship is complete without an absolutely fantastic crew, and no book comes into this world without an armada of people behind it. So, this is my attempt to thank everyone who steered our ship to victory, one milestone at a time.

First and foremost, thank you to the God through whom all things are possible. You heard the prayers of a ten-year-old little girl all those years ago and turned her dream into reality. Every word I write is for you and because of you.

Next, to my incredible agent, Andrea Morrison: who knew a tweet and a like would be the start of something this amazing? You believed in Ximena and me from the very beginning, and you are the best champion, cheerleader, and helmsman this writer could ever ask for. A huge thank-you also goes out to the entire team at Writers House, especially Alessandra Birch, Cecilia de la Campa,

Hayley Burdett, and Sofia Bolido, for bringing Ximena to the world. #LatinxPitch, I wouldn't have found them without you!

My wonderful editor, Karen Chaplin, you made a writer girl's dream come true with an email and a Zoom call all those months ago. (Remember when I was still calling from my college dorm room? Craziness!) Your vision, commitment, and feedback sharpened this story like a rapier, and made the world of Luza that much more magical. If anyone deserves a Cazador Cloak, it's you! The team at Quill Tree Books and HarperCollins truly has my whole heart: my publisher Rosemary Brosnan, designer Laura Mock, Audrey Diestelkamp and Shannon Cox in marketing, Tim Smith and Heather Tamarkin on the managing editorial team, and Samantha Ruth Brown in publicity, you are all incredible!

Of course, the only thing better than having one amazing publishing crew is having *two* amazing publishing crews, which is why a heartfelt thank-you must go out to the entire UK team at Hot Key Books and Bonnier. To my ever-fabulous editor Ella Whiddett, the champion and friend I always hoped to have for my books, I am eternally grateful for your insight, Instagram DMs, and endless enthusiasm. I can't wait to come back to London and fangirl over YA releases together again! Thank you to my publisher Emma Matthewson, publicist Amber Ivatt, Kate Griffiths in sales, Emma Quick, Jas Bansal, and Olivia Jeggo in marketing, and Dominica Clements and Freencky Portas in design.

To Micaela Alcaino—finding out that you would be *Capitana*'s cover artist was the ultimate pinch me moment. If only I could tell younger Cass that the artist she fangirled over/low-key Instagram stalked would illustrate the cover of her dreams someday!

I wrote *Capitana* while I was still a sophomore in college, traveling around the state of Florida researching the history of piracy and the Spanish Armada's involvement. None of that research would have been possible without the tremendous generosity of Princeton University through the Dale Summer Award grant, along with the support of the Program in Creative Writing. Professor Yiyun Li and the CWR 303 workshop, thank you for encouraging me not to give up on Ximena and her story.

I also have to thank the wonderful people who helped me during the research process at the Mel Fisher Maritime Museum, the Castillo de San Marcos National Monument, the St. Augustine Pirate and Treasure Museum, and the Museo Naval in Madrid. Your insight and knowledge were invaluable in creating the Empire of Luza. To Captain Brian from Captain Brian on the Water—you told me that a frigate bird would make an excellent pet for a pirate, and I'm so very glad I took your advice.

Friendship is at the core of Ximena's story, and for good reason. I couldn't have completed this publishing journey without my loving, patient friends who read all my terrible first drafts, cheered me on, and drank absurd amounts of coffee with me throughout this process. Christy, Molly, Sarah, Alexis, the Larson family, Rosy, Selena, Claire, Jayne, Jenna, Faith, Anna, Leah, Caro, Courtney, Lexi, Tyler, and Danielle—I love you all.

To my writer friends, Alexis Maragni, Ayngelea Stevens, and RJ Valldeperas—if I'm even half as cool as you are when I grow up, I'll consider myself a success. Oh, and O.O. Sangoyomi, I'm pretty thrilled that we traded law school for solo-traveling and writing the books we wanted to read as kids.

Family is *Capitana*'s beating heart, just as it has always been mine. To the Arias side of the family, thank you for your love, your wisdom, and for teaching me to pass down stories. Pop and Becky, thank you for coming on every crazy research trip, no questions asked, and supporting me wholeheartedly with hugs, prayer, and cheese pita.

Now, to the James Family Five, who have inspired every book I have every written: we did it!!!! Nikko and Kate, the Marquesa to my Ximena, you are my best friends and favorite readers. I truly write plot twists just to watch your reactions. Mama, thank you for always pointing my eyes to the Lion of Judah and for insisting every day of my life that I was going to publish a book and have it turned into a movie. Daddy, I would give up a galleon of gold just to celebrate with you in person, but I know you're throwing the biggest pirate-themed party in heaven right now. Romeo, giver of besitos, I couldn't ask for a better (or fluffier) writing buddy.

And to my real-life Dante: I never knew how to write a love story until I met you. I would follow you to the horizon.